D0210692

CLIMB
THE
WIND

Also by Pamela Sargent

NOVELS

Cloned Lives
The Sudden Star
Watchstar
The Golden Space
The Alien Upstairs
Earthseed
Eye of the Comet
Homesmind
Venus of Dreams
The Shore of Women
Alien Child
Venus of Shadows
Ruler of the Sky

SHORT FICTION

Starshadows
The Best of Pamela Sargent

NONFICTION

Firebrands: The Heroines of Science Fiction and Fantasy
(with Ron Miller)

ANTHOLOGIES

Bio-Futures
Afterlives (with Ian Watson)
Women of Wonder: The Classic Years
Women of Wonder: The Contemporary Years

Climb the Wind

A Novel of
Another America

Pamela Sargent

■ HarperPrism

■ HarperPrism

A Division of HarperCollins*Publishers*
10 East 53rd Street, New York, NY 10022-5299

Copyright © 1999 by Pamela Sargent. All rights reserved. Printed in the United States of America. No part of this book may be used or reproduced in any manner whatsoever without written permission except in the case of brief quotations embodied in critical articles and reviews. For information address HarperCollins Publishers Inc., 10 East 53rd Street, New York, NY 10022-5299

HarperCollins books may be purchased for educational, business, or sales promotional use. For information please write: Special Markets Department, HarperCollins Publishers Inc., 10 East 53rd Street, New York, NY 10022-5299.

FIRST EDITION

Designed by Elina Nudelman

Library of Congress Cataloging-in-Publication Data

Sargent, Pamela
    Climb the wind : A novel of another America / Pamela Sargent. — 1st ed
      p. cm.
    ISBN 0-06-105029-6
    1. Indians of North America—West (U.S.)—Wars—Fiction.
    I. Title.
    PS3569.A6887C57 1998
    813'.54—dc   98-30783

Visit HarperPrism on the World Wide Web at http://www.harperprism.com

99 00 01 02 03❖/RRD 10 9 8 7 6 5 4 3 2 1

To the memory of my father,

Edward H. Sargent, Jr.

"The history of the United States would have been very different if there had been an Indian Genghis Khan."

—Louis L'Amour

ONE

Five days ago, White Buffalo Woman's husband had mounted his horse and gone east, telling her that he would return in two days. She did not begin to worry until the fourth day after he had left her. In the days when she was suckling her youngest child, and in the time before the visions had come to Touch-the-Clouds, she would not have worried at all when Soaring Eagle was often gone with the other men for many days, but she worried now.

Her husband had gone alone this time, and after a man had ridden here from the camp of Touch-the-Clouds. Soaring Eagle had gone east to be his chief's eyes and ears. He had ridden east to be a spy for Touch-the-Clouds.

White Buffalo Woman scanned the horizon to the east. Outside the circle of tepees near her, other women tended their fires or scraped with their bone chisels at buffalo hides laced to wooden frames. The camp looked much as camps had when she was a girl, but her people were not the same.

Everything had changed for them after Touch-the-Clouds had seen his third vision. That vision had come to the chief during the great war among the Wasichu, when the white men in the north had been fighting the Wasichu to their south. The whites had already been growing more numerous on the plains, and the buffalo herds were thinning. The Tsistsistas—the Cheyenne—spoke bitterly whenever they camped near the Lakota of the way the Wasichu shot at the buffalo along the Iron Horse trail to the south, of how they left most of the animal to rot.

In his vision, Wakan Tanka and the spirits had told Touch-the-Clouds that he and his people would have to make peace with others, even with those who had been enemies of the Lakota for generations, if they were to keep the Wasichu from stealing all of their lands.

In only five years, Touch-the-Clouds had won treaties with the Shawnee, the Cherokee and the other red men who tilled the soil in the manner of Wasichu, and even with the Crow, who did not. White Buffalo Woman had hoped that securing promises of peace and friendship from the Comanche, a treaty even Soaring Eagle had not believed could be won, would be enough to keep the Wasichu from taking more of the land.

"To fight the Kiowa, to hate the Crow, only makes us weaker," Touch-the-Clouds had said many times. "Together we can keep the Wasichu from this land." White Buffalo Woman's husband had agreed with him, as nearly all of the Lakota had. As for those who disagreed—she did not want to think of them. Touch-the-Clouds demanded loyalty. He had killed his own brother for raiding a Crow village, for forgetting that the Crow were now their brothers.

Still the whites came to the Plains, more of them now that their war among themselves was over. Even some of the allies of the Lakota had made their marks on the treaties offered to them by the Wasichu, only to find out later that they had promised to give up lands that were never mentioned in the treaties that had been read to them. The visions of Touch-the-Clouds, even the fear some of his allies had of him, would not be enough to hold their hunting grounds. For that, they would need more weapons, more guns, more bullets.

Touch-the-Clouds had a way to get such weapons. White Buffalo

Woman's own son was one of those who had gone northwest with other men, and with the yellow-haired Wasichu who called himself a friend of the Lakota, in order to secure more weapons. She did not want to think of the tales she had heard, of Lakota and Cheyenne who had begun to scar the land near the sacred Black Hills, the center of the world.

She looked to the north over the flat grassland and saw a rider. Her eyes were not as sharp as they had been in youth, but she saw that the rider was her husband, and knew that he had ridden north of here to the camp of Touch-the-Clouds before returning to her. Others in the camp, among them her son's wife, also watched the approaching rider, obviously curious about what news he might bring.

By the time Soaring Eagle reached their camp and had entered their tent, White Buffalo Woman had a supper of dried meat mixed with wild cherries ready. He sat down in the back of the tepee, opposite the entrance, near their small stone altar.

"You went to Touch-the-Clouds," she said as she set out her husband's food.

"He heard that there were two red men journeying up the Missouri River, red men wearing the blue coats of the Wasichu soldiers but who call themselves our friends. I went to see if it was so and to tell him what I found."

"So that was what he wanted." She chewed her meat. "And did you find such men?"

"I did. They have Wasichu names, Parker and Rowland, and they live among the white men and are said to know their medicine. They even fought in the Wasichu war—Parker wears a blue coat with eagles on the shoulders, like one of the Wasichu war chiefs. Yet he calls himself a friend, and says that he wants to help us. That is what I was told—I saw him myself only from a distance."

"And how will they help us?" White Buffalo Woman asked.

"By helping us to settle our differences. By finding out which of the agents on our lands are cheating us and seeing that they are stopped."

"And how can they do that?"

"I do not know," Soaring Eagle replied.

"Does Touch-the-Clouds think that he can help us?"

Her husband's mouth twisted. "Touch-the-Clouds says that he already has a Wasichu who calls himself his brother and does not need red men who follow white ways. But I heard him speak to his yellow-haired Wasichu as I was leaving, and he spoke the name of Parker. I think that he was asking his Wasichu brother about this red man in a blue coat. He will also let the one called Rowland stay in a Lakota camp to learn some of our ways, but he does not want to see this Rowland himself. He doesn't want him to find out too much."

White Buffalo Woman shook herself. "You should not be thinking so much of this."

"That is true. I shouldn't be thinking of it at all, or speaking of it to you. Touch-the-Clouds will listen to the spirits, and to the other chiefs, and I don't have to know what he is thinking."

It was not wise to know or even to guess at what Touch-the-Clouds was thinking, White Buffalo Woman thought. The more allies and treaties he won, the less he wanted others to speak of what he had accomplished to any who might repeat it to the Wasichu. There was some wisdom in that. If the Wasichu felt that one chief was getting too strong, they might send more of their soldiers against the Lakota.

"Since the yellow-haired Wasichu was in the camp of Touch-the-Clouds, you might have asked him for news of our son."

Soaring Eagle looked up, and she saw anger in his eyes. "I do not have to ask about our son," he whispered, so softly that she could barely hear him, and then he suddenly got to his feet and went to the open tent flap, then stooped to peer outside. He turned back to her, letting the flap fall behind him.

He sat down next to her and his fingers closed around her wrist. "The yellow-hair saw our son not two moons ago," he said, still in that same soft voice, "in the place where the sky weapons are made. And I should not be speaking of this to you."

That was all he had to say. She knew enough not to ask any more questions. That the place of creating sky weapons was somewhere to the north and west, far from where the Wasichu had made trails for their Iron Horse or put up poles for their talking wires, hidden from any who might try to find it, and that sometimes those weapons were brought in secret to the Black Hills—that was all she had to know. Others knew even less, and everyone knew that to speak of it was dangerous. They would need more weapons, and more powerful ones, than what they had or could trade for or could steal to defend themselves.

It had come to that, she thought, some of her people keeping secrets from others. That was almost like the evil of telling a lie.

Soaring Eagle said no more until they were lying on their hides, ready for sleep. "Touch-the-Clouds has had another vision," he said in a low voice. "He spoke of it after I told him of the red men who wear the white soldier's coats. He sees another war coming, one in which we will drive the Wasichu from our hunting grounds for good."

"And then perhaps we can have peace," White Buffalo Woman said wearily.

"If the Wasichu keep to their promises, he won't fight. But he does not expect them to keep those promises."

It was none of her concern. The men decided on matters of war, and Touch-the-Clouds was making himself the head and putting himself in front of the men. He had grown greater than Crazy Horse, perhaps greater even than Sitting Bull, who turned more and more to Touch-the-Clouds for counsel and who called his vision a true one. The men would not come to her for advice on when and where to fight.

But she was not a foolish woman, and she saw what her husband refused ever to say openly, what others would not even whisper, although she could sense their thoughts. Touch-the-Clouds was thinking of more than simply holding the Wasichu to their promises, to keeping the hunting grounds of the Lakota. He wanted more than that. She wondered what his next vision would tell him.

TWO

Lemuel Rowland left Washington in the night. Grigory Rubalev would be waiting for him at the train. A spring rain fell, making the streets muddy and slippery. The clatter of horses' hooves over what cobblestones were left in the torn-up streets and the creaking of buggies and wagons was a constant din, even at this late hour. The carriage in which Lemuel rode creaked and swayed from side to side, shook, and finally shuddered to a halt. He heard another carriage rattle past, and then the sound of boots squishing through mud.

The driver peered in at him and opened the door to Lemuel's right. "Wheels are stuck," the driver said. Water dripped from the brim of his hat. "Too many ruts in the road. You'll have to walk the rest of the way, but it's close by."

Lemuel reached for his two carpetbags, handed one to the man, then climbed out of the carriage. The wheels had sunk into a rut in the road. Lemuel set the carpetbags down on the carriage's step as he felt for his wallet.

"Going north or south?" the driver asked.

"West."

The other man shook his head. "Heard tell it's quiet for now, but that might not last long." The new commissioner of Indian Affairs had said much the same to Lemuel in his office; it was one of the reasons he was returning to the West. "Good luck to you."

Lemuel paid the man, picked up his bags, and continued down Second Street toward Pennsylvania Avenue and the Baltimore and Ohio station. He had thought, vaguely, of going home, but Ely Parker had suggested that he go west and Lemuel had readily agreed. Commissioner Ely Samuel Parker, apart from the bond they had in common, had been his comrade, his sponsor, and his commanding officer. But Lemuel had grasped at the notion of going to St. Louis because he would have work there and he did not know where else to go. He could not go home; the home he remembered no longer existed. The Rowlands would be relieved to get his most recent letter telling them that he was not coming home after all.

In front of the station, a few carriages waited. The trees that had been torn down from around the station during the war had still not been replaced. Lemuel made his way inside and threaded his way through the crowd to the doors on the other side of the station. Grigory Rubalev was supposed to meet him. Lemuel had seen him only once in Washington, but the Russian was an easy man to spot. He wondered again why Ely Parker had suggested that he travel with Rubalev, and what the commissioner wanted from him.

"I might need you out West, Poyeshao," Ely Parker had told him during their last meeting in the commissioner's office. "Poyeshao"— only Ely Parker called Lemuel by that childhood name, although he had abandoned his own childhood name, Hasanoanda, long ago. Poyeshao and Hasanoanda—they had done well for two Seneca boys, better than many whites would have expected them to do. Parker's example had inspired Lemuel, who had admired the older man enough to follow him into the ranks of the army and onto the staff of General Ulysses S. Grant.

Now Grant was president, and Ely Parker had been appointed commissioner of Indian Affairs. The honor of that appointment had given him an office that oversaw some of the most corrupt men in

Washington, as well as an opportunity to make more enemies among those who would resist Parker's efforts to clean things up.

"I may not care to stay in St. Louis for too long," Lemuel said.

"I'm not your commanding officer now," Parker muttered. "If you don't stay there, you're free to go elsewhere. All I ask is that, if you see or hear anything that might be of interest to me, you pass it along." Lemuel sensed what the commissioner had not said: Whatever happens, whatever you discover, I know that I can trust you.

Lemuel nodded. "I'll probably stay for a year, at least." He doubted that he would learn much in St. Louis, certainly nothing about any unrest among the Indians of the northern Plains. Even after a few months in one Sioux camp, he had picked up nothing except some knowledge of the Lakota language and customs and the distinct impression that he was being told as little as possible. He had finally left, writing a report of his observations for Parker before traveling east to his home, not knowing then how unwelcome he would be there.

"Grigory Rubalev is also traveling to St. Louis," Parker continued. "I can arrange for you to travel together. It would ease the tedium of the trip."

Lemuel, feeling that he had no reason to object to this, had agreed. But what did the commissioner want? Why was he to travel with Grigory Rubalev? An adventurer, some called Rubalev, while others murmured that he must be a spy for the tsar, sent to Washington on some secret mission. Lemuel had found out that the Russian had been seen often in Washington during the war to preserve the Union, appearing and then dropping from sight for months at a time, and suspected that he was a profiteer. He had seen Rubalev leave Parker's office one time, in the midst of a small group of men; the Russian had towered over all of them.

He was to travel to Louisville in Kentucky, then go on to St. Louis from there. Rubalev was to meet someone in Louisville, where they would rest and recover from the first part of the journey. Lemuel thought of the hours and days ahead, sitting on a hard wooden seat as the train bumped and bounced him west. Maybe he should not have agreed so readily to travel with Rubalev.

Passengers were already boarding the Baltimore and Ohio; perhaps the train would leave on time after all. He walked under the overhang, looking for Rubalev. The Russian, Parker had told him, would have Lemuel's ticket as well as his own. Lemuel had objected at that point. He was not so poor that he could not purchase his own passage, and did not like the notion of accepting a stranger's largesse.

"Rubalev asked to make the arrangements," Parker had replied. "He wants it to be easier for you to talk, and he also prefers to travel in as much comfort as possible with you."

Comfort, on a train? The man had set himself a difficult task.

"Mr. Rowland?"

Lemuel looked up. Grigory Rubalev stood on a step leading into one car. A conductor was just below him. "Mr. Rowland?" Rubalev said again. The Russian wore no hat. His blond hair fell over his shoulders, and his eyes were as dark as Lemuel's.

"Yes, I'm Rowland."

"I thought that it was you. I saw you one time, from a distance." Lemuel was surprised that the man remembered such a brief glimpse. "Please come inside." The Russian's English held only a trace of an accent.

Lemuel followed Rubalev into the car. The seats were upholstered and larger than he had expected, the car decorated with red curtains, brass fittings, and wood inlay, and he saw only three other passengers, all men, all at the other end of the car. "It is one of the new cars," Rubalev said. "There are not many of them." He glanced at Lemuel. "This Pullman car, I mean. We will be able to sleep without having to sit up." He sat down on one of the seats near the front of the car.

Lemuel set down his bags and seated himself across from the other man. The Russian had two large leather valises stowed under his seat; a third, smaller leather bag sat next to him. "Perhaps you would like to go to the smoking car, have a drink," Rubalev said.

"I don't drink." Lemuel thought of the father he barely remembered, who had tried to follow the ways of the Iroquois prophet

Handsome Lake by giving up whiskey, and who had failed. Drink had ruined too many of his people.

"And I suppose that you do not play cards."

"No, I do not."

"It is nothing." The Russian waved an arm. "It might have been more interesting if you played cards, but—" He shrugged.

"I am grateful for the chance to travel in some comfort," Lemuel said.

"It was Donehogawa who made the request. He proposed that I travel with you. I was happy to oblige."

Lemuel looked away for a moment. Donehogawa, the Russian had called Ely Parker—Donehogawa, the Keeper of the Western Door. Almost no one called the commissioner by the Seneca chief's name given to him in adulthood; Lemuel was one of the few who did. The commissioner did not like to remind the whites around him of his origins.

"I tire of Washington," Rubalev said. "I tire of the East. I have gone from New Archangel to San Francisco to the Plains and Missouri, and to Cincinnati and to Washington, and back and forth, and now—" He closed his eyes for a moment and rubbed his forehead. "Now it is time to go back again."

"To Alaska?" Lemuel asked.

"Alaska is no longer a Russian colony, Mr. Rowland. It is an American colony now." A distant look came into Rubalev's dark eyes. "And you are going to St. Louis. Commissioner Parker says that you are to work there."

"That is my hope. I have a letter of introduction from General— from President Grant. There's work for engineers on the Mississippi levees. Much of the damage the war inflicted there still hasn't been repaired."

"I wish you well, then. If you seek something else, I am certain there will be other opportunities."

Not as many, Lemuel thought, as there might have been had he been a white man. Donehogawa had found work on the levees, before the War Between the States, but only because engineers had been so badly needed along the capricious, everchanging river.

Rubalev's eyes narrowed slightly. The Russian seemed to be studying him. What was Donehogawa's interest in this man? Lemuel thought then of the times when he had seen a distant look in Ely Parker's eyes, a keen and observant look, the look of a hunter stalking his game. Rubalev had the same look.

Other passengers passed them along the aisle, a gray-haired man in a black suit, a woman and child in matching pink ruffled dresses. "You have known Donehogawa for some time," Rubalev murmured.

"Since the war," Lemuel said. "He was an example to me, to several of us—the Seneca boy who worked in an army stable, who learned how to read and write and speak English as well as any white man." He spoke carefully and precisely, as he had trained himself to do. White men could afford to be informal or careless in their speech; he could not. "He wanted to be a lawyer once—did he ever tell you about that?"

Rubalev shook his head.

"He worked in a law office for three years. Then he was told that no Indian could be admitted to the bar. So he became an engineer instead. I followed that path because Donehogawa showed that it was possible. He knew General Grant in Illinois, before the war. When he came back to New York, to Tonawanda, he was looking for Iroquois who would fight for the Union, and I volunteered."

"I understand that the Union forces were not overly eager to enlist you. The commissioner did tell me that."

Lemuel kept his face still. "The New York Volunteers had no place for us. General Grant had to go to some trouble to get us ordered to his staff. We joined him just before Vicksburg."

"Fools." The Russian shook his head. "Fools and idiots!" The vehemence with which he expressed his sympathy surprised Lemuel. Would a profiteer and a spy have such feelings? His suspicions that Rubalev might be just another of the corrupt vultures circling Ely Parker, hoping for some way to take advantage of the Indian Affairs commissioner, faded.

The train began to move. It creaked and shook as Lemuel rested against the back of his seat.

* * *

Soon after the conductor came through to check their tickets, a porter arrived to make up their beds. Their seats were transformed into berths to hold mattresses. Rubalev took the upper berth, groaning a bit as he settled his tall form onto the shorter bed. By the time Lemuel had stretched out on the lower berth, the Russian's breathing was deep and even.

The porter had closed off their compartment from the aisle with a curtain. Lemuel lay in the stuffy, hot darkness, unable to sleep, then got up to make his way along the aisle to the washroom at the other end of the car. After relieving himself in the facility jutting from one wall, he washed his hands in the tin basin and went back to his compartment. Rubalev started from his sleep as Lemuel opened the curtain, stared at him for a moment, then stretched out again.

The man, he saw, could fall asleep quickly and yet be awake in an instant. Lemuel had been able to do that during the war, but had lost the skill during his civilian life. He lay down again, shifting himself on the hard bed. He had slept on rocky ground and in wet mud during the war; this bed signified ease and comfort in comparison.

"If you decide to come back East," Ely Parker had told him in his office, "then let me know what you've heard and seen. Information is always useful."

"You sound as though you want a spy," Lemuel had replied. "But we're no longer at war." Ely Parker had smiled at that. "I'll write to you as soon as I get to St. Louis."

"There's something else." The commissioner frowned. "When you write to me, do it in our old cipher, and send the letters to this address." Parker pushed a piece of paper with an unfamiliar name and a New York address across his desk. Lemuel managed to conceal his surprise at the request. They had used the cipher, based on their own Seneca tongue and in a script Parker had devised, to pass messages to each other during the war, knowing that any Confederate who might intercept them would not be able to read them. Perhaps Parker, surrounded by people who resented his efforts to put an end to the corruption in his office, was simply being cautious, but Lemuel had wondered. This seemed an excess of caution, the request of a man suspicious of everyone, or fearful of what others might uncover.

And Donehogawa had wanted him to travel with this Russian who was sleeping so soundly above him now. Did the commissioner want him to report on Rubalev, to spy on him?

The bed shuddered and bounced under him as the train moved along the tracks. This bed would not make for an easy rest, but it was better than trying to sleep upright. For a while after the war, he had feared sleep, but the dreams of war, the wails of the besieged in Vicksburg, the flames raging through Richmond, the screams of men torn apart by cannon, had not come to him in some time. Dreams were sent to men and women to guide them, so his people had always believed. Now he would welcome a dreamless sleep in which the spirits remained silent.

He and Donehogawa had served together on the staff of General Grant. Despite the need for engineers, Grant had fought hard to get them both orders to join him. But they had proven themselves, with Donehogawa becoming Colonel Ely S. Parker and Lemuel breveted to the rank of major. Lemuel had believed that the tolerance shown toward them by the whites among whom they served would last only as long as the war did, and he had not stayed in their society afterward in order to test his suspicions.

Now, as commissioner of the Bureau of Indian Affairs, Donehogawa was in a position to help other Indians; or so he still hoped. He had brought Lemuel to Washington, telling him of his plan to form a board to keep watch over the bureau, but his efforts to put Lemuel and other Indians on that board had failed. Lemuel had expected such a result, while still hoping that he might be wrong. He had not come to Washington with any faith that his old comrade could change things. He had come there knowing that he had made a mistake by going home earlier and thinking that he could pick up the threads of his old life.

His chest contracted as he remembered how the hills around

Tonawanda had looked in autumn, the deep green of the pines amid the changing leaves of red, yellow, and orange. Sometimes the surface of a lake near those lands would grow so still that he could see the hills mirrored clearly in the water. He would imagine then that below the water, there was an upside-down land, where everything mirrored this world yet did not happen in quite the same way.

In the upside-down land that he envisioned, men would hunt by calling out to the deer instead of silently tracking them. There, the Three Sisters of corn, squash, and beans began as fully grown plants before shrinking into the ground. People grew younger as they aged, and died as babies in the arms of their mothers. When the people of the False Face Society donned their masks, instead of going to those who were ailing, they went instead to the houses of the hale and healthy to burn coals and to chant. The white people lived in longhouses, and followed his peoples' ways.

Lemuel had not thought of his imagined upside-down land in years. He had been a boy when he first imagined the land under the lake. Not long after that, his mother had died and he had soon lost his father to drink. The Rowlands had taken him in and sent him to school with their youngest son. By then, he had learned of Donehogawa, the man the whites called Ely Parker, the Iroquois who could read and write in English and knew law and engineering, and he had decided that he wanted to be like him.

The Rowlands named him Lemuel, and he had tried to live in their world, but there were others who often reminded him that he was not really one of them. Even in the eyes of his foster family, he sometimes glimpsed doubts. In a bout of homesickness, torn by the realization that he would always be an outsider in their world, he ran away from the Rowland farm and made his way back to the lake he remembered, longing for his old home, but the longhouses were poorer and shabbier than he saw them in memory, food was hard to come by, and his people were still struggling to keep their land from being taken by the whites.

"There is no place for you here," one of his cousins had told him, and Lemuel had returned to the Rowlands and their farm. Gideon Rowland had pleaded with his father to take Lemuel back.

Once, while he and Gideon were sitting by a pond, Lemuel had conjured up the upside-down land in words. The other boy had not laughed at him, and after that they had whiled away many pleasant hours in telling stories about the people who lived there. Gideon was his friend, and the Rowlands had finally come to care for him in their quiet way. They had done what they could for him even when others made their lives harder because of him. He could imagine himself, at times, to be their true son.

Gideon had left their home first, during the frenzy of volunteering at the war's beginning. The two of them had been full of fighting words then, talking of courage and the Union and a quick end to the war. By the time Lemuel had won a place for himself in the Union forces, with the help of Ely Parker, richer men were paying for poorer men to take their places in the ranks. He did not have the money to pay for another to do his fighting, but would have enlisted even if he had. As a man who had fought to preserve the Union, he might finally win acceptance among the whites.

After the war, when he had feared sleep and the dreams it would bring, sleep would come upon him even against his will. Now he often could not sleep, however much he longed for rest. The elusive, dimly seen dreams that had vanished when he woke, trembling and damp with sweat and hearing still the cries of dying men, had been replaced with memories from which there was no escape.

Mary Rowland had stood in the doorway of her house, staring past him with her gray eyes, refusing to speak, to cry, to make any sign of welcome. Inside, Ezekiel Rowland sat with a younger man and woman Lemuel did not know.

"My brother Benjamin," Ezekiel said. Lemuel had never heard Mr. Rowland speak of a brother. "And his wife, Polly." The brother had thin red veins in his nose; his wife had reddish hair done up in sausagelike curls and a pregnant woman's bulging belly. "Come back to help us on the farm." The couple had been given the room he and Gideon once shared.

Lemuel had not stayed there long. He had seen the sharp look in Benjamin's eyes that said, This farm will be mine someday, not yours.

Since then, he had received two letters from the Rowlands, brief ones scrawled in Ezekiel's shaky hand. The letters had told him of a cow lost in a storm, a neighbor's marriage, and the birth of Polly's boy, but the letters had seemed empty to him. They had not wanted him back, he knew, because he would only remind them of Gideon, the son they had lost at Gettysburg. In their grief, perhaps they had even wished that Lemuel had died in their son's place.

At last sleep came. Lemuel woke when he heard voices from the other end of the car. Soon the porter was coming through to put away the mattresses and adjust their seats.

He waited until the others in the car had used the washroom, then went there himself. Rubalev was outside the door when he left, looking as though he had slept soundly. "We must eat," the Russian said without preamble. "I will see you in the dining car—there is one on this train. Tell the waiter I want eggs—ham, too." He disappeared into the washroom before Lemuel could reply.

He managed to get to the dining car without getting dirt spattered in his face when between cars or being thrown against a wall by the train's shaking. It would have been easier, he thought, simply to buy some food when the train stopped at the next station. He ordered some breakfast and wondered if Rubalev meant to pay for it. He was already in the man's debt, and felt uneasy about being in the debt of someone he did not know.

Rubalev soon arrived, sat down, finished his ham and eggs, ordered another plate, drank more coffee, and gave the waiter a silver coin, enough for both their meals.

"Thank you for the breakfast," Lemuel said.

"It is nothing," Rubalev replied. "When I had little food, when I was close to starving, I told myself that when I had the means, I would eat as much as I liked. But I do not like to eat alone."

"You've paid for my ticket. You're under no obligation to feed me as well."

"You make so much of money. It is of no use if it is not spent." The Russian leaned back, resting his hands on the arms of his chair.

He had been so long about his eating that the dining car was now half-empty. "I think we have something in common, Mr. Rowland," Rubalev said in a softer voice. "We are both exiles of a sort, both men who must live in a world that is not ours. Perhaps you sometimes wonder, as I do, if there are ways in which we might make it ours."

The man was probing at his mind; that made Lemuel wary. He said, "I would be content to live out my life without being seen as—as what you call an exile."

"I wonder if that is possible," Rubalev said.

"As it is," Lemuel said, "you don't have to live as an exile. Surely your money would go as far in Russia as it does here."

"Russia!" Rubalev's dark eyes narrowed. "What of Russia? I was born in New Archangel Sitka, it is called now. People here think of me as Russian, but it is not so. I was a subject of the tsar, one of his subjects in his colony, but I was of Alaska, not Russia." He paused. "One of my grandmothers was a native, an Aleut." He raised his brows. "You see that we have more in common than you thought, Mr. Rowland."

Lemuel felt no such kinship. Any natives that lived that far north were as strange to him as the Russians who had once shared their Alaskan land. Then he recalled how Donehogawa had said that this was a problem of all Indians, that they did not and could not think of themselves as one people, because of their tribal differences, and that the whites still used that against them.

"My home was Alaska," Rubalev continued. "I thought Alaska would always be my home when I was young. And then, at the beginning of your war between the states, we learned that our Russian-American Company, which had the duty to preserve our colony, had tried to sell it to Washington." He tapped his fingers against the tabletop. "There is that difference between us, Mr. Rowland. My land was sold. That of your people was stolen."

"We have land still," Lemuel said. "Not all of it was stolen. We were allowed to buy some of it back." He looked away, poured some water from the pitcher on the table, and took a sip. The man's frankness and open expression of feeling disturbed him. Lemuel had always taken much effort to control himself, to see that he betrayed none of his inner feelings to most of those around him. Practicing such restraint could make him forget, for a while, that there was anything for him to resent. Now this man seemed to be trying to provoke feelings that he had usually been able to put aside.

"That first effort to sell our colony failed," Rubalev continued. "Many in New Archangel were reassured. Many of us, we were told, lived as well as minor court officials in Saint Petersburg—we would, it seemed, keep our gardens and our tea houses, our theater and our library. We had a gracious and beautiful life, Mr. Rowland, and it was a life led by people who in Russia would have been no more than the dirt under the tsar's boots. So many of us wanted to believe that we would keep that life."

He sighed. "I think that I knew even then that we would lose it all, that our colony would be taken from us in the end." He was silent for a few moments, as if recalling that old life, and then his eyes were suddenly wary. Rubalev glanced quickly around the car, but no one was listening to them; the only diners left were five men a few tables away.

"I left New Archangel in 1860," Rubalev went on, "and I went to California, to Fort Ross and San Francisco, and to other places, and eventually I found my way to Washington. During your war, you see, I knew that there would be opportunities, and I was looking for something to do." He lowered his voice. "I will confess that even though my tsar and his Russia supported your Union, I do not know if I would have mourned its passing. If the South had won its independence, Alaska might not have been sold. I could have abandoned my enterprises here and returned to my home and left whatever I began in the hands of others."

Lemuel was very still. Rubalev watched him with an unexpectedly mournful, almost gentle look in his dark eyes.

"You are wondering now if I worked against the Union somehow," Rubalev said.

"No," Lemuel said truthfully. "Ely Parker would never have trusted you or become your friend if you had."

Rubalev sighed. "It does not matter now. In the beginning, I had enough to live on without exerting myself, so I waited and watched and met many people and learned what I could—perhaps it was then that people began to whisper that I was the tsar's spy." He smiled for a moment. "I believed that if the South was to win, such a victory would have to come early in the war. When the war did not end early, it became obvious to me that the Union would likely not lose unless it made tremendous mistakes. I had nothing to gain by aiding a Confederacy of rebels that would be vanquished. I also knew that if the Union was preserved, I would not see New Archangel again. I made my peace with what was and turned my thoughts to—"

Rubalev stopped talking and then smiled again. His smile made Lemuel uneasy. The man, he realized, might be dangerous; perhaps he should not have agreed to travel with him. He steadied himself. Donehogawa had put him at this man's side; if he could not trust Rubalev, he would have to doubt his old comrade as well.

Rubalev poured himself a glass of water, pulled a flask from his jacket pocket, poured some amber liquid into the glass, and downed the drink in one gulp. "A friend wrote to me, toward the end of your war." His voice was so low now that Lemuel had to strain over the creaking of the wooden car to hear him. "He told me that Dmitri Petrovich Maksutov was to be our colony's governor. His letter told of Dmitri Petrovich's reassurances to the people of New Archangel, his promise that the Russian-American Company would grant us a new twenty-year charter, that our colony would be preserved, that Dmitri Petrovich had spoken of this to the Grand Duke Constantine himself."

He took a breath. Already, with only one drink, the man sounded a bit drunk. Lemuel waited for him to go on.

"Dmitri Petrovich was to be our governor," Rubalev said, "a man with a noble wife, a man with the ear of the tsar. And I hoped, when I read this in the letter of my friend, that he was right. I hoped that those in Washington who thought of my home as a worthless wilderness would prevail, and put an end to talk of buying it, and leave our land to us."

Lemuel sympathized with this strange man, while still embarrassed to be listening, to hear a stranger picking at his wounds so openly.

"And then, two years ago, my home—our colony, my people's land, Russian America, was sold." Rubalev reached for his flask again, then thrust it into his pocket. "Seward and others in Washington were happy, for they had rewarded Russia for supporting the Union by relieving the tsar of a large piece of worthless land and the expense of supporting a colony there. The tsar was free of a costly burden. And my friend wrote to me to say that New Archangel rejoiced, because the Americans had promised to treat us fairly, that they would leave us our colony."

Lemuel knew little of this. During his time in Washington, he had heard that almost all of the Russians in Sitka—in New Archangel— had chosen to return to Russia. It had been one of those small facts of no great consequence to him or to those around him.

"And then my friend sent me his last letter." Rubalev's face sagged. "The Americans sent their soldiers. They sent men who wanted to get rich, to steal what they could for themselves. Shanties to house them went up, and more soldiers came, and before long they were looting our churches and taking our houses and using our women. They sold liquor to the Tlingit people, something we had always forbidden. And when the winter of 1867 came, those Russians who were left in New Archangel left with Dmitri Petrovich Matsukov." He paused. "Only a few were left behind."

Lemuel said, "I know of broken promises."

The waiter was watching them. He would be waiting for them to leave so that he could clear the table and prepare for the next meal. Lemuel, unlike many of those he had met in Washington, had never been able to pretend that servants and porters and other help were invisible.

"My friend left for Russia with the rest," Rubalev said. "They are now lost to me. When I was younger, while I still lived in New Archangel, I used to hear that those who left Alaska for our motherland, for Russian cities, did not live long."

"I am sorry," Lemuel said, feeling the inadequacy of those words.

"Being sorry is useless, Mr. Rowland. I am happy that I left when

I did. I am relieved that I did not have to see it and that my time in this land has been profitable." He rested his hands on the table. "And you, Mr. Rowland—what is it that you seek in the West?"

"I told you—there will be work for me there."

"Or perhaps you are another like me who does not want to see what has become of his old home." Lemuel heard the sadness in his voice. There was, he thought, a deep sorrow in the man, the kind of sorrow he had seen in others during the war, a sorrow that flowed from him like a dark current.

"And what is it you seek in the West, Mr. Rubalev?" Lemuel heard himself say.

Rubalev was silent for so long that Lemuel thought he might not answer him at all. "The fate of this land will be decided there, in the West, not in the triumphant North or the conquered lands of the South. I would prefer to be in a place where fate can make use of me. Perhaps you feel that too, Mr. Rowland." Rubalev stood up. "The train will stop soon. There should be time for a walk at the depot."

In Cincinnati, a bearded middle-aged man boarded their train and came to the Pullman car. Lemuel saw the look of recognition that passed between the stranger and Rubalev, and then they left him to go to the smoking car. The stranger had muttered a greeting before going off with Rubalev, and Lemuel had heard the accent of a Southerner. He wondered about that after Rubalev returned to the car alone, and about why he had not been introduced to the man.

"An old friend?" Lemuel asked.

Rubalev nodded, but did not elaborate. The man, so voluble in the beginning, now fell into a somber silence. He reached toward a valise, extracted a small leather volume bearing gold letters in an unfamiliar alphabet, and began to read.

They passed the rest of that day that way, Rubalev intent on his book and Lemuel gazing out the window at the green, gently curving Kentucky hills, until the train came to a sudden stop at a small town station. After an hour, passengers left the train to stroll under the depot's overhang. Lemuel got out to stretch his legs and heard someone mutter about a problem with the locomotive. Rubalev paced restlessly, clearly impatient to be on his way.

After they reboarded the train, the blond man fell into a brooding silence. During the few times Rubalev bothered to speak, it was to tell tales of his early life in New Archangel. He had, he said, been educated in one of the colony's schools, where he had learned both French and Russian. He had also studied at the colony's zoological institute, and might have continued his studies in Russia had he not chosen to leave Alaska for California. He claimed descent from a Russian noble as well as from an Aleut woman. He had made some of his money through various ventures in San Francisco, but did not offer any details about those pursuits.

Lemuel did not know how much of what Rubalev told him was true. The man seemed hesitant about answering any questions about exactly what he had studied at the zoological institute or what he had done between leaving California for the East and the end of the war. But in his voice, Lemuel heard him mourning for what was lost. The place he had known was gone; only the dream of memory was left.

When they had come to the outskirts of Louisville, Rubalev looked up from his book and said, "Mr. Rowland, what would you say if I told you that another war is coming, a war in the West?"

Lemuel looked up, startled. "Are you speaking of another war of secession? I have heard nothing—"

"That is not what I am asking."

"If you are talking about Indians and settlers, I can only say that such a war would soon be over. It wouldn't even be a war—only a few pitched battles."

"That is what some think, but perhaps they are wrong. There is a chance that such a war may go on for some time, ten years, perhaps twenty."

"Both the North and the South are drained by war," Lemuel said, "and my hope is that Donehogawa can help to keep the peace in the West." He kept his composure, even though the man's talk was making him uneasy. He did not know why Rubalev had suddenly spoken of the West and of war.

"Let me know what you hear," Donehogawa had asked him. Had the commissioner put him in the company of Rubalev in order to find out more about him? But the man would not reveal anything important, certainly not anything that he might want to hide, to a stranger.

"I have been through one war," Lemuel continued. "I don't have the stomach for another."

"Even if you can find some—shall we say—purpose in the fight? Some worthy end?"

Lemuel leaned back. "I was full of noble thoughts eight years ago, all fired up to volunteer, going to Ely Parker to say that I would join his Iroquois volunteers if the Union would ever let us fight. Even when we were told that it was a white man's war, that didn't dampen my enthusiasm. Those were my ends preserving the Union and proving myself to the whites around me. And if I sought an even nobler purpose than that, I could think of enslaved Negroes yearning for their freedom." He glanced out the window at the darkening landscape. "That war is over. And if it didn't quite turn out as some might have hoped, it's over."

Rubalev closed his book. "The war never ends, Mr. Rowland. It may stop for a while in one place before beginning again in another, but it does not end. A war is not ended merely by the signing of a surrender or victory in a few battles. It can end only when the enemy no longer has the will or the power to fight."

THREE

She was a child, ten summers in age, when the dream came to her one night during the Leaf Moon. Men on horseback were riding down on her father's camp, shouting war cries. The men were Wasichu, like the men in the fort near the agency.

When she woke, she told her dream to her mother. "You have been listening to stories," her mother said. "The white men will not come here. We have a treaty with them, we're at peace with them. Why should they ride against us now?"

"We should join Touch-the-Cloud's band, Mother. There are too few of us in this camp to be safe if the whites come against us."

"It is not up to a girl to tell the men when to move camp, and how to fight is for men to decide, not for you. They will join Touch-the-Clouds when it is time to hunt together."

A few days later, a band of Wasichu came to the camp of her father, before most of the men were awake. She was about to go fetch water from a nearby stream when she spied the Blue Coats in the distance. Her father left their tent as the blue-coated men approached, and before he could call out a greeting, the men fanned out around the camp on their horses and took aim with their fire-sticks. There was a sharp sound, a sound like the crack of dead wood, only louder, and then her father fell, clutching at his chest.

She threw herself to the ground and crawled under a hide. Her gorge rose and filled her mouth with bitterness. Something fell across her, pinning her down. Even under the hide, she could hear screams. A woman cried out, begging for her child's life, and then her voice was cut short.

She struggled for breath under the hide, then held the air inside herself, fearing that her lungs would burst. She kept expecting one of the Wasichu to find her, to pull her out from under the hide and the body lying over her, and then there was silence.

She waited for a long time after she heard the sound of the white men's horses carrying them away from the encampment. She huddled under the hide until there was silence and she was certain that the Wasichu were gone.

Pushing against the weight that lay over her, she crawled out from under the hide and saw that night had already come. The moon was up, silvering the grassland. She shivered in the cold, then looked down at a body near the hide and saw that it was her mother. In her dream, she had seen her mother's death, but had not told her that part of the vision, fearing that she might call her mother's death to her if she spoke of it aloud.

Everyone had died in her dream, but at first, wandering past the torn and ripped tepees, the tools and clothing strewn about the land, she thought that some of her people might have fled into the hills and escaped. Then she saw the bodies, twisted shapes lying by tents and dead fires, some of them with black bloody scalps where their hair had once grown. Her brother was dead, and her cousin Fleet Foot, and her father's younger brother along with his wife and infant son, and she thought of how her cousin would cry, waking them all in the night, always hungry, always crying for his mother, and she wondered that he had not cried at all while the whites were going about their killing and had not cried even when they were killing him. Soon she stopped counting the bodies.

All of the horses were gone. She wondered if the Wasichu had stolen them or had only driven them off. She sat down, wrapping herself in a blanket against the cold, and then saw the flap of a ruined tepee move. Someone crawled out of the tent and crept toward her. Old Black Cow, she thought, suddenly disappointed that of all those who were here, only that old woman still lived.

Black Cow sat next to her and wailed, chanting for the dead until the moon was higher in the sky, then got to her feet. "The camp of Touch-the-Clouds lies west," the old woman said.

"We have no horses."

"Then we must walk," Black Cow replied.

"It is too far to walk."

"We cannot stay here, little one. We must try to find other people. We cannot stay alive by ourselves."

They took what food and water they could find and began to walk toward the west. By dawn, Black Cow had spied one of their horses in the distance, and so they were able to ride to the camp of Touch-the-Clouds. That was where she first saw Grisha, in the tent of the chief, sitting with Touch-the-Clouds and some of his warriors, his yellow hair falling over his shoulders.

She had somehow kept herself from screaming at the sight of a Wasichu inside the tent of Touch-the-Clouds, had stilled the spirit within her as Black Cow spoke of what had happened, and when the old woman was finished, she said, "I dreamed it before it happened. I dreamed that the Wasichu came to my father's camp. The spirits were warning me. I spoke of my dream to my mother, but she would not listen to me."

A couple of the men shook their heads, but Touch-the-Clouds said nothing, nor did the yellow-haired Wasichu. That night, another dream came to her, and she saw herself riding far from this land on a roan horse much like the one her father used to ride. A man sat behind her on the horse, but she could not turn around to see who he was.

In the morning, she found the yellow-haired Wasichu outside the tepee of Touch-the-Clouds. She came up to him, pulled at his sleeve, and said, "I had another dream. Someone is going to take me away from this place."

The Wasichu made a sound in his throat. At first she thought that he might not understand her words. Then he said, "You are right, small one." The Lakota words sounded strange in his mouth, as if he did not quite know how to say them. "Touch-the-Clouds has decided to send you away with me. Are you brave enough for that, to live among the Wasichu?"

"I do not know."

"If you are not, I will send you back here. Touch-the-Clouds will see that you are cared for."

"He would see me as a coward if I came back when he thinks I should leave," she said. "Why does he want to send me away?"

"I did not understand everything he told me," the Wasichu replied, "but it has something to do with your dream. You may have a gift for certain visions, for seeing what will come, and Touch-the-Clouds has to know what the Wasichu may bring to his people. You saw that some would break the treaty before they broke it. Touch-the-Clouds thinks that such a gift may be even more useful to his people and yours if you learn the Wasichu ways."

She was silent.

"Not all of the Wasichu are like the ones who killed your father's band. I am not like them—I am here, and call myself the friend and brother of Touch-the-Clouds." He paused. "And now your dreams have shown you that you are to come away with me."

But I do not want to leave my people, she longed to say, but kept silent. The spirits had already shown her what she would have to do.

"What are you called?" she asked him.

He made a sound that sounded like a laugh. "Yellow Hair. What else would your people call me?"

"What do your own people call you?"

"Grigory Sergeievich Rubalev." The sounds were strange, and the name had no meaning. "But that is too much for you to learn all at once. Those close to me call me Grisha."

He had taken her away from the camp of Touch-the-Clouds two days later, to a place of many wooden dwellings and what seemed to be a horde of whites. They left that place in a wagon with sides and openings to look out of after Grisha had given her other clothes, a garment with a wide skirt and leather boots that pinched her feet and made it hard for her to walk. They came to a place where there were even more whites, all of them crowded together in their high buildings with narrow dirt-and-stone-covered trails that wound among them, and she wondered how they could all bear to be so crowded together. She had not imagined that there could be so many Wasichu in the world.

By then, she had learned a few words in the Wasichu tongue, words of greeting and farewell, and how to ask for food or water. Their journey was still not over, even in this place by a great lake that held so many Wasichu. From there, they had climbed into one of many wagons pulled by an iron creature that made her think of a big black buffalo. This buffalo ran along a trail made for it, pulling the wagons and puffing loudly from its efforts as clouds poured from its top, and whenever it stopped, the buffalo still sighed and gasped as if struggling to catch its breath.

That was, Katia told herself, a long time ago. She waited under the overhang, looking down the tracks as another black iron buffalo moved toward her. She had lived in Grisha's world for eight years now, and could no longer remember her old name, but had not much wanted to recall it after her old life was over. She might have forgotten her people's speech by now if Grisha had not continued to use it whenever they spoke alone. The spirits had not spoken to her in all that time, and she often thought that they would never speak to her again, that they had forgotten her long ago.

Grisha had sent her to a school in New York, and then another in Boston. After the War Between the States was over, he had brought her to Washington; by then, she could read and write and sew and pour tea, as Wasichu women did, and knew how to say the Christian prayers, although she still thought of the Great Spirit and not of Christ whenever she said them.

She had also learned the truth of what Grisha had often told her:

"There are two kinds of Wasichu, Katia—those who will accept you and tolerate you as long as you act and think and believe exactly as they do, and then there are those who will hate you no matter what you do."

But this was not true of Grisha. He spoke Lakota words to her and told her not to forget them. She discovered that he had brought two Lakota boys and a Cheyenne into the Wasichu world and had sent them West after the war. She did not know what his dealings were with the men who came to his house in Washington, or where he went during his months-long disappearances, but she knew that they had something to do with her people. Sometimes, when he spoke to her in Lakota, more fluently than he had when she had first seen him, he hardly seemed like a Wasichu at all.

He had sent her to Louisville a month ago with Denis Laforte, telling her that he would come for her soon and travel with her to St. Louis. She did not know what his purpose was, but she had never questioned Grisha about anything he did. A telegraph message from him had reached her five days ago, with information about the train he was to take.

The train was very late, but she had never known one to be on time. Denis Laforte craned his neck as the train puffed and shrieked and groaned to a stop. He was a tall man with pale brown skin and hair as dark and wooly as a buffalo's. Denis, a freeman originally from New Orleans, had been with Grisha for three years now, obeying him as unthinkingly as she did.

The iron buffalo sighed to a halt. Katia moved toward the Pullman car, searching for Grisha. She might have waited for him at the hotel, and the prolonged waiting at the station had wearied her, but Katia had felt that he would want her to meet him here. He would not have sent a telegraph message to her otherwise, and often she felt that, no matter what she did, no matter how hard she tried not to disappoint him, she could never show him enough gratitude for what he had done. So she had waited, refusing to return to the hotel to rest even when it was clear that the train would be late. Grisha had been kind to her; she owed him everything.

A foolish thought, she told herself. He would not have schooled her and cared for her simply out of kindness. Grisha's kindly gestures always had some purpose.

A woman passed them and glanced from her to Denis with a narrow-eyed expression that told Katia they did not belong there. She had seen the same look at the hotel, among the guests in the lobby and even on the faces of some of the staff. Only Grisha's money could have bought them even that much forbearance. For days now, she had taken her meals in her room, afraid to leave it for the hotel dining room downstairs.

Two men left the train, and then she saw Grisha. A dark-haired man followed him out of the car and stood with him, looking awkward and out of place.

"Katia," Grisha said, "how kind of you to meet me." His face was drawn, and the skin under his eyes sagged. She had rarely seen him looking so tired. He gestured at the man next to him. "This is Mr. Lemuel Rowland. He is a friend of Ely Parker's—of the commissioner of Indian Affairs."

Katia nodded at the man, recalling that Ely Parker had occasionally come to Grisha's house. She had not known that Parker was an Indian until Grisha had told her.

"Katerina Rubalev," Grisha continued, waving a hand at Katia.

The man called Rowland looked puzzled for a moment. "Your wife?" he asked.

"My ward. And Denis Laforte, my valet."

Denis signaled to a porter, then reached down to pick up the bags Rowland had set down on the walkway. "Come with me, sir," Denis said to Rowland as the porter hefted Grisha's bags.

The three men hurried on ahead. Katia felt Grisha's hand on her arm. "Lemuel Rowland was an officer in the northern armies," Grisha said in Lakota. His voice was so low that she could barely hear him above the noise of the station. "He also belongs to the same people as does Donehogawa—they are both Seneca."

Katia lifted her brows. So he was one like her, another Indian who wandered in the Wasichu world like a ghost.

"Donehogawa wanted the man to come with me," Grisha said. "I believe that he thinks this Rowland will be a spy for him."

"And will he be?" she asked.

"I do not know. I have been talking to him. I would like to find out more about what kind of man he is."

"He is going to St. Louis?"

"Yes."

"And where are we to go, Grisha?" He had not told her yet, not in his letters, and not before sending her to Louisville.

"What would you say if I told you that we may go back to the camp of Touch-the-Clouds?"

She halted, not knowing what to say or how she felt. He stopped next to her. "Do you not want to return to your people?"

"I have forgotten too much," she said softly. "I don't belong here, but I will be out of place there."

"I will not leave you there if you do not want to stay. And it will be Touch-the-Clouds who decides your fate. I think that he may decide that you will be more useful among the Wasichu in the end."

They resumed their pace, keeping Denis and the man called Rowland in sight. Katia thought of what she had heard from a visitor to Grisha's house, the night before she had left for Louisville. She had not seen who the visitor was, and had heard him only because the door to Grisha's study was open.

"You cannot advise Touch-the-Clouds." The man was speaking in English, but with an accent she did not recognize. "He allows others to speak to him, but hears only what he likes."

"It does not matter." That was Grisha's voice. "He wants what we all want."

"To defend his people, to protect them, to see that the whites live up to their treaties—I know that he wants all of that. But that isn't all he wants."

"He may have to—" Grisha began, and then the door was closed and she could hear no more.

"There is something I want you to do for me before we leave here," Grisha said to her now. "Watch Lemuel Rowland, talk to him when you can and tell me what he says, and tell me what you think of him."

"Yes, Grisha." She had expected him to ask that. In Washington, he had occasionally asked her what she thought of a visitor to his house, what she might have seen that he had not. Sitting silently in a corner, moving only if a guest needed more tea or a stronger drink, she might notice that a man talked too much or too little, or that he seemed uncertain, or that his eyes shifted when he spoke of particular matters. Often she knew right away that a man was not to be trusted, but could not say how she knew that. She did not know whether Grisha ever made use of her observations.

"And another thing," he said. "If he asks you how I found you and came to care for you, you may be honest with him. You do not have to dodge his questions—say what you please."

He did not have to tell her that. She knew almost nothing of importance to reveal to anyone.

"Your mother had visions," a dimly remembered voice whispered. Katia stopped walking, wondering why this voice had come to her now. She put out a hand and felt Grisha take it.

"Your mother saw visions, and spoke to the spirits." The voice was Black Cow's. She had spoken those words to Katia while they were riding to the camp of Touch-the-Clouds.

"I never heard of her speaking to spirits," Katia had replied.

"It was when she was younger, before she became your father's woman," Black Cow said. "After that, she became as you knew her. After that, the only visions that mattered for our people were those of Touch-the-Clouds."

Katia came to herself, saw the concern in Grisha's face, then noticed that a few people were staring at them. "I was remembering," she said. "It is nothing." But she suddenly knew that the spirits must have carried that memory to her.

Grisha had their dinner brought to their suite, and Katia saw that Lemuel Rowland was not used to the rich food or to having a waiter hover over him to serve him. When she excused herself to go to her own room, she noted the surprised look in his eyes when Grisha told him that he had secured another room for himself and for Rowland. Clearly Rowland had expected her and her guardian to share the same room. Several of Grisha's acquaintances had also assumed that she was his woman, but in fact he had never touched her except to take her hand or elbow. Once she had been grateful for that. Now she wondered at his restraint, at his lack of interest in her, and found herself disturbed by his indifference.

That night, she dreamed, and found herself in the midst of a great camp of tepees. It was time for the Sun Dance, and her people had gathered to renew their ties to the earth. In the center of the camp, she saw Touch-the-Clouds, and another man was with him, dressed in unfamiliar clothing—dark boots, and a long robe that was belted at the waist. He turned, and showed her a broad flat face with narrow dark eyes.

She walked among the men, the Crow Owners, the Owl Feathers, the Strong Hearts, the Foxes, the Dog Soldiers, the men of the Lakota and the Tsistsista who were gathered together in their warrior societies, and she wondered why she was there, what had brought her here. "My brother is here," Touch-the-Clouds said, and she knew that he meant the man standing with him. "He has come to us from the lands across the water far to the west. The hoop was broken, and now it will be joined once more. Our brother has come here to lead us into battle. The circle will close at last."

Waking, Katia knew that the spirits had spoken to her again, but she did not know what they were trying to tell her. She had once seen a picture of a man who had looked like the one standing with Touch-the-Clouds, a painting in a book of tales about faraway lands, but she recalled no more than that.

She slept again, but no more dreams came to her. In the morning, she dressed and left her room to find Lemuel Rowland sitting alone at a table set for breakfast.

He got to his feet as she approached, looking awkward. "Good morning, Miss Rubalev," he said. He was courteous; she had met some who did not call her by name at all, who treated her as even less than a servant.

She went to the table and sat down. "Denis Laforte has gone to secure our passage to St. Louis," he continued. "Mr. Rubalev wants to leave as soon as possible—he has gone to pay our bill and make arrangements."

"We are leaving today?" she asked, surprised.

"Tomorrow or the day after."

She poured herself a glass of water from the pitcher, then helped herself to some bread. "Mr. Rubalev has been generous to me," the man continued, "paying for my travel, putting me up here. I don't quite know why, unless as a favor to Commissioner Ely Parker. I served with Mr. Parker during the war, in the Union forces."

"I have seen Mr. Parker," she said. "Sometimes he came to see Grisha at his house."

"Grisha?"

"It is what I call Mr. Rubalev." She took another sip of water. "It is what he asked me to call him."

"He's told me something about himself without actually saying what he does. I suppose that he must be in some kind of business venture."

She drank her water, saying nothing.

"And that he has been successful at it," Lemuel Rowland went on.

She said, "If you have any questions, you should ask them of Grisha."

"I have asked him a few. He's talked about his past and how he came to Washington, but not much else. I suppose it's none of my concern." He paused. "Would it be unmannerly of me if I asked you how you came to be his ward?"

She lifted her head. He was gazing at her, looking as if he might actually be curious about her.

"You are a Seneca, an Iroquois," she said. "Grisha told me that. I am Lakota—a Sioux, the whites would call me."

"I know something of the Sioux," he said. "I lived among them for a short time, when Ely Parker and I were on a mission to investigate complaints about the agencies on the reservations. It's a hard life, it takes strength and courage to live it."

He paused. "I was brought up by a white family," he continued. "They were kind to me in their way. They were the people who gave me my name." He sat back and she saw that he was still waiting for her to answer his question.

"My people are dead," she said, "my father and my mother and uncle. We had a treaty with the whites, but a band of Blue Coats came to my father's camp and killed everyone there except for me and one old woman. We were spared only because they didn't find us, or else they would have killed us, too."

She saw sorrow in his eyes and looked away. He would have seen a lot of death during his time as a soldier; she wondered that her story could move him. He had, after all, admitted to having worn the blue uniform of the men who had killed her father and mother. "We rode to another camp, and that was where I first saw Grisha. I have lived with him ever since. He has been kind."

"It might have been kinder to leave you in the East instead of bringing you West again."

She glanced at him. "I do not know why you say that."

"It must remind you—" He fell silent.

"I do not have so many memories, Mr. Rowland. I recall only what I care to of my early life, and those things that I do remember do not cause me pain any more. And if I had not wanted to come, Grisha would not have forced me to go." She said that without knowing if it was true. Grisha had never forced her to do anything. Her gratitude to him and her knowledge that, without him, she could neither live in the white world or return to her own people had made it impossible for her to defy him, to do anything except what he wanted of her.

"How long are you to stay in St. Louis?" she continued. "Do you plan to settle there?"

"I don't know. I'm already thinking that I should have stayed in the East and found work there, perhaps in New York. There will be more fighting in the West, fighting that's futile. I would rather not be close to it."

He had to mean that he was tired of fighting. She did not think that he was a coward.

The door opened, and Grisha entered from the hallway. "It is settled," he said as he took off his hat. "We are leaving as soon as we can." He came to the table and sat down, then glanced at Rowland. "I heard you speak to Katia of fighting."

Rowland tensed. "I didn't mean to say anything that might upset her. I was saying only that—"

"I understand, Mr. Rowland. And you cannot upset Katia with talk. And what fighting is it that you regard as futile?"

"That of the red men trying to hold on to their lands in the West. Please don't misunderstand me." Rowland looked at Katia for a moment. "My sympathies are with them, but they'll be lucky if they can keep even some of their land."

Grisha leaned back and folded his arms. "I would like to hear your reasons for believing that."

"They are outnumbered, greatly outnumbered. Their weapons are no match for those of soldiers and settlers. They have no industry at all, no places to make the things they would need to fight people with many more resources. They would be even worse off than the Confederates were toward the end. The most that they can hope for is to hold off the settlers and miners and all the others after their land for a few more years, and then to be allowed to live on their reservations in peace."

Rowland's words were those of a man who was resigned, but there was still a hopeful sound in his voice. He does not want to believe his own words, Katia thought; he is fighting them even as he speaks them.

"Your comrade Donehogawa is their voice in Washington," Grisha said. "He will try to hold the government to its treaties."

"It won't do any good," Rowland said, "not in the long run. The best he can do is to keep the peace long enough for the Indians there to agree to stay on the lands allotted to them. If the commissioner stands in the way of too many men who covet the western lands, they'll find the means to get him out of their way."

Grisha rubbed his chin and was silent as Katia poured him some coffee. He sipped from his cup, then said, "I have a story to tell you, Lemuel Rowland, a story of what happened in a place far from here. Would you care to hear it?"

"Surely," Rowland said, "if only to pass the time."

"This is something that happened hundreds of years ago in the lands bordering the motherland of my ancestors."

Rowland gazed steadily at Grisha.

"Far to the east," Grisha began, "there was a rich empire inhabited by millions of people. To the west, outside the wall that bordered the empire, bands of horsemen roamed. The wealthy empire had great candles that could be fired into the air, siege engines, all manner of weaponry, and trained armies as well, while the horsemen, who were poor and lived in tents, had only their swords, bows, and lances. The empire's soldiers were many, while the horsemen were few, and yet the horsemen conquered the empire and became its rulers."

Rowland looked doubtful. Katia had heard the story once before, and knew that Grisha had told it to a few others.

"I see that you do not quite believe me," Grisha said, "but it is the truth. These horsemen also conquered the lands that lay west of them. They took those of my own ancestors, as it happens. I have often thought that I am in part a descendant of those conquerors— my grandfather had claimed to be such."

Some of the doubt left Rowland's face. "You wouldn't be telling me this tale," he said, "unless you thought it had some bearing on what we said earlier."

"That is perceptive, Mr. Rowland."

"You say that this happened long ago."

"Yes."

"These horsemen didn't have to face Springfields and Enfields and Spencer repeating rifles."

"That is so, Mr. Rowland, but they were still greatly outnumbered and without weapons that were the equal of the eastern empire's—yet they conquered it."

Rowland looked thoughtful. "Then I must assume that this great empire, despite its wealth and its weapons, had weaknesses that allowed the horsemen to win—a lack of the will to fight, perhaps, or a loss of morale among their troops."

"That is part of it," Grisha said, "and also that the eastern empire was divided and had three rulers, and that some of their armies chose to go over to the invaders. And these horsemen were quick to learn." He paused. "Before this time, the horsemen had fought among themselves, but one chief united them and led them to conquer much of the world. This chief was called Genghis Khan."

"An inspiring story," Lemuel Rowland murmured.

"And you are thinking that it is only something that happened long ago and far away." Grisha finished his coffee and poured himself another cup. "I have another story for you, one about a people long ago who left one land for a new land—who settled in this land long ago."

Rowland frowned. "I've heard enough stories about the early white settlers."

"I am talking about something that happened long before that, Mr. Rowland. An old man who was one of my teachers told me this tale. He believed that, long before these horsemen I spoke of became conquerors, some of their ancestors had left their land for this one. It must have been a long and difficult journey—they would have had to go through Siberia and then find a way to cross over to Alaska."

Katia tensed; she had not heard this story before. Siberia and Alaska—she had only the dimmest notion of where they were, although she had seen them marked on maps.

"They would have had to use boats," Rowland said, "and the ice and cold surely would have made such a crossing difficult. Unless it was so cold, and the strait so frozen, that they could walk across it."

"My old teacher had reason to think that Siberia and Alaska were not separated by water, that a land bridge once connected them. He believed that these people long ago crossed that bridge and came to this land. This should be of some interest to you."

Rowland raised his brows, looking doubtful.

"How do you think the ancestors of your people came to be here?" Grisha glanced at Katia. "Or the Lakota, or the Cheyenne, or any of the tribes who were here before the white man came?"

"I've heard a number of stories," Rowland replied. "All of them come down to this—the Creator, or Divine Providence, put us here, or perhaps we were always here, from the time God made the world."

"Or you came from elsewhere," Grisha said. "My teacher believed that the peoples here might have come from the same place where these horsemen I spoke of—the Tatars—lived later. He had reasons for believing this. One was the physical resemblance of the Aleuts we knew to Tatars, and another was tales that he heard from a few old natives. So there you have it—the red men here might be the brothers of men far to the west, across the Pacific. And the men of the Plains are horsemen, as were the Tatars."

"There were no horses here before the white man came," Lemuel said.

"But they are horsemen now. It is as if they recalled what their ancestors once knew, is it not?"

Katia gripped the arms of her chair. A sharp pain bloomed inside her head; she closed her eyes, afraid that she might faint.

"Miss Rubalev," she heard Rowland say.

"I'm all right," she whispered.

"Do you wish to rest?" That was Grisha's voice.

"Yes. I shall be in my room." She got to her feet and stumbled toward her room, waving Grisha away before he could help her.

She lay on her bed in the darkness, waiting for the pain to leave her. In a while, she heard a soft knock on the door and then it creaked open.

"Katia?" Grisha said. "Denis came back. I sent him out again with Rowland, to amuse him and show him the city."

She opened her eyes. Grisha came inside and sat down in a chair near the bed. "Will you be well enough to travel?"

"Yes. Of course." The pain was fading. "It is nothing."

"What happened, Katia?"

"It was something you said." She swallowed. "I had a dream last night. I thought that the spirits were trying to speak to me again."

"What did you dream?"

"I saw Touch-the-Clouds, at the Sun Dance, but another man was with him. Touch-the-Clouds spoke of the circle closing and said that the man with him was his brother, come to him from far to the west, across the water."

"Ah."

"I didn't know what this meant," she went on. "Then you spoke of those—those horsemen, and how—" She rolled her head from side to side on the pillow. "It made me think of my dream."

"You have not lost your gift, then. Touch-the-Clouds will be happy to hear that." He was silent for a while. "Your vision was not unlike his own, the vision that showed him his purpose. Do you know what I was in the years before I found you?"

Why was he asking that question? she wondered. He never spoke of those years.

"I was an adventurer," he continued, "my only skill that of thinking up ways to make the money of others my own, along with some small talents that could aid me in this business—a good memory, a strong body, an ear that helped me to master other tongues. I left San Francisco in the company of scouts and trappers, thinking that I might find ways to make more money in the East when the war came, as I was certain it would, and that along the way I would learn a few things from my companions. And then I met Touch-the-Clouds, and knew that he—"

Grisha cleared his throat. "There are times when one is seeking without knowing it, looking for what it is one must do without knowing what it is. One of the brothers of Touch-the-Clouds told me of his first vision, when he had gone out alone as a youth to seek it. He came back with his name and his vision of a brother far away, one who would come to him and fight at his side. And then Touch-the-Clouds told me himself of the hoop that would be mended, and of the brother who would aid him. He described his vision to me—the man on horseback with his tunic and belt and sword and bow and the shaven head and black braid coiled behind his ears—and I knew that he had seen a Tatar. And I knew what it meant. Now the same vision has come to you."

"But I do not know what it means," she murmured.

"Genghis Khan conquered China and Russia. Other khans followed him, his sons and grandsons, but he was the khan who ruled most of the world. And Touch-the-Clouds is his brother, the man who can be the American Khan."

"What are you talking about?" Katia whispered.

"The American Khan, the ruler in these lands."

She raised herself on one elbow, frightened by the tone in his voice. "Grisha, if he can keep the Lakota hunting grounds, that will be enough, and he will need the consent of the other chiefs for that."

"Ah. Yes, perhaps." He sat back in his chair, and she had the feeling that he regretted his words to her. "What do you think of Lemuel Rowland?"

"That he is unhappy. That he will soon forget us. If you were hoping that he would come west with us, I am sure that he will not."

"Do you think he is trustworthy?"

"Yes. I don't know how I know that, but I see it. Grisha—" She sat up. "Let me stay in St. Louis." He gazed at her steadily. "Or send me back to Washington."

"What is it, Katia? Are you afraid?"

"It isn't that. I'm of no use to you here."

"I will leave it to Touch-the-Clouds to decide that. You will come with me, Katia."

Of course she would. She had nowhere else to go, no means of supporting herself. "I am of no importance to him," she said, "but I will go."

"Yes, you will. Do you think I took you in for nothing, for no reason? I think I know what Touch-the-Clouds intends for you. I think that he intends to make you his wife."

FOUR

Caleb Tornor thought of Fort Riley as the ends of the earth. He had grown up amid Pennsylvania's green hills, but even a boyhood passed in a desert might not have prepared him for this desolation. The wind blew so hard across the flat Kansas plateau that the blowing sand could scour pots. To the west was emptiness and Indians—Cheyenne, Sioux—not that it mattered much to him which particular tribe of redskins he encountered.

Now, riding out from the fort, he began to appreciate Fort Riley. There was something of civilization inside its walls. There was nothing civilized out here, on the empty flat land stretching to nowhere, nothing but Indians and the buffalo they hunted.

He could not for the life of him figure out why the Negro soldiers had deserted, but they had, and his orders were to bring them back, one way or another.

Buffalo soldiers, the Indians called them. The redskins were afraid of them, some said. Caleb had heard that they wouldn't scalp a black man they had killed because they thought it was bad medicine, although maybe it was only because the hair wouldn't make for an impressive scalp. Maybe the deserters thought that the redskins would be too afraid to come after them, but they wouldn't be too fearful of ten men to kill them all, even if they did leave them their hair.

And if we find the niggers first, Caleb thought, they're not much better off than they would be with the redskins. George Armstrong Custer wasn't an officer to let men get away with desertion. Some had tried it a couple of years ago and been shot for their trouble, and they had been white men. "Bring them back dead or alive" was the colonel's order, not that Caleb would have cared all that much about what happened to the black men.

Caleb had fought in the war, not to free darkies or to preserve the Union, but because he had lacked the money to buy himself out of the draft. As a soldier in the Army of the Potomac, he had expected to be afraid most of the time, terrified of dying and maybe even more afraid of losing a limb and having to drag through the rest of his life with a shattered body. He had seen men lying on the battle-field with their own bloody entrails clutched in their hands, had heard them scream in pain as their damaged legs and arms were cut away from the rest of them. He had known dark fear, but also the exhilaration of knowing that he was alive while others were dead, and that some of the dead had died at his hands. His comrades had longed for their homes, but Caleb soon realized that he was not like the other soldiers. The longer he was away from the farm where he had grown up, the more pallid and tiresome and tedious his past life became. He had not gone home when the war ended, but west.

He had been with Custer and the Seventh ever since the winter campaign against the Cheyenne, when they had been ordered to kill all the warriors in the camp of one of the chiefs. It had been eas-ier simply to shoot at any Indian rather than to try to sort out women and children and old people from the fighting men. Custer had found himself a girl in that camp, although he had been quick to abandon her before rejoining his wife. Caleb still did not know how Custer could have wanted a redskin girl in his bed, however pretty she was. Some of the men might sink that low, but he never had, not yet.

Young Jebediah Kearns rode up ahead, peering at the ground. Most of their Indian scouts had run off long ago, disappearing into the Plains. Caleb cared for Indians considerably less than he cared for blacks, but a few of the Crows could be tolerated, and once they had been useful. Now they preferred even the company of their old enemies the Cheyenne and the Sioux to that of the United States Cavalry.

Caleb knew that the Indians could be beaten. Custer was itching to go after the Cheyenne for their raids; General Sheridan was ready to mount a campaign against their winter camping grounds. But Washington was holding them back. Some said that the expense of fighting Indians, especially in the wake of the War Between the States, was draining the Union treasury. Others claimed that the commissioner of Indian Affairs had talked the president into holding the troops back.

And while Washington dithered, the Indians grew more stubborn in their resistance, more bands disappeared from the reservations and the lands near the agencies, and it was rumored that more of the tribes were smoking the peace pipe with old enemies.

The men riding behind Caleb were quiet now, but he had heard their grumbling back at Fort Riley. The blacks were not the only soldiers capable of deserting. If they kept letting the redskins get away with more raids without striking back severely, other men would lose heart. Presumably any other deserters would have enough wit to flee east instead of west, to safety instead of into territory full of savages.

What bothered him about this bunch of deserters was that they hadn't deserted all of a sudden, but with some forethought. They had to have been thinking about it, planning for it. Given that niggers did not, as far as he could tell, have much natural equipment to think with, he was struck by the care they had put into their desertion—the stolen food they had taken with them, the extra weapons and horses. The blacks who had come back to the fort, who had refused to run off with the deserters, were soon looking as if they regretted having made the choice to return.

The trail of the deserters was fairly easy to follow. They had not buried the evidence of their fires, or made much effort to hide their tracks as they rode west. He and his men kept on the trail until the sun had set and it was time to make camp.

They were up before dawn, shivering in the cold as they mounted their horses. The flat land soon gave way to small hills, which made Caleb more wary. He preferred a flat plain where he could see what was coming from far off; men could be ambushed from hills.

"Bunch of niggers," a man behind him said. Caleb knew his voice for that of Bob Tenefer. "I say maybe we oughta let the red-skins have 'em."

Jeb Kearns was riding back to them. "Saw something up ahead, sir . . ." he gasped out as he reined in his horse ". . . ain't gonna like it." He caught his breath. "There's tracks of Indian ponies up ahead. There's the tracks of Washburn's men, and then they meet with these redskin tracks, and then they go on like they're riding together, Washburn's men and the Indians."

Washburn was the black sergeant with the deserters. "Hold on," Caleb said. "Riding together? Like they been captured?"

Kearns shook his head. "Like they just met up with each other. Like they stopped there a bit to rest up and then rode on. No sign of somebody trying to get away, or a fight."

It sounded like a trap. Caleb felt a prickling at the back of his neck. Given his druthers, he would have ordered his men back to the fort right now.

"Kearns," he said, "your platoon's coming with me. The rest of you wait here two hours and then come after us." He didn't like dividing his forces that way, but liked the idea of leading them all into a trap even less. "If we haven't caught up with them by tomorrow night, we're heading back to the fort."

He rode on with Kearns, the other men behind them. The trail was now leading them northwest. There were more hills around them. By evening, they stopped to make camp. After sunset, the second column had caught up with them.

Caleb posted guards, then tried to sleep. In the middle of the night, one of the sentries came to his tent to wake him. "Sir," the man whispered, "I think they're out there. Do you hear it?"

He threw off his blanket and sat up. For a moment, he could hear the distant sound of chanting and wailing, and then it died.

"I think we better get ready to meet them," Caleb said. It was too late to turn back and hope that they could outrun them. The men dug makeshift barricades of dirt, cleaned their rifles again, and waited.

At dawn, they saw the tiny shapes of men on horseback against the horizon. Caleb squinted, counting them, seeing that they greatly outnumbered his men. Then the strangers began to ride toward them, dust billowing around the legs of their mounts.

He threw himself behind one dirt ridge and took aim, then saw that one of the Indians in front was carrying a white banner. "Hold your fire," he shouted to his men. "Looks like they want to talk."

Most of them were Cheyenne; he could tell that by their war bonnets. Others were Sioux, and a few he recognized as Kiowa. The sight of them all together made him even more uneasy, and there was another man with them, one with light brown skin and a black man's woolly hair.

Caleb stood still as they rode toward him. Most of them reined in their horses and halted two hundred feet away while a group of five, the woolly-haired man among them, trotted toward Caleb. His men were ready to shoot if anything went amiss, but taking on this band would be suicide; they outnumbered his men at least four to one, possibly more. Also in their favor was that every one of them, as far as he could see, had a rifle and wore an ammunition belt, and several had pistols at their waists. Where had they stolen all that firepower?

The woolly-haired man, who looked like he might be a light-skinned Negro, raised one arm. He wore a loose cloth shirt, leather leggings, and the leather shield of an Indian brave hung from his saddle. "I'll speak for my comrades," he said without preamble. "You are in pursuit of ten deserters—am I correct?"

Rough as the man looked, he had a precise, almost prissy, way of talking. "You got that right," Caleb replied. "Lieutenant Caleb Tornor of Company F of the Seventh Cavalry. I've got orders to bring those men back dead or alive. If they've changed their minds, we'll take them back with us. If they're dead, I'd be obliged if your—comrades—" he almost spit the word "—would let us take back the bodies."

"They are not dead," the Negro said, "and they would prefer not to ride back with you."

A nigger with airs, Caleb thought as he listened to the man talk; a nigger with airs running around with a pack of savages. "I don't know that unless they tell me so themselves," he said.

The Negro smiled. "Then you'll just have to take my word for it. They're not in your country anymore. They have decided they would rather be part of another nation."

"I don't know what kind of nation that would be," Caleb said. "There's nothing out here except for Indians and buffalo—maybe a few coyotes."

"There are people who have been granted these lands by treaty. If others choose to join them, they are welcome here. That's the message we give you to take back with you if you leave peacefully. Keep your soldiers and settlers east of Fort Laramie, and keep your railroad tracks away from the buffalo grazing grounds in the northern Plains, and there is no reason for us to fight. And, as I said, anyone who wants to live among us is free to do so."

"Renegades," Caleb muttered. "I thought the Indians didn't want settlers out here."

"They wouldn't all be settlers. They could be—" The man paused. "They could be Cheyenne, Kiowa, Lakota, Comanche, Crow—depending of course on which people they chose to live among."

"Renegades, you mean." Caleb spat, filled with disgust and contempt for this pale-skinned smooth-talking darkie and the black deserters. "I've got to talk to my men."

"Fine," the Negro said. "We'll wait yonder." He said something else to the Indians with him in another tongue, and then they rode back to where the other Indians were waiting.

"Sir," Jeb Kearns said, "I seen him before, the one talking to you."

Caleb tensed. "Where?"

"Junction City—and I seen him talking to Josiah Washburn. They was standing out in the street, just talking. And a month later, I seen them talking in a saloon."

"You're sure it was the same man," Caleb said.

"I'm sure."

He could put it together now. Washburn and the others had not only decided to desert, they had known where they were going. His stomach knotted. He could understand the black soldiers wanting to desert. Army life got to some men after a while, and there had been more discontent among the troops lately as they waited for their commanders to act. He could even understand a bunch of men making for the frontier and hoping they could stay alive out there. But these men had joined the savages. Whatever he thought about darkies, whatever other lacks they had and however inferior to the white man they were, he had always assumed that they hated Indians as much as he did.

Caleb looked around at the other men. "All right," he muttered. "They outnumber us. They've got enough firepower to wipe us out, and we can't outrun them. We'll have to go back without the deserters."

Bob Tenefer whistled. "Glad I won't be in your boots when you report to Custer."

Caleb did not want to think of that. Maybe this time, he told himself, somebody'll do something when they hear about this. Maybe they'll finally turn Sheridan loose.

He left his men and beckoned to the Negro and the Indians. The man began to ride toward him, with two braves on either side. Caleb swallowed the anger that suddenly welled up inside him.

FIVE

A few days after Katia came to the camp of Touch-the-Clouds, she had a dream in which she heard a woman's voice speaking her old name, the name she had forgotten. When she woke, she remembered that her name was Graceful Swan and that the voice she had heard in her dream was her mother's. She spoke her name to the wife of Touch-the-Clouds and the other women, only to find out that they had known it all along, that the chief had given it to them, but had been waiting to see if she would discover it for herself.

Things were a little easier for Graceful Swan after that. White Cow Sees, the wife of Touch-the-Clouds, brought her into her tepee and told her that their mothers had been the daughters of two sisters. As she looked after the dogs with the other women, worked at buffalo hides, watched over the younger son of White Cow Sees, and cooked game, Graceful Swan felt some of her old life coming back to her. Sometimes she could imagine that White Cow Sees was the mother she had lost, and that little had changed for her since her childhood. At other times, when she watched White Cow

Sees fashioning an adze from bone, sewing beads on deerskin in elaborate patterns that Graceful Swan had forgotten how to read, or spreading fat on a hide to prepare it for softening, she thought of how much lore she had lost, how much she might never master. Often, she was too tired even to think of whether she was happy or unhappy.

Grisha left two days after they arrived, to ride west with Denis Laforte and two Lakota men, saying only that he would come back before the Moon of the Shedding Ponies. In his absence, Graceful Swan went about her work, making herself as useful as she could to White Cow Sees. She saw no sign that Touch-the-Clouds intended to make her his wife, as Grisha had predicted. Instead the chief seemed indifferent to her presence.

Perhaps Grisha had been mistaken. Maybe Touch-the-Clouds, despite his horses and his followers and the means to care for more than one woman, preferred to keep only one wife. White Cow Sees had given him two sons, and was growing heavy with her third child.

After seventeen days, Grisha returned to the camp. He went into the tepee of Touch-the-Clouds, and the two men spoke for a while. That night, the chief asked Graceful Swan if she would become his wife. She searched his face for some sign of longing or passion, but saw only the same distant indifferent gaze she often glimpsed in Grisha's eyes.

She and Touch-the-Clouds were married in early summer, during the Moon When the Ponies Shed. White Cow Sees, her nearest female relative, provided her with a tepee and some household goods, although Graceful Swan was certain that Grisha had come to some sort of bargain with the chief in payment for them. She was carried on a blanket to her own tepee, where a feast was held, and she listened in silence as the men told stories of past battles and the women spoke of their children.

Graceful Swan's new husband spent one night with her before leaving the camp to meet with a Kiowa chief to the south. He was silent during their lovemaking and said nothing to her afterward before he rode away, but Graceful Swan knew from the sounds she had often heard in the night that Touch-the-Clouds felt more passion for his other wife. Perhaps more time had to pass before her husband could show the same feelings for her.

When Touch-the-Clouds returned, he spent one night with White Cow Sees and the next with Graceful Swan. This time, he was gentler with her, and held her face between his hands after he had spent himself.

"You have not been unhappy here," he said as he stretched out at her side.

"No, I have not," she said.

"My other wife has a liking for you." His words warmed her. "Were you unhappy in the world of the Wasichu? Or were you content to leave it?"

She did not know what to tell him. There had been many moments of unhappiness among the whites, especially during her years at school, when the other girls had whispered about her behind her back and sometimes openly insulted her, but nothing that had evoked deep sorrow or despair. She had been reasonably content in Grisha's house, living on the fringes of his life. Sometimes she wondered if all the feeling had been burned out of her by the massacre at her father's camp.

"The world of the Wasichu seems far away now," she said at last.

"It is coming closer to us," he said softly. "I must find out more about it before it swallows us," and then she heard a sound from him that might have been a laugh.

Two days later, when she was outside working at a hide with White Cow Sees, the great chief Crazy Horse came to his camp with ten of his warriors and said that he wanted to talk. Graceful Swan had heard from the others about how strange Crazy Horse looked, with his pale skin and reddish-black hair, and he looked strange even to her, after all of her years spent among palefaces. As Crazy Horse dismounted, Touch-the-Clouds made a short speech of welcome, invited the other chief into his tepee, and told Graceful Swan and White Cow Sees to remain outside.

* * *

Grisha was walking toward them from a tepee at the edge of the camp. In exchange for a couple of bundles of cloth and some metal pots, one warrior and his family had given him a place in their tent.

"You are not to enter," White Cow Sees said to him as he neared the chief's tepee. "Our husband and Crazy Horse have much to say to each other."

Graceful Swan saw Grisha's eyes widen as White Cow Sees spoke the name of Crazy Horse. Crazy Horse, Tashunka Witko . . . she sounded his name to herself silently. He was a great chief and a fierce fighter—that much everyone knew. He was said to possess strong war medicine and often wandered off by himself to seek visions. Some of the people who had spoken of him to her sounded both admiring and fearful. Now she knew from the look on Grisha's face that he was afraid of Crazy Horse.

He said, "I have heard that Crazy Horse is a man of few words."

White Cow Sees motioned toward her husband's tent with her head. "That is so, but he has many words to speak to my husband today." She walked off, her baby strapped to her back.

Graceful Swan looked away from Grisha. "What is it?" she whispered in English.

"I think that Crazy Horse came here to tell your husband that he cannot trust me." He paused. "That he should not trust me."

"But you are his friend."

"Crazy Horse does not think so."

At that moment, the entrance flap of the tepee was lifted. Crazy Horse came outside, followed by Touch-the-Clouds. When Graceful Swan looked at the two Lakota men, they kept their eyes from her, as though refusing to see her.

"In your camp," Crazy Horse muttered, "I feel farther from the real world than ever."

"The Crow have made peace with us," Touch-the-Clouds responded. "Some of the buffalo soldiers, the Wasichu Sapa, have decided to join us. Even some of the Wasichu will fight with us."

"The Wasichu are our enemies," Crazy Horse said.

"Not all of them. The Yellow Hair in my camp is my ally."

Crazy Horse looked directly at Grisha then, raising his head to gaze at the taller man with his black eyes. "It is this Yellow Hair in your camp who brings you to violate our sacred places. He has brought men from far away. He disturbs the spirits. He brings bad medicine to the Paha Sapa, the Black Hills, the center of the world."

"He is doing what my visions told us we must do. He is carrying out what my visions showed me we had to do to keep our lands, and I saw those visions before I ever laid eyes on him."

I should not be here listening to this, Katia thought. She wanted to run away from the men, but could not bring herself to move.

"Your visions did not tell you to violate our sacred places," Crazy Horse said, "to rob the ground of its yellow metal and dust, to bring in men and wagons from far away."

"Our sacred places have not been violated. We are taking only what the spirits have given to us so that we can win our war with the Wasichu."

Crazy Horse motioned at Grisha. "Is that what the Yellow Hair tells you? We should be at war with his people, too."

"We are not at war with him. The Wasichu to the east took his people's northern lands from them. We are not at war with his comrade, the man called Laforte." Touch-the-Clouds stepped back from the other chief. "I will tell you what the Yellow Hair is. His people came here from far to the west, but others of his people came here long ago, at the beginning of the world. They are both our ancestors and the ancestors of the Yellow Hair."

Crazy Horse shook himself.

"His ancestors and ours come from the same chief," Touch-the-Clouds went on, "a great chief who lived long ago on the other side of the world. This chief lived among bands of horsemen who warred with one another. He forced them to make treaties, and they became a nation of warriors. And when they were bound together, they rode against an enemy who lived to the east of them, a people with weapons and riches that were greater even than those of our Wasichu enemies."

"Did he drive them from his own lands?" Crazy Horse asked.

Touch-the-Clouds touched the small medicine bag of amulets

hanging around his neck. "He did more than that. He became their chief. He took their lands for his people."

Crazy Horse pressed his lips together. "We do not need the lands to the east," he said at last. "That is not why we fight. We fight for our sacred hills and our grazing grounds and to save the buffalo—we fight for what is ours, for what even the Wasichu call ours in their treaties before they break their promises. We fight to live as men should, to be free and to wander our hunting grounds."

Grisha seemed about to speak, but Crazy Horse looked at him then, and he kept silent.

"That is also why I fight," Touch-the-Clouds said, "to preserve what we have. But sometimes a man must strike at his enemy, and take more from him even than he wants to take, in order to keep what he has."

Crazy Horse said nothing.

"After I had my first vision, this Yellow Hair came to me and told my vision to me, told me what I had seen, before I had spoken of it to him. Have we not made allies of old enemies? Are we not stronger than we were? Does that not prove the truth of what my visions have shown me?"

"I remembered something before riding here," Crazy Horse said in a low voice. "I say remember because that is how it seemed, that my thoughts were turning to the past and what had happened then. I remembered a man riding to me to tell me of a long-haired Blue Coat and his men who rode down on Black Kettle's camp and killed everyone there—the women, the children, the old men. But I also remembered Black Kettle being left in peace, and a strong feeling—a knowing—that he was still alive came over me."

Touch-the-Clouds murmured, "Black Kettle and the Cheyenne who camped with him were killed at the Washita River by the Blue Coat called Long Hair Custer."

"I know that." Crazy Horse shook back his hair. "Yet this memory that he was still alive came to me, and that is what it was—a memory. It was not a vision, taking me from this world and showing me what is true, and yet it held the power of past truth. It was as real to me as my memory of my first buffalo hunt, or my first vision. I recalled the words of the warrior who told me of the massacre clearly. I knew that Black Kettle had left this world, and yet it was not so. I saw a world where he still lived, where his people still lived, and only after a while did I remember that it wasn't so. And I do not know what this means, this memory that was not a true memory."

Katia made a small sound in her throat. The gaze of Touch-the-Clouds shifted to her. "Get away from here, woman," he said harshly.

She fled.

Near sunset, Crazy Horse rode away with his band. The men, Grisha among them this time, had gone back inside the tepee of Touch-the-Clouds. Graceful Swan followed White Cow Sees back to their husband's tepee, wondering what had passed between the men.

Grisha came out of the tent, stood up straight, and said, "Crazy Horse is still our brother."

White Cow Sees smiled. "Of course he is. He only had to speak to my husband again to know that."

"I will be leaving soon," Grisha said to Graceful Swan in English as White Cow Sees stooped to enter the tepee.

"Where are you going?" she asked.

"I do not know yet, but Touch-the-Clouds will be more at ease if I leave his camp for a while."

That night, Graceful Swan's monthly bleeding came upon her. She kept away from her husband for four days until the bleeding stopped. Grisha had remained in the camp. On the day he was to leave, at the beginning of the Moon of Red Cherries, he came to her tepee.

"Go to your husband," Grisha told her, "and tell him that you are coming away with me."

She gaped at him, too startled to speak, wondering if Grisha had grown jealous of her husband. Perhaps he had come to love her, to regret seeing her married to Touch-the-Clouds. She felt confused.

"Have you lost your wits, Katia?" He spoke in English now. "He thinks that you now may be of more use to him away from here. You will still be his wife—he knows that there is nothing between us. Even if there were, you would have the right to leave him."

"I don't know what to tell him," she said softly.

"Tell him that it has been hard for you to live your old life, that you have grown used to the white world, that there are people and places you want to see before you return to him. Tell him whatever you like, Katia. He wants you to go, and I have agreed to take you. He is only trying to save you from being shamed in front of others by letting you leave him, instead of having him hand you over to me."

For a moment, she could not breathe. Something swelled inside her and she began to shake. She wanted to scream, to rage at Grisha and her husband for what they were doing, for treating her this way.

"You take me away and teach me how to live in your world," she said, keeping her voice low. "Then you bring me back here and I have to remember my name and find my old life and now that I've found it, you want to take me away again."

"Are you so sorry to leave? Have you not tired of the work? Do you love your husband so much?"

Katia looked at him from the sides of her eyes. "I know that he does not love me."

"You can see visions. You have medicine in you, strong medicine, that the chief might be able to use. You know how to live in the world of the Wasichu, and perhaps he can use that, too. If he wins his battles, you will be honored and rewarded for any part you play in his victory."

She made her hands into fists. "You care nothing for me, either."

"I am concerned for you. I would not willingly see harm come to you." Grisha showed his teeth. "It is true that if you had been an ordinary, simple girl with no gifts and no beauty and nothing I could use, I would have left you in this camp when you were still a child. Do you think you would have been happier then?"

She was still trembling. Her gorge rose; she wanted to lash out at Grisha, to strike him and curse at him. She had not known that she could feel such rage.

"You have a chance now," he went on, "to help Touch-the-Clouds avenge your mother and father and all of your people, to see that the Wasichu never commit such crimes against other red men again, but you must let others decide how to use you in that struggle."

She struggled to control her anger. Rage would not help her. If Grisha and Touch-the-Clouds planned to use her, then she would have to find a way to gain something for herself in whatever they intended for her.

Grisha said, "Go to your husband and tell him that you are leaving him."

She turned and walked toward her husband's tepee. It was strange that she felt no pain at knowing that Touch-the-Clouds wanted her to leave him, but she had seen all along that he did not care for her. She was not carrying his child, so he did not need her here, she was useless to him here. He needed her for some purpose of his own, something connected to Grisha and the Lakota battle with the Wasichu.

It came to her then that she would miss White Cow Sees much more than she would miss her husband. Leaving her would be like losing her mother all over again.

SIX

Black Eagle had encountered many wonders in Washington. In the house of the Great Father, he had seen tiny fires flickering inside crystal ornaments that glittered on the sides of walls and hung down from high ceilings into vast rooms. He had seen places with more houses and walls and people than he had ever believed could exist in the world. He and Red Cloud and the other chiefs had ridden the Iron Horse from their lands to the place called Chicago, and Black Eagle had marveled that one city could hold so many people. Later, he had traveled through other cities that were even bigger than Chicago.

The Iron Horse, with its shaking and its panting and its thick black smoke, had at first terrified him, and the masses of people rushing about in the Wasichu cities had made him even more fearful. But nothing on the journey to the East had frightened Black Eagle as much as returning to his own land knowing that he would have to ride to Touch-the-Clouds to tell him of what he had seen.

Touch-the-Clouds, he told himself as his horse trotted over the grassland, was one of the greatest of the Lakota chiefs, surely as great as Crazy Horse or Sitting Bull. He was, many now said, the equal of any chief who had ever lived, but Black Eagle preferred to admire his greatness from a distance.

Black Eagle reined in his horse. By the time the camp of Touch-the-Clouds was visible on the western horizon, thin gray streams of smoke rising from tepees crowned by the fans of the poles that supported them, his mount was moving at a trot. He now wished that he had never promised Touch-the-Clouds that he would report to him on his journey. When he had made that promise, he was expecting to see Wasichu in settlements much larger than their forts and outlying towns, and more signs of their power and wealth, but not the mobs of white people, the buildings that seemed to touch the clouds, and things that he did not understand, ornaments of glass and metal and tubing that made strange sounds and that he could stare at for a long time without being able even to guess at what they were. In the great rooms where they had lived while in Washington—he and Red Cloud and Spotted Tail and all the other chiefs who had gone there at the Little Father's invitation—he would stare at the carpet under his feet and the pictures on the walls and wonder how they had been made. He had wondered at times if he were still in the real world.

How could he speak to Touch-the-Clouds about that? How could he tell the other chief that his visions might have misled him about how to fight the Wasichu?

His horse slowed to a walk. Touch-the-Clouds would wonder why Black Eagle had come alone, why he had not brought his brother, his son, or some of his men with him. It was because he was far more afraid of Touch-the-Clouds than of anything he had seen among the Wasichu, and did not want anyone close to him to suffer if Touch-The-Clouds grew angry with him about what he would have to tell him. Touch-the-Clouds, everyone knew, had killed his own brother for raiding a Crow village, even though the Crow had long been their enemies before promising peace. No Lakota had dared to call his brother's death a murder, or to point out that his brother had had unfinished business with the Crow chief he had attacked, and that some would consider his raid justified.

Black Eagle did not want to think of what Touch-the-Clouds might do to a man who was riding to him to tell him that his battle was lost before he even fought it.

Touch-the-Clouds welcomed Black Eagle into his tepee, seating him in the back, in the place of honor, under a leather shield that hung from a horn set into a pole. His wife, White Cow Sees, set out food. Black Eagle expected that others would come there to make speeches of welcome and to hear what he had to say, but when they had finished their meal, Touch-the-Clouds looked directly at him and said, "Tell me about this new treaty between Red Cloud and the Wasichu."

"It is not a new treaty," Black Eagle replied, dismayed that the other man obviously wanted to speak to him alone. The presence of other men and the smoking of a ceremonial pipe might have brought Touch-the-Clouds to swallow his anger and restrain himself. "It is the same treaty offered to the Lakota before we went to Washington. Since we and the Wasichu are in agreement about what it says, Red Cloud and any of the Lakota who wish to live in their hunting grounds may do so. It says so in the treaty, whatever we were told before. We can stay by the Powder River, and do not have to live by the Missouri. We do not have to stay on the reservation or trade there."

"That is what the Wasichu say now," Touch-the-Clouds said in a small voice. When his voice got that small and that soft, Black Eagle was even more afraid of him than when he shouted. "Later their interpreters will tell us that the treaty says something else again."

"It was the Little Father who told us we were right about what the treaty says," Black Eagle said, "and the Great Father agreed with him."

White Cow Sees sat in the shadows to their left with her two sons, one of them a baby and the other a boy of five years. "Tell us of what you saw in the East," she said after a long silence.

He spoke of the Iron Horse and the cities that were like anthills and the strawberries and cream they had eaten at the Great Father's White House, and then Touch-the-Clouds waved a hand impatiently. "I don't want to hear tales of one wonder after another and of how you filled your bellies. I want to know what you think of the Wasichu."

Black Eagle had been dreading that demand. His eyes shifted uneasily toward the large medicine bundle on the right side of the tent as he silently sent up a prayer for protection. "What I think of them?" he asked, trying to put off what he must say.

"What you think our chances are against such an enemy. How strong you think they are. How the chiefs who traveled with you think we could fight such an enemy if the treaty is broken again."

"We would fight them as we have before." Touch-the-Clouds would have seen that answer coming; he was probing for something else. Black Eagle had seen him do it before when meeting with other chiefs, asking questions that everyone else believed were already answered, as if the true answer to what he was asking had to be flushed from the thicket of words like a rabbit from under a bush.

Touch-the-Clouds leaned forward. "You mean that we must fight them here, drive them back from our lands."

"How else can we fight them?" Black Eagle asked. "All we can hope to do is to keep what lands we have and make the Wasichu honor their treaties. But we may be able to do that without fighting, with the Little Father to speak for us in the councils in Washington. He is our friend."

"When he was traveling near our lands, up the Missouri, I did not go to see him. Perhaps I should have, so that I could see for myself what kind of man he is. His comrade stayed in another camp for a short time, and I did not go to see him, either. The Little Father, Ely Parker, calls himself our friend, but what I see is that he is asking our people to live on only whatever lands the Wasichu will allow us to have. He wants much the same thing as the Wasichu want from us. The only difference is that he does not lust to kill us and will give us more time to resign ourselves to giving up whatever the whites want to take from us before we are forced to live as diggers of soil, as men tilling the ground." Touch-the-Clouds turned his head and spat.

"He is our friend," Black Eagle said again, but the words sounded more hollow this time.

Touch-the-Clouds drew up his legs and rested his arms on them. "Tell me of your meetings with him."

"But you know what happened. You know of the treaty, and—"

"I want to hear it in your words, Black Eagle."

"It is very simple." Black Eagle sucked in some air. "When the treaty was first said to us in our own tongue, by the white chief called Secretary Cox, Red Cloud said that it was not the treaty he had agreed to earlier. He said that the words were wrong, that the interpreters were wrong. The Wasichu Cox disagreed. Red Cloud grew very angry. At last we went back to the rooms in the great house where we were living and Red Cloud said that we had been lied to and would have to go home. I said that if we went home then, we would have to tell everyone that we were deceived, and that I would rather die in Washington than do that." He let out a sigh. "But the Little Father Parker told us that he would set things right, and so he did. We went to another meeting with the man Cox, and were told that the treaty was as we understood it, that the interpreters had been wrong when they translated it for us."

Black Eagle paused. "Go on," Touch-the-Clouds said.

"That's all there is to say. From Washington, we went to New York, and Red Cloud went before many Wasichu, and he saw that many of them were willing to be our friends. You would have marveled at the sight of so many, crowding into a big room to hear the words of Red Cloud, to hear him say that all he wanted was peace and what is already ours. Many of the Wasichu stood up at the end and shouted that what he said was the truth."

"And now Red Cloud is inviting all the chiefs to a council at the Wasichu fort of Laramie, and they think they will decide on where we will go to trade." Touch-the-Clouds frowned. "They think that they will get the Wasichu to agree to a post along the Platte, and not force more of the Lakota to live near the Missouri. Red Cloud has already sent Man Afraid of His Horses to ask me to ride to the fort, to give in and say that I will agree to this new wording of the treaty."

Black Eagle heard the hardness in the other man's voice and wished again that he had not promised to ride here. "And what did you say?" he managed to ask.

"Tell me what you agreed to do, Black Eagle."

"I said that I would go to Fort Laramie. What else could I say?"

Touch-the-Clouds leaned closer to the fire. "I said that I would not go, that the Wasichu have cast bad medicine over Red Cloud's eyes, and that now he sees only what they want him to see. When I said that, Man Afraid of His Horses told me that Sitting Bull had said the same words to him, that Sitting Bull won't go to Fort Laramie either."

"And I would have given the same answer as you did," Black Eagle said quickly, "if I had not gone to Washington and seen the Little Father for myself. We do not have only the word of the Wasichu, but also the promise of Parker. He is on our side."

"And how long do you think his promise will last?" Touch-the-Clouds stared into the fire. "Yes, the Little Father Parker may be our friend. At least he sees himself that way. That much I believe, because he is also the friend of the Yellow Hair Rubalev. But Parker has enemies, and they will not let him stand in the way of what they want forever. So Yellow Hair Rubalev has told me."

"You won't trust the Little Father, but you will listen to that Wasichu Rubalev."

"I think that the Little Father spoke truly to Red Cloud, but also that the Wasichu will work against him. I trust Rubalev only because I can use him."

"We have to live in peace," Black Eagle said, "and hope that the treaty is kept, because I know now that we can't fight the white man if he ever decides to use all his power against us. I rode their Iron Horse trail and saw their cities, I saw with my own eyes how much the Wasichu have and how many of them there are. They have sent only a small part of their people and weapons against us so far. If they ever send even a few more against us—"

"You are saying that we are helpless as we are," Touch-the-Clouds said.

Black Eagle was silent for a long time, afraid now that Touch-the-Clouds would grow enraged at any moment. The chief was like that, holding in his anger until it burst from him the way the smoke burst from the top of the Iron Horse.

"I happen to agree with you in part," Touch-the-Clouds went on. "As we are, we are helpless. If we go on as we have, we can hope only that the treaties are kept. If they are not, we can hope that the Wasichu will find it too much trouble to fight us and leave us our lands."

"If you believe that," Black Eagle said, finally finding his courage, "then you should have agreed to go to Fort Laramie with the other chiefs, and agree to this treaty, because we lack the power and the medicine to fight the Wasichu."

"We don't have the power or the medicine to fight them as we are. But we can fight them in new ways. Long ago, we had no horses, only dogs—so the tales of our old men tell us. Not so long ago, we had no rifles, only bows and arrows and lances and knives." Touch-the-Clouds lifted his head. "We cannot fight as the white man expects us to fight. There are ways to fight him that he will not expect us to use."

"I hope we don't have to fight at all," the wife of Touch-the-Clouds murmured. Black Eagle glanced at her, surprised by the strength in her voice. "I am hoping that the treaty is kept."

"I hope that it is kept for as long as possible," Touch-the-Clouds said, "but it will be broken in the end. Let us hope that we have enough time to prepare ourselves for what must come."

If there were more men like the Little Father Parker, Black Eagle thought, perhaps there would be peace. Then he saw a cold look pass over the face of Touch-the-Clouds, a look he had seen only once before, on a man afflicted by a spirit that had brought him to curse his mother and raise his hand against his father, a man so enraptured by what the evil spirit inside him was saying that he could not hear anything else.

The strange look on the face of the other chief passed, but Black Eagle felt himself grow cold. It came to him then that Touch-the-Clouds was hoping for war, for a war greater than any they had ever fought.

"It isn't enough to win one victory, Black Eagle," Touch-the-Clouds said. "There must be other victories."

He no longer knew what Touch-the-Clouds wanted. Once, he

had believed that the other chief wanted only to keep their lands, to follow their path, to live as they always had while the Wasichu left them alone. But Touch-the-Clouds was dreaming of more than that.

If we can keep our lands, Black Eagle thought, if the Wasichu will keep their treaties, what other victories must we have? What kind of battle would we have to fight? But he did not ask his questions aloud.

SEVEN

Lemuel Rowland picked up a letter from Ely Parker at the post office, just after his return to St. Louis. He recognized his old comrade Donehogawa's clear, elegant writing on the envelope. News traveled more swiftly from east to west now, and he had overheard talk about recent events in Washington from other passengers boarding the riverboat at Cape Girardeau. He had some notion of what the letter from Donehogawa might say even before opening it.

He had traveled to New Orleans out of restlessness, having saved enough to make the journey and telling himself that he might find work there, that he was not simply indulging himself by visiting that city. He had not written to Donehogawa to tell him that he was leaving St. Louis temporarily, promising himself that he would send a letter to his old friend when he got back. He had posted his occasional letters in cipher to Donehogawa since settling in St. Louis, reporting on rumors he had heard about events on the Plains, but to write such insignificant and unenlightening correspondence in a kind of code seemed unnecessarily cautious.

He did not spend much time looking for work in New Orleans, seeing quickly that the men there were unlikely to hire an Indian when there were so many white men in search of work. He had too much pride to try to pass himself off as something other than what he was, and did not want to live in fear that an old acquaintance might expose him, however unlikely that possibility might be. The fleshpots of New Orleans held few attractions for him; his upbringing by the Rowlands and his own need to prove himself as upright as any respectable white man left him unable to indulge himself in vice anymore, or even in the milder indulgences of a whiskey or a cigar.

His journey back up the Mississippi to St. Louis had also evoked somber thoughts that he was unable to dismiss. Gazing at the cliffs of Vicksburg had brought back the memory of the long bombardment and siege of the Union forces against that Confederate stronghold. He and his comrades had learned how to live on the land and take what they found around them, and doing so had been part of the battle, since it deprived the enemy of food. Vicksburg still looked as it had during the siege, with its battered buildings, earthworks, and trees downed or scarred by cannon. Lemuel, looking out from the deck of the steamboat, could almost imagine that Vicksburg's citizens were still hiding in the caves in the clay precipices below the town. Grant's men had turned the course of the war there, many claimed, cutting the Confederacy in two. The ruin of the South, the ravaged towns and impoverished farms, had been clearly visible along the Mississippi from his steamer. Lemuel, surprising himself, had felt pity swell up inside him for the people he had fought to defeat, and had wondered again at his desperate need to volunteer for that war.

He slipped Donehogawa's letter into his pocket, deciding that he would read it in his room. He had been living in the same boardinghouse since coming to St. Louis over two years ago, telling himself from time to time that he would either look for larger quarters or move on to another part of the country. For a while, he had shared some of the restlessness of those around him, the men who passed through St. Louis by train, boat, coach, or on horseback, to head west and north along the Missouri, or north and south along the Mississippi.

But people seemed less restless these days, more willing to settle at last in one place; so it seemed to him. On his way back up the Mississippi, Lemuel had found himself looking forward to his cramped but comfortable room, his lessons with Virgil Warrick, and to dining on the widow Gerhardt's beef and cabbage or her potato soup.

A miasma of smoke hung over the city, obscuring the sky; the air was thick with the odor of burning coal. Lemuel's rooming house was one of a row of stone houses, their exteriors darkened and soiled by smoke, that overlooked the rail yards near the waterfront. As he climbed the steps to the entrance, Virgil Warrick suddenly opened the door.

"Suh," the black man said, "din' 'spect to see you back so quick."

"I arrived early this afternoon."

Virgil reached for Lemuel's bag.

"I can carry it upstairs myself," Lemuel objected; the man was obviously leaving the house on an errand.

"Don't mind totin' it, suh." Virgil took the bag from him. He had been one of the laborers at the levee when Lemuel first came here, and one of the hardest workers. Lemuel had quickly seen that the Negro was not the slow-witted man he had at first seemed to be, and had noticed how the other blacks among the laborers deferred to him.

Soon Lemuel was relying on Virgil to manage the other black workers. He might have been helpful in handling the white laborers, too, but too many of them already resented doing anything that resembled "niggers' work," so it had been better to leave the white men their signs of authority over the colored workers. St. Louis might have been held by Union forces during the war, and many of its people had been fervent in their support of the Union during the conflict that had divided the people of Missouri, but that did not mean that most of them were ready to grant too much to the freedmen and former slaves among them. Still less were they likely to tolerate any affronts against the natural order by an Indian. Had the

South won the war, Lemuel had often reflected, St. Louis's once-flourishing slave trade might well have been revived.

One of Lemuel's first observations here had been that the farther west one went, and the closer one was to the Plains, the more open hostility and hatred one found directed toward red men. "Those Easterners can say what they like about the Indian," one man had told him during his first weeks in St. Louis, "but they're too far away to know what's out here. Savages, that's what they are—wild men riding around half-naked, scalping people and attacking settlers and raising hell." That man had been one of the exceptions, an articulate man who probably thought of himself as civilized and who had been careful not to include Lemuel in his general condemnation of the red man. Many others said far worse, and talked of extermination, but Lemuel was not often in the company of such people. His society in St. Louis was limited to the very few who could overlook his race and patronize him because he had mastered the ways of a white man, to the widow Gerhardt, who seemed not to care what color he was, and to Virgil Warrick.

The house was filled with the odor of stew. Lemuel could hear Hannah Gerhardt out in the kitchen, talking to her colored girl Laetitia, as he climbed the stairs behind Virgil. The two blacks were Mrs. Gerhardt's only help, and Virgil was her servant because she could not have given him a place to live there without such an arrangement. To hire a colored man as a house servant was one thing; to let him a room in a house such as hers was something else altogether, and the widow Gerhardt would not let her kindliness overrule her good sense. Virgil still labored down at the waterfront, to supplement his meager servant's wages, and did odd jobs for Mrs. Gerhardt when he was not needed at the levee to haul stone, load cargo, or unload baggage from an arriving paddleboat.

Virgil opened the door to Lemuel's room, stepped inside, and set down the bag. "Enjoy the trip, suh?" he asked.

Lemuel nodded.

"Usta be more boats," Virgil said. "Before the war, they was all over the river. Not so many now." Lemuel, thinking of the steamers, boats, rafts, and small craft that he had seen from the deck, a veritable armada of river-going vessels, tried to imagine how any more could have crowded onto the river. But the trains, he knew, had affected the traffic on the Mississippi; the trains were, many now said, the future. The trains also threatened the Plains Indians, whose lands might have been largely left alone had those moving west been content to settle along the rivers. He wondered how much longer it would be before the railroad men finally had the means to build their long-postponed northern route through the lands of the Sioux.

The black man waited while Lemuel opened his bag and began to unpack. "You be needin' anything, suh?"

"No, thank you," Lemuel replied.

Virgil lingered, apparently wanting to say more. "Heard some talk, suh," he continued, "jes' after you left. This colored man showed up in St. Joseph, with some gold in his pockets and a story." He lifted his brows.

"Go on," Lemuel said.

"He say there's a Sioux chief out West who don't mind having colored folks out there, who treats 'em same as his own kind." He lowered his voice to a conspiratorial tone. "Say a friend of this chief give him the gold and tole him to say the chief is lookin' for black brothers. Say it might be wise to be a friend of this chief, 'cause he hellfire on his enemies." Virgil paused. "Heard it from a teamster, suh, and he only tole it to me 'cause he knew I wouldn't see him no more and wouldn't get him in no trouble. Ain't the kind of story to spread around, it ain't. The teamster said that colored man only talked to a few coloreds in St. Joseph, ones he could trust, 'fore he drop out of sight. Wouldn'ta tole that tale to no whites, that's certain."

"An interesting story," Lemuel said, "and I won't pass it on." Virgil trusted him, partly because Lemuel had been teaching him to write. The colored man had learned the rudiments of reading in a school set up by the Freedmen's Bureau, although the two had kept that accomplishment, along with the reading lessons, a secret from the widow Gerhardt. Knowing that her black servant was literate might test even the limits of her tolerance, an acceptance that seemed to Lemuel to depend at least partly on pity for those people she viewed as her inferiors.

"Dunno, suh," Virgil said then, "but that I wouldn't mind livin' in a place where one man's as good as another." He laughed softly. "More chance of findin' that inside the Pearly Gates than out on the Plains, and maybe even heaven's got its Niggertowns. Wouldn't be no heaven for the white man if they wasn't."

Lemuel shook his head and smiled. "Tell Mrs. Gerhardt that I want to rest now, but that I'll be down for supper later."

The black man left the room, closing the door behind him. Lemuel finished unpacking, lit a lamp to read by in the shadowy room, and sat down by the window, where there was still a little daylight, to read the letter from Ely Parker. Downstairs, he heard Virgil informing the widow Gerhardt that he had returned to St. Louis. He slipped the letter from his pocket and slit open the envelope.

The letter was in English. Donehogawa had not used their cipher this time. The date of the letter—30 August 1871—was neatly written at the top of the page. Donehogawa had always had excellent penmanship; it was one reason that General Grant had asked him to write down the terms for surrender at Appomattox.

"Our military chieftain is still head and front of the American people," he had written, "but I am no longer at his side. Too many accusations have been leveled against me for me to be of any further use in Washington. I have been slandered until I can no longer discharge my duties. The only way that I can serve my chieftain now is to leave his service. I am going to New York City to live, where there are opportunities for me to secure a living in business. I shall write to you again when I am settled."

None of this was a surprise, but Lemuel still felt angry and disheartened. Donehogawa had stood in the way of too many who wanted to make profits on Indian lands. Lemuel had read in the newspapers that winter about the attacks on the commissioner, the accusations that he had broken regulations trying to get food to reservation Indians who would otherwise have starved. Clearly Donehogawa had resigned as commissioner of Indian Affairs rather than let himself be forced out, or allow himself to be used against the president.

"A man who is but a remove from barbarism." That had been

one of the slanders directed at Donehogawa, perhaps the most wounding one. It came to Lemuel then that his old comrade had in fact had good reason to use a cipher in their communications; he had made enough enemies to feel threatened. Clearly his enemies had done their damage and could threaten him no more, since Donehogawa was now writing his letters in English.

He glanced at the bottom of the page and saw that the letter was unsigned.

"All that I want now," the letter concluded, "is to live out my life in peace and quiet." Lemuel peered at the letter more closely and saw, in the dim light of his candle, a faint mark after this sentence; Donehogawa had apparently begun to sign the letter but had stopped. Instead, in scratchier letters unlike his usual clear hand, he had scrawled, "Your former traveling companion has written to me from St. Joseph. If you should find yourself there, give him my regards."

He had to mean Grigory Rubalev. Lemuel had not thought of the man in a while. Rubalev had stayed in St. Louis for only a few days, leaving for Kansas City with his ward Katia and servant Denis three days after Lemuel had let his room from Mrs. Gerhardt. In the company of Katia and Denis, Rubalev had not been as talkative; he had brooded during the journey from Louisville to St. Louis, leaving Lemuel more time to dwell on what the Russian might be. A man who sold guns to Indians, a trader looking for profit, a gambler, a man dreaming of his lost Alaska and resenting those who had taken it from him—he might be any or all of those things. Lemuel might have tried to find out more about him had he stayed longer in St. Louis, but his curiosity had faded after Rubalev left the city.

He also did not want to think of Katia. Whatever Rubalev said, however respectably he had acted toward her, Lemuel was certain that the young woman was more to him than a ward. Being certain of that had bothered him more than he had wanted to admit at the time.

He had made a life for himself here, simple and largely solitary as it was, and his old comrade Parker was apparently welcoming his chance for peace and quiet. He could do nothing for Done-hogawa now except to write back to him and extend his sympathy and good wishes. There was no reason for him to go to St. Joseph, to seek out Rubalev.

The odors of stew and baked bread had reached his room. Lemuel folded the letter, slipped it into his pocket, and went downstairs.

In Lemuel's absence, Joe Wiegand had taken on more authority. By the end of his first day back at work, Lemuel had seen that the other man intended that he be little more than the boss of the Negroes shoring up the stone face of the levee, while Wiegand supervised the rest of the workers.

He did not dwell on the matter as he made his way home. He had grown used to working for men like Wiegand. Some of them came to respect him more in time, while others never would.

He was on the street leading to the widow Gerhardt's rooming house when the door to another house opened. A woman emerged, glanced from side to side, then descended the steps toward him. She wore a plain blue dress, black bonnet, and short black cape; Lemuel caught a glimpse of her face before she looked away.

Katia, he thought. For a moment, he was certain that he had spoken her name aloud. He stood there, expecting her to look back and say something to him, but she was already crossing the street. Perhaps she did not recognize him. He was about to follow her when she glanced back at him, then hurried on, disappearing around a corner.

He thought of following her. If she was in St. Louis, then surely Rubalev was as well. Something stirred inside him. His small, uneventful life, a life it had cost him some effort to find, suddenly seemed more precarious, but also more empty. He saw himself going on as he was, doing his work, living on the edges of the life of this city, never thinking further ahead than the next day or week. Such a life had been enough for a while, and maybe he had needed that calm during the years after the war, but now—

Lemuel steadied himself. He had not felt this restless and dissatisfied for some time. He had not allowed himself to have such feelings. Perhaps the trip to New Orleans had awakened his restlessness.

He would not follow Katia. He did not know what she was doing in one of the modest dwellings on this street, but perhaps Rubalev knew people here and had sent her to that house for some reason. If Rubalev was in St. Louis, he was most likely staying at one of the better hotels, and would soon be leaving the city once more. Better, Lemuel told himself, not to seek the man out.

He continued toward Mrs. Gerhardt's house, feeling uneasy with himself.

There was a knock on Lemuel's door. "Come in," he said.

Virgil entered the room and thrust an envelope at him as Lemuel rose from his chair. "Letter came for you, suh," he said.

Lemuel had sent the black man out with a letter to Ely Parker and enough money for the postage. His life was becoming more eventful than it had been in a while, with two letters in less than a week. He peered at the envelope and saw that it had been mailed from Fort Kearney in Nebraska; the spidery handwriting was unfamiliar.

Lemuel sat down. Virgil shifted from one foot to another. "Mr. Rowland," he said slowly, "don't know how much longer I be livin' here."

Lemuel looked up quickly. "Is Mrs. Gerhardt giving you any trouble?"

"No, suh. I—" The black man was gazing at him directly, without the usual blank expression he wore in front of most other people. "I guess I can tell you. I's thinkin' of going west. Don't got much, but I got enough to go somewheres and then think about where I might go after that."

"I'll be sorry to see you leave," Lemuel said.

"I can write some now. I can send you a letter from where I end up." Virgil's pronounciation was more precise than before.

"You do that," Lemuel said. He would need the practice; Virgil could write out short sentences now, but his spelling made them hard to decipher.

"You want a good man, put Moses in my job. The other darkies'll listen to him."

"Thanks for the advice. I'll probably take it." Lemuel paused. "When do you plan to leave?"

"Not for two or three days, suh."

"Well." He did not know what else to say. In two or three days, maybe Virgil would change his mind again. Perhaps Mrs. Gerhardt could be talked into raising his wages for the odd jobs a little. He realized just how much he would miss the colored man, how few friends he had here.

Virgil left the room, closing the door. Lemuel suddenly felt exasperated with himself. He had grown softer during the past years, and lazier. He wondered if he would still be able to endure a day's march with a rifle and a knapsack or spend days on horseback, as he had during his brief time among the Lakota. He had accepted the limits others had put around him and fashioned his quiet, small life inside them.

He thought of the young man who had taken Ely Parker for an example, who had learned and struggled and made the whites around him allow him a place in their world, however grudgingly. He would have despised what Lemuel had become. Even Virgil, with more obstacles in his path, was willing to chance following a new trail.

He opened the letter in his hand and glanced at the signature. Colonel Jeremiah Clarke, one of his former comrades in arms, was writing to him. Jeremiah Clarke had remained in the army after the war, but Lemuel had lost track of him some time ago. He leaned back in his chair. Jeremiah was one of the few men he had known who seemed to possess no bigotry. Indeed, the colonel had numbered Donehogawa among his closest friends.

The letter was short; he read it quickly. Jeremiah had heard that he was living in St. Louis. He himself would be in St. Joseph next month, in case Lemuel had any business there. A few of his black troopers had recently deserted, apparently lured by stories of an

Elysium on the Plains run by a Sioux chief who called all men brothers. Jeremiah and Lemuel's former brother-in-arms Custer were wondering why Washington was holding back from sending forces against the growing number of Indians who refused to keep to reservations and lands near the trading posts, and Jeremiah suspected that their old friend Ely Parker was urging restraint. But sooner or later, the officers would have to lose patience. The next provocation by the Indians would bring severe punishment. Jeremiah hoped that it would not come to that, but feared it would, and if it did, he would have to do his duty.

Lemuel stared at the letter for a while. Donehogawa might have told Jeremiah Clarke that he was living in St. Louis; how else would Jeremiah have known where to send the letter? It seemed more than a coincidence that both men were suggesting that he travel to St. Joseph.

"There was a woman here," Mrs. Gerhardt said at breakfast, "looking for you last night, after you went to bed."

Lemuel sat down, averting his eyes from the two other boarders at the table. The widow Gerhardt sounded disapproving; he felt the other two men watching him.

"Did she give you her name?" Lemuel asked, pouring himself some coffee.

"No, she didn't. Don't get me wrong—she looked respectable enough, not all painted up, but she seemed upset and worried about something. I said I wasn't going to wake up one of my roomers in the middle of the night and told her to come back another time."

It had not been quite the middle of the night; he had gone to bed right after supper, feeling unusually tired. But a strange woman, coming here to see him—the two men across the table were probably already wondering if he had a secret sweetheart, maybe even if he had got her into trouble.

"I don't know who she could be," he said as he reached for some eggs and ham. The skeptical, amused looks that passed between the others around the table told him that no one believed him.

Lemuel ate quickly and left the house. Two horses pulling a wagon trotted by, followed by a buggy and another horse and landau; he waited for them to pass. Some rain had fallen the night before, making the road even slicker than usual. He was about to cross the street when he saw Katia on the other side. She wore the black bonnet and cape he had seen her in before, but her dress was gray this time, with a mud-stained hem.

She walked toward him before he could cross; he waited. "Mr. Rowland," she said as she came up to him.

"How do you do, Miss Rubalev," he responded, touching his hat and taking refuge in formality. "I didn't know that you were back in St. Louis."

"You know. You saw me the other day, on this street. I did not know what to say to you, that's why I didn't say anything. I thought you might follow me, but you didn't."

"Were you the woman who came to see me last night?" he asked. "I was told—"

"Yes, I came here. I have to talk to you, Mr. Rowland. I don't know anyone else in St. Louis." Her face was more drawn than it had been two years ago, and she seemed thinner, but her large dark eyes were still lustrous, her pale brown skin still flawless and unmarked.

"Isn't Mr. Rubalev here with you?"

"No." Her fingers tightened around the small purse she carried. "I am here alone. Mr. Rowland—" She swayed; he caught her by the elbow.

"I was on my way to work," he said.

"Mr. Rowland, I am out of money. I have nowhere to go. I can no longer pay for my room where I am staying, so I must pack my bag and leave today."

"Where are you staying?"

"At the house where you saw me the other day. You look surprised, Mr. Rowland."

"I suppose I thought that you would be living at the hotel where you stayed before, or at another as well appointed." But of course she would not have had the money for that, not without Rubalev.

"Miss Rubalev, I must go to work." He let go of her arm and reached into his pocket. "I can give you a little money." He quickly pressed the coins into her hand. "That ought to be enough for at least a week's rent."

Her cheeks reddened. "I am too much in need to refuse it." She thrust the coins into her purse. Lemuel wondered if anyone was watching them from Mrs. Gerhardt's sitting room window, but did not look back to find out. "Will I see you again?"

She sounded both artless and desperate. "I'll meet you later— this evening," he said. There could be no harm in that. "I'll wait for you here, in front of the house." By now Mrs. Gerhardt, or anyone else watching from the window, would be assuming that there was something between him and Katia. "There's a fairly good restaurant two streets from here—the food isn't fancy, but it's plentiful and not too dear."

Her face brightened. She probably had not eaten for a while, either. He did not have time to go inside and get her more money for some food.

"I must go now, Miss Rubalev."

"Katia," she said, "please call me Katia." Her eyes narrowed. "I do not want you to call me by his name."

"At six o'clock," Lemuel said. He was already late. He tipped his hat to her and strode away.

Lemuel was descending the steps of Mrs. Gerhardt's house when he saw Katia walking toward him. He murmured a greeting and took her arm to lead her down the street. She said nothing as they walked, and he decided not to ask her any questions until later.

He had a number of questions that he wanted to ask. Why had she left Rubalev? Or was it he who had asked her to leave, and she was simply afraid to admit it? He recalled the harder look he had occasionally glimpsed in the man's face. Rubalev was probably capable of abandoning a woman without a qualm, but he could also have followed her to St. Louis.

Only half of the tables at Morrissey's were taken. Lemuel guided Katia to a table next to one wall, away from the other diners. A waiter with an unfamiliar accent took their order.

"I have my room for another week," Katia said. "You were kind to give me some money."

"It was nothing."

"I have been here for only two weeks—I didn't think I could spend so much money so quickly. It isn't that I cannot do anything, Mr. Rowland. I know how to sew and to do some cooking, I can read and write and keep accounts. But I do not know how to find any work."

He was about to ask her to address him by his Christian name, then decided against it. Better, he thought, to keep his distance until he knew more. She had been here for two weeks. Rubalev might already be in this city, looking for her.

The waiter came back with a pot of coffee and cups. Lemuel poured some for them. "Why did you come here?" he asked.

"I didn't know where else to go." She tapped her fingers nervously against her cup. "When I came here, I went to the hotel where we stayed before. I soon found out that I could afford only two nights with the money I had left if I was to keep anything to live on. Fortunately, I have a good memory—I remembered the name of the street where you told us you had let your room." She kept her eyes down. "It isn't that I was looking for you, Mr. Rowland. I thought only that around here, I might find lodgings that I could afford. I didn't think that you would still be living here."

"I assumed you were in St. Louis with Mr. Rubalev. That's one reason I didn't follow you. I didn't want to meddle in any of his business."

"I found out where you lived a day later," she continued. "I saw you go into that house. I thought—" She lapsed into silence; he did not press her.

The waiter returned with two plates of chicken and biscuits and a bowl of collard greens. Katia had finished half of her plate by the time Lemuel had taken a few bites. "You needn't answer this," he said. "Perhaps it's none of my concern, but why did you leave Mr. Rubalev?"

"He is angry with me, and I know why. He thinks that I haven't been as useful to him as he had hoped I might be."

She ate the rest of her supper in silence. Lemuel finished his food, restraining himself from prodding her with more questions. At last he said, "I have heard that Mr. Rubalev is in St. Joseph."

She raised her head; her eyes widened.

"So presumably you came here from there," he continued.

She nodded. "I took the train to Hannibal, and a boat from there to St. Louis. It cost more than I expected. I'm not used to handling money—Grisha always took care of that." Her mouth tightened. "He trained me so well for some things and so poorly for others."

"What did you think you would do after you left him?" He tried to say the words gently.

"I don't know. I didn't think, I simply had to get away from him. I thought of going to my people first, but I would have needed someone to guide me, I could not have ridden there alone."

Lemuel was surprised. "You mean that you were ready to ride to a Sioux camp? That's hard to believe. It would have been extremely hard on you. You might not even have survived it."

She gazed at him steadily. "I am more used to Lakota ways than you realize. I passed some of the past two years among my own people. That is part of what troubles me, Mr. Rowland. I live one way, and then another way, and neither way is truly mine. Grisha has made me an outsider among both the Lakota and the Wasichu, and then he grows angry with me because—"

Her voice has risen slightly. She glanced around the room, but the other diners were paying them no mind. Lemuel was beginning to see how this evening would end. Katia, with no one to turn to and no way to make a living—apart from a manner not fit to mention in respectable company—would prevail upon him to help her.

And, he told himself, he probably would help her, out of pity and also because she had touched his heart.

"I shouldn't say any more to you," she said, "not without knowing that you will keep it to yourself."

He leaned back and folded his arms. "Katia, I know almost no one here. The closest I have to a friend in St. Louis is a colored man who's going to be leaving here tomorrow or the day after. There's no one I talk to, and the only man I write to regularly is Commissioner Parker in Washington." He corrected himself. "The former commissioner."

She lifted her brows slightly.

"He resigned his post recently," he continued. "Perhaps you hadn't heard. The people who were using the Indian Bureau to line their own pockets finally forced him out, it seems."

"I didn't know," she said. "Grisha is still corresponding with him, too."

"Ely Parker informed me that Mr. Rubalev was in St. Joseph. He even suggested that I give him my regards if I found myself there."

"Then I can speak openly to you," Katia murmured. "Grisha might have written to Ely Parker about his disappointment with me and about what he is trying to do. Now Mr. Parker is perhaps thinking that you may be more useful to him and to Grisha." Her mouth twisted. "I have a husband, Mr. Rowland. My husband is a Lakota chief. Some say that he may become the greatest of our chiefs, and some say that he is already."

Lemuel was too surprised to feel disappointment that another man had won her.

"His name is—" She shook her head. "You would call him Touch-the-Clouds." Lemuel kept his face still. "He has alliances with the Kiowa, the Comanche, even the Crow. He has more allies than the Wasichu know about. But he needs other friends."

The waiter approached their table. Lemuel asked him to bring more coffee and two pieces of apple pie and sent him away again. The chief called Touch-the-Clouds, he realized, was probably behind the letters from Donehogawa and Jeremiah Clarke, and maybe even behind Virgil Warrick's decision to go west. He remembered the way Rubalev had talked to him about a war that might start in the West. Why was Touch-the-Clouds welcoming others to his lands? To have peace, or to find more allies for a war?

"If I may ask this," he said, "what brought you to marry this Sioux chief?"

"It was Grisha's doing. I think he had it in mind all along, making me a wife to Touch-the-Clouds. My husband had one wife already, but Grisha brought me to his camp, and I was soon married to him. I think Grisha thought that he might come to care more for me, or that I would give him a son, so that I could win some influence over him. Perhaps he thought that my husband would take some counsel from my visions." Katia frowned. "But my husband heeds no visions except his own, and no more visions have come to me. I also have given him no son."

She fell silent when the waiter returned with their coffee and pie. Lemuel calculated how much the supper would cost him. Katia would need some more money for food and to keep her room. He would have felt happier about helping her if something might have come of it.

"So you left your husband," he said.

"He allowed me to leave him. I had the right, and he had no use for me—he wanted me to go. Grisha and I went to Chicago and then back to Washington—he would leave me alone in my rooms while he wrote his letters and met with various men. A year later, we were back in my husband's camp, and this time Grisha had a use for me. Touch-the-Clouds wanted to learn English. I was his teacher. He learned it quite quickly, more quickly than I expected."

"Why did he want to learn it?" Lemuel asked.

She looked away from him and did not answer for a few moments. At last she said, "He knows that he must learn more of the white man's ways to get what he wants. Grisha taught him that."

"And what does he want? To hold the whites to their treaties?"

"I don't know what he wants, but I think it's more than keeping what was promised to our people by treaty. You heard Grisha's story about the great chief on the other side of the world. Touch-the-Clouds has heard it, too. He and Grisha have the same dream, I think. But Grisha has lost some of his power over him. He thought that I could help in winning back his influence, and that didn't work, and now I think that he is looking for someone else to use."

"And then, presumably, you left your husband again," Lemuel said.

"Yes, with Grisha, as I had before. This time, my husband told me that I could cut my ties to him completely if I wished." She glared across the table at him. "I replied that I was still his wife, that I would be his wife for as long as I pleased, whether I lived under his tent or not. Grisha thought that he would get very angry with me, but he didn't. I think that my words might have given him a little more respect for me."

Perhaps they had; the man would have seen that she had some pride. Or perhaps she was only deluding herself.

"I didn't think that we would stay in St. Joseph for long," Katia said, "but things were worse between Grisha and me after that. So I left him. I will tell you what his greatest cruelty was to me, Mr. Rowland. He taught me just enough to live on the edge of the Wasichu world, and let me recall just enough to live on the edge of the Lakota world when I had returned there, but I cannot truly live in either."

Lemuel finished his pie and coffee. He had grown used to living on the edges of things. Katia pushed away her plate, and after a few moments he saw that she had nothing more to say. What had she left out? What had Rubalev done to her to drive her from his side? Again he had the feeling that she was concealing as much as she had revealed.

Katia said little as Lemuel walked her back to the house where she was staying. He filled the silence with some talk about his life here and his trip to New Orleans. When they came to the house, he pressed a few greenbacks into her hands.

"Thank you, Mr. Rowland." She put the money into her purse. "I cannot live like this for very much longer."

"No, you can't," he admitted.

"I think now that I should have gone back to Touch-the-Clouds." She hurried up the steps and into the house before he could reply.

What could he possibly do for her? Mrs. Gerhardt had Laetitia; she did not need another servant.

As he walked down the street, he thought of the letters from Donehogawa and Jeremiah Clarke. Events were conspiring to push him out of his small, safe life; now there was Katia to upset things. The discontent that he had kept at bay was troubling him again, feeding his restlessness. He thought of spending more years enduring Joe Wiegand's insults and living on the fringes of life here, and the prospect suddenly repulsed him.

Lemuel recalled the dream as he woke. He was on horseback, riding across a grassy plain. The figures of men on horseback were visible on the horizon, then abruptly he was in the midst of the riders. He reined in his horse and watched as the riders fanned out around him to form a circle.

He could not see the other men clearly. Some wore the feathered headdresses of the Cheyenne and Sioux, while others had bandannas tied around their heads and still others wore long loose shirts. He watched as the circle closed, and saw a man in a long feathered headdress riding toward him. The man's black eyes commanded his attention; his gaze was direct and implacable.

"The circle has closed," the man said, and then Lemuel was awake, his memory of his dream so vivid that for a moment he did not know where he was. Somehow he had expected to wake under the vast blue sky of his dream, not in this cramped, darkened room.

He got up, used the chamberpot under his bed, poured some water from a pitcher into the basin on his wash stand, and washed quickly before getting dressed. Then he left his room, knowing what he had to do and vowing silently to himself that he would act on his decision before he could have second thoughts.

The banging of pans from the kitchen told him that Mrs. Gerhardt was still making breakfast. He came to the stairs and saw Virgil standing near the door.

"Still thinking of leaving St. Louis to head west?" Lemuel asked.

The black man nodded. "Yes, suh."

"If you can wait two or three days more," Lemuel continued, "you may have company. I've decided to leave St. Louis myself."

* * *

Joe Wiegand, who had never hidden his contempt for Lemuel, suddenly seemed distressed at losing his services. "I'll find another man," he said, rubbing at his balding head, "but you knew how to get work out of the niggers."

"I couldn't have done it without Virgil," Lemuel said, wanting to give the black man his due.

"And that nigger's running off, too. If you ever come back this way—" Wiegand did not finish the sentence. There would always be work here, levees to rebuild and shore up with stone; the changing, unpredictable Mississippi made that inevitable.

Katia's talk of her Sioux husband might have fed his dream of last night. The dream might simply be a reflection of his discontent. There were many ways a white man might explain such a dream, but the vision still held him, as rich and real as a memory.

He left the waterfront and headed up toward the house where Katia was staying, knowing what he would have to tell her. It came to him that he was sorrier about leaving her behind than about his impending departure from St. Louis.

A young woman with a broad freckled face answered the door, then went to get Miss Rubalev. He waited in the sitting room until the young woman returned with Katia. As he stood up, she nodded to him.

"Good morning, Mr. Rowland," she said. The other woman left.

"Can we talk here," he said, "or would you rather go for a walk?"

"We can talk here," she replied. He sat down again on the settee; she seated herself in a chair near him.

"I have something to tell you," he said. "I've decided to leave St. Louis, but before I go, I'll make certain that you are taken care of."

"I see." She lowered her eyes; her hair was pulled up on her head, but a few black locks had escaped confinement, falling past her shoulders. "Mrs. O'Brien seemed a little suspicious when I gave her more money for my room. She must wonder where I got it, and how. She's probably already wondering who you are. I don't know how much longer she'll want me here as a boarder."

"It doesn't matter," he said. "You can take my room at Mrs.

Gerhardt's. I'll speak to her about it. She'll be pleased at getting another roomer so quickly, and if she chooses to think of you as a sweetheart waiting for me, so much the better." He tried to say it lightly, but felt a pang of regret. "You'll be safe there. I'll give you the money before you move, so Mrs. Gerhardt won't have to know that I gave it to you."

Her head was still bowed. "When will you come back?"

"I don't know if I am coming back," he said.

She looked up, widening her eyes.

"I can pay for your room and board for six months," he said. He would have enough left for his needs, and surely half a year was a long enough time for Katia to find a situation for herself. "My advice is to make yourself useful to Mrs. Gerhardt in whatever ways you can. She's a good-hearted woman in her way. She may find other work for you later on, or help you find another place." Katia might meet a man who would make a good husband; her marriage to the Sioux chief could be conveniently forgotten, and had no legal standing here in any case. He ignored the qualms such thoughts brought to him.

"Where are you going?" she asked.

"West." He glanced toward the door. "An old friend wrote me to say that he would be in St. Joseph. I thought to meet him there."

She pressed her lips into a thin straight line. "And what will you do there?"

He was not obligated to tell her anything. "I'll probably look for your guardian, if he's still there," he replied. "Ely Parker did ask me to give Rubalev his regards. I promise you that I won't tell him where you are, or even that I've seen you."

"He'll guess." The skin of her face was taut; he saw her throat move as she swallowed. "He'll know that I would have come to St. Louis. I'm not very good at making my way in the world, Grisha made sure of that, so he'll know what I would have had to do."

"Katia—"

"Why are you going to him?" She whispered the question, but he still heard the anger in her voice. "You don't have to visit him just because Ely Parker wants it. You needn't see him at all."

"I have to see him." There was no reason to conceal what he was hoping to do from her. "The friend I may meet in St. Joseph is Jeremiah Clarke, the commander at Fort Kearney. He told me that sooner or later he and others will be ordered to punish any Indians who are too troublesome—meaning, of course, any Indians who happen to be in the way of whatever the government in Washington wants. Ely Parker is no longer in any position to try to prevent that."

"What can you do about it?" she asked.

"I don't know. That's what I'm going there to find out, and I may need Rubalev's help. He obviously knows more about what may happen out there than I do—maybe even more than does Colonel Clarke."

Her dark eyes stared at him. Her hands trembled slightly; she looked angry. Then she said in a soft voice, "If you can do anything to help my people, I would of course be grateful." She averted her eyes once more. "If you find that there is nothing you can do, will you come back?"

"I don't know. You would be wise not to wait here hoping that I might return." He paused. "Shall I speak to Mrs. Gerhardt?"

"Yes," she murmured.

"I'll bring you some money to pay for your room later." He stood up, knowing that he had done all he could for her. "Good morning, Katia."

"Good-bye, Mr. Rowland."

EIGHT

Lemuel carried his valise onto the train, leaving his carpetbag to Virgil. The Negro had only one bag of his own, and it would be easier for Lemuel to travel with Virgil if he allowed others to think that the colored man was his servant. The North Missouri Railroad would take them as far as Macon; from there, they would travel on the Hannibal and St. Joseph to their destination.

Lemuel sat down in one of the wooden seats, stowing his bag under it. Virgil handed him his other bag, then made his way to the back of the car, where two other black men were sitting. Lemuel had spoken to Mrs. Gerhardt about letting his room to Katia; his landlady had readily agreed to the arrangement, as he had expected. He had also, without actually saying so, allowed the widow to think that he might be coming back in a few months or a year and that he and Katia had an understanding.

The young woman would be moving to the house in a week. He recalled how solemn she had looked during their last meeting. He had introduced her to the widow Gerhardt and then taken her to the Southern Hotel for an early supper, justifying the extravagance by hoping that he might cheer her. She had said little and her face wore a resigned look as he spoke of the trains he would be taking to St. Joseph and the arrangements he had made on her behalf.

Only toward the end of the meal had she grown more animated. "Will you write to me?" she asked.

"I shall when I can, if I'm able to post a letter." It was easy enough to make that promise.

"It would help me if you do," she said. "Mrs. Gerhardt will be expecting you to write."

"And when—if—I stop writing and don't come back, she'll likely take pity on you and be even more solicitous of a girl abandoned by her intended." Katia had actually managed a smile at that remark.

More passengers came aboard the car. Lemuel shifted in his seat; the wood was hard against his backside. Some of the seats near him were still empty, which was unusual; he knew how crowded the trains often were. More people would grow restless again and be lured west, especially now that the Union Pacific could take them across the entire continent. The trains would decide the fate of the people who lived in their path. He wondered if it was already too late to do anything about that.

A slender woman in a black cape and bonnet came down the aisle, her head bent forward as she struggled with the weight of her bag. He got up to help her. She straightened and his eyes met Katia's brown ones.

"What are you doing here?" he asked.

"What do you think?" She handed him her bag and sat down in the seat across from him. "I bought a ticket to Macon."

"And where do you intend to go from there?"

She said, "To St. Joseph."

He was too surprised to speak for a moment. "When did you decide to do this?"

"Last night. That's when I finally decided to leave, but I was thinking of leaving all along. I saw what it would be like for me, living in that house with Mrs. Gerhardt and her boarders. What a small and poor life it would have been. If I have to live in a city, I would rather live as I did when I was with Grisha."

"I see."

"You're angry."

"Of course I'm angry," he said, hearing the tremor in his voice. "I went to some trouble and expense to secure that situation for you. I suppose you used some of the money I gave you to buy your ticket."

She nodded.

"Apparently it didn't take you long to start missing the luxuries Rubalev provided. Maybe it will now be worth it to you to go back to him and put up with his ill treatment as long as you regain your comforts."

"That's not why I'm going to St. Joseph," she said. "I intend to go back to my husband. I can find someone to guide me to him—perhaps even Grisha, if he's stopped being angry with me. And you—" She leaned forward. "You say that you want to help my people." She was whispering her words now. "You may need me."

None of the boarding passengers had taken seats near them, and no one else had come aboard. "Will your husband take you back?" he asked.

"I think so. If I bring you to him, he might. You may be able to tell him more of what he wants to know."

His anger was a hard knot inside him. The knot might have loosened if he could believe that she was on this train because she wanted to be with him.

"A dream came to me," she said, "last night, and that was when I knew what I had to do. Perhaps you can understand that."

"Yes," he said, thinking of his own dream, "I can." He had been sorry to leave her; perhaps he should be relieved that she had thrown in her lot with him. "Rubalev didn't leave you so helpless after all." He tried to keep the bitterness out of his voice. "You've learned how to use someone else to get what you want, and without having to give anything in return." He had the small mean pleasure of seeing her flinch before she looked away.

* * *

Lemuel had written to Jeremiah Clarke just before leaving St. Louis, saying that he would be going to St. Joseph. There was a good chance that he would arrive there before his letter reached Clarke at Fort Kearney. Presumably Jeremiah would know how to go about looking for him, and it was possible, given what he had told Lemuel in his letter, that he might already be in St. Joseph himself.

In the meantime, he would have to seek Rubalev out.

After Lemuel was settled in his room, he sent Virgil with a message to the considerably more sumptuous hotel where Katia said Rubalev had been living. The black man returned with a scrawled message from Rubalev saying that he would expect Lemuel to join him later for supper at his hotel.

"Now you done what you want, suh," Virgil said as Lemuel put Rubalev's note in his pocket, "think I'll nose around some, see what I can learn."

"Do as you like," Lemuel said. They had maintained the pretense that Virgil was Lemuel's servant, although the black man would be staying in a boardinghouse in the colored section of town.

"If'n I hear anything, I'll let you know." Virgil was speaking more clearly and distinctly now, as he often did when there was no one to overhear them. Sometimes Lemuel felt that Virgil had more learning than even he suspected. "But I think I's going to stick with you for now, suh. You might discover somethin' I should know."

The black man left. Lemuel put on his one black suit, the only outfit he possessed that might pass muster at Rubalev's hotel, then went down the hallway to Katia's room.

He knocked on her door. "Who is it?" she called out.

"Lemuel Rowland."

She opened the door. Behind her, he saw that her room was even smaller and more modest than his simple quarters. She glanced down the hallway before admitting him, perhaps out of worry over what others might think of a woman admitting a man to her room, perhaps because she was afraid that Rubalev might have found her and be lying in wait for her.

"I sent Virgil to Mr. Rubalev with a note," he said as she closed the door. "He sent a message back inviting me to have supper with him, so I'm going there now."

She turned away and sat down in the room's only chair. "What will you say to him?"

"That's what I came to ask you about."

"I can't go there, not until I know—" Katia twisted her hands together. "Perhaps you should tell him that you saw me in St. Louis, and then see what—"

"Are you so afraid of him? Has he been violent? Is he likely to beat you?"

Katia shook her head. "He never touched me. He never had to— I always did what he wanted me to do."

"You had better decide what to do before your money runs out, Katia. I can't afford to give you any more."

She pointed her chin at him. "Tell Grisha whatever you like. Tell him that I want to go back to the camp of Touch-the-Clouds."

He turned around and left the room without agreeing to her demand, slamming the door behind him. He would at least have the satisfaction of leaving her to worry about what he might say to Rubalev.

Grigory Rubalev remained seated as Lemuel approached his table. He was also dressed in a tailored black suit that fit his tall frame perfectly. His blond hair still fell to his shoulders, and he had grown a mustache.

"I am pleased to see you again, Mr. Rowland," Rubalev said. "I have taken the liberty of ordering for both of us, since the beef stew is one of the few dishes fit to eat in this establishment."

Lemuel sat down. A bottle of whiskey was on the table with two glasses, one half full and one empty. Rubalev was about to pour some whiskey into the empty glass when Lemuel shook his head.

"Ah," Rubalev said, "I forget that you are not a drinking man." He leaned back in his chair. "Perhaps you are here at the suggestion of our friend the former commissioner."

"He did write to say that you were here, and that if I found my-self in St. Joseph, to give you his regards." He paused, unsure now of how much to say to Rubalev. Somehow he sensed that he should not say anything about Jeremiah Clarke's letter. Jeremiah and he had, after all, fought together. He still knew almost nothing about Rubalev.

"It is unfortunate, what happened to Donehogawa," Rubalev said. "I expected it, of course. Did he write to you before or after he resigned?"

"After."

A waiter came to the table with dishes and some bread, followed by another with a large bowl of stew. The second waiter quickly ladled out the stew. Rubalev waved them both away. "I have not had much of an appetite lately," the blond man said. "If you wish to eat anything more, I will be pleased to order it for you."

"This is fine." Lemuel tasted the stew; Mrs. Gerhardt could not have done nearly as well. "I've left St. Louis, Mr. Rubalev. I'm not planning to go back."

"And what do you intend to do?"

"I'm not sure yet."

"Come now, Rowland. I know that two days ago, the command-ing officer of Fort Kearney arrived in St. Joseph and asked if a man by your name was staying at this hotel. I am guessing that you came here in the hope of seeing him."

Lemuel's fingers tightened around his fork. He managed to swallow his food without choking.

"I also know that when my ward Katerina ran off, she used some of the money she took from me to buy a ticket to Hannibal. She would not have stayed in that town, she would have gone to St. Louis, and she would have taken a steamer from Hannibal because that's how we traveled before. So perhaps she found you in St. Louis, because she would not have known anyone else there and she would have been frightened and desperate by then. How long did it take her to find you?"

"Not very long." Katia had told him that Rubalev would know what she had done, but Lemuel had not entirely believed her. Now he wondered exactly how much about his doings the man already knew.

"You need not look so shocked," Rubalev said. "Had Colonel Clarke of Fort Kearney not come to this hotel, I might still be unaware of his presence in St. Joseph. As for Katia, it is easy to see what she would do—her choices were limited, as was the sum of money she stole from me."

"Then you have probably guessed that she came back to St. Joseph with me."

Rubalev drew in his breath sharply.

"Not on my account, I assure you," Lemuel said. "She claims that she wants to go back to her Sioux husband."

Rubalev threw back his head and laughed. The men and women dining at the tables nearest them glanced in their direction. "That does surprise me," Rubalev said. "What did you do—refuse to help her?"

"I gave her money and found her a place to live, in a respectable house with a kind-hearted woman. She decided to follow me here instead."

"Well." Rubalev poured himself another drink. "So Katia wants to go back to her people. A pity she will not be of much use there. I suppose that she told you everything."

"She told me very little," Lemuel said. "I know she has a husband, a Sioux chief named Touch-the-Clouds, that you took her to him, and that she left with you and then went back to him one more time before leaving with you again."

"You may tell her this." Rubalev set down his glass. "I will see that she gets back to her husband. It may take me a bit of time to arrange for this. In the meantime, she may stay wherever she is now—I assume at your hotel."

Lemuel nodded.

"She will come looking for me when she runs out of money. I hope that you were not too generous." Rubalev stood up. "Finish your supper, Mr. Rowland. There is nothing more that I have to say to you until you have spoken with your friend Colonel Clarke." He walked away from the table.

* * *

"Lem Rowland," the voice called out behind him.

Lemuel turned, recalling that voice, so resonant that it could be heard above the noise of the wagons passing in the street. "Jeremiah Clarke," he said.

The man in a cavalry officer's blue coat with a colonel's gold eagles on the shoulders came up to him and shook his hand. "You haven't changed much, Lemuel." Jeremiah had changed; his beard, once a rich brown, was streaked with gray, the strands of hair visible under his hat were thin and silvery, and his face was browner and more creased. The hollows under his jawbones showed that he had also lost more teeth.

"I happened to be coming this way," Lemuel said. "I posted a letter, but perhaps it didn't reach you."

"It didn't, leastwise not before I left Fort Kearney, but I had a feeling you'd show up. Don't expect it was just my letter that brought you here, though."

"No, it wasn't." Lemuel hesitated, wondering how much he should admit. "I was tiring of St. Louis," he said. "Your letter reached me when I was thinking of leaving anyway."

"Come with me." Jeremiah led him along the wooden sidewalk to a saloon. "Started asking at the better hotels where you might be staying, and figured I'd work my way down to the worst."

"Then it's a good thing we met," Lemuel said, "or it might have taken you a few days more to find me."

They went through the doors into the saloon. "Things been that hard for you?" Jeremiah asked.

"No, but I'm not in the habit of throwing money away."

"Yeah—you never were." They stood at the bar while Jeremiah ordered a sarsaparilla for Lemuel and a whiskey for himself; he downed the whiskey at one gulp and ordered another. Lemuel swallowed some of the sarsaparilla. Men were playing cards at two of the tables; Lemuel followed Jeremiah to a table in the far corner.

"I'll get to what I have to say now," Jeremiah said as they sat down. "Some come to St. Joe to settle, or work at the rail yards, but a lot of them are on their way to somewhere else. I'm guessing that you're going somewhere else."

Lemuel nodded.

"Ely Parker wrote me a while back, told me you were in St. Louis. That was before he had to leave Washington. Sometimes I think it was a wonder he lasted there as long as he did." The colonel rested his arms on the table. "I made him a promise. I said I would try to keep the peace out here. I think I've done all I can, but maybe you can help me out."

"Is that why he told you to write to me?" Lemuel asked.

"He didn't tell me to write to you. He told me where you were, that's all. I don't know if you heard this in St. Louis, but there's talk of strange things going on out West, Indians making peace with enemies, saying they want their own nation, like the South wanted to have. I need to know more about what's going on."

"Send out some scouts," Lemuel said.

"The scouts I sent out deserted. Then it was some of the colored troops. I sent out one detachment and they disappeared. I don't know if they deserted or got wiped out—it's like they just vanished."

Lemuel was silent.

"You don't know what it's like out on the Plains now," Jeremiah continued, "but I'm still thinking you might be able to find out a few things for me, if you're willing. Ely Parker wants the same thing. I'm guessing you got a letter from him suggesting that you come here."

"Yes." There seemed little point in denying it.

"You came west with Parker a while back. And I know you had supper two nights ago with a Russian—Rubalev, he's called. He's a gambler and a drunkard, and I suspect that he's a profiteer of some kind—he made money out in California, probably by fleecing miners, given that he doesn't look much like a miner himself. But I know Ely Parker had dealings with him, and that he knows some of the redskins' ways. So I'm guessing that Parker told you to give Rubalev his regards."

"Yes," Lemuel said, knowing that there was no reason to deny that, either.

"I won't ask you what he said, or what you said to him, but maybe you can help me out. I need somebody who's willing to head out to the Plains and report back to me about what's going on there."

Lemuel leaned back. "Any number of scouts could have done that for you by now."

Jeremiah shook his head. "You're wrong there. Either they come back saying that they couldn't find out anything, or they don't come back at all. And then there's a few like Rubalev, men who probably know more than they're letting on."

"Have you tried talking to him yourself?" Lemuel asked.

"I wouldn't get anywhere with him. I know that already. He didn't get what he has by telling what he knows. Besides, I wouldn't trust a man like that to be straight with me."

Jeremiah had finished his whiskey; a solemn look passed over his face. "We could have struck four years ago," he went on. "Sherman was champing at the bit, ready to turn Sheridan loose. Custer was out raiding when he thought he could get away with it—what he needed was more reinforcements. But they held them back—first it was because it was too soon after the war, and then it was because the government thought maybe we'd have to fight in Canada. Then it was Grant listening to Parker. Don't get me wrong—I would have rather settled this Parker's way, but that probably isn't going to work now."

The colonel suddenly stood up, went to the bar, and returned with another whiskey. "It's the railroads that are getting impatient," Jeremiah said as he sat down again. "They want to lay more tracks, and bring more people out, and they won't let the Indians stand in the way. If the Indians can't be bought off and be content to settle where they're allowed to live, they'll be forced off their land."

"What is it that you want to do, then?" Lemuel asked.

"Figure out some way to find out what they're up to and then see if they can be made to see reason. Maybe I shouldn't have come out here, maybe I don't have the stomach for this. See, after knowing you and Parker, I don't like the idea of killing them, even if you two are a lot more like white men than those Sioux savages are. I just don't like the idea of slaughter. I can admit that to you. Don't know as I could say it to anybody else." He propped his elbows on the table; the whiskey had no doubt contributed to his frankness. "If you've got any idea of riding out there, maybe with Rubalev, I wouldn't mind if you reported back to me later."

Lemuel kept his eyes on the other man. He could have trusted Jeremiah Clarke with his life when they were both fighting under Grant—had trusted him with it on a few occasions—but that was years ago. Jeremiah, it seemed to him, might be looking for a way to defeat the Indians with a minimum of effort and bloodshed, but he still wanted a victory. The struggle would still end with the breaking of treaties and with Indians being forced onto ever smaller parcels of land.

Unless the Indians had more resources than he expected, and more ways to fight. He thought of Rubalev. The man did not strike him as someone who embraced hopeless causes.

"It might work with you," Jeremiah said. "I mean, they might trust somebody who's an Indian and a friend of Parker's. You might be able to find out more about this chief who thinks he can make a country. Maybe there's nothing to it. I've heard a lot of strange rumors that didn't amount to much in the end."

"I think I have a way to ride out there," Lemuel said, "if I decide to take it. Rubalev can help me. That's all I can tell you." He paused. "If I can find out anything that might save lives, I'll try to get that information to you."

"You do that," Jeremiah said. "I'd send a couple of men I can trust with you, but they might just get in your way. I'll have to tell you where you can go to get a message to me, but it might be better if, once you learn anything, you put a lot of distance between you and those Indians. The Sioux and the Cheyenne don't take kindly to betrayals."

Wiser, Lemuel thought, not to ride out there at all, where he might, if he were not careful, find himself in the middle of whatever conflict was to come. Rubalev had promised to get Katia back to her people and her husband. Virgil would have come to St.

Joseph with or without him. There was nothing to stop him from going back to St. Louis and resuming his old life, except his reluctance to live that closed-in safe and small life again.

"I'll see if I can find out anything," Lemuel said at last, knowing that those words committed him to nothing.

"Good. I think that calls for another drink." Jeremiah got up and headed for the bar.

As evening came on, the streets of St. Joseph grew more lively. Men dismounted from horses or stepped down from wagons to enter saloons and bawdy houses. Lemuel made his way past the knots of people to his hotel. Jeremiah might have called Rubalev a drunkard, but the colonel was drinking fairly heavily himself. Drink had not affected his ability to walk a straight line from the saloon to his horse and the hitching post, meaning that he was probably used to taking in that much whiskey.

Lemuel decided, as he entered the hotel, that he would tell Rubalev about his meeting with Jeremiah Clarke. Rubalev probably had ways of finding out that they had been seen together. It was in his best interests, at the moment, to be honest with both Clarke and Rubalev. Presumably they were all after the same end.

He went to the desk clerk to get his key. The man handed it to him and said, "That lady, the dark-haired one who came here with you—she checked out this afternoon. Thought you might want to know."

Lemuel was surprised for only a moment. "Did she say where she was going?" he asked, knowing where she had to have gone.

"Didn't say anything. Just paid her bill and left." The clerk had an amused look on his face. It was easy to read what he was thinking, that Katia was a loose woman who had decided to look for more promising prospects.

He walked toward the stairway. If he asked Rubalev to reimburse him for what he had spent on Katia, the man would probably give him the money. The thought of asking for it repelled him.

He was in front of his door, just about to unlock it, when he recalled that he had promised to meet Virgil later, just outside the hotel door. The colored man might have heard something he should know.

Lemuel turned to go back downstairs. For a moment, standing in the shadows of the hall, he felt suspended, without firm footing, as if the floor under his boots had vanished, leaving him standing on air. The walls around him were suddenly formless and indistinct.

It came to him that he had felt this same sensation long ago. He searched his memory, and then remembered the time he had run away from the Rowlands as a boy. He had been in the forest when the trees around him grew transparent; he had waited, stiff with fear, trying to recall who he was and where he was bound. The world he recalled had seemed insubstantial, the Rowlands and their farm only spirits he had glimpsed in a dream.

I am not here, Lemuel thought, expecting to find himself back in his room in Mrs. Gerhardt's house, I don't belong here, this isn't the world I know, and then the feeling was gone. He was standing on the staircase, looking down into the gas-lit lobby of his hotel; yet the feeling persisted that he had dreamed this life, that his true life had taken another path.

Virgil was walking toward him as he went back outside. The two men sat down on a bench. "Heard anything I might like to know?" Lemuel asked.

The black man shook his head. "Ain't heard nothin'. Nobody wants to talk."

Lemuel was silent for a while, waiting until a group of men rode by on horseback, then said, "If I could find someone willing to take me to this chief you heard about, the one who supposedly treats colored people same as whites, would you come with me?"

Virgil sat up. "Damn right I would, suh."

"It could be dangerous—probably will be."

"Mistah Rowland, ain't nothin' as dangerous as bein' a black man tryin' not to let white folks see you know more'n they think you do. And the longer I live, the harder it gets."

"Then I'll see what I can do." Lemuel stood up. He might not be doing Virgil any favor by offering him the chance to ride out with him.

* * *

A bellhop led Lemuel to Rubalev's room; the other man had said that he would speak to him there. Rubalev answered the door. Behind him, Lemuel saw Katia sitting on a settee.

"Come in," Rubalev said, handing the bellhop a coin. As Lemuel entered, Katia suddenly stood up, as if preparing to run from the room, then abruptly sat down again. She wore a dark blue silk dress, one he had not seen her in before, probably one of the garments she had left behind when she ran away from Rubalev.

"Are you here on Katia's behalf?" Rubalev asked as Lemuel sat down. "I told you that I would see that she was returned to her husband. I am of course willing to pay you for anything you may have spent on her."

"I don't want any money," Lemuel said. "If you are going to take Katia back to her people, all I ask is that you allow me to come along."

Rubalev smiled. "I see. I must assume that this is not because you harbor chivalrous impulses toward my ward." Katia averted her eyes from both of them. "So perhaps you have met with your friend Colonel Clarke. I think that I know what he wants—for you to spy for him."

Lemuel did not respond.

"I will tell you this now, Mr. Rowland. Whatever Clarke told you, he would use whatever information you bring to him against the Lakota and their allies."

"I'm well aware of that," Lemuel said.

"Then I must tell you this. If you ride out with Katia, you cannot come back. Do you understand? You may be a friend of Done-hogawa's, or even his blood brother, but you cannot come back until you win the trust of the Lakota. For until you do, I cannot risk trusting you, either."

Lemuel thought of the moment of strangeness that had come to him before, when he had felt himself apart from the world, uncertain even of his own reality. To follow this trail meant leaving everything he knew, and for what?

"Perhaps you will change your mind," Rubalev said. "Done-hogawa may be disappointed, but there is nothing he can do, and perhaps he is only asking you to take risks that he can no longer take himself, or that he is unwilling to take. You may leave this room, go back to St. Louis, even travel back East if you like. I will not stop you if you leave St. Joseph now. You do not yet know enough to have any effect on events."

"I've made my decision," Lemuel said. "A Negro named Virgil Warrick is willing to travel with us. I hope that he can come along."

Rubalev frowned. "Already you are asking for more conditions. I know nothing about this man."

Katia said, "He's the black man who came with us on the train." Lemuel turned toward her, surprised to hear her speak. "Mr. Rowland appears to know him fairly well and to trust him," she continued, "and if he turns out to be useless, he won't live long anyway."

Rubalev's eyes narrowed. "You make a good point, child."

Lemuel wondered why she was speaking up for what he wanted. "Then perhaps," he said, "we can now discuss when we are to leave with you and what I might need to take with me."

"You will not be traveling with me," Rubalev said. Katia's eyes widened with astonishment. "I will see that you have a guide, but I cannot go with you. There are matters I must tend to elsewhere." He was silent for a few moments, and Lemuel did not ask where Rubalev intended to go. He probably would not have told him anyway.

"My husband," Katia said, "will be disappointed at not seeing you with us."

"You may tell him that I am securing our alliances," Rubalev replied. "I trust that he will be happy to see you again, but if he is not, then the arrival of Mr. Rowland will perhaps be some consolation. Touch-the-Clouds can always use skilled men."

Katia's hands fluttered.

"She would be safer with you," Lemuel said.

"She wants to go back to her people. In any case, she is of no more use to me here."

Katia got up and hurried from the room, slamming a door behind her.

Rubalev leaned back in his chair. "Now, Rowland, let us talk about the arrangements for your journey."

* * *

The street leading to his hotel, usually lively even late into the night, was almost empty. Lemuel passed a row of saloons and saw only a few men in each, sitting at tables or standing at the bars. He had been in Rubalev's suite for some time, talking of the route he would take and the way he would travel, to Omaha on the Missouri by boat and by horseback after that.

He had better start getting used to long hours on a horse again, Lemuel told himself; he was out of practice. Rubalev, after telling him that it might take some time for him to arrange things, now seemed anxious to get him away from St. Joseph as quickly as possible. He would have to wait in Omaha for his guide to meet him. The guide would probably be Rubalev's colored man, Denis Laforte, if everything went as Rubalev hoped.

He would be putting himself in the hands of strangers, people who seemed to hope for some justice for the Indians of the Plains and some sort of action that would preserve their lands. He did not know what else they wanted. Rubalev had promised to give Lemuel enough money for the journey, but if he reached his destination safely, it was unlikely that he would need any greenbacks and coins among the Sioux.

He was risking his life. He could still turn back. Rubalev had made that statement several times, repeating it so often that Lemuel began to think the words were a test. "You can go back, Rowland. Even after you get to Omaha, you can turn back." To take Rubalev at his word might involve just as many risks as keeping to his decision. By turning back now, he would be showing Rubalev that he could not be trusted after all. He thought of Katia, helpless to go against him. Lemuel did not want to find out what the man might do to someone he could not trust.

The hotel lobby was as empty and quiet as the street. Lemuel got his key at the desk and went up the stairs to his room. He was closing the door when the thought came to him: I must write to Donehogawa.

Lemuel lit the lamp on the nightstand, then sat on the edge of the bed to write his letter. He had brought ink and paper with him, intending to send a brief note to Katia at Mrs. Gerhardt's in order to maintain that charade. He would use the cipher for his letter, since he could write in that as easily as in English.

He dipped his pen in the inkwell and wrote quickly, telling Donehogawa that he would be traveling to Omaha and then from there to the camp of Touch-the-Clouds. He set down everything that Rubalev had told him that evening; after hesitating for a moment, he wrote a short version of his meeting with Katia in St. Louis and what had followed. Rubalev would assuredly send Donehogawa a report of what had passed, but Lemuel wanted the former commissioner to have a letter from him as well.

The letter came to two pages in length, on both sides of the paper. Lemuel was about to fold up the letter and slip it into an envelope when he realized that he had left something out.

If you are wondering why I decided to come here and seek out Rubalev, he wrote quickly in the cipher, *it is because a dream told me that I had to ride out to the Plains.* There was no need to tell Donehogawa anything more than that.

Lemuel got up early. He would go to the livery stable near his hotel to see about a horse, and then mail his letter to Donehogawa. It came to him then that perhaps one of the reasons he had written that letter was to have a thread connecting him to his former life. He might ride out to the camp of Touch-the-Clouds only to disappear from the world he knew as completely as though he had never existed. He might die out on the Plains before he even reached his destination, or—perhaps worse—discover that he had given up his old life for no reason. He wanted at least one person back East to know where he had gone.

In the daylight outside the hotel, he felt more hopeful. A wagon rattled by, and then another; a knot of men had gathered in front of the general store down the street from the stable. Lemuel waited for a buckboard to pass, then hurried across the road.

"Came in on the telegraph last night," one white-bearded man was saying as Lemuel approached. "They called in a doctor right after it happened, but it was too late. Died yesterday morning, it said."

Lemuel slowed his pace, then turned. "Was he drinking?" a young man asked. "Always heard he was a man what enjoyed his liquor."

"I don't know," the older man replied, "but maybe it wouldn't have mattered one way or the other. Maybe it was too dark to see the carriage coming. Maybe there weren't enough time to get out of the way—I mean, that congressman was hurt, too."

Another man shook his head. "The Rebs couldn't kill him, but a carriage in Washington City could."

"Washington?" Lemuel said before he could stop himself.

"Guess you ain't heard, son." The white-bearded man folded his arms. "President Ulysses S. Grant's gone to meet his Maker. Seems he was crossing the road not far from the White House when a couple of panicked horses hitched to a carriage came around a corner. They carried him into a boardinghouse nearby, and the doctor came, but the president died a few hours later."

Lemuel opened his mouth, but no words came.

"Going down to the *Journal* office," a man in a duster said. "Maybe they ran off the new edition by now."

Lemuel turned away. Schuyler Colfax was president now. The man from Indiana had been Speaker of the House before becoming vice president. The vice president was a man enamored of the sound of his own voice, which was why he had spent much of his time traveling around the country to lecture, and he had a weakness for both flattery and money. Donehogawa had always regarded Colfax with some amusement, especially after the vice president had announced his intention to retire from public life in the hope that a groundswell of popular support would dissuade him. When his announcement was greeting with silence, Colfax had quickly retracted his promise. He was a man who would likely not have been invited to run with President Grant a second time, and now he was president.

How would the country fare with President Colfax at its head? Lemuel walked toward the stable, too stunned to feel any grief as yet for his former commander. Again he had the feeling that the world around him was insubstantial, that the news of Grant's death was something he had only imagined.

NINE

Two weeks after word of President Grant's death had reached him, Lemuel was in Omaha with Katia and Virgil Warrick. To reach the city, which stood on bluffs overlooking the Missouri, required crossing from Council Bluffs on the eastern side of the river in a ferry that seemed ready to capsize into the muddy water at almost any moment. Omaha was a crowded, rapidly growing city of muddy streets with newly planted trees and dust-covered buildings, of horse-drawn omnibuses and mud-spattered carriages, of restless people on their way to someplace else.

Denis Laforte met them in Omaha, telling them little except that they would be leaving in a few days to travel northwest up the Missouri, and then west toward Dakota. Snow would be coming to the Plains soon; Denis wanted them to reach the Sioux camp before the worst of the winter set in. It occurred to Lemuel again that he might not survive the harsh winter.

He could turn back. The money Rubalev had given him would be enough for him to go back to St. Louis. The thought crossed his mind for only a moment before he pushed it aside. He had survived as a Union soldier; he would make himself live through this.

He left Omaha with his companions early one morning. By now, he had grown used to seeing Katia on a horse. Rubalev had gone riding with the two of them on the outskirts of St. Joseph, obviously wanting to make certain that they would be prepared to make a long journey on horseback.

"Katia can ride without a saddle as easily as with one," Rubalev had told him, "but of course she has been riding since childhood. I saw to it that she did not lose the skill, although she is somewhat out of practice. But you will see. By the time I see you again, she will be a better rider than either of us."

"When will we see you?" Lemuel had asked.

"I do not yet know. That depends on how long it takes me to settle matters with those who may be helpful." Lemuel had not asked Rubalev what he meant by that, and who the people were that he was to see; the man would tell him nothing. He knew only that word of Grant's death had disturbed Rubalev greatly.

The colder weather had held off, and the air was warm for late autumn. Lemuel felt grateful for that. Once they left the Missouri, and headed into territory unsettled by the white man and unmarked by railroads and wagon trails, there would be no more small towns or encampments at which to stop for a meal and a bed. They would be dependent on their scouts and on whatever hospitality the Sioux were willing to offer.

The Plains grass had grown dry, and the farther they rode from settled lands, the more monotonous the landscape became. The short yellowing grass rippled and rolled like the waves of a vast sea. Four days after they had left Omaha, there were no sightings of a distant cabin or sod dwelling on the horizon to mark their passage, only an isolated tree, a rocky outcropping, or a slight rise in the land. At dusk, as they pitched their tents and settled down for the night, the wind wailed, died, and then picked up again. Lemuel slept to the sound of the wind, hearing it in his dreams, and when he woke, he recalled only fragmentary dreams of horses and riders on the western horizon, always moving ahead of him, never allowing him to catch up.

Virgil Warrick was awkward in his saddle, and when out of it, walked stiffly and sat down gingerly, obviously sore and aching from the long ride. It was clear that he did not have much experience as a rider, but he refused to complain and did his best not to slow the rest of the party down.

Katia did not complain, either. By the third day, she was easily able to keep up with Denis and Lemuel. By the fifth day, she was riding ahead of them, reining in from time to time to allow them to catch up with her. On the sixth day, after they had struck camp, Lemuel was preparing to saddle his horse when he saw Katia leap onto the blanketed back of her mount.

"I'll ride this way," she said as she swung one leg over the horse and dismounted.

"Without a saddle?" Virgil asked.

"I rode that way as a girl, before I had a woman's saddle." Katia picked up her saddle and lifted it to the back of one of their three spare horses. "We are being followed," she went on.

"I know," Denis said.

"We have been followed for the past two days at least," Katia murmured, "perhaps longer."

Lemuel wondered how Katia could be so certain of that. Someone could track them; he had no doubt of that. There would be their trail to follow, the droppings of their horses, the places where they had camped. He had seen no one at a distance, so whoever was tracking them was keeping well out of sight.

"Cavalry?" Lemuel asked.

Denis shook his head. "If they were soldiers, they would have shown themselves by now." Lemuel did not think that they would rouse any suspicion even if soldiers crossed their path. He and Katia could pass for young homesteaders with two black servants, and if they were brought in to any fort, he would have a message sent to Jeremiah Clarke. Still, he was relieved that they were apparently safe from being waylaid by soldiers.

On the seventh day, Katia took down her hair and braided it in two long plaits. She still wore a plain brown woolen dress and a thick sheepskin coat, but there would be no mistaking her for a settler now.

The wind had tanned her skin and brought color to her face; when she reined in her horse to lean forward and scan the horizon, she looked like what she was, a Sioux. He had feared that she might slow them down, that he would see regret in her face. Instead, she seemed to be looking forward to her return.

On the eighth day, as they were about to ride on, Lemuel finally spotted two riders in the north, across the treeless plain of rippling yellow grass.

Lemuel sat on his horse, waiting as the riders approached them. They were Sioux, clothed in ragged leather jackets that looked as though they might have once belonged to white men, leggings, and boots made of hide. Their long black hair fell to their waist.

When the two riders were near, Denis held up a hand, then glanced toward Katia. As the two strangers reined in their horses, Katia said a few words that Lemuel recalled were a greeting.

"She is saying that she is the wife of their chief," Denis murmured, "riding back to her husband, and that you and Virgil were sent here by their friend Yellow Hair."

Yellow Hair, Lemuel assumed, was Rubalev. He heard Virgil suck in his breath.

Katia said another word that sounded to Lemuel like "magaskawie." He guessed that it was a name, perhaps her own in Lakota. The men responded with more unfamiliar words and sounds.

"They are saying their names," Denis said, "what they are called. Magaskawee is what Katia is called here—it means Graceful Swan. The two men are Hotahwambee—White Eagle—and Kohana Tashunka, or Swift Horse. I do not know these men, but they are the men who were sent to meet us and to take us to the camp of Touch-the-Clouds."

Lemuel nodded. Once he was among these people, more of their words would return to him.

"Was you the one tole them we was coming?" Virgil asked.

Denis shook his head. "Mr. Rubalev sent someone else to tell them." He did not explain how that had happened.

"I can speak."

Lemuel tensed. One of the Indians had said those words. "I can speak your words," the Sioux said again, looking directly at Lemuel. "So I will speak in words we can all hear and know."

Again Virgil inhaled sharply. "We hope you can be trusted," the man continued. "If you are not trustworthy, it will not go well for you."

"You can trust them," Katia said.

"It is not enough for you to say it," the man replied. "We will see if they are trustworthy." He sounded as though he was not quite certain that he could trust her, either. "You will follow us now."

The man who spoke English was the one named White Eagle. Lemuel found it easier to think of his name in English than in the still unfamiliar sounds of the Lakota tongue. They rode in silence, stopping at intervals to graze and rest the horses. When night came, Lemuel and his companions pitched their tents. The two Sioux slept under a makeshift shelter of a blanket and branches.

In the morning, they set out at dawn. By late morning, the dry and grassy land was giving way to small hills. By midafternoon, Lemuel saw several tepees in the distance.

Swift Horse and his mount were soon galloping toward the camp. White Eagle rode after him, quickly leaving the others behind. "It is my husband's camp," Katia said. "I can see his tent."

The tepees looked much the same to him. Only when they were closer could Lemuel see that each was painted with different colors and patterns. His horse moved alongside Katia's. "You will have to tell me what to say to your husband."

Katia made a sound that might have been a laugh. "Greet him, and tell him that you have come as a friend," she said. "Nothing else you can say will make any difference." She glanced at him from the sides of her eyes. "If he has forgotten some of his English, and you most of your Lakota, I'll translate for you."

They continued toward the camp. By the time they reached it, a number of people were gathered in front of their dwellings to stare at them. As Lemuel dismounted, he saw the look of apprehension in Virgil's eyes.

White Eagle called out something in his own tongue, too fast for him to grasp it, then stooped to enter the nearest tepee. Katia dismounted and came to Lemuel's side. "He is greeting my husband," she said softly. "I don't know if he will invite us inside or come out to meet us." Her voice shook slightly; he realized that she was frightened.

Perhaps her husband did not want her here and would not welcome her. He wondered what Touch-the-Clouds could do with her. Divorce her? Give her to someone else? Force her to leave his camp once more? He could probably do any of those things.

White Eagle emerged from the tepee, followed by another man, clothed in a simple robe and with only one feather in his hair. "Welcome," White Eagle said in English.

"Welcome," the other man with him said as he straightened.

Lemuel gazed at the second man's face. For a moment, he could not speak. He knew this face. This was the face he had seen in his dream, the dream that had told him to come here.

The man stared back at him and said in English, "You have seen me before. That is what your eyes say."

"Yes, I have seen you before," Lemuel replied.

"Lordy," Virgil muttered behind him.

"I had a dream before I rode here," Lemuel went on. "I was on a plain, riding, and I saw a circle of warriors. One of them said to me, 'The circle has closed.' The man who said those words had your face."

The man continued to stare at him. Perhaps he had not understood all of his words. "You are the chief I came here to see," Lemuel said in halting Lakota, "the one called Touch-the-Clouds in my tongue."

"The Yellow Hair Rubalev sent you. He thinks you might be of use." The chief gestured at Virgil. "Who is this man?"

"My friend," Lemuel said.

"That is good. You are friends. We will see if you are my friends." Touch-the-Clouds gazed indifferently at Katia; she lowered her eyes. "And my wife is with me. I am pleased to see her again." His voice was flat. Lemuel knew then that he would take her back, and felt a pang, but also knew that Touch-the-Clouds was saying that he was pleased only out of courtesy. He was looking at her as though she was less to him than one of his horses, which was perhaps understandable. Maybe he would keep her only until Rubalev came here again.

Denis murmured a few words in Lakota, and then Touch-the-Clouds beckoned to Lemuel with one arm. "You will come inside, you and the Buffalo Man Laforte and your friend. Yellow Hair Rubalev has told me about you. He says that you are one who can build a wall and say where tunnels can be dug and tell in what places an Iron Horse trail can be made."

"An engineer," Denis Laforte said.

"Yes, that is what it is," Touch-the-Clouds said, "an engineer. I have some now. I need more of them—these men who build."

Lemuel tried not to let the surprise show in his face. "I have some now," this chief had said. What would he be doing with engineers? He wondered what other surprises the man had in store, and felt more adrift from his own world than ever.

TEN

White Eagle looked up as the Flowers of Fire blossomed in the clear blue sky overhead. A few moments later, he heard the sound of thunder, and grinned. Watching the arrow-rockets arch toward the sky and then burst forth with their fire and thunder always gave him pleasure.

Five years ago, he had come here with his father and his comrade Swift Horse to become one of those who guarded Paha Sapa, the Center of the World. The Flaming Trees and Flowers of Fire had terrified him; his frightened horse had neighed and reared, thrown him to the ground, and then galloped away in panic. Now White Eagle loved to gaze at the arrow-rockets streaking across the sky and opening into blazing blossoms.

These devices, the ones that bloomed in the sky and made showers of colorful sparks, were the harmless arrow-rockets. Glorious Spirit and his brother Victorious Spirit also made other arrow-rockets, ones launched from pony drags carrying the long flared nests they called Herd of a Hundred Buffaloes Running Together or Eagles in Search of Martens. Those arrow-rockets could make craters in the ground and even shatter rocks. White Eagle smiled when he thought of what they might do to the ene- mies of the Lakotas. He imagined them arching into the sky and then falling toward one of the forts of the blue-coated Horse Soldiers.

Glorious Spirit and Victorious Spirit could make strong war med- icine with their arrow-rockets. White Eagle knew that when Sitting Bull and Crazy Horse had first learned of the fire-flowers that were beginning to bloom above Paha Sapa, they had grown angry at such stories. To shoot arrow-rockets at the heavens from this sacred place, to disturb the peace of the warriors who came here to seek their visions, would enrage the spirits. There might even have been a war over the matter if Touch-the-Clouds had not brought the other chiefs here to see the strong medicine of the arrow-rockets for themselves. If the Wasichu would not leave them their lands and keep the peace, the fiery arrows would bloom against the walls of their forts and more whistling and shrieking arrows would fall upon the wagons that followed their Iron Horse.

What Touch-the-Clouds had left unsaid was that if Sitting Bull and Crazy Horse and their warriors chose to fight him, the rocket- arrows might be aimed at their camps. White Eagle, were he a chief, could not have brought himself to use such arrows against others of the Lakota, and especially such respected men, but Touch- the-Clouds was not like other chiefs. He had seen the arrows in one of his visions, flaming arrows that shot across the sky and made thunder. Touch-the-Clouds had known long before meeting Glori- ous Spirit and Victorious Spirit that he would find men who could make such weapons.

To the south loomed the high sharp peaks of the Black Hills, dark- ened by the ponderosa pines that covered their slopes. In the north, the land sloped more gently. Glorious Spirit and Victorious Spirit made their camp in the circle of tepees to the east of the sacred places, in the hilly pastureland.

Sacrilege, many had called it, to make rocket-arrows so near the Paha Sapa, to mark this land with the making of such alien things. White Eagle suspected that his father Soaring Eagle still had many questions and doubts about what went on here. But when it was time for the Sun Dance and for warriors to go into the Hills to seek visions, this camp was moved, all signs of it erased, and the men who lived here did what they could to protect and guard from view those areas in the Hills where caves had been dug and the land was scarred. It was better if most of the Lakota never saw what had been done in those places.

Better also, White Eagle told himself, to make sure that no Wasichu ever had a chance to learn of the existence of this camp, and of the places in the Hills where others dug for the yellow nuggets they traded for what they might need. The Lakota and their Cheyenne brothers had kept the white men from finding out what was here so far; at least two parties of soldiers and surveyors lay under the land bordering the Black Hills. But White Eagle wondered if they could continue to keep the Wasichu out if they ever found out about the gold. The yellow metal was a substance that maddened the Wasichu, that always brought them to come in great numbers with their tents and tools and wagons to dig at the ground.

White Eagle hoped that his people never fell victim to such madness, but already a few men had tried to sneak away with nuggets or bags of gold dust. No one ever found out what the thieves wanted with the gold, whether they planned to trade it for firewater at one of the Wasichu agencies, or simply wanted to keep the shiny pieces of Paha Sapa for their medicine bundles, but it did not matter. To use the yellow metal for anything other than the defense of their land was an evil Touch-the-Clouds would not allow. The few who had tried to leave with bits of the metal now lay under the ground with the Wasichu.

Someday, White Eagle knew, a Wasichu, a trapper, or even a warrior who still thought of the Lakota as his enemy would discover that there was gold here and carry that news back to the Blue Coats or to others of the Wasichu. After that, White Eagle was certain that the Lakota and the Cheyenne would have to fight to keep their lands. Some men doubted that, believing the Wasichu would keep their promises, especially if a battle for the Black Hills threatened to be long and bloody. But White Eagle thought that only merciless actions and a series of victories would have a chance of keeping the whites away. In that, he was in agreement with Touch-the-Clouds.

Glorious Spirit and Victorious Spirit, with the aid of a few of the men, were readying a portable quiver of rockets. The two brothers wore long dusters, taken from the bodies of two dead Wasichu, over their long woolen shirts and baggy leggings; each had a long thin black braid down his back. Even after almost seven years of living among the Lakota, the two brothers remained poor riders. No one had to worry that Glorious Spirit and Victorious Spirit might try to get away with stolen gold. They would never be able to ride far and fast enough to escape.

Victorious Spirit made a sign with one hand. The man holding the quiver, who still wore the worn blue coat of a Buffalo Soldier, was about to loose the first of the hand-held rocket-arrows. White Eagle leaned forward on his horse to watch, then saw a distant speck on the hilly green horizon.

He let out a whoop and waved an arm at Victorious Spirit. "I see a rider," White Eagle called out, shouting the words in English, the only tongue he and the two brothers had in common. "Two riders," he added as the tiny, faraway forms became more distinct. There were two men, leading three more horses with packs.

The dark-skinned man with the quiver hurried toward the nearest tepee; Victorious Spirit threw a hide over the basket from which the Flowers of Fire had been launched. The two approaching riders were almost certainly friendly. White Eagle doubted that any enemy scouts could have ridden this far without being seen, but even friends could pose a danger. Even their Apache, Comanche, and Kiowa allies to the south knew little of this place except that it was a place of strong medicine and powerful spirits.

The encampment, in only a few moments, had taken on the appearance of an ordinary circle of tepees. Not quite ordinary, White Eagle reminded himself, since there were no women here most of the time. Glorious Spirit and Victorious Spirit did not seem to feel any shame when doing the women's work of preparing food or putting up a tent. White Eagle tried to do as little women's work as possible out here.

He now saw who the riders were. Even at this distance, he recognized the long yellow hair of Rubalev that flowed from under his hat over his shoulders. The second man's black hair was now almost long enough for a braid. That man was Poyeshao, the Orphan. Yellow Hair Rubalev had found out somehow that Orphan was the man's childhood name, given up after he had begun living in the world of the Wasichu. Poyeshao was in fact an orphan, having been adopted by a Wasichu family after losing his own parents. The white people had given him the name of Rowland, but White Eagle still thought of him as the Orphan.

And, he admitted to himself, the man, even after a year and a half among them, seemed as solitary and strange as he had when White Eagle had first led him to the camp of Touch-the-Clouds. The Orphan came from a people who called themselves the Keepers of the Western Door and who were one of six nations known as the People of the Long House; so he had told them. They made their camps in the northeast, among forests, where deer, beaver, waterfowl, and other game could be found, but they lived also as tillers of soil. The Orphan had admitted that his Long House People had dug at the ground and raised crops even before the Wasichu came. Perhaps they were not Wasichu, but they were also not anything like the Lakota. What kind of Lakota would choose to till the ground? The Orphan Rowland might call himself a brother, but he seemed apart from everyone around him.

Perhaps it was all the time he had lived among the Wasichu that made him that way. He was like the second wife of Touch-the-Clouds, who was always watching the other women as they went about their tasks, as if she were still a girl learning how to do a woman's work and unsure of her skill.

Touch-the-Clouds needed something from this man; that much was clear. Whether he trusted him or not did not matter. If Poyeshao tried to leave this place after seeing what was here, he would end up with the others under the ground. As White Eagle rode back to the encampment, he wondered why Yellow Hair Rubalev was bringing the Orphan here now.

Rubalev reined in his horse and took a deep breath. "A good day," he said expansively.

They had been lucky, Lemuel thought. Each day of the ride had been warm but not hot, breezy but without the strong winds that so often swept the Plains. The land around the Black Hills yielded plenty of grass for their horses. In the distance, he glimpsed a small circle of tepees. Rubalev had not told him very much about their destination, only that he would see some of the weapons the Lakota might have to use in any future battles with the white men. But Lemuel had now lived among the Lakota long enough to know that they were not depending solely on their bows and rifles and whatever weapons they could steal.

They had a base somewhere, maybe more than one. Somewhere, perhaps in northern California or near it, weapons were being made for them, purchased with the gold of which the Sioux seemed to have an unlimited supply.

"You will find this place interesting," Rubalev said. He had said almost nothing about their destination so far, mentioning only that Touch-the-Clouds wanted him to see it. He had not even mentioned how long they would be here, but Lemuel knew that the Sioux and Cheyenne would soon be gathering here for the Sun Dance. He might be invited to join them for the ceremony this year. Lemuel had witnessed one Sun Dance, and only briefly, and the mutilations he had seen made him hope that the Lakota would not show him that much esteem.

It was easier to think kindly of the Sioux at a distance. Once he had dismissed that notion; now he saw its truth. Perhaps Rubalev found it easier to be their friend because he spent so much time away from them.

That was what it came down to, now that he had lived longer among the Lakota, learned more of their customs, even attained proficiency in their language, thanks largely to the efforts of Katia and the persistence of Touch-the-Clouds. He could not be like them, not on the inside. He and his own people had grown too far away from what they once had been, and he had lived too long among whites. Underneath the daily doings of these people was a complicated web of rituals and ceremonies, of warrior societies and taboos, of lengthy speeches and councils, and of gestures that could inadvertently offend someone. He could feel sympathy for the

Lakota and want to see justice for them, but part of him, in keeping with their white enemies, still thought of them as mysterious, alien, beings unlike himself.

"It is good to be here again," Rubalev continued. "Things have grown hard in the cities. It would not surprise me to learn that there had been more riots by now." The blond man looked happy at the thought. The recent financial panic Rubalev had told Lemuel about, the tarring of so many politicians with scandal, the shakiness of President Colfax's hold on power—all of it made the Sioux safer. Lemuel wondered if Rubalev still burned with his longing for revenge against the people who had destroyed his home, still dreamed of the rise of his American khan, or had simply been plotting and planning for so long that his schemes had become an unbreakable habit.

Rubalev had been in Touch-the-Cloud's camp for only a few days before deciding to come to the Black Hills with Lemuel. Touch-the-Clouds had intended to send Lemuel with Swift Horse, but Rubalev had asked to ride out with him, and the chief had agreed. Rubalev might have wanted the chance to talk to someone who could understand the implications of what he had to say about recent events.

There had been much to tell. The collapse of the powerful bank of Jay Cooke and Company, the exposure of the fact that stock in Crédit Mobilier had in effect been given to President Colfax and much of the Congress in an effort to ensure that they supported the interests of the railroads, and the ensuing bankruptcies and scandals, had all shaken the United States. People outside Washington were now afflicted with bankrupt railroads, lost jobs, labor unrest, and financial panic. Plans for surveying along the planned route of the Northern Pacific Railroad, yet another threat to the Lakota lands in the north, had come to a halt, and workers were refusing to work on the other railroads to the south.

Donehogawa, according to Rubalev, had weathered the financial storm. He had said no more than that, but Lemuel suspected that Donehogawa still did what he could to lend aid to Rubalev.

"There were rumors when I left," Rubalev continued, "that the South was growing discontented again. President Colfax was perhaps too willing to give in to those around him who wanted a firmer hand there." Another piece of good luck for the Lakota, Lemuel thought. More soldiers would be needed in the South to dampen any rebellion; fewer would be sent west to fight Indians.

The East, and his life there, seemed far away and insubstantial, a hazily recalled dream. He had come to understand Katia's anger and her feelings of displacement. She had come back to a husband who was indifferent to her; she seemed incapable of giving him a child. Her main use had been to teach Lemuel more Lakota and to instruct the first wife and the sons of Touch-the-Clouds in English, since the chief seemed to think that they should also learn the Wasichu tongue. Perhaps she would ask Rubalev to take her back with him when he left these lands again. However unhappy she had been in that world, she was clearly unhappy here.

There was nothing that he could do for her. Lemuel reminded himself of that fact often, and avoided her as much as possible, knowing that otherwise he might be tempted to offer her more comfort than he should. He had welcomed the chance to get away from her.

Something was different about the small encampment they were approaching. The tepees disappeared behind one hill, then reappeared as Lemuel, leading one of the pack horses by the reins, followed Rubalev along one stream and up the slope of a hill. He was closer before he realized what was different. There were no women tanning hides on frames outside the tepees, or sending their children to the stream to fetch water.

"Not many ride to this place," Rubalev said, "and Touch-the-Clouds makes certain that those he sends here are trusted. If they prove to be treacherous in the end—" He turned his head toward Lemuel and smiled. "I do not think he has to worry about you. If you try to leave this place, you will not get far. I would go after you myself if you did, and bring your scalp to Touch-the-Clouds, and then beg his forgiveness for ever bringing you to his camp."

"I'm sure you would." Lemuel had no doubt about that. He had learned quickly that Touch-the-Clouds was not a man anyone wanted to offend. He had never seen the Lakota chief raise his voice in anger, or even utter a threat, but he did not have to do so. Whatever he had done in the past to ensure obedience had obviously worked.

"I would of course be very sorry to have to kill you." Rubalev chuckled.

"I assume that this camp up ahead is a base of some sort," Lemuel said. "I don't see any women outside the tepees, so I'm guessing that some kind of special training for warriors goes on here. Is it training as soldiers, or perhaps something more spiritual?" He had seen how devoted these people were to their prayers and their rituals in which they appealed to the spirits; it was one of their more attractive qualities.

Rubalev twisted around in his saddle. "You will see."

Lemuel thought of the sound he had heard not long before, a sound that had reminded him of an explosion. "You're making weapons here," he said. "They must be something different from the weapons the Lakota usually steal. I heard—" He paused. What he had heard might only be thunder, although it had sounded more like fireworks. "An exploding sound," he finished.

"Yes," Rubalev said.

A man rode toward them; Lemuel recognized White Eagle. In the camp, standing near one of the tepees, were two men with light brown faces and almond-shaped eyes who did not have the look of the Lakota. They were also much shorter, although their clothing made them look bulky.

"Those two men aren't Sioux," Lemuel murmured.

"No, they are not. They are the Chen brothers—I think you will find them interesting. Wing-shen and Shing-shen, they are called, but they know English and are used to answering to the English meaning of their names."

"And what are those?" Lemuel asked.

"Glorious Spirit and Victorious Spirit. They are most suitable names, are they not? They are men who make things, as are you. I think you will enjoy their work."

* * *

"And this," one of the Chen brothers said softly, "is the Flying Eagle with Magic Fire."

Lemuel peered at the basket of reeds and wood. It looked more like a winged chicken than an eagle. The basket had been filled with gunpowder and sealed with paper; two rockets were attached under the wings.

"Light fuse, here," the man continued, "and then he flies, and when he lands—" He threw out his hands and made an explosive sound. "Big fire. Big noise."

"Sides of hole must be straight," the other brother said. Glorious Spirit or Victorious Spirit? Lemuel could not tell the two apart. "Too deep hole here—arrow lose too much fire from back when bird flies. Too shallow, and will fall before reaching enemy—maybe on top of us."

The two had taken him to their tepee and shown him some of their devices soon after dawn. Lemuel had slept badly, after an early supper of dried buffalo meat and the effort of trying to suppress his curiosity. He had expected to see something unusual. He had not expected this. He looked around at the other rocket launchers, the Pack of Fifty Wolves Running Together, the Mountain Lions Who Scatter, and the Eagles in Search of Martens.

"Better with bamboo than wood and reeds," Victorious Spirit— or was it Glorious Spirit?—said. "But still work good."

Lemuel nodded. He had no doubt of that. Rubalev had told him a little about the Chen brothers. They had come here from China and found work building the western tracks of the Union Pacific. They had come here with, apparently, much more learning than most of their fellow Chinese coolies; Rubalev had hinted that they had been in flight from powerful enemies in their homeland. Rubalev had met the Chen brothers near San Francisco and had found out enough about them to think that they might be of use.

"I did not know what to do with them in the beginning," Rubalev had admitted. "I gave them some money, found them a place to work, and told them to make what they liked. After I saw what they could do, I brought them here."

Rubalev stood near Lemuel; White Eagle was fingering the

shafts of one arrow-rocket. "These will be good to use in battle," the Lakota said. "Hitting the enemy at a distance—it is not the right way, not a good way to fight, but the rocket-arrows will not kill them all. We will still have some men to fight against hand to hand. We will still count coup."

"What do you think?" Rubalev asked.

"The Lakota can probably win a battle with these weapons," Lemuel said. "They might even win a few battles, but they won't win a war. The main advantage they'll have in the beginning is that the Blue Coats won't expect such weapons to be used against them, since they don't know these Indians have them. But once they find out, they'll throw even more of their weaponry against the Lakota. They've kept these weapons secret so far, but once they fight their first battle, the secret will be out, and they'll lose that advantage."

"That is what I think," Rubalev said.

"And I don't know how they can be brought into action," Lemuel continued. "If the Lakota wait until the Blue Coats come after them, they may not have time to bring these rocket-arrows to the scene of the battle. If they engage the enemy and then retreat, to lure the Blue Coats here, they had better win an overwhelming victory and kill every last man, because otherwise—"

"—they will know what is going on here," Rubalev finished.

"And at that point, they will send everything they have against the Lakota," Lemuel said, "and they'll win."

"Touch-the-Clouds knows that," Rubalev said.

"We raid," White Eagle said. "The spirits want us to use these weapons—not let us make them here in Paha Sapa if they did not want us to fight. We attack agencies, first Red Cloud Agency and then Spotted Tail. We can take what we want there and then go to Fort Laramie." He glanced at the Chen brothers. "We bring rocket-arrows with us and fire them at the fort."

"That is not a bad idea," Rubalev said.

"It might be a good idea to go on the offensive," Lemuel said, "instead of waiting for soldiers to come after you." He was surprised to hear the notion from White Eagle. Touch-the-Clouds might have convinced many of his people that they would have to find new ways to hold on to what they had, but some of them still clung to older ways. They thought of battles as efforts to win some individual glory, not as parts of a larger campaign with a purpose. They still raided and stole horses from outlying, isolated farms and ranches when they thought they could get away with it. Some of them would say that as long as the whites kept away from the lands given to the Lakota by treaty, there was no reason to attack their forts.

"We fire rocket-arrows," White Eagle said, "and kill everyone inside the fort." He smiled. "But only if treaty is broken."

Rubalev turned toward White Eagle. "You will need more of a plan than that," he said.

Lemuel moved toward the open tent flap. "Thank you for showing me your inventions," he said to the Chen brothers. "I have no doubt that they'll prove useful." He went outside and had reached his horse before Rubalev caught up with him.

"Where are you going?" Rubalev asked.

"For a ride. I'll be back by evening."

"You should not go alone."

"I thought I was trusted."

"You are trusted." Rubalev showed his teeth. "But you should not go alone."

"Then have someone follow me," Lemuel said. "Ride after me yourself if you like, but keep behind me. I need some time to think."

"About tactics?" Rubalev asked.

"About a lot of things." Lemuel saddled his horse and tightened the girth. Rubalev watched him in silence, then went back inside the tepee.

Lemuel rode along the side of a small stream, then up a hill. He knew that he was being followed, but did not look back.

He had not thought of escape until now. During his early months at the camp of Touch-the-Clouds, he had thought only of keeping himself alive. The winter had been harsh, although the old men in the camp had implied that other winters had been much harder, and Lemuel had been given enough to eat. It might have been easier for him if Virgil had stayed in the encampment with him, but the black man and Denis Laforte had left after only a few days, and he did not know where they had gone.

He had mastered the Lakota tongue quickly, sensing that the men around him would grow more impatient with him if he did not. He had survived the winter while brooding about what might become of him if Touch-the-Clouds decided he was of little use. There was little he could do to prove himself. He did not know the land and the game well enough to hunt, and he had no other useful skills. All he could do was to practice his Lakota and help Touch-the-Clouds with his English while answering any of the chief's questions about the Wasichu. Lemuel had never been able to tell if his answers satisfied Touch-the-Clouds or not. Everything he said was met with the same silence, brief nod of the head, and steady, merciless gaze.

By the summer after his arrival, when the bands of Oglalas, Brulés, Wahpetons, Hunkpapas, and other bands of Lakota were gathering at the Black Hills with the Cheyenne for their annual Sun Dance, he already suspected that the source of the Lakotas' gold had to be near here. He had seen the nuggets passed from hand to hand, the bags of gold dust given to riders to take to unknown destinations. Some of it, Lemuel knew, had been taken to Rubalev, to be used to buy weapons and friends and whatever else was needed.

There had been rumors about gold in this region for years, even before the war. There had also been too many hostile and dangerous Indians in the territory to attract miners looking for strikes. But sooner or later, some of the gold that might be here would find its way into enemy hands. Perhaps it already had.

Anyone seeing the gold would want to know where it came from, and perhaps they already knew. The provisions of the treaty with the Lakota would not keep prospectors from this region if anyone even suspected that there was gold here. The Sioux were right about the yellow metal driving the Wasichu to madness. If times were as hard as Rubalev said they were, people would be even hungrier for gold.

Miners and prospectors would swarm into the Black Hills and the Lakota would kill as many of them as they could. The army would have to retaliate and there would be a war—a true war, not just isolated raids and battles and revenge killings.

A comet had been sighted that spring, growing into a streak of starry light near the Great Bear. Most of the Lakota seemed to regard it as an evil omen, a sign of the Great Spirit's disapproval. Touch-the-Clouds was not so certain. The comet might be a sign of anger, or it might have been sent to guide those warriors who died in any upcoming battles to the heavens. Touch-the-Clouds had insisted on this forcefully enough that soon most of the men had come around to his view. Lemuel wondered if the Lakota chief was expecting a war soon.

He reined in his horse. The animal lowered its head to drink from the stream. Lemuel glanced over his shoulder and saw a Lakota warrior, bare-chested, with a necklace of beads and bear claws and his black hair streaming down his back. White Eagle was following him. Maybe sending someone after him had nothing to do with a lack of trust; perhaps they only wanted to keep him safe from any danger. He wondered which would shame him more, not being trusted or having these men so certain that he could not protect himself.

The sun danced on the water as his horse drank. The thought that he had been avoiding suddenly floated to the surface. He had made a mistake in coming here. The Lakota did not need him to fight their war. Better for him to try to find some way of getting word back to Fort Kearney and Jeremiah Clarke from Bismarck or Fort Abraham Lincoln. He could ride that far, have a chance of outrunning any pursuers. There was no need to betray the Lakotas. He could tell Jeremiah truthfully that any war with the Sioux would be bloody, that it was not worth fighting, that the Indians had more weapons than they realized, that there had been enough wars.

He suppressed his thoughts immediately. He had grown used to doing that, afraid that somehow Touch-the-Clouds might sense his hidden musings. Foolish to think that even Jeremiah would be persuaded by his plea to honor the promises in the treaties.

He would look at the missiles Glorious Spirit and Victorious Spirit had built, and see if he could find ways to improve them. That would be useful to the Lakota. He drew on his reins, guiding his mount toward White Eagle.

The sound of voices woke Lemuel before dawn. He sat up and realized he was alone; Rubalev had already left the tepee they shared.

He got up and went outside. Men were taking down the tepees and tying packs to horses. He expected to see them looking angry or ashamed at doing this women's work, but instead their expressions were grim. Others were loading the rocket-arrows and their baskets, onto hides attached to poles. Two men Lemuel had not seen here before were in the camp. He recognized one of them: Soaring Eagle, the father of White Eagle.

Rubalev was talking to the newcomers. "What's going on?" Lemuel asked as he approached them.

"We are leaving," Rubalev replied. "Some will go southeast with Glorious Spirit and Victorious Spirit. Others will hide in the mountains and wait to see what we have to do."

White Eagle turned toward them. "My father rode here with Iron Hawk to say that Blue Coats are riding to Paha Sapa. Many pony soldiers." He held up his hands. "Not to fight. They are not war party here to fight us. Here to look."

Lemuel frowned. "And they weren't stopped?"

"They are being followed," Rubalev said. "There's no point in attacking until—" One of the men loading the horses motioned to the blond man. Rubalev strode over to him.

He did not have to finish the sentence. Lemuel could guess what the intentions of Touch-the-Clouds were. He would spy on the expedition, assess their strength, see how far they went and what they found. Maybe they would not travel too far, and perhaps they could be left alone. If, however, the Lakota decided to attack, they would have to kill them all. They could not risk having any of them return to their post with tales of gold and strange activity in the Black Hills.

Lemuel said, "They are breaking the treaty if they come here."

Rubalev sniffed. "Of course they are breaking the treaty. They do not care. So the Lakota will not be breaking the treaty if they attack."

White Eagle's father muttered a few words in Lakota, something about the Morning Star. Rubalev scowled. "He says that the Long Hair Custer is with the expedition, the one the Crows call the Son of the Morning Star."

"They rode out from Fort Lincoln some days ago," White Eagle added. Then, Lemuel thought, Jeremiah Clarke was not likely to be with them. "My father says that is what our spies there told Touch-the-Clouds."

Of course the Lakota would have spies, Lemuel thought. No one had ever mentioned such spies to him, but there was no need to give him such information. He wondered who the spies were; some were probably among the Indian scouts. Not many would scout for the Blue Coats unless they were also spies for the Lakota and Cheyenne; they were too afraid of Touch-the-Clouds for that.

"Many," Soaring Eagle said. "Many wagons, many men."

"How many?" Rubalev asked.

"One hundred wagons," Soaring Eagle replied. "Men—many hundred." He held up his hands, stretching out his fingers. "This many hundred."

Lemuel let out his breath, seeing how many the Lakota meant; nearly a thousand. Could Touch-the-Clouds attack them and have any hope of winning? He did not think so.

"Come with me," Rubalev said then. "Touch-the-Clouds gave his orders for us. We are to ride east and stay with White Eagle and his father and keep watch for the Blue Coats along the Belle Fourche River."

"You'd do better without me," Lemuel said. That sounded cowardly. "I don't know this territory," he said in a more forceful way.

"You do not have to know," Rubalev replied. "We will watch out for you. You are coming along in case we have to speak to them."

ELEVEN

Martha Jane Cannary tightened her hands on the reins, urging along the mules that pulled her wagon. Up ahead of the canvas-covered wagons, out of sight, she still heard the band playing. She cupped an ear, trying to recognize the tune; the sound of brass echoed from the hills. The reverberating echoes of the trumpets made it impossible for her to know what the song was.

They were probably playing "Garry Owen" again. The Seventh Cavalry's band played a lot of tunes, starting first thing in the morning after "Reveille." General Custer—he was actually a colonel, but everyone addressed him by the breveted rank he had earned during the War Between the States—enjoyed music and pomp. Only Iron Butt Custer would think of bringing a sixteen-piece brass band on white horses along with the Seventh on an expedition into territory few white men, except for maybe some traders or trappers, had ever seen.

The sound of the trumpets and the other brass instruments might scare the redskins, though. The Indians had probably never heard a brass band before.

The territory here was beautiful country. The flowers were thick around Jane, many reaching past the tops of her wagon's wheels. The men had been picking the flowers as they rode by and there were still enough left for hundreds of bouquets. To the southwest, in the distance, lay the dark, forbidding peaks of the Black Hills.

Jane was sure that they were being watched. Trailing the expedition in the last of the wagons, keeping well behind Hard Ass Custer and most of his men, she felt eyes watching them from the hills. The band had finally stopped playing. The Indians had to be waiting, maybe thinking of picking off any stragglers among the soldiers bringing up the rear.

The wagonmaster back at Fort Lincoln had hired her as a driver. She was used to passing as a man, and he had not been looking at her any too closely anyway. The Seventh had been on the move for five days before she gave herself away. It was the whiskey, always her weakness. She had been drinking with a couple of the mule packers and had left the campfire to take a piss. One of them, growing suspicious, had followed her. If she had been sober, she would have taken more trouble to keep her voice low, conceal herself from view.

The driver in charge of the wagons might have sent her back to the fort, but they were five days out by then and, as she had pointed out, she had been a rider for the Pony Express, and would also be useful as a scout. Calamity Jane, they called her, and the other driver had heard the name before. He had kept her on, but grudgingly. She expected that he would send her back to Fort Lincoln with the next scout carrying dispatches and letters from the men to their wives.

They had come to a Sioux camp a couple of days ago. Custer had ridden ahead with a few of the men of E Company to assure the Indians that they were not there to attack them. That was true enough. Custer had smoked a pipe with the Sioux in that camp, and they had said nothing about the treaty of 1868 that Custer and the Seventh were violating by simply coming into this territory. Any fighting would come later, after the soldiers had returned to Fort Lincoln with their reports and people started moving into the territory around the Black Hills, as they inevitably would. The railroad engineers were itching to survey the land for tracks, and lately there were more rumors of gold. That past winter, a badly injured scout had shown up at Fort Laramie with a few gold nuggets he had found on the body of a Sioux he had killed. The man had died before he could say anything more.

By itself, Jane thought, that story might not have meant much. But there were other stories, tales that had been going around for a while, of Indians who used gold-tipped arrows and of mysterious men who traded the gold for weapons.

Lately, there were also a lot more stories of the Sioux chief who called himself Touch-the-Clouds. It was said that he was the one who had brought about peace between his people and the Crows. Even the Crows who still hated the Sioux had come to hate their white enemies even more. Now it was rumored that the other Sioux chiefs had given Touch-the-Clouds the power of a general over them all, even though Jane found that hard to believe. The Sioux did not fight the way white men did, by following the orders of officers and planning for the battle. It was hit and run with them, and each man fighting the enemy in his own way.

That was one reason Custer could beat the Indians, if it came to that. To hear him tell it, he could whip the entire Sioux nation, and the Cheyennes and their other allies to boot, with just the Seventh Cavalry.

Up ahead, in the foothills, was yet another valley alive with flowers. The men leading the way had stopped to rest and to pick more blossoms. A few had decorated their hats with flowers. One of the drivers up ahead waved his bouquet in her direction.

The procession came to a halt. Men began to set up mess tables for the midday meal. Tom Custer, the general's brother, had caught yet another snake with a forked stick; he lifted the snake and then threw it from his stick into the high grass.

Jane felt uneasy. She had been feeling uneasy ever since they had left the Sioux camp where Custer had smoked the peace pipe with a couple of chiefs and a few braves. She did not like the way the general was so readily assuming that they could now move through this land safely, that the Indians would not attack. They had broken the treaty by riding here, and at last she felt the weight of that fact.

She reminded herself that the Sioux probably lacked the men to attack them. That thought did not console her.

The game was plentiful here. The members of the expedition had been adding venison and duck to their repasts of beans, hardtack, dried meat, and coffee. Jane, climbing down from her seat, noticed a few men creeping around the wagons, out of sight of Custer and his officers, to drink whiskey. Custer, although he didn't partake of liquor himself, had to know how much liquor the expedition was carrying, but the men still preferred to drink it where Iron Butt could not see them.

John Burkman, Custer's orderly, handed Jane a filthy shirt and pair of breeches, then let her have a few sips from his flask. In return for the whiskey, she would wash the clothes; it was a trade she had going with a few of the men. She swallowed slowly, knowing that the whiskey would have to last her at least until nightfall.

"Luther got back," Burkman said at last, "just before we stopped." Luther North was one of the Seventh's scouts. "Said he saw signs of a small camp that'd been moved maybe two days ago. Found something odd there, too, a piece of painted wood."

"What's so strange about a piece of painted wood?" Jane asked.

"Didn't look like something an Indian would make. It had these markings on it, sort of inky, almost like letters, but not like any letters I ever seen."

"Redskins can't write," Jane muttered.

"Maybe they weren't letters," John Burkman said. "Maybe they were just some of their marks."

"Hey, Calamity," another man called out. Jane looked up to see Isaiah Dorman, another of the scouts, walking toward her, his dark face split in a grin that showed his white teeth. That was what most of them called her, Calamity Jane, because it was said that she brought calamity to any two-timing man she ever caught fooling around behind his woman's back. Her aim was so good, it was rumored, that she could hit her target from a long way off; it was said she had shot one man through a saloon window and creased his buttocks while he was two-timing his wife with a loose woman. She let people believe the story, even though the only part of it that contained any truth was that she was a damned good shot.

"Isaiah," Burkman said, "didn't expect to see you before dark."

Isaiah Dorman sat down, then glanced at Jane. "You're drinking again, Calamity," the Negro scout said. "Ain't good for you."

"Ain't good for anybody," Jane said, "but that never stopped no one from indulging." She sat back as Burkman put away his flask.

"Have to talk to the general," Isaiah went on. "Saw something I don't like." He rested his hands on his knees. "Thought I saw someone following me, but every time I turned around, he wasn't there. Finally doubled back and headed up the way we come."

Jane handed Isaiah a plate of beans. The black man forked them into his mouth. "See anything else?" Burkman asked.

"Found another place where the Lakota broke camp. Some headed north with the tepees and their goods. That has to be most of the women and children. The others are following us."

"The braves, you mean," Jane said.

"Yeah." Isaiah shoveled in more beans. "So I'm wondering if we might have a fight on our hands."

Jane thought about that. The Sioux, if they had the chance, would do their best to get their women and children safely away from any battle. But there were other reasons for the Indians to send the women in one direction and the men another. Still, she didn't like it. Isaiah seemed to be having the same worries.

"General Custer smoked the pipe with two chiefs," Burkman said.

"I know," Isaiah said.

"They wouldn't have passed the pipe if they meant to fight," Burkman said. "Couldn't fight us anyway—they don't have the men or the firepower. Anyway, they know we're not here to attack them, just to look around."

Isaiah frowned and was silent. Jane kept her eyes on him. The black man had gone to the Sioux camp with Custer as an interpreter. Isaiah had been a courier after the war, riding between forts, and then had disappeared to go and live among the Sioux for a while. She did not know much about his life with the Indians, but it was rumored that he had become a squaw man and taken an Indian wife. He had worked for the Northern Pacific surveying team for a while, until plans for tracks west of the James River to Bismarck and beyond were abandoned in the wake of the railroad's bankruptcy and the collapses of the banks back East. Since then, Isaiah had been an interpreter and scout for the U.S. Cavalry.

"Spotted Eagle and Fast Bear promised peace to the general," Isaiah said at last, "as long as we leave these lands and abide by the treaty." He would know exactly what was said, Jane thought, given that he had translated all of it. "That was after General Custer said we weren't here to fight."

The two chiefs had surely known that if the Seventh was here to fight, they could have let the Indian scouts take a few scalps in that small encampment. Jane knew that Bloody Knife and some of the other Arikaras were disappointed at being held back, and some of the troops were impatient, too, men like Caleb Tornor who were always ready for killing, maybe even too ready. She was not so sure about White Man Runs Him and others of the Crow scouts, whose loyalty seemed to be to whiskey as much as to the Seventh.

"What's worrying me now," Isaiah went on, "is the way Fast Bear and Spotted Eagle said what they said to General Custer—as long as we leave these lands, go away from Paha Sapa, we still be at peace. I think they was telling us—warning us—to leave right after smoking the pipe with them, and we ain't done that." He sighed, then finished his beans. "And now we goin' to have trouble if there's a heap of Indians following us."

"The general can lick the whole Sioux nation with just the Seventh," Burkman said, "hell, with just these companies here." He was only saying what Custer himself would have said.

"I need to scout around some more," Isaiah muttered.

"Talk to Varnum, then, or Hare. They'll send you out again." Burkman stood up, stuffed the bouquet of flowers he had picked inside his hatband, and walked away.

* * *

The sky was still blue at evening, but a few clouds had formed, hanging over the valley and the tree-covered slopes of the Black Hills. The air smelled of ozone, and occasionally there was the sound of distant thunder. Jane did not think there would be a storm, but it was hard to tell. The weather could change suddenly out here, and a storm could hit without much warning; hail, even snow, could fall in late spring or in the middle of summer.

Jane sat by one of the campfires with three of the other wagon drivers and young Ned Banks. The men were being stingy with their whiskey; she had nagged at Ned and wheedled him and got only a small sip for her trouble. Now the others had put away their flasks. At last she got up and walked to her covered wagon.

Isaiah Dorman was leaning against the back of the wagon. "I'm riding out tomorrow," he said. "Lieutenant Varnum heard what I had to say and said I could go."

Jane wondered why he was telling this to her. "What exactly did you say to him?"

"That maybe some of the Lakota is looking for a fight. The lieutenant shook his head at me, but told me to scout around, so I guess he ain't so sure I'm wrong."

"Good luck."

"I asked him if you could come with me, Calamity. You's a better shot than any of the other scouts, and I can trust you. He say if you's crazy enough to go, I can bring you."

He was admitting that he could not trust the others. Maybe he couldn't trust some of them, the Indian scouts in particular. Crows, Arikaras, half-breeds—a lot of times a black man wasn't any better off with them than he was with whites.

"I'll ride out with you," she said. "Ned can drive my wagon when the Seventh moves on."

"We won't be gone long if I'm right. And if I am right, they's already getting ready to attack us."

Jane said, "They can't win, and they'll lose too many braves if they try."

"We'll lose men, too."

"Not as many as them," she said.

"That's what I keep telling myself. I just hope it's what the Indians think." Isaiah turned up the collar of his blue coat and walked away.

Before dawn, just as Jane was ready to ride out with Isaiah, it was discovered that White Man Runs Him had disappeared in the night with two of the other Crow scouts, Goes Ahead and Hairy Moccasin, and five horses. Lieutenant Luther Hare went to report that news to Custer, while Jane and Isaiah waited to find out if they would be given different orders. If White Man Runs Him had deserted, which was possible if not likely, they might be told to follow him and find out why.

Hare was in the general's tent for a while. The men had broken camp and loaded the mules and horses by the time the sun was up, and Hare was still talking to Custer and Benteen and the other officers inside the tent. Jane could hear their angry voices even from the hill overlooking the clearing, where she waited with Isaiah and their horses.

At last the tent flap was lifted and Colonel Benteen stomped out, slapping his hat against his thigh before pressing it down on top of his thick gray hair. Benteen hated Custer and the feeling was mutual. They didn't do a very good job, Jane thought, of hiding their disagreements and hatred of each other from the men.

Hare left the tent and waved an arm in their direction. Jane trotted toward him, followed by Isaiah. "See what you can find out about where the Sioux are moving," the lieutenant said. "Don't bother about White Man Runs Him and the other God damn Crows—probably just got restless and decided to ride out and take a look-see. They'll come back if they see anything we should know."

"What was all that hollering about in there?" Jane asked.

The heavyset Hare gave her a look that told her that this was none of her business. Along with about half of the men, he was of the opinion that she did not belong here. Most of the others grudgingly tolerated her because she would wash their clothes in exchange for some of their whiskey. Only a few treated her as just another member of the company.

"I'm just asking what they said," Jane added, "in case there's anything we should know afore we ride out."

"General Custer wanted to divide us up," Hare replied, "send Troops D, C, and B to the east while the rest of us continued south. Colonel Benteen strongly advised against it."

"I heard how strongly," Jane said. "Folks down along the North Platte must have heard Benteen advising the general. For once, I agree with Benteen. No point dividing our forces if there's any chance of an attack."

Hare gazed at her even more contemptuously. "There's no chance of that. We're not here to fight and the Sioux know that. They won't attack unless they feel threatened, and we haven't given them any cause to worry about that. Varnum just thinks it won't hurt to have you scout around." He cleared his throat and spat. "Maybe you can find some of that gold that's supposed to be in these parts."

Hare stomped away toward a string of horses. Isaiah flicked his reins lightly against the neck of his horse. Jane followed the black man up the rise. They had one horse each and some rations in their packs; they were traveling light. Lieutenant Varnum wanted them to rejoin the company in four or five days.

Their horses continued to climb until they had a view of the clearing. The band, mounted on white horses near the head of the column, had finished "Boots and Saddles" and was playing "The Girl I Left Behind Me." The Seventh was a long serpent of blue and butternut-colored buckskin with splashes of bright color; those were the flowers tucked in the men's hats and tied to their saddlebags.

Isaiah said, "I reckon White Man Runs Him and the other Crows deserted."

Jane turned in her saddle, surprised. "You think they did? Why would they? Hellfire, White Man Runs Him hates the Sioux more than any white man in the company."

"He hates them, all right. But he's a-scared of them, too. Now he might be more scared than he is hateful—I think that's why he might have run out. Goes Ahead and Hairy Moccasin must be even more scared if they went with him. That's what's worrying me, Calamity, why they're that scared."

They rode in silence for a while. Soon they came upon fresh tracks leading away from the valley clearing where they had made camp the night before. They had to be the tracks of White Man Runs Him and the other Crows. The Indian scouts had not tried very hard to hide them, and it looked like they had been moving fast. Jane wondered why they were heading northeast instead of west.

Isaiah lifted his head. In a soft voice, he sang what sounded like a chant.

Jane did not know the words. "What's that, Isaiah?"

"It's a prayer to Wakan Tanka, the Great Spirit." Isaiah sighed. "Thought we might have need of it right about now."

By noon, they had come to a creek. They watered the horses and Jane fed them some of the grain they had brought in their saddle-bags. Indian ponies could live on just the grass; the Seventh's horses could not.

They were still on the trail of White Man Runs Him when they reached another spot where some Sioux had camped. This party had been larger, with about forty horses, and apparently all of them were braves, since she saw no signs of pitched tepees and lodges, or any droppings from the dogs that could always be found in Sioux camps. Jane wondered what would happen to the Crow scouts if they ran into any Sioux. That would most likely depend on the number of Sioux and on how much of a match they were for the three Crows. Most of the Crow, it was said, were now at peace with the Sioux, but there were still diehards like White Man Runs Him who would happily kill as many Sioux and Cheyenne as they could.

She sat down by the creek and gnawed at a piece of hardtack. Isaiah sat near her, chewing on some dried meat. He swallowed his food, wiped his mouth, then said, "I think White Man Runs Him may be trying to join the Sioux."

She tensed. "Why would he do that? They'd as soon kill him as look at him."

"Maybe I's wrong. I hope I is wrong. Maybe he's just heading for one of the forts, or an agency, but I don't think so. Think he's riding to the Sioux to give himself up."

Jane thought about that for a moment. "Wouldn't that be kind of like putting his head in their hands and telling them to help themselves to his scalp?" she asked.

"Not if he goes to them in peace. Not if he promise to ride with the Lakota and fight with them against the Seventh." Isaiah turned toward her. "I live with the Lakota. I live with them for years. Maybe I would have still been living with them if my wife hadn't died."

She knew all of that, but could tell that he needed to talk. It was probably easier for him to talk to a woman, even a woman like her, than to one of the men.

"I don't know," he went on. "They called me Wasichu Sapa, the black white man, but they didn't treat me like I was colored, not after I was living with them a while. I kept finding reasons not to leave. Told myself I would someday, and then kept putting it off. Maybe I'd still be living with them and thinking about leaving if she—"

He fell silent. Jane said nothing as she looked from west to east, scanning almost without thinking for any signs of danger. Isaiah's dark eyes shifted from side to side; he was doing the same thing.

"I went back to the army in '71," Isaiah continued. "They sent me out with the Northern Pacific survey team, to be a guide, but I was just as glad when they decided not to build those tracks. You see—" He frowned and rubbed his chin. "I ain't disloyal, not to the army, and not to the Lakota. That's what I told myself, that I could be a friend of the Lakota and an army man both. The Lakota'd have their lands, and we'd have ours. Now I know that ain't gonna happen. People goin' to come flocking into these parts once they find gold, and that means war."

"So you think all those stories about gold being here are true," Jane said.

"I knows it." Isaiah reached down and put his hand in the water, then brought it out again and opened his palm. She saw two bits of yellow metal, hardly bigger than flecks of dust. "That's what's here," he said, "and it ain't much, but the Seventh is sure to find more."

"You're so sure of that?" she asked.

"I knows it. The Lakota—" He turned and gazed directly at her. "I passed some time with the Hunkpapas, in Sitting Bull's camp. The older braves said he might have been the greatest of the chiefs, and others said Crazy Horse would have been, except for Touch-the-Clouds and his vision of the hoop being joined and all the Indians, even old enemies, being one nation."

"I heard about Touch-the-Clouds," Jane murmured. "Not much, mind you, just that he brought a lot of tribes together."

"He did more than that, Calamity. He give them all a new vision. The old men told me things changed a lot after that. I don't understand a lot of it, because they didn't let me find out much. Wasn't just that I was a Wasichu Sapa—a lot of the Lakota didn't seem to know what was going on, either. The old men didn't like that much, but they couldn't do much about it."

Jane leaned forward, waiting for him to say more.

"I thinks it was after the Lakota smoked the pipe with the Crows that things really started changing," Isaiah said. "Touch-the-Clouds told them that the Black Hills were sacred to both Lakota and Crow, and the only way they could keep them was to stick together. By then, the Lakota had a peace with the Kiowas and the Comanche, so the Crow was ready to listen to him, I reckon." He stared at the bits of gold in his hand. "Touch-the-Clouds told them the buffalo was dying in the south, that the white men was killing them, that they would keep on killing them until no buffalo was left, and there was only one way to stop the killing."

"Go on," Jane said.

"He said the Black Hills was given to the Lakota, to all the Indians, by Wakan Tanka so that they would have weapons for their fighting. I think maybe they was digging up some of the gold for buying weapons. Never could find out much, because except during the Sun Dance in the summer, the Lakota and everybody else was keeping away from here. Some men would leave their camps and go into the Black Hills for a while, but nobody talked about why."

"Maybe they went to look for visions," Jane said.

"They'd stay away too long for that, for visions and making medicine." Isaiah let out his breath. "Too many secrets. That's what the old men said, too many secrets, too much that Touch-the-Clouds and the men he trusted the most wanted to keep to themselves. But things turned out the way Touch-the-Clouds said they would. The Lakota still had the buffalo to hunt. The treaty wasn't broken."

"Until now," Jane said dryly.

"And now I has to pick my side and stay with it, just like White Man Runs Him and anybody else. Can't run from one side to the other. Got to make up my mind to fight for the Seventh or for the Lakota and not look back."

He was admitting that his loyalties were still torn. She tensed, suddenly wary of the other scout. For a moment, Jane thought of reaching for her gun and making up Isaiah's mind for him. She would not have to shoot him in the back, she could outshoot him even if she gave him a fair chance, then blame his death on the Indians when she rode back to rejoin the Seventh.

She could not do it. Isaiah was as much of a friend as she had found with the Seventh Cavalry. He would not betray a friend, any friend, even her; of that she was certain.

"If White Man Runs Him is heading for the Sioux," she said at last, "then we might as well keep following him."

"Yeah. For now." Isaiah stood up and let the tiny bits of gold fall from his hand.

They mounted their horses and rode on, moving east, following the creek and the trail of the Crow scouts. If the Sioux were on the warpath, she hoped that Isaiah's old ties to them would give them some protection.

Isaiah reined in his horse. He motioned to her, then dismounted. Jane leaned toward him from her saddle. He pulled a slender wand with a tiny pouch attached to it from the ground, then held it up.

"What is it?" she asked.

"An offering to Wakan Tanka. It ain't been here for long—maybe two days or three. There's tobacco in the bag, and a little bit of willow tied under it. Someone came here to pray and make medicine."

Jane found herself scanning the hills. She did not feel anyone watching them. She hoped that she could trust her instincts.

Isaiah stuck the wand back into the ground. "There's another one over there," he said, pointing, "and another." He mounted his horse. "Somebody was praying a whole lot, and I wonder what for."

They made camp for the night under a stand of pine trees on a hill overlooking another small creek. There were some horse droppings under the trees; White Man Runs Him and his companions had not stopped here for long.

Isaiah, having unburdened himself to her earlier, was silent as they ate. Jane thought longingly of hot coffee followed by whiskey. There was no sense in making a fire, and she had not bartered for any whiskey to bring along, knowing that she would need a clear head.

They used their saddles as pillows and their horse blankets as their beds. Isaiah slept with his back to her. Once in the night, she heard him let out a sound that sounded like a sob, and wondered if he was dreaming of his dead Indian wife.

They woke just before dawn and ate hardtack for breakfast, then followed the creek upstream. By midmorning, they had come to more hilly ground. The trail of the Crow scouts led up a grassy hill. Jane was behind Isaiah. He was at the top of the hill when she heard him curse.

He lashed at his horse and galloped down the other side of the hill. Below them lay an expanse of grassy pastureland, and in the grass there lay three small, lifeless bodies. Jane's eyesight was damnably keen. The corpses, she saw, had been stripped of clothing. Their chests were bloody hollows, their legs gashed with deep cuts, and their scalps were gone.

She galloped after Isaiah and caught up to him. He slowed his horse as they neared the bodies. She recognized the face of White Man Runs Him, now twisted and staring at her with lifeless eyes.

The Sioux had cut open his chest and stuck a willow branch into the gaping wound. Someone else had pushed a long quill into his groin, where a lot of his male equipment was missing. By the look of him, White Man Runs Him had taken a while to die. She did not want to look closely at Hairy Moccasin and Goes Ahead.

Isaiah dismounted and stared at the dead men for a while. Jane studied the grass. A large party of Sioux had camped here, but not for long. Some had gone west, the others south. The Indians going west had left the parallel tracks of poles being pulled over the ground, so they had been using pony drags to move tepees and lodges, and had to be women and children moving to safety. The others—the warriors—were heading south.

"They's headed toward the Seventh," Isaiah said, although Jane could already guess at that.

"Can we warn them in time?" Jane asked.

"I don't know. There's only two of us. If we wears out our horses, we'll never make it. The Indians should stop for a while, put on paint, pray for animal powers, get ready for battle. Maybe we could reach the Seventh if they don't move too fast."

Jane mounted her horse quickly. "Then we better get moving, Isaiah." There was no time to do anything for the dead Crows.

The colored man's lips moved as he whispered something. He looked like he was saying a prayer. She wondered if it was a prayer to the good Lord or one to Wakan Tanka.

"Isaiah," she said more sharply.

He swung himself into his saddle. They rode away from the mutilated bodies of the Crow scouts.

There were two of them on horseback, coming down the pine-covered slope, one a Sioux with a feather in his long braided hair. Caleb Tornor could not make out whether the second man was an Indian or not. He carried a piece of white cloth attached to a stick and wore a worn blue army jacket that might have been stolen off a dead man, but he couldn't be a Sioux or a Cheyenne, not with black hair that reached only past his collar.

The Seventh had just finished setting up tents for the night. "Halt!" Lieutenant Donald McIntosh called out. They were to treat any redskins they ran across as friendly, as long as the Indians showed no hostility. Those were the orders. Caleb regretted those orders and would not have minded picking off this Sioux if he thought he could get away with it. He wondered what the pair wanted.

Sergeant Smith was walking toward the two men when Captain Tom Custer, the general's brother, rode past the nearest tents. The Sioux with the feather in his hair held up one hand. "We have come to talk," the Indian said in English. "We wish to speak with your chieftain, the one called Long Hair, the man the Crow have named Son of the Morning Star."

Caleb narrowed his eyes, surprised to hear the red man say the words so easily. The Indian was wearing only a breechcloth and leggings, but he also carried a Winchester and had a Colt pistol at his waist; an ammunition belt hung across his chest.

"I am the brother of Long Hair, the Son of the Morning Star," Captain Custer said. "What do you want?"

"I have told you," the Sioux replied. "We come here with a message for your chief Long Hair."

"Sergeant," Tom Custer said to Smith, "go to the general's tent and—"

Caleb had caught sight of the general. "He's already riding this way, sir," Caleb said.

Custer rode toward them on his favorite sorrel horse. He wore his favorite buckskin jacket and the blue yellow-striped trousers of his uniform. He had cut his hair before setting out on this expedition, but a few reddish-blond curls poked out from under his hat. He glanced toward the two strangers before reining in his horse in front of his brother.

"What is it, Tom?" the general asked.

Tom Custer gestured at the Sioux and his companion. "They want to talk to you. One of them speaks English."

"Both of us do," the man in the officer's blue coat said. Still seated on his horse, he extended his arms, palms out.

"My name means White Eagle in your words," the man with the long braids said. "The man with me is called the Orphan."

"I know him," Custer said, "by another name." He stared at the stranger in the blue coat for a bit. "I am the man you call Long Hair. We came here in peace, not to attack your people. I smoked a pipe with Spotted Eagle and Fast Bear of the Sansarc Lakota."

"You may have smoked the pipe with them," the man wearing the feather said, "and you may say you come here in peace, but you have broken our treaty by coming to Paha Sapa."

"We came to explore," General Custer said, "to see what is here, and then we intend to leave." He gazed at the two with his cold blue eyes.

"Will you leave and never come back?" the man in the blue coat said. "When the army comes into Indian lands, surveyors and settlers usually aren't far behind. These lands are sacred to the Lakota, and were promised them by treaty."

General Custer frowned. "You're not a Lakota, Rowland." Caleb looked from Custer to the stranger.

"I am not a Lakota, but I have lived among them for some time now."

General Custer frowned still more. "You don't belong here."

Caleb shifted uneasily on his feet. Maybe this Lemuel Rowland was actually a deserter. There had been enough of them.

"And how exactly did you come to be out here?" General Custer asked.

"Colonel Jeremiah Clarke asked me to live among the Lakota for a while and then report back to him," Lemuel Rowland said. "And now I have come here with a message from the chiefs Sitting Bull, Crazy Horse, and Touch-the-Clouds. They are asking you to leave the Black Hills and to promise not to return. They want your pledge that you will abide by the treaty the United States government and the Lakota signed in 1868."

"The Orphan named Rowland carries a talking paper with these words," White Eagle said. "He will give it to you now."

Rowland reached into his blue coat and took out a folded piece of paper. Tom Custer nodded at Caleb, who went to get it. "I wrote these words out myself," Rowland said. "They were given to me by a warrior who rode to me with this message from Touch-the-Clouds. The words are set down exactly as he spoke them. By now they will have been said to Sitting Bull, Crazy Horse, and others of the chiefs."

The general's lip curled. Caleb could almost believe that Iron Butt Custer was amused. "Read the message to us," Custer said.

Rowland's horse carried him closer to the general. There was still enough light to read by, but Caleb wondered why the man had written the message down; the Sioux with him probably could have repeated it word for word from memory.

"By coming into the Black Hills," Rowland read, "you have broken the treaty between our peoples. If you leave now, and swear never to return, we will remain at peace. If you refuse to leave, we will consider ourselves at war with you, and with anyone else who comes into the Black Hills without having first pledged himself to us as our brother."

Rowland fell silent. General Custer was looking at him contemptuously. Lieutenant McIntosh fidgeted.

"Is that all?" Tom Custer asked.

"That is the message," the Sioux called White Eagle added.

Rowland handed the piece of paper to General Custer, who took it and held it by two fingers, as if longing to throw it away. "There's something I don't understand," Custer said. "'Pledged himself to us as our brother'—what does that mean?"

Rowland glanced at White Eagle. The Sioux said, "This land is Lakota land. Other land is ours by treaty. If the Wasichu want to come to these lands, they must come as friends of Lakota and live as we allow them to live instead of taking our land from us and driving away the buffalo."

General Custer was reddening, angered. Behind Caleb, Sergeant Smith cursed softly. No self-respecting white man, Caleb thought, would make any promises to a bunch of red savages to live as Indians wanted him to on land that should belong to whites anyway. Sooner or later the Indians would have to get out of the way or face extermination. That was a law of nature; Caleb had heard that somewhere. It was the destiny of white men to have all of this land, from east to west.

If God had not wanted white men to have this land, He would not have allowed them to take it.

"And what will happen," General Custer said, "if we remain here to complete our exploration?"

Rowland looked even more uneasy. White Eagle said, "If you stay, you will never leave the Black Hills."

"Sounds a lot like a threat, Autie," Tom Custer muttered to his brother.

"We'll do what we were sent here to do," General Custer said, letting the paper Rowland had given him fall from his hand. "Tell them to leave us unmolested, and we'll ride out of this territory. If the Sioux want a fight, we'll fight, and give no quarter. Tell that to your chiefs. Lieutenant McIntosh—see that those two ride out of here before dark." He dug his knees into the sides of his horse and rode toward his tent.

"You heard the general," the officer named McIntosh said to Lemuel. He picked up the paper that Custer had dropped. One of the other Blue Coats brought a horse to McIntosh; he mounted. "I'll ride with you as far as that rise."

Lemuel flicked his reins lightly against his horse's neck. "You will see nothing from there," White Eagle said to the lieutenant. "Our fighting men are not here—not now. Not yet."

"Why did you write all this out, anyway?" McIntosh asked.

"For the record," Lemuel said. "I don't suppose General Custer might change his mind and decide to leave the Black Hills."

"Never," McIntosh said. "The Sioux haven't got a chance against the Seventh." His eyes shifted toward White Eagle. "You'd better make that clear to them."

Lemuel's insides knotted. Throughout the ride here, he had been telling himself that there was a chance the expedition would leave peacefully. That everything could go on as it had, with the Lakota in their territory and the treaty being kept—he clung to that hope without reason. He remembered the last time he had seen Custer, at Appomattox, carrying off the desk on which Lee had signed the

South's surrender as a souvenir. He wondered if Custer had brought the desk out west with him.

McIntosh slipped the paper inside his coat. Rubalev, after hearing the message carried to them from Touch-the-Clouds, had insisted on having Lemuel set it down in writing. "The Wasichu use written words to rob you of what is yours," Rubalev had said to the Lakota messenger. "Tell Touch-the-Clouds that we will use a talking paper against your enemies." The Lakota with them had looked happy at that, as if the piece of paper held strong medicine that would give them victory over the Blue Coats.

Lieutenant McIntosh stared intently at Lemuel. "You say that you served with Ely Parker," the lieutenant said.

"And with General Custer," Lemuel said.

"And which of the Six Nations are you from?"

Lemuel felt surprise at the question. "I am a Seneca, as Parker is."

McIntosh nodded. "I am also a member of the Six Nations, a Mohawk. The Seneca who fought with General Grant was a man I could admire."

Lemuel might have been in the other man's place if he had remained with the army. Get away from here, he wanted to say to this officer, desert and join the Lakota. If Custer's men don't leave the Black Hills, too many will die.

"Ely Parker traveled the white man's road," McIntosh continued, "as I have also. I know that he hoped for peace in the West, but there will be no peace in the end until the Sioux move to the lands allocated to them. Ely Parker knew that, too."

"Lakota will never live that way," White Eagle muttered.

"You cannot survive in the white man's world unless you live as he does," McIntosh said. "I am a red man, like you, and I learned that long ago. You must already be coming to understand it, or you would not speak English as well as you do, or troubled to learn it. You already see that you may have to follow the white man's trail."

White Eagle grunted. "I don't know what you're doing here, Rowland," McIntosh said. "Maybe you're living out here spying for Jeremiah Clarke, or maybe your loyalties have changed. You wouldn't be the first who deserted and went over to the Sioux."

Lemuel could not help this man. Custer would be expecting the Lakota to attack as they had in the past. He did not know himself what Touch-the-Clouds was planning, but had the feeling that it would come as a surprise to these soldiers.

"They can't win, you know," McIntosh went on. "You must know that."

"I came here with a warning," Lemuel said, knowing that trying to sway this man was a hopeless effort. "You'd be wise to convince your commander that he should take heed of it."

"I wouldn't try to convince Custer to cut and run even if I could," McIntosh replied. "He won't do it, and he won't listen to anyone who tells him that's what he should do. He despises cowardice." He paused. "It isn't that I don't have some sympathy for the Indians here." He glanced at White Eagle. "I tell myself sometimes that maybe it would have been better to leave these lands to the red man. But there's nothing I can do if settlers start coming here except to protect them. I chose my path a while ago. The men of the Seventh are my comrades."

The man was loyal; Lemuel could respect him for that. "The Sioux shouldn't have warned us," McIntosh went on. "If they were going to attack, they would have done better to surprise us. Now we'll be ready for them—not that we can't defeat them anyway."

"Touch-the-Clouds was warning you," Lemuel said, "so that you'd have a chance. He has a sense of honor. He wanted to give you a chance to abide by the treaty and leave."

McIntosh shook his head. "Let me give you some advice. Do your best to talk the Sioux out of fighting. Even if they succeed in making us retreat, which I doubt they can, we'll just come back with an even stronger force."

There was nothing more to say. Lemuel wondered if Touch-the-Clouds had meant to fight all along, if he in fact welcomed the chance for this attack. Maybe the Lakota chief had only been waiting for an excuse to fight.

"Farewell, brother," McIntosh said before he rode back down the hill.

* * *

By late afternoon, Jane and Isaiah were following the tracks of many Indian ponies. They were on the trail of at least one hundred braves, possibly more. She did not want to ask the black man exactly how many he thought there might be.

Isaiah led them away from the pony tracks and toward a piney slope. The Indians might be getting ready to halt and rest for the night. Keeping near the trees was one way for her and her companion to conceal themselves.

Their horses slowed to a walk as they made their way up the hill. An evening breeze made the pines around them give off a sound like a sigh.

"Isaiah," Jane said softly, "we got to rest these horses."

"I know."

So he could still talk. Jane had been worrying that the sight of White Man Runs Him's mutilated body might have robbed Isaiah of the power of speech. She reined in her horse and dismounted. Isaiah's horse halted near hers; he slipped from his horse's back.

Jane took some oats from her saddlebag and fed them to her horse. "The Lakota'll wait," Isaiah said, his voice close to a whisper. "They won't attack at night. Can't fight in the dark—the Great Spirit might not be able to pick up the souls of the dead if it ain't light enough to see who they are."

"Then maybe we'll have a chance to reach the Seventh before they do." Jane handed the small bag of oats to Isaiah. "We'll rest up a while, and then move on." They would have more cover in the dark.

They tied their horses to the lower branches of one tree, then sat down. Isaiah passed her a bit of dried meat; she ate it and sipped from her canteen. The water they had should hold them, she thought, until they reached the Seventh.

Isaiah had lapsed into silence again. That was just as well; smaller groups of Indians might pass near them on their way to join the other braves. The Sioux couldn't beat the Seventh, no matter how many of them there were. She had to believe that.

"Strange," Isaiah's voice said softly from the darkness, startling Jane, and she realized that she had been dozing.

"What's strange?" she asked, keeping her voice low.

"The Lakota picking a fight now. It ain't their usual way of fighting. That's what's worrying me, Calamity. They could have let this go. It might be breaking a treaty, coming in here, but they ain't been attacked. That's when they fight, when they're attacked. Maybe sometimes for glory, or stealing horses, things like that, but not this."

Now that he had broken his long silence, he seemed anxious to talk. "There'd be glory aplenty in taking on Custer and the Seventh," Jane said.

"Ain't no glory in a fight that can't be won." He sighed; she could not see his face in the darkness. "I don't know. The Lakota ain't like they were back before more and more of them started believing that Touch-the-Clouds was the chief they had to follow."

They were silent for a while longer, and then she heard Isaiah get to his feet. "Better ride on," he said.

She stood up. If they kept to a canter, the horses wouldn't tire for a while, and they still had a chance of reaching the Seventh in time to warn Custer.

The two miners who had come along with the Seventh, William McKay and Horatio Nelson Ross, wanted to talk to General Custer. Caleb Tornor happened to be the sentinel outside Custer's tent when the two rode up and asked for permission to speak to the general.

"Can't it wait till later?" Caleb said to them, wary of disturbing Custer now. Custer and Benteen had been arguing again about whether or not to divide their forces and then trap the Indians between them, and Benteen had come storming out of the tent not more than a few minutes ago. Did he think Custer was just going to wait here until the Sioux showed up? The general had already sent out Luther North and a couple of the half-breed scouts to find out where the nearest Indian camp was. Attack there, and the braves getting ready to make war on the Seventh would rush to the aid of their women and children. That seemed to be what Custer was thinking, anyway.

The Seventh had moved up the side of a nearby mountain to higher ground, not wanting to be caught by the Sioux in the valley by the stream where they had been camped. The Sioux, according to one of the scouts, called this peak Mountain Goat, or Hean-ya-haga—at least that was how the outlandish Indian name sounded to Caleb. Charley Reynolds, one of the white scouts, was already riding to Fort Laramie to report on the expedition's progress and also that the Sioux had threatened to attack. The miners had stayed behind, moving upstream in their search for gold; McKay had seen signs of yellow color in the creek's bed, and had wanted to look around.

"Son," McKay said to Caleb, "this news can't wait," and Caleb was suddenly sure that the man had found gold, that the old stories about the Black Hills were true.

He called out to the general and heard Custer order that the two men be admitted. Caleb followed the two men inside. If Custer ordered him to leave, he would. Otherwise, he might as well linger here and find out what McKay and Ross thought was so important.

Custer sat at a candlelit table, a pen in his hand and with a notebook and writing paper in front of him. Two of his dogs were asleep under the table, while the third sprawled by his chair. He had been preparing dispatches and articles for newspapers and magazines about the expedition, and making notes in his journal, as well as writing long letters to his wife, but did not look as though he had done much writing this evening.

Without preliminaries, Ross said, "General, white people are going to be rushing to the Black Hills now," and then held out his hand, opening his fingers. A small glass bottle lay in Ross's palm. Even in the candle's dim light, Caleb could see the yellow color of gold dust.

Caleb let out a whistle.

"Well, now," Custer said.

"Isn't much there," McKay said, "maybe ten or fifteen cents' worth, but there's got to be more where that came from."

"Charley Reynolds is riding to Fort Laramie," Caleb said. "It'll take him at least four days to get there. Too bad you didn't get here sooner—he could have told the commandant there about this gold." Folks would have been rushing here after that. Maybe it was just as well to have the news to themselves a bit longer. The men of the Seventh might have a chance to stake out some claims and pocket a few nuggets.

"Time enough to spread the word," Custer said, "when this approaching battle is past." He knew that they would win out over the Sioux; Caleb could hear the assurance in his voice.

"That isn't all we found," Ross said, stepping closer to the general. "There's gravel washed down from upstream that looks like it's been sluiced, like somebody was panning for gold."

"Maybe even doing some mining," McKay added. "That water wasn't running as clear as it should have been."

"Do you think some prospectors are out here already?" Custer asked.

"If there was a lone prospector here or there, maybe a couple of men or some fellow who isn't too afraid of Indians—that I could believe." Ross shook his head. "But that creek looked like there was more than just a few men digging around farther upstream."

"So maybe they're keeping it a secret," Caleb said, "until their claim's tapped out."

Ross looked amused. "The more men you've got, the less chance of any of them keeping it a secret. Anyway, if you had fellows going into any of the nearby towns with gold nuggets or dust, going in there regular, don't you think somebody would have followed them back here before now?"

Caleb thought of how little they knew about this territory, and about the deserters and others who had vanished into Indian country. Could some of them already be prospecting for gold? Maybe they could keep any finds a secret from folks in the towns and cities, but they couldn't hide what they were doing from the Indians for long, not here on land the Sioux called sacred. The Indian scouts serving with the U.S. Cavalry would have found out long ago if anything like that was going on.

"If those redskins weren't getting ready for a fight," McKay said, "I'd almost think it might be a good idea to skedaddle back to Fort Lincoln about now."

"We can carry word about the gold back to civilization," Custer said, "after thwarting the Sioux attack." He rubbed his chin. "We can strike at one of their camps, draw the braves to it, and make quick work of them, and then we'll send another scout after Reynolds to Fort Laramie with news of our victory."

Confident as the general sounded, Caleb found himself agreeing with McKay. If they left now, they could outflank the Indians and make it safely back to Fort Lincoln. If the Indians saw them leaving, they might assume that Custer was retreating, and leave them alone. After that, they could return with a larger force and catch the redskins off guard.

But Iron Pants Custer would not retreat, would not even pretend to retreat. He would want to attack, inflict punishment upon the Sioux, and return with a victory and news of a gold strike as well. That would bring him even more of the glory he craved.

Charley Reynolds had left the Seventh in late afternoon. He rode just far enough to see that no Indians were yet in the region below the slopes of the Mountain Goat, and then he holed up in a rocky hollow with his horse to rest for a while. Traveling at night would keep him and his horse from overheating in the hot summer sunlight and also from being spotted by hostiles.

After sunset, Charley ate a little of his bacon and hardtack, drank some water, and then mounted his horse. The sponge and leather coverings he had put on his feet would keep him from leaving any footprints, but he would have to ride fast tonight. Any Indians who saw him were likely to guess that he was riding south to warn of their attack. He wanted to be away from the Black Hills before any of the Sioux spotted his horse's trail.

Flatter land lay ahead. Every so often, he reined in his horse and looked around for signs of Indians. Luther North claimed that he could smell an Indian from far off, but that was just brag, and Charley was already higher-smelling than any Indian.

The crescent of the moon was up when Charley looked back and saw a lone rider behind him. He guided his horse toward the shadow of the trees, took out his rifle, loaded it from his cartridge belt, got out his Colt and cocked the hammer, and waited.

The rider was soon close enough for Charley to make out his long light-colored hair and buckskin jacket. If he was another member of one of the Seventh's companies, sent after him for any reason, Charley did not recall ever seeing him. He held his breath and watched as the man reined in his horse and leaned from his saddle to peer at the ground.

He was no redskin, not with that yellow hair, but he could be a renegade. It looked as if he was looking for signs of Charley's trail. Charley was pretty sure that he had not left tracks, but maybe the stranger had caught a glimpse of him after he rode out from the rocks.

He knew that he had not been spotted leaving Custer's encampment, and he had not seen any signs of hostiles since then. But maybe he should have been a tad more cautious.

The stranger was very still, and then Charley heard him say, "I must talk to you."

Charley kept very still.

"I have something to say." The words were accented in a way Charley did not recognize; he wondered what part of the country the light-haired man came from. "I must warn you." Still mounted on his horse, he held out his hands, palms up.

Warn him of what? The stranger might know something about the movements of the Indians preparing to attack the Seventh. Maybe he was a squaw man who, after learning what the Indians intended to do, had ridden out to warn Custer's men.

It would have been safer for the stranger to lie low, Charley thought, instead of risking his neck to warn them. Another thought came to him: the man could tell him what he knew and then be on his way while Charley rode back to alert the Seventh. A stranger might risk giving a warning without wanting to help in any fighting later on.

The stranger said, "You have to know this. A party of Sioux warriors is riding out to attack the soldiers who have come to the Black Hills."

Charley could see him pretty well, even in the dim light. The stranger could not see him. He aimed his Colt at the man's chest and waited for him to say more.

"They are moving southwest," the man went on, "and they have forded the Belle Fourche."

How many Indians? Charley wanted to ask. What kinds of weapons have they got—Springfields, maybe Winchesters? Some of them would have Colts or other revolvers for sure. The stranger hadn't told him very much.

"More than a thousand of them are riding against the soldiers," the man continued.

That, Charley thought, was worth knowing, not that the Seventh couldn't handle even a thousand. If they picked off even twenty or thirty redskins, the rest were likely to scatter. The Sioux could not afford to lose even that many men.

"We must warn them," the stranger said. "Where are they now camped?"

Charley was silent.

"I cannot wait here any longer." The man slowly reached for the reins of his horse. "You will have to warn them. Now I must make my escape." He rode off, heading in the same direction Charley had been riding.

He would have to decide what to do, whether to ride back with this information or continue on his way. How could he even be certain that what the stranger told him was true? Even if the man had not been lying, he might still be mistaken.

Again Charley wondered what the stranger was doing in this territory. He might have been prospecting for gold. The rumors had brought other lone prospectors into the Black Hills in the past. A few, from what he knew, had returned to civilization empty-handed. Others had never returned.

He could wait here under these trees with his suspicions while the Sioux war party prepared to attack the Seventh, or he could ride on. Custer would have sent out scouts already to find out more about what the Indians might do. Calamity Jane Cannary and Isaiah Dorman might already be riding back with more reliable information than he possessed.

He holstered his Colt, touched the neck of his horse lightly with the reins and left the trees. The stranger's horse was moving at a canter, putting distance between them. Charley rode after the man and saw him look back. The stranger's horse began to slow its pace. Charley was closing in on the other man when he saw the man's arm move toward him.

The shot caught him in the chest. He swayed in his saddle, reaching for his gun when another bullet caught him in the arm. The horse under him kept moving and then the ground was rushing up to meet him.

"Jesus," he heard himself say, "I'm a God damned fool." He was lying on his back. A large shadowy shape loomed over him. Charley was about to say that he already knew he was done for when another shot struck him.

"Shit," Jane said under her breath.

From near the top of the hillside, under the pines, she had a good view of the flatter land below and the campfires of an Indian war party. The fires flickered on the darkened plain like oversized stars. She guessed that there might be as many as three hundred warriors, possibly more.

"And that's just one group," Isaiah said next to her. They had veered east, leaving the trail of another band of Indians, only to discover that there were even more of them in their path. "Looks like they mean to come at the Seventh from two sides."

Jane leaned against her horse. "Isaiah," she said softly, "I just damn well don't know what all to do now."

"If Custer found out they's coming," Isaiah said, "he'll already be moving against them."

"He wouldn't know unless he sent out more scouts."

"Maybe that's just what he did. Wouldn't have moved far without sending scouts out, even after smoking a peace pipe."

Jane shook her head. Isaiah sounded like he might be looking for reasons not to rejoin the Seventh. Well, she couldn't blame him for that. At this point, it looked as though the redskins would probably get there first. She wondered what would give them a better chance at staying alive—riding to the Seventh in time to fight at the side of the men, or getting as far away from this territory as possible. Fort

Laramie had to be at least five days away; Bismarck and Fort Lincoln were farther away than that. A hard ride toward Laramie through the dry badlands would likely kill the horses.

Isaiah said, "Calamity, maybe you oughta think about riding out of here as far and as fast as you can go." He was thinking the same thing, then. "Nobody'd think any the worse of you, being a woman and all."

"Hell, being female never kept me from doing anything before. Ain't going to be what tells me what to do now. Our horses couldn't take a hard ride out of here anyway." She was silent for a while. "What are you going to do, Isaiah? Try to find the Seventh?"

"Damn right."

"You're a good man."

He turned his head. She could not see his face. "You saw what happened to White Man Runs Him," he said. "That's what they'd do to me if I get caught. Don't have nothing to lose by going to fight with Custer."

"We'll split up," she said. "That way, we'll each of us have a better chance of getting through." It came to her that Custer might have divided his forces. "You keep heading east around those redskins, and I'll go the other way." The Indians would be on the move at dawn, and she and Isaiah would lose time trying to avoid them. There was a good chance that one of them, maybe both of them, would find their way blocked by another band of redskins. Their horses were already tired, and they probably would not reach the Seventh in time to do any good. None of that would stop her from trying.

Jane led her horse on foot, keeping under the cover of trees. The fires were going out; the Indians would be riding out soon. She crept down a hillside and kept going until another hill hid the hostiles from her, then pulled herself into the saddle.

They had to be close to the Seventh, she and Isaiah. She could get to the valley where they had been camped before dark, and from there she could easily follow them to wherever they were now.

Custer's men could not have gone far, not in the time since she and Isaiah had left them. The Indians might stop to sing their war songs and put on war paint and make medicine, and that would give her more time.

The weather was growing cooler; the wind rose and then died. Jane's eyelids felt gritty. Isaiah and she had been riding for most of the night, stopping only once to rest and water their horses, before they saw those hundreds of Indians. She might not sleep for a while. She urged her horse on, trying not to think about sleep.

It was almost noon when she came to more tracks. They showed a small band of Indians moving south. She followed them down to a small creek and saw, on the other side, the pale bloated body of a white man lying on his stomach.

They had stripped the dead man of his clothing. Jane crossed the stream and dismounted next to the corpse. They had scalped him, but the body was largely unmarked. Maybe they had not had time to torture him. She turned the body over and looked into the twisted face of Luther North.

He had been shot twice, once in the chest, once in the head. Jane let go of him and straightened. Several paces away, she saw two more bodies lying in the grass, also stripped. For a moment, she thought they might be the bodies of Indians, but they couldn't be Sioux or Cheyenne. Those redskins would not have stripped one of their own and left him here; they would have taken the body with them. So they had to be scouts, ones who had ridden out here with Luther North.

So Custer had sent out more scouts. She wondered if Iron Pants already knew that hundreds of Indians were massing against him. If he didn't, he wouldn't find out anything from Luther now. Her heart thumped against her chest. She looked down at Luther North's body and was suddenly terrified.

The Indians were gathering below the Mountain Goat, on the other side of the river. Caleb Tornor could make out their feathered war bonnets; a lot of the redskins were wearing the headpieces, while others had feathers in their hair. The men near him were still digging earthworks and getting ready to hold their position.

Bloody Knife, one of the Arikara scouts, had ridden out in the night. He had returned with the news that hundreds of Sioux and Cheyenne would be near the Mountain Goat by dawn. The Seventh had quickly dug in for the battle, setting up barriers with wagons and digging defensive trenches. They held the higher ground, Caleb thought; they still had the advantage. If they killed enough Indians, the other redskins would retreat.

The sun was high, noon already past, and the Indians still had not attacked. Maybe they realized that trying to fight with the Seventh holding the high ground would be a costly battle, and a lot more costly for the redskins than for Custer. They would try to rush the cavalry eventually and draw some men off into an ambush. That was the way Indians fought. They could lose a lot of braves that way.

Caleb and Captain Yates's F Company were dug in below Tom Custer and C Company. One of the men near Caleb, an Irish trooper named O'Hara, leaned forward, cupping a hand over his eyes.

"What the hell is that, now?" O'Hara asked.

Caleb saw where the man was looking. Near one group of Indians stood what looked like a small platform; on this platform sat several colorful cylindrical objects. Narrowing his eyes, Caleb noticed then that the platform was made up of several poles, much like the pony drags the Sioux used to transport their tepees and goods from one campsite to another. The cylinders were painted with bright colorful designs; two men in loose blue jackets squatted near the platform. Unlike the other redskins, they each had one long black braid hanging down their backs. The two, unlike the bare-chested men around them, were also not stripped down to their leggings and breechcloths. They were smaller than the redskins, too. They didn't, he realized, actually look much like Indians.

"Damn," an officer behind Caleb muttered, "wish we'd brought a fucking Gatling gun."

More Indians were riding in from the west, along the opposite side of the creek below the slope. Caleb saw dust clouds in the north, marking more riders. There might be at least as many as two thousand braves massed against them, maybe a lot more. He had never expected to see so many Indians in one place.

The Indians chanted. Caleb could barely hear them over the rising wind. "Hoka hey," they were singing, "hoka hey." It was their usual chant before going into battle. "Hoka hey—it is a good day to die."

Suddenly the chanting stopped. Caleb kept expecting them to cross the creek and ride toward the mountain, to charge up the hill and attack as they usually did. Instead, they waited, mounted on their horses, gazing at the hill in silence.

"I don't like it," a man behind him whispered.

Caleb did not like it much himself. It almost looked as though the Indians were grouped in a kind of defensive formation, although he had to be imagining that. Were they planning to sit there and wait the Seventh out? Indians wouldn't be that patient. Anyway, they would run out of food before Custer's men ran out of water. They could not have brought much food with them, and would have to hunt for more to feed so many men.

Suddenly the wind died. At that moment, a chief in a war bonnet lifted his arm and pointed at the platform with his war club.

One of the blue-jacketed men jumped up and leaped onto the platform. A bright light flared from one of the painted cylinders that the Indians had brought with them. The cylinder shot toward the sky, shooting off sparks, and then separated into three missiles.

Caleb, still clutching his Springfield and too stunned to move, watched the three rockets silently arch toward the mountainside, then drop toward the Seventh. One exploded, sending a shower of black debris toward the regimental flag. He heard the clap of the explosion just as the second missile struck near a wagon, sending up a geyser of dirt and grass. Caleb could not see where the third one had landed, and then the sound of the blast nearly deafened him.

He threw himself to the ground. Somebody shouted, and another blast tore at the air, a sound he had not heard since the War Between the States, and he realized that one of the ammunition wagons had been hit. Several men were screaming.

A lucky hit, he thought, and bad luck for the Seventh. His hands were still locked around his rifle; he waited for someone to shout an order, not knowing what to do. The Indians still waited below, and then another cylinder rose from the platform and arched toward the slope.

Lemuel sat on his horse, to the rear of the fighters, far out of range of the Seventh, too far from the action even for the Lakota and their allies to have him within range of their weapons. He was far enough away from the battle for Custer's men to be tiny, indistinct shapes in blue or buckskin crawling on the mountainside. He watched as a third rocket shot toward the sky and then fell toward Custer's forces.

The sound of the explosion reached him a few moments later. Glorious Spirit and Victorious Spirit had done well with their arrow-rockets, their Eagles Hunting for Martens and their Flaming Flowers. The sight of the missiles had probably been enough to throw Custer's men off guard, but seeing an ammunition wagon explode had shown Lemuel how this battle was likely to go.

Touch-the-Clouds would have to kill them all. He had said it himself, that they would all have to die for coming into these lands. Anything less would be a defeat, and would only bring more Blue Coats into the Black Hills later on to avenge the Seventh. At least a few of the men with Custer would have found traces of yellow metal by now; they would have to be blind not to see the evidence that there was gold here. Lemuel sat on his horse watching the battle, sick at heart.

A company of troopers was massing on the slope. He guessed that they were preparing to attack the Indians. They had to be wondering why the Sioux and Cheyenne were not fighting in their usual fashion, why they had not tried to rush the hillside to win glory and count coup or to draw men away from the slope.

They would fight by using the ways that Touch-the-Clouds had seen in his visions and had heard about from Rubalev. He had sent other chiefs among the men to repeat what he had told them before, what he had been telling them ever since having his earliest visions. Trap the Blue Coats, let them waste themselves and their bullets in attacks, use the rocket-arrows against them—there would be chances enough later for counting coup on the bodies of the enemy.

The front row of troopers coming toward the Lakota warriors stopped, then raised their rifles. Other Blue Coats were behind them, holding their horses. Before they could fire, the Lakota nearest them brought up their rifles in one swift movement and fired. Lemuel watched as several cavalrymen fell; others fired and were brought down by answering shots from Lakota Winchesters.

Another rocket-arrow shot toward the sky, then fell toward the Blue Coats, sending up a spout of earth near a flagpole. Lemuel gazed at the red, white, and blue flag hanging from the pole and remembered when he had fought for that flag. Another company of the cavalry was preparing to attack the Lakota below. Lemuel supposed that they would try for the platform holding the rocket-arrows, but the Lakota would fiercely defend both the weapons and their designers.

Soaring Eagle rode toward him. The older Lakota man was prepared to fight if necessary, but Lemuel very much doubted that he would have to ride into battle. The men on the mountainside could not have known what they would be facing. He reminded himself that they had deliberately violated the treaty by coming here, that they had brought this punishment upon themselves, but could not stop thinking about Custer and about McIntosh, the Mohawk officer. McIntosh would be up there now, preparing to fight with his men. Maybe he was among those getting ready to attack the rocket-arrow platform.

"It is a good day to die," Soaring Eagle said in Lakota as he reined in his horse.

Soldiers rode down the hillside toward the platform, firing from the saddle. More soldiers followed them, covering them with their rifles. Another rocket-arrow shot out from the platform, but this one was traveling in a straight line toward the attackers. Victorious Spirit and Glorious Spirit had released the Buffaloes Running Together, one of the rocket-arrows that moved close to the ground and was packed with what the Chinese brothers called their Thunderclaps. Lemuel's mouth grew dry as an explosion brought down a few of the charging men and horses.

"It is a good day to die," Soaring Eagle said again.

Lemuel looked away and then bowed his head.

If, Caleb thought, they could hold the redskins off until night— His thoughts did not go much further ahead than that. The Indians would not fight after dark. It might be possible to slip away under cover of night. He was thinking of deserting. Probably most of the men were considering that, ready to take their chances fleeing through Indian territory. He wondered if it was too late to surrender.

Behind a wagon near him, Captain Williams, one of the medical officers, was tending to the wounded. Five men lay there, and two of them looked like they wouldn't be around much longer. Williams had given them some of the whiskey, which would probably do them as much good as the doctor's epsom salts or quinine. Caleb suddenly longed for a swig of whiskey himself.

Still the Indians waited on their horses, remaining out of range. Maybe they could wait there until the Seventh had exhausted its rations and water. They were not shooting off their rockets now. He wondered how they had come upon such weapons, along with the Winchesters and Colts and ammunition they seemed to have in such abundance.

Caleb heard a shriek to his right. More of the men were suddenly charging down the hill on foot, firing away with their rifles. From the way they ran, in all directions, he could tell that no one had ordered the charge. Some of the Sioux opened fire, and he watched them fall, one by one. The last man to fall almost made it as far as the creek.

He heard another shriek, and then voices calling in words he did not know. The voices were calling from farther up the hillside. Shots rang out from behind him. "They're behind us!" somebody shouted, but Caleb had already figured that out. He turned his head to look back and glimpsed a movement near one rocky precipice.

Somehow some Indians had sneaked up behind them and were now shooting at them from higher ground. Caleb spun around, loaded his rifle again, and took aim. A man near him pitched forward before Caleb could hear the shot that had struck his brother-in-arms.

Caleb fired, and an Indian tumbled from a rock.

Some of Custer's men were deserting, trying to escape. That was how it looked to Lemuel as five blue-coated cavalrymen galloped away on gray horses. Maybe those men had some other strategy in mind, but he doubted it.

A band of Cheyenne galloped after the five men. One of the Cheyenne warriors suddenly fell from his horse; a soldier firing from behind a wagon had wounded him, perhaps killed him. Other Indians had fallen, and Lemuel wondered how many more Touch-the-Clouds was prepared to lose. The Cheyenne were closing in on the fleeing cavalrymen when another Indian was shot from his mount.

The Cheyenne quickly surrounded the men trying to get away. Two of the Blue Coats swung rifles at the Indians, almost knocking one from his horse. I knew what the Lakota and their allies would have to do when I rode here, Lemuel thought; I knew what might happen when I was riding to Touch-the-Clouds with Katia. He covered his eyes for a moment, unable to watch the fighting.

When he looked up again, another arrow-rocket was arching toward Custer's men. It fell toward a wagon, lighting its canvas covering. The flames danced, and then the wagon exploded, sending a geyser of rocks and dirt into the air and curtains of earth over some of the men near the wagon. Glorious Spirit and Victorious Spirit had been lucky once again in their aim.

The Lakota who had crept up behind the Blue Coats were still firing down upon their enemies. Soldiers were scattered over the slope like broken toys; Lemuel guessed that over a hundred were dead or wounded, perhaps more.

"Hie!" a woman's voice shouted behind Lemuel. "It is a good day to die!"

He turned in his saddle. Walking Blanket Woman, one of the women from the camp of Touch-the-Clouds, sat on a roan horse. She held a war club and wore an ammunition belt around her waist. The war club had belonged to her brother, but someone, perhaps a man who had known her brother or her father, must have given her the Colt and the rifle she also carried. Walking Blanket Woman had not come to the battle alone. Next to her, on a black horse, was the Cheyenne woman Young Spring Grass.

"Why are you here?" Lemuel asked in Lakota.

"I have come to fight," Walking Blanket Woman replied.

Young Spring Grass said in Lakota, "I have come to see the father of my son die."

Lemuel restrained a shudder. These two women frightened him as much as almost any man. Walking Blanket Woman had lost her father and brother, and did not yet have a husband; there was no fighting man alive in her family. The men allowed her to ride into battle because of that.

Young Spring Grass was another matter. She was here because of her son, a light-haired boy called Yellow Bird. Young Spring Grass had once lived with General Custer, the man her people called the Son of the Morning Star, and then had been abandoned by him. Perhaps she had loved him; perhaps she had gone away with him after the death of her family at Black Kettle's camp along the Washita because she had no choice. But Lemuel saw, as he gazed at her implacable copper-colored face and onyx eyes, that she now had only hatred for Custer, the father of her son.

He thought of Katia, who in her own way was as out of place among these people as were these two warrior women without men. Katia was still the wife who had given Touch-the-Clouds no son. Whatever medicine she possessed, and there were still rumors that Touch-the-Clouds trusted in her visions, had not been powerful enough to give her any children. Katia probably could have come to the battle with Walking Blanket Woman and Young Spring Grass and no one, not even her husband, would have stopped her. Such bravery might have earned her a bit of respect. He felt relieved that she was not here.

"It is a good day to die," Walking Blanket Woman called out, and then she kicked the sides of her horse with her heels and rode away. Young Spring Grass let out a cry and galloped after her.

Caleb saw where Custer stood. He was up by the flagpole, firing at the Indians above them on the slope. A bloodstain covered the left buckskin sleeve of his jacket.

Raise the white flag, Caleb thought; it was time to surrender. If you stay, the man Rowland had said, you will never leave the Black Hills. Caleb wondered if that meant that the redskins would accept a surrender and make prisoners of them, or if this was to be a fight to the death. It did not matter; Custer would never surrender anyway.

On the hillside below, wounded men lay dying. Soon the Indians would try to take the slope and kill the rest of them. "Look there!" a soldier near Caleb shouted, pointing to the east.

A man galloped toward them along the riverbank, whooping and shouting as he fired his Colt wildly at the Indians. Caleb did not know who he was at first, until his Stetson fell from his head and revealed his wooly hair and dark brown face. Isaiah Dorman, Caleb thought; the nigger scout would get himself killed that way.

"Hoka hey!" Dorman shouted. "Hoka hey!" He kept firing his gun; miraculously, the Indians shooting back at him kept missing him.

"Damn black fool!" a man near Caleb said, his voice tinged with respect. Dorman had to have seen signs of how many Indians had gathered here during his ride, and yet he had come back to fight with the Seventh. He was a damned fool, Caleb thought, admiring the scout in spite of himself.

A Sioux galloped straight toward Dorman. "Hoka hey!" the black man shouted, waving his gun. The Indian closed in on him. Dorman swung his gun at the Sioux brave's head, and Caleb realized that the scout's Colt had no more bullets. The Indian swung his club, catching Dorman in the chest.

The Negro swayed in his saddle, then fell. The Indian jumped from his horse as other Indians rushed in to strike at Dorman and count coup.

"Shit," Caleb muttered, and then heard a shriek behind him. An Indian was standing on top of an open wagon just up the hill. He aimed his rifle at Caleb and fired, hitting him in the chest.

"Shit," Caleb said again. He was lying on the ground, staring up at the sky. An Indian stood over him. "Damn it all to hell." The Indian brought down his club on Caleb's head.

The sun was setting. Lemuel felt grateful for that. Soon darkness would hide the carnage of the day.

He had seen Custer fall. The general had leaped on a horse and begun to ride down the hill, surrounded by other men on horseback. Lemuel supposed that Custer had decided to die fighting hand to hand, since he would have seen that escape was impossible. Custer had been struck by an arrow, then by a rifle shot. He had looked oddly graceful as he toppled from his horse.

The other Blue Coats had lost heart after that. One group had waved a piece of white cloth, perhaps in an attempt to surrender, but had been cut down. When the Lakota stormed the hill, Lemuel had seen a few men raise their revolvers to their own heads. Perhaps they had feared torture at the hands of the Lakota, although there had been no reason to fear it. Touch-the-Clouds and his allies were too intent on killing the Blue Coats as quickly and cleanly as possible to bother with torturing them.

Touch-the-Clouds, Lemuel thought, had inspired his men to be more efficient.

Walking Blanket Woman rode along the creek, waving her rifle and rallying the men. Young Spring Grass was just behind her, shaking a scalp in one hand. Maybe one of the warriors had given it to her; maybe she had taken the scalp herself.

Lemuel could watch no longer. He tightened his legs around the barrel of his horse and rode up the hill behind him.

* * *

Jane reached the top of the hill by late afternoon, in time to see that the Seventh had already lost their battle. Trees dotting the hillside gave her cover as she dismounted and crept forward, leading her horse by the reins. She had watered the animal that morning and fed it the last of her oats, forcing herself not to think any further ahead than the next hour. Now the thought she had been avoiding came upon her so suddenly that she was unable to push it from herself.

She had known as soon as she saw the trails of the Sioux, and how fast they seemed to be traveling, that it was useless to ride to the Seventh. Nothing that she could do would change the outcome of any battle; to warn Custer's men, even if she could reach them before the Indians did, would accomplish nothing. The size of the Indian force had told her that the battle would be hard fought; the blue-coated and buckskin-covered bodies lying on the mountain slope to the east of the hill, and the sporadic gunfire of the few defenders who were still alive, showed her that the battle was nearly over. The Indians were already moving over the slope to count coup and take scalps.

She might have tried to get out of Sioux territory, but the ride would have killed her horse and her both. Better to die here, to at least go through the motions of trying to warn Custer's men. No one could say that she had deserted, that she had acted like some lily-livered woman in the end. No one, she thought grimly, was likely to remember her at all.

She wondered what had happened to Isaiah. He would not have turned yellow and made a run for it; she was sure of that. Anyway, dying in the fight would have been better than being captured by the Sioux.

Her vision blurred. She let go of the horse's reins and sat down. "Damn it all," she muttered, then began to cry. Her horse nickered at her side. Someone would find her here. She did not care.

A rider was below the trees, moving in her direction. The rider wore an old blue soldier's coat. As the horse he rode made its way up the hillside, Jane reached for her pistol. The man could not be one of the Seventh; he would not have been able to ride here out in the open without being shot. He might be an Indian who had taken his coat from a dead man's body; she could not tell. His hair was too short for a Sioux's, but that might not mean anything.

She took aim, then let her arm fall. Shooting him would likely bring a pack of redskins galloping over here to see what was going on. Maybe it made more sense to shoot herself.

Jane got to her feet, not troubling to conceal herself. The man had seen her. He was reaching for his Colt when her forefinger tightened on the trigger of her gun. In that instant, she knew that she had him, that her bullet would hit him right between the eyes.

"I'm not a Lakota," he called out. Hearing him talk in American startled her, nearly making her flinch. She kept her Colt trained on him. "My name's Lemuel Rowland."

He could be a renegade, she thought. The stranger held out his hands, apparently seeing that he could not draw his gun before she shot him. "I don't want to shoot," he went on. "I've seen enough killing for one day." He paused. "Who are you? What are you doing here?"

She was silent.

"You won't gain anything by shooting me," he said.

That was true enough. Already a few of the Indians had ridden toward this hill; she glimpsed them through the trees.

"You're right about that," she said, lowering her right arm. "Just do me a favor, stranger. Shoot me right here—don't leave me to those redskins. I saw some of their handiwork, riding here."

He frowned. "Why, you're hardly more than a boy."

She had forgotten to keep her voice low. If she didn't mumble, or remember to lower her pitch, her voice often gave her away. "Hell," she said, "I ain't no boy, mister—I'm Calamity Jane Cannary, and I might as well tell you that so as there's somebody to remember my name. Now go ahead and shoot."

He still had not reached for his gun.

"Go on," she said, "don't drag it out. I'd do it myself, but I don't know how the good Lord would take to that. I always heard He

didn't much cotten to folks who died by their own hand, and I got
enough sins on my conscience already."

The man did not move. At last she dropped her gun. "Hell," she
said, steadying herself, "that ought to convince you."

"I don't know if I can shoot an unarmed woman."

"Mister, those redskins won't exactly treat me like a lady." Her
legs shook under her. She sank to the ground once more. "They're
all dead, aren't they—Custer and his men, all of them, they're all
dead, the redskins killed them."

"I think so. Yes. They were warned. They could have left the
Black Hills and nothing would have happened."

Tears trickled down her face. Damn it, she thought, despising
her own weakness. Here she was, facing death like one of those
soft silly women she had always scorned.

The stranger had his gun trained on her now. "It'll be dark
soon," he said. "I'll wait here with you."

Jane tried to understand what he was saying. "You think I can
ride out of here?" she asked, startled at how quickly she grasped at
that futile hope. Maybe she wasn't so ready to die after all.

"No. You can't ride out of here, but I think I can keep you alive."

More tears flowed; she could not stop herself from crying.

"Damn it all," she whispered. "Keep me alive—what the hell for?"

"You can't leave. You won't be able to leave for a long time, and
if you tried, I don't want to think of what would happen to you.
But I'm pretty sure I can keep them from killing you."

Jane forced herself to look up at him. "I ain't going to be no
squaw," she said. "If that's the deal, you might as well put a bullet
in me now."

"You won't be a squaw. I don't think any of the men would force
that on you. Hell, just about every Lakota woman I've seen is a far
sight prettier than you are."

She made a choked sound. The man had almost made her laugh,
even in the midst of this horror. "I won't argue that with you,
mister."

"Anyway, we might need you to identify some of the bodies,"

Lemuel Rowland said. "Touch-the-Clouds will want to know that Custer is dead."

Jane covered her face. Custer dead, the rest of them dead—Isaiah was probably dead, too. She was the only one left alive to mourn them—Calamity Jane Cannary, lone survivor of Custer's Seventh after the Battle of the Black Hills.

TWELVE

Katia and White Cow Sees followed the tracks of their husband and his men to the Mountain Goat a day after they were told of his victory over Long Hair and the Blue Coats. They brought little with them, so did not have to walk with horses pulling pony drags. Red Deer, an uncle of Touch-the-Clouds, rode with them; the rest of the people in their husband's camp would follow them soon to the site of the battle.

White Cow Sees had her youngest child tied to her back; another of her sons, on a roan pony, trotted ahead of them. Red Deer was one of the oldest of the men, too old to fight. He spoke of past battles as they rode, of raids against other red men to steal horses or to avenge a slight, of wars fought before there was peace with the Crow and with the Arikara and the other peoples near these hunting and grazing grounds. Katia listened, thinking of the three scouts who had deserted the invading Blue Coats to join the Lakota, and of how merciless Touch-the-Clouds had been in his treatment of them.

"I would have welcomed you if you had come to me many

moons ago," Touch-the-Clouds had said to the Crow called White Man Runs Him and his two comrades, Hairy Moccasin and Goes Ahead. "I would have trusted you if you had come into this land by yourselves, instead of with the Blue Coats. But if you run away from them now in order to join me, how can I trust you? How do I know that you haven't come to me out of fear of what will happen? How do I know that you won't desert me in times to come?"

Perhaps, Katia thought, her husband was right about the three men, but others had changed sides and he had made his peace with them. He might have granted the three scouts a quicker death.

They rounded a bend along the creek bed. Ahead, a few of the young warriors were watering their horses; one of them wore a soldier's hat and another a blue jacket. The Mountain Goat lay to the east. Even at this distance, Katia saw that bodies of the dead still covered the slopes. Other women were already there, taking what they could from the corpses.

One of the warriors by the creek shook his war club at Katia and White Cow Sees. The wind carried the chants of the young men's kill songs to them. "Let go of your guns, Long Hair. You brought us more weapons and we thank you, for you have need of them no more. You make us dance with joy." The son of Touch-the-Clouds smiled at his mother, put back his head, and laughed.

Katia reined in her horse and rested her hands on the high pommel of her woman's saddle. "These are the wives of Touch-the-Clouds," Red Deer said to the men as White Cow Sees halted near him, "and they have brought his two youngest sons along with them."

"He will be pleased to see them," one of the men replied.

"Then our husband will have to come here to visit with us and to see his sons," White Cow Sees said, "because this is as far as I go." She gazed toward the mountain. "My husband's victory makes me happy, but I would rather not rest too close to where it was fought."

Katia gazed gratefully at the other woman. Maybe White Cow Sees did not want to be near the carnage, the stink of the bodies, or perhaps she had seen into Katia's thoughts.

It had been right, Katia thought, to try to live among her own people, and certainly better than being a largely useless companion to Grisha Rubalev. She might have failed to give Touch-the-Clouds children, but he had learned something of the Wasichu ways from her. There had been few happy moments for her in the Wasichu world, and the Lakota had given her little more happiness, but living among them had hardened her and made her stronger than the weak woman she had once been, living in the white world. The triumph of the Lakota over the Blue Coats who had come into the Black Hills was right and just, but the sight of tortured men and bloated, rotting bodies tempered any joy she might have taken in the victory.

I still don't belong among them, she thought. Now she thought of herself as Katia Rubalev almost all of the time, and no longer as Graceful Swan, the wife of Touch-the-Clouds.

Lemuel watched as Rubalev danced. "He rode alone," Rubalev sang in Lakota, "and I found him. We have kept our promise to Long Hair Custer, for he will not leave Paha Sapa." He shook the scalp as he sang.

Jane Cannary had recognized the long reddish-brown hair of the scalp. "Charley Reynolds," she had told Lemuel. "Nobody else had hair like that. It has to be Charley. I guess they must have sent him out after Isaiah and I rode out after White Man Runs Him."

Rubalev had said that the scalp's owner was riding south, presumably aiming for Fort Fetterman or Fort Laramie, and that he could have been riding there only to report on the plans of the Lakota to attack. For the time being, it was necessary to keep any word about the fate of Custer and his men from spreading, so that scout had to die.

Lemuel understood that necessity. Once the fate of the Seventh was known, many would want to avenge the dead soldiers, and the Lakota were not yet ready to face that kind of battle. Lemuel could grant all of that, and still find himself repulsed by the joy with which Rubalev was displaying his trophy.

Already some of the stronger men, and several of the women, were digging graves so that the dead soldiers could be buried. Horses would be ridden over the graves in an effort to hide any traces of them. Old men on horseback and women with pony drags would ride back along the route the Seventh had taken, concealing marks of their trail. Custer's superiors would have to know, when he did not return, that he had met with misadventure; they would be certain that he and his men had been attacked. They would have to guess at his fate sooner or later, but meanwhile it was better to have as much mystery surrounding Custer's fate as possible. To have him and his men vanish so completely would terrify the Wasichu. Terror, Touch-the-Clouds was learning, could be a useful weapon.

"Poor Charley," Calamity Jane muttered. "Maybe I shouldn't be saying 'poor Charley.' Maybe he's better off dead than I am alive." She took a sip from her flask of whiskey. Lemuel had found some liquor among the dead, and she had asked for some, and he had not had the heart to deny her its solace.

The woman had been useful, and that had mollified Touch-the-Clouds, who had been furious to discover that there was even one enemy survivor. Jane had known all of the scouts and had confirmed that all of them, including the ones whose bodies she had seen while scouting with her comrade Isaiah, were dead. She had drunk a lot of whiskey while pointing out this man and that, speaking their names in a clear voice as if wanting to make certain that Lemuel and Touch-the-Clouds and all of the warriors would hear them. She had kept her composure in the midst of the carnage until they had come upon the body of a Negro, and then she had dropped to her knees, whispering his name: "Isaiah." Someone had taken the dead man's scalp; others had stripped him of his clothing. Lemuel had expected her to cry. Instead, she had screamed out his name, over and over again, until her voice was little more than a rasp.

Jane tilted the flask again. "I am a coward, Rowland," she said. "I know I'd be better off dead myself, but I'd still rather be alive."

"That isn't cowardice," he said.

He had asked Touch-the-Clouds to spare her, and the Lakota had been reluctant to show any mercy, but he had finally agreed. She would not be allowed to leave Lakota territory, at least not for now, and would be killed if she tried to escape. Jane had accepted this command passively, and then Touch-the-Clouds had given her to Lemuel, obviously wondering why he wanted her. Her face was plain and weather-worn, wisps of drab blond hair hung down from under her hat, and her skinny body was that of a boy; about the best Lemuel could say for her looks was that she had all of her teeth. She cursed like a soldier and had, he was beginning to see, too much fondness for whiskey. Still, she had been a scout and claimed to be a good shot. At least she now had a chance to survive out here.

Glorious Spirit and Victorious Spirit sat by another campfire. The two brothers were watching Rubalev, their usual half-smiles on their faces. They were, one of them had said to Lemuel, pleased that their arrow-rockets had worked so well. "We make more better ones," Victorious Spirit—or Glorious Spirit—had told him. "Make with bigger noise, more boom, bring down whole mountain next time!" The Chinese man had showed his teeth in a broad smile.

Rubalev was singing his kill song again. "You were alone," he chanted, "and so was I, but it was you who fell, and I who struck you with my coup stick."

Jane said in a low voice, "That yellow-haired son of a bitch has the devil in him."

Lemuel got up and climbed the slope, suddenly wanted to be away from the kill songs and the dead.

White Cow Sees and Katia had raised a small wickiup of hides and branches by dusk. The sun set behind the hills to the west and still their husband had not ridden to them. Soon a rider came and said that Touch-the-Clouds would come to them the next morning. He gave the older son of Touch-the-Clouds a doll that he had made with some of the green picture paper he had taken from a dead soldier's pockets, before Yellow Hair Rubalev and the Orphan of the East had told the men that the paper had value and should be saved, and used later to buy more weapons.

The two women ate some dried meat and then curled up under their buffalo robes to sleep. Katia woke abruptly in the night. At first she thought that one of the children was murmuring in his sleep, and then realized that the sound was coming from outside.

She slipped from under her robe, pulled on deerskin boots, and crawled out of the shelter. Someone was singing in the distance. She could barely hear the song, but knew at once that it was not a Lakota or a Cheyenne chant.

There was light on the slopes of the Mountain Goat. Tents had been raised near the mountain, tents of white cloth unlike the Lakota dwellings made of painted hides. Several campfires were burning, and brightly enough so that she could make out the forms of blue-coated men sitting around the flames. She found herself walking toward the mountain, following the stream that led toward it, unable to turn back. The music had changed; instruments accompanied the singing, instruments that sounded like trumpets.

The men around the fires were not Indians. She saw that when she was closer. They were soldiers, seated by covered wagons, leaning against the wheels. Several of the men had tucked flowers into the headbands of their hats.

I am seeing ghosts, Katia thought. The fires began to die, one by one, until the mountain was dark and the tents hidden by night. The only fires she could see now were those of the warriors camped below.

Katia kept walking toward the mountain, following the black snake of the creek in the moonlight. She was near one of the wagons when a man's voice called out her Lakota name. "Graceful Swan!" The voice sounded as though it came from a great distance. "Graceful Swan!"

She moved away from the wagon and climbed past the bodies that still lay on the slope. "Katia," a voice said behind her, the same voice that had been calling her Lakota name before. She knew that voice. Lemuel Rowland was calling to her.

Katia turned to see a man's shadowed dark shape standing just below her. "I heard them singing," she said. "I saw them on the mountain."

"The warriors?"

"The dead soldiers. The Blue Coats. They were here. I think their ghosts are still here. Why did you come here?"

"Because I heard men singing," Lemuel Rowland said. "It was a dream I was having. I fell asleep and heard them singing and then I found myself climbing up here with no memory of waking up." He shook himself. "Maybe I am still asleep."

"You're not asleep." Katia turned away from him and continued to climb until she saw the glow of a fire above her. She moved toward the fire, thinking that it might be another vision, and then saw two women seated near the flames.

"Walking Blanket Woman," Katia said to one of the women, "why are you here?"

"I sit with the dead chief of the Blue Coats." Walking Blanket Woman waved an arm at the darkness beyond the fire. Something lay there, under a robe. Katia could smell it now: a rotting corpse. "I came here," Walking Blanket Woman continued, "with Young Spring Grass to sit with the dead chief who is her kinsman, who is the father of her son."

Young Spring Grass smiled. Katia could see by the light of the fire that the Cheyenne woman's arms and legs bore several bloody gashes.

"He is dead," Young Spring Grass murmured. "I rejoice that he is dead, but he is also the father of my son, so I have cut at myself with a knife in mourning for him." She lifted her head. "He would not listen when he was told to ride away from here, to leave this place with his men. Now his Long Knives are all dead because he would not listen. I have pierced his eardrums with my awl, so that he will hear better in the next world." She picked up a stick, thrust it into the flames until it caught fire, then held it toward the dead man.

His face was now visible above the robe that covered him. Katia had seen his face before. She said, "I know this man."

"You know him, too?" Rowland asked, moving closer to the women; he was speaking to her in English now. "Did you meet him when you were living with Rubalev? He was in Washington from time to time—perhaps you saw him there."

.

"No," she replied. "I didn't meet him in the Wasichu world. I saw his face in the real world, the world my visions show me. I saw him last summer, when we camped near the valley of the Greasy Grass River."

"But how—"

She sat down. "I hear the ghosts again," she whispered.

Rowland said, "I hear them, too," and took her hand. The voices swelled around them, the voices of men singing "The Girl I Left Behind Me," singing as though they knew that they would never see those girls again. Katia could not see the men, but she felt the presence of bodies crowded together and heard them cough and clear their throats and make gulping sounds as they drank.

"They're here," Katia said, "they're with us." They were still alive somewhere, not in this world, not in the world of spirits, but in a place that was near, that was real, but that she could not reach. "They didn't die," she murmured. "That was an illusion. The bodies we saw here aren't real. They came to the Black Hills and they left again and then they died somewhere else. I saw that man—"

"Custer," Rowland said. "That dead man lying near us was Custer."

Katia took a breath. "This is what happened last summer," she said. "I was out riding, alone. I left our camp and rode out alone. It was so sudden, that feeling that I had to be by myself." Her hands were shaking; she pressed her palms together. "White Cow Sees didn't stop me. No one tried to stop me. Later I was told by a medicine woman that she had seen from the look on my face that a spirit had taken possession of me."

"Go on," Rowland said.

"I rode toward the river and then I heard cries and then I was in the midst of a battle. Lakota and Cheyenne warriors were all around me, screaming war cries. I rode with them and bullets flew around us, but somehow I knew that none of those bullets could touch me, that I was protected. The warriors were riding toward a ridge where some soldiers—" She covered her face, remembering how fiercely the blue-coated soldiers had fought. It had been hand to hand in the end, the Blue Coats fighting with rifles and bayonets.

"He was there," Katia continued, "the man called Custer. I saw him fall when a bullet struck him in the chest. I saw him die."

She fell silent for a while. The invisible men that she could not see were still singing, but more faintly.

"What happened then?" Rowland asked.

"I don't remember. I think that I fell from my horse. When I came to myself, I was lying on the ridge where I saw the man Custer die. My horse was grazing near me. I rode back to our camping circle to find my husband waiting for me. He was angry. I told him what I had seen, and he grew angrier."

Her hands were shaking again as she remembered how furious her husband had been. Telling him of the battle in her vision had only made him angrier. What did it mean? he wanted to know. Was it a warning? Was it something that would come to pass, or something that had already happened? When she could not answer, she had feared that he might beat her. He had not, but his rage had terrified her more than any beating.

Katia struggled to compose herself. "He said that it might be a vision," she said in a low voice, "or that it might be the work of evil spirits. He said that he had been patient, that he had waited to see if I had any of the power and strong medicine he had seen in me when I was a girl, but that all I had brought to him was a vision he could not understand. But now I think I may know what it was telling me."

The invisible soldiers were no longer singing. Behind her, Walking Blanket Woman and Young Spring Grass were chanting softly: "You did not listen, Long Hair. You did not listen."

"What does your vision mean?" Rowland asked.

"Tonight, when I came here, and saw the soldiers and heard their singing, I knew that they were still alive somehow, in a world we can't reach. Then I saw the body of Custer here, and the same face I saw at the Greasy Grass." She paused. "I think it means that these men weren't meant to die here, that they were meant to die somewhere else, in the place where I saw them in my vision. What my husband has done here has changed what will happen, and I don't know whether that will help him or destroy him." Katia plucked at her long braids. "Maybe this can all be explained another way. Maybe it only means that I have gone mad."

"If you're mad," Rowland said, "then so am I." He turned toward her. "I heard these men in my dream, I saw them. I had—" He rested a hand lightly on her arm. "I've had the feeling before that something that has happened in this world hasn't truly happened at all. It's a feeling that doesn't come upon me often, but when it does, it's powerful enough to make me think that much of this world is an illusion." He shook his head. "Illusion seems the wrong word, but I don't know how else to say it."

She said, "It felt to me as though this battle happened and also didn't happen."

"Yes," he said, "that captures how I felt."

"But that is impossible." She drew away from him. "My husband is right. My visions, whatever they may mean, are useless to him."

"You may have another vision, my wife. That may make the meaning clear."

That was her husband's voice. Touch-the-Clouds had said the words in English. He stepped out of the darkness into the dim light of the fire. He had put aside his war bonnet, and wore only one eagle feather in his hair. Katia wondered how long he had been standing there, how much he had heard.

"This was a victory," Touch-the-Clouds continued, "to strike fear in the hearts of the Wasichu and to keep them away from Paha Sapa. Now you tell me that it may not be the victory we were meant to win."

"I do not know—" Katia began.

"If it had been only you, my wife, who saw and heard the ghost of the Blue Coats who lie here, I might doubt that your visions have much to tell me. But the Orphan has also seen and heard them."

Katia glanced back at the fire. Young Spring Grass and Walking Blanket Woman were watching and listening, but they would not have understood what was being said. It did not matter; they had probably heard the hardness in her husband's voice. She was suddenly afraid of what he might do.

"You had a vision here," Touch-the-Clouds went on. "Perhaps to find out what it means, you must go back to the Greasy Grass, where your earlier vision came to you, and seek another vision."

His words had the sound of a command. "And when must I do this?" she asked.

"Soon. Before the next moon. I must know if there is anything to this before we fight again."

She lacked the power to protest. What was she to him? A childless woman, one he had taken as a wife only because he had believed that she had good medicine and that her visions might show him what would come to pass. If she could not be a true woman to him, then she would have to seek visions, as a warrior did. He would have to send her on a quest for another vision, even if it might mean her death. She had grown stronger among the Lakota, but she doubted that she would survive a solitary quest. She was not likely to reach the Greasy Grass and the ridge where she had last seen Custer until near the end of the Moon When the Geese Shed Their Feathers. The weather would grow colder after that, the autumn winds would begin to howl.

Rowland said, "I also saw the ghosts of the Blue Coats here, and heard their songs."

"So you tell me," Touch-the-Clouds said.

"Searching for visions of how to fight should not be the business of women. Perhaps I am the one who should go on this quest."

"It is not the business of most women," Touch-the-Clouds responded, "but my wife Graceful Swan claimed to see visions of what would come to pass as a child, and now she tells me that she saw this battle in another place."

"We shared this vision," Rowland said, "so perhaps I should seek another vision with her."

"Then go," Touch-the-Clouds said, "and search together. Leave tomorrow at dawn. Do not stop at any of the camps you may see along the way, for I want nothing to cloud any visions that may be sent to you. We will hunt buffalo and then camp by the Crazy

Woman Creek during this moon. If you have not returned to me by the Moon of Falling Leaves, I will send someone after you."

He climbed swiftly to where the two women sat with the body of Custer, took out his knife, cut at the dead man's head, then made his way back down to them.

"Here." He put a lock of Custer's hair in her hand and closed her fingers around it. "Perhaps this will help to guide you."

"I have no choice," Lemuel Rowland was saying to the man called Rubalev, the man with the devil in him. "She can't come with me, so I have to leave her with you."

Jane looked from one man to the other. Rowland stood near the impaled corpse of one of Custer's dogs. Rubalev closed the box in which he was collecting greenbacks scavenged from the dead, then looked up. "If she even thinks of escaping," Rubalev said, "I will kill her."

"Hellfire," Jane muttered, "don't you think I know that?" Lem Rowland had come to her with a story of having to ride northwest with a wife of Touch-the-Clouds. He had said something about dreams and visions that she did not really understand. She had been persuading herself that maybe having to stay with him would make captivity more tolerable, and now he was turning her over to the Russian. She would never be able to look at Rubalev without remembering how much he had enjoyed dancing with Charley Reynolds's scalp.

"She's been a scout," Rowland said, "a Pony Express rider, and a wagon driver. You might find her useful."

Jane had not slept much, and Rowland looked as though he had not slept at all. The sky was growing light in the east; he would be riding out soon on his mysterious journey. Rubalev glowered at her, as if trying to decide whether keeping her alive might be too much trouble for him.

"You are telling me," Rubalev said, "that if she attempts to escape, she has the skill to survive."

"Damn it all, Rubalev," Jane said, "I know enough to know

when I have a chance and when I don't, and right now I don't. I know what you did to Charley. I know what you'd do to me."

"He won't shoot you," Rowland muttered, "unless you try to get away, and if he does, he'll have to answer to me." He stared at the light-haired man until Rubalev looked away.

"I wish you luck, Rowland," Rubalev said, "but I think you are foolish to go. If no vision comes to her, she will be of no further use to her husband. I am hoping that she has not lost the powers he values so much, but if she has, you would have been kinder to leave her to her death."

Rowland said, "You care nothing for her."

"You are wrong. It is she who has failed me."

Rowland's face was grim. The anger in his eyes was enough to make Jane skittish. He'd kill that blond devil if he could, she thought. Rowland spun around quickly and strode away.

Katia had put the reddish-blond lock of Custer's hair into her medicine pouch. Her husband had given her and Rowland two horses each and food enough for four days. They would run out of their provisions before they reached their destination; they would have to hunt and gather more food. Perhaps Touch-the-Clouds thought that hunger would aid in bringing her another vision.

She turned in her saddle and looked back. White Cow Sees was still standing by her lodge, her baby in a cradle near her feet. She had not looked pleased to hear that Katia was being sent away by their husband, but had said nothing.

Rowland was ahead of her. His horse slowed as he waited for her to catch up to him. They rode for a while, not speaking, until at last she said, "You didn't have to come with me."

"I did have to come with you."

"Because you think we'll find what my husband wants us to find?"

"That, and other reasons."

"For a while," she said, "I wondered why I had no more visions, why the spirits no longer revealed anything to me. I longed for visions. Now I wish that I had never been given the power to see them."

Among the pine-covered Black Hills, there were valleys of bright flowers and lush green grass. They had soon left them behind for the flatter, more desolate land of the Plains, yellow with buffalo grass and empty of trees. Katia supposed that, as a child, she and her family had wandered over this land, but had no recollection of that. The first time that she had seen it as the wife of Touch-the-Clouds, the emptiness and the big empty sky had frightened her.

Rowland scanned the horizon. He cupped one hand over his eyes, and she wondered if he had learned to see this land the way a Lakota man did, full of wakan beings and spirits living in healing plants and buffalo and all of the life of the world, or if he saw it more as the white man did, as ground to be tilled and surveyed and parceled out and scavenged for nuggets of gold.

He turned toward her as his mount began to nibble at the grass. "When you saw Custer's men, and heard them singing, were they as real to you as anything in this world?"

"Yes." His question puzzled her. "Of course they were. That was what made me feel that our battle with the Blue Coats had not happened."

"I felt the same way," he said, "but now—I have more doubts. Perhaps it was only a dream after all."

"The spirits can speak to us through dreams."

"And sometimes a dream is only that, Katia—a dream." He tugged at the brim of his hat. "I saw what won that battle. It wasn't any vision that came to Touch-the-Clouds or Sitting Bull or to the other chiefs. It wasn't just that the Lakota and their allies have learned something more about tactics and fighting together. It was the Chen brothers and their rocket-arrows, it was the guns and ammunition the Lakota have stolen and bought and are learning how to make."

She rested her hands on her pommel. "Are you saying that you don't trust your vision?"

"I suppose I am."

"Then why did you decide to come with me?" she asked.

"Because you would have had no chance to survive if I hadn't."
He looked away quickly, as though he had said too much.

Touch-the-Clouds had given them dried buffalo meat and some of
the hardtack from the provisions of the dead soldiers. They ate the
food sparingly, trying to make it last, but had eaten almost all of it
by the time they came to the Powder River. A small herd of buffalo
were crossing the winding river to the north. Katia stared after
them as they moved over the yellow land, their legs disappearing
in clouds of dirt and dust.

Their horses had to swim the river. After crossing, Katia and
Rowland filled their waterskins and canteens while their horses
rested. The ridge of the Wolf Mountains lay ahead, and Goose
Creek, and then the Greasy Grass River, a journey of three or four
days, and she was already feeling lightheaded. They would still
have to cross the mountain divide. She told herself that crossing the
Wolf Mountains would be easier this time, with only four horses,
than it had been when her husband's entire camp was on the move.

Rowland had said almost nothing during the past days. They
rode, stopped at intervals to rest, graze, and water the horses, and
then moved on. At night, they slept under blankets, nested next to
each other against the cold. Twice they had come to trails that
would have led them to the camps of Lakota or Cheyenne, and she
had found herself longing for the sound of another voice, but did
not dare to go against her husband's wishes. Touch-the-Clouds had
told them not to stop in any camp; he would be certain to find out
if they had. She forced herself to put aside thoughts of talk, of food,
of a warm space inside a tepee.

Katia moved her arms, waiting for her clothing to dry. The sun
was high and hot today, but the air would soon grow cooler.

"Katia." For a moment, she did not recognize Rowland's voice.
"We need food. I saw deer tracks along this side of the river, going
south. You'll be safe here for now. I'll take one of the horses and
ride back to you before dark."

"If you have luck," she said.

"Even if I don't have any luck. Better not to waste what strength I still have, and I won't leave you to face the night alone."

He mounted his bay horse and rode away. She gazed after him, thinking of when she had first met Rowland, how he had looked at her as if wanting to shield her from the world. She had known that he would try to help her when she went to him in St. Louis. He had not known what she had truly wanted then, what she had refused to admit even to herself.

She had wanted Grisha to come after her. She had hoped that he would finally see what was inside her and would come to her, that what she felt for him was more than gratitude. He would tell her that she no longer had to be the wife of Touch-the-Clouds. She had gone no further than that in her thoughts, vaguely imagining that she might live among the Lakota and that Grisha would make a life there with her, and if they had gone back to the Wasichu world, she could have borne that, too. Now she saw how little she meant to him. If she died out here, he would find someone else who could serve his aims.

She walked along the river, searching for edible roots. There were berry bushes up ahead, near a bend. I will not die, she told herself. Her visions at the Mountain Goat and the Greasy Grass had been true visions, even if she was not sure of what they meant. The wakan spirits would come to her with another vision.

Rowland returned at dusk, as he had promised to do, with a small young deer slung over his saddle. Katia had dug a hollow in the ground with a long stick and gathered enough grass and dry twigs for a fire. They butchered the carcass together, cutting the meat into long strips and spreading them on a few of the flat stones along the riverbank to dry, then cooked some of the meat for their supper along with the wild onions and turnips she had found.

Katia slept uneasily. During one dream, a voice whispered to her in Lakota, but she could not make out the words, even whether the voice belonged to a man or a woman. At dawn, she woke and saw that Rowland was already awake, sitting by the dying fire.

He looked back at her and said, "Someone spoke to me in a dream. I couldn't sleep after that."

"What were you told?" she asked.

"I can't remember."

"A voice spoke to me, too." She took a breath; already the air was growing warm. "It's going to be hot today," she said.

"I know. We'll stay here, wait for the meat to dry some more, and ride out in the evening."

They gathered more twigs and grass, fed the fire, and cooked some more meat. They would not be here long enough for her to tan and finish the deerhide. Katia rested by the fire as the horses drank; the weakness and unsteadiness she had felt were gone. She was not used to such idleness, to having so little to do. Idleness gave her too much time to worry about what might happen to her, and to think about Grisha. Maybe he would come to care for her more if she could bring back a vision that would prove her worth. That was not a thought to have; a vision was not something to use as love medicine, a way of binding Grisha to her.

From a high place in the Wolf Mountains, Katia and Rowland could see the valley of the Greasy Grass River. The grass, green when Katia had last camped here, was turning yellow and tan. To the southwest lay more mountains that bordered the Greasy Grass. Keeping the mountains at their left, they followed the well-traveled trail to Goose Creek and then toward the Greasy Grass River. They rode at night and rested during the day, since the days remained hot and sunny, the air still. It might almost have been the Moon of Red Cherries, Katia thought, instead of late in the summer.

Rowland rarely spoke. She heard his voice more often when he slept than when he was awake. When he was sleeping, she would hear his whispers, sometimes in English and sometimes in words she did not know, and wondered what his dreams were telling him.

They came to the twists and turns of the Greasy Grass River and followed it north, toward the place where Katia had seen her vision of Custer's soldiers. Shallow gullies and ravines ran down to the river from the undulating line of a ridge. The only trees on this land were willows and cottonwood trees along the river's course; the rest of the brown rolling land was sparsely dotted with bushes and lay open under the vast sky.

The Sun Chief rose in the sky. As they rode toward the ridge where she had had her vision of Long Hair Custer and his Blue Coats, a buffalo came down to the river to drink. Rowland reined in his horse, signaling to Katia to wait, and then the buffalo lifted its head and gazed directly at them.

Katia met the animal's eyes. *"Pte,"* she said, using the Lakota name of their buffalo brother. The buffalo turned and began to move up the river, passing a small grove of cottonwood trees. Somehow she knew that the buffalo wanted them to follow, and then realized that it was leading them toward the ridge. The animal quickened its pace, moving into a run and disappearing around a hill near a riverbend.

Katia pulled at her reins; her horse halted. She dismounted and handed the reins to Rowland. "I will walk there," she said.

"I'll come with you."

She shook her head. "I have to go by myself."

She walked toward the ridge. She could feel Rowland watching her. If any vision came to him, he would have to face it alone.

When she reached higher ground, she turned and looked back. Rowland had tied their four horses to the trunks of two cottonwood trees and was now sitting on a blanket.

The buffalo had disappeared. Katia could not even find his tracks. The lock of Custer's hair her husband had given to her was in a small pouch at her waist, with her other medicine; she put her hand on the pouch and continued to climb until she came to the jutting point of the ridge.

A Lakota man sat there, a pipe in his hands, a bonnet of many eagle feathers on his head. In front of him, a few slender wooden wands, hung with small leather pouches and bits of bark, jutted from the ground, offerings to the spirits. Katia knew this man. She had seen him with her husband and the other chiefs during the war talks. All the Lakota and Cheyenne and their allies respected this man. There were a few among the older men who still considered him as great a man as Touch-the-Clouds, perhaps greater.

"Tatanka Wotanka," she whispered, "Sitting Bull." At first she thought that he must have followed her and Rowland here, that perhaps her husband had sent him after them, and then she saw the strange glow that suffused his face. Sitting Bull was here as part of her vision. The buffalo had led her to him.

"I saw many soldiers falling into our camp," the chief said to her. "That was what the spirits showed me ten days ago, before the Sun Dance. The soldiers wore their blue coats and were falling toward us, but their heads pointed toward the earth. That was how I knew we would have a victory. In gratitude, I sacrificed part of myself to the Creator." He held out his arms and she saw the marks of scars where pieces of flesh had been torn away.

"Is our victory at the Mountain Goat, in the Black Hills?" she asked.

The creases at the edges of his thin lips deepened. "No, child. Our victory will come here, at the Greasy Grass. Crazy Horse will bring us a victory. I see that now. Long Hair, the chief of the Blue Coats, will fall here. He and his men will come to attack us, hoping to surprise us, and then they will die."

"No," she whispered, "he cannot die here. He fell on the slopes of the Mountain Goat. I saw him there with his men, I saw his body."

Sitting Bull held out his pipe and lifted his head to the sky. "Wakan Tanka, hear me! I ask you to save my people. We want to live, and to be protected from all danger and misfortune. Hear me!"

Katia sat down a few feet away from him. Sitting Bull prayed for a while longer, and smoked his pipe, then stood up and walked toward the edge of the ridge. She closed her eyes for only a moment, and when she opened them, he was gone.

She stood up and went to the ridge. Below, in the valley, soldiers were fighting hand-to-hand with Indians near a hill, while others were shooting at the massed warriors on horseback from higher up on the slope. She saw them all as if through a mist.

"We will have a great victory here," the voice of Sitting Bull said behind her.

"My husband won a victory in the Black Hills," she said, "but you say that Custer fell here. I must ask you—what will happen now?"

"I cannot see it clearly," Sitting Bull murmured, "but the spirits show me a victory that will later turn into a defeat for our people. The Blue Coats will grow angry. They will seek vengeance for the death of their chief and send even more of their warriors against us. They will take our lands from us and kill all of the buffalo. They will force me and my Hunkpapas into exile in the north, in the country of the Great Mother."

He was speaking of having to flee into Canada. "And then?" Katia said.

"I cannot see further than that, child. I do not want to see further than that, because I know that what I see will only bring sorrow. Our medicine has grown weaker. Once, before the white man came, our medicine was strong, and the spirits spoke to us, but they have become much weaker. Now they grow silent. As we took our land from the Crow and the Arikara, the Wasichu will take our land from us."

"But we are at peace with the Arikara and the Crow," Katia said. "There are a few who have gone over to the Wasichu, but most have smoked the pipe with the Lakota."

"The Crow are our enemies. They have always been our enemies."

Katia blinked, and when she could see again, the battle was over, the ground covered with dead soldiers. The wind lifted her and carried her over the battlefield, away from Sitting Bull. She spread her arms, soaring, climbing on the wind, then plummeted to the ground.

She had alighted amid bloating horse carcasses and the naked bodies of dead soldiers. There was no sound in this world, only silence; the hot air, reeking of death, was so thick that she could hardly breathe. Above her, on the ridge, the pale body of a man lay amid a circle of dead horses. Two women and a boy with pale reddish and blond streaks in his long hair sat with the body. The boy lifted an arm and beckoned to Katia.

She walked toward them, making her way around the fly-covered carcasses. The boy was Yellow Hair, and next to him was his mother, Young Spring Grass. Katia did not know the third woman, who seemed as ghostly and insubstantial as mist.

"You did not listen, Long Hair," Young Spring Grass chanted. "You did not listen."

"Monahseetah," Katia whispered, "Young Spring Grass."

The other woman looked up. "I do not know you," Young Spring Grass said.

"You know me as Graceful Swan, the wife of Touch-the-Clouds."

"I do not know you." Young Spring Grass made signs with her hands. "I have seen the wife of Touch-the-Clouds, and you are not that wife."

"What of him?" Katia asked. "What can you tell me about him?"

"He rides with Crazy Horse," the second woman replied. "Have they not been friends since the time Touch-the-Clouds saved his life?"

Katia had never heard such a story. "When did he save the life of Crazy Horse?"

"When the husband of Black Buffalo Woman grew jealous," the woman said, "and rode after Crazy Horse to demand that his wife be returned to him. It was Touch-the-Clouds who stood between them and kept them from coming to blows."

Katia did not understand. The wife of Crazy Horse was named Black Shawl, not Black Buffalo Woman.

"You did not listen, Long Hair," Young Spring Grass said, "you did not listen. You came into our lands when your people had promised to keep away. You came to Paha Sapa, and thousands of the Wasichu followed you there. Now you have died here, at the place you call the Little Bighorn."

"They can tell you no more," a voice said behind her.

The voice was that of Sitting Bull, but when Katia turned around, the buffalo that had led her to the ridge was standing near her.

"Why did you come here?" the buffalo asked.

"To seek a vision."

"A vision has come to you. It has shown you what you must see."

"But I don't understand what it means."

"You are not a medicine man," the buffalo said. "You have the power to see, but someone with stronger medicine will have to tell you the meaning of your vision."

She held out her arms. The buffalo vanished; the air abruptly grew cold. The ground was covered with snow and the mutilated bodies of many people, and as she moved among them, she glimpsed Blue Coats fanning out around them, their rifles aimed at them. She sank to the ground and lay there as the snow sifted down, making a white blanket over her. She closed her eyes, surprised at how warm the blanket of snow felt.

"This is where the victory at the Greasy Grass will lead your people," the buffalo's voice murmured. "This is where the Lakota way will end. Our people will do the Ghost Dance, to summon the spirits of our dead and to sweep away the Wasichu, and the Wasichu will kill them for dancing the Ghost Dance at a place called Wounded Knee. The hoop will be broken, and the people scattered."

"Katia," another voice murmured, and after that, "Graceful Swan."

She opened her eyes. The shape of a man, black against the bright blue cloudless sky, loomed over her. She groaned as she struggled to sit up; her body felt stiff and bruised. It took a few moments for her to realize that she was sitting on the ridge where she had first seen Sitting Bull.

"I waited for you," Rowland said. "I waited until dark, and then I was going to come up here and look for you, but—" He paused. "I couldn't do it. I could not make myself get up and climb up here to you. I don't know how else to explain it."

He sat down next to her. "I must have slept," he continued, "and I know I dreamt, but I can't remember much about the dream." He rubbed his face. "Except for this—I was walking along the river there, and I think I heard the sound of guns. I started to run toward the sound, but something was holding me back. A voice told me,

'You do not belong here, you do not live here, you do not exist here.'" Rowland shook his head. "And for a moment, I—was not."

"I don't understand."

"I had no memories, no place, no being. I don't know how else to say it."

Katia pressed her hands together. "I saw Young Spring Grass," she said, "and she told me she didn't know me. I saw things that can't happen and was told of events that didn't happen. And Sitting Bull spoke to me."

"Tell me of what you saw," he said.

She spoke to him, telling him everything she could recall. By the time she was finished, the bright noontime sun was lower in the sky, the wind picking up. Rowland went to water their horses and brought her some of the dried meat from his saddlebag. His face was solemn as he watched her eat.

"We can't stay here by ourselves," she said.

"There must be people camped not more than two or three days' ride from here," he said. "We'll rest tonight and ride tomorrow. I'll find someone to ride to Touch-the-Clouds or else go to him myself." He looked toward the river. "I thought attacking the Blue Coats was a mistake," he continued, "not that any of the chiefs would have been interested in my opinion. Whether he used his own methods, or fought as the white soldiers do, I didn't think Touch-the-Clouds could win that battle either way."

"You were wrong about that," Katia said softly.

"His victory might still turn into a defeat for him. There will be many who will want to punish all the Indians now for what happened at the Mountain Goat. Maybe that's what your vision was telling you, that they will now come after us and take their revenge."

Katia and Rowland left the banks of the Greasy Grass at dawn and rode east. Already the weather was turning sharply colder. Not far from the foothills of the Wolf Mountains, they found the trail of people moving their camp southward, and followed it. Five days after leaving the Greasy Grass, they came to a circle of Lakota tents.

The chief in this camp had just returned from the battle with Custer's Blue Coats. Katia, weakened by her ordeal, stayed in the tent of his wife and helped her with her work while he and Rowland rode to Touch-the-Clouds.

Seven days later, the two men returned with Touch-the-Clouds, Sitting Bull, and a rider in buckskin clothes who was the size of a boy. Katia, working at buffalo hides outside the circle of tents with the other women, saw no other men with them, not Grisha, not even any of the young men who had left their families here to join Touch-the-Clouds.

My husband is planning another battle, she thought. Touch-the-Clouds wanted to keep his warriors together, most likely so that he could fight again before winter set in. She remembered what Rowland had told her, and wondered how much wrath her husband might bring down upon his people.

Touch-the-Clouds greeted Katia with one nod of his head and no words. The rider in buckskin clothes was the white woman Rowland had found after the battle, the only member of Custer's group who had survived. Rowland left her with Katia and went inside the council tepee with the other men.

The white woman sat on her heels as Katia scraped at the hide. "Lem Rowland says you talk American," the woman said.

"Yes, I do."

"Just like the chief," the woman said. "Fact is, seems a few of the braves know at least a little of our lingo."

"My husband thinks it is wise to learn what he can about his enemies." Katia paused. "I should not have said that to you. You are not my enemy. I know what you must have endured. When I was a girl, soldiers came to my father's camp and slaughtered everyone—my mother, the babies, everyone except for me and an old woman, and we lived only because they didn't find us."

The woman stuck out her hand. Katia gazed at the hand, then clasped it for a moment. "I go by the name of Martha Jane Cannary," the white woman said. "Got the right to call myself Martha Jane Hickok, but my husband Wild Bill took off and I ain't seen him for a while. Some call me Calamity Jane, but you needn't."

"Calamity Jane?" Katia asked.

Martha Jane Cannary shook her head. She had blond hair poking out from under her hat, a pointed face darkened by sun and dust, and pale blue eyes. "Hell, calling me Calamity's even more fitting now than it was. I witnessed the worst damned calamity I ever hope to see."

Katia did not know what to say.

"Lem told me I could stay with you a while," Jane continued.

"I'm sure we won't be here for long," Katia replied. "My husband will expect me to leave with him, to stay in his camp with his other wife."

"You talk good American," Jane said. "Hell, you talk it better than I do."

"I lived in the East," Katia said, "in Washington and other places. Grigory Rubalev found me among the Lakota when I was a child, after the Blue Coats killed my father and my mother. He named me Katia Rubalev and brought me up in the East, and when I was older, he brought me back to my people so that I could marry my husband." She was saying too much. The Lakota women near them could not have understood what she had said, but she saw the concern in their eyes.

"Rubalev," Jane muttered. "Lem left me with him. Told Lem I'd take an oath not to even think of escaping if he just got me away from that man." She shook her head. "Wasn't anything he did to me, you understand, but I couldn't help seeing he'd gun me down if he could get away with it."

Katia was about to say that Grisha was not always hard, that there was some kindness in him, but did not speak. Grisha did not need her to defend him, and she had never really known him. Maybe he had already lost what little kindness he had possessed.

"Didn't tell him I had a daughter," Jane went on, " 'cause then he'd likely be expecting me to try to run, just to get back to her."

"A daughter?" Katia asked.

"Her name's Jean. Couldn't keep her, and she's better off with the good folks who took her in, but I wasn't about to explain all of that to that blond devil."

"I'm sorry," Katia said.

"Ain't much for you to be sorry about," Jane muttered.

"Graceful Swan."

She looked up. Touch-the-Clouds was coming toward them. Katia got to her feet.

"You will come with me, wife," her husband said in Lakota. "Sitting Bull will speak to you of your vision." He turned toward the other women and motioned at Jane. "Keep this Wasichu woman with you," he told them, then took Katia by the arm and led her away.

Touch-the-Clouds made Katia sit inside the council tepee and speak of her vision, and Lemuel found himself watching the stern face of Sitting Bull as Katia spoke. He wondered what the great Hunkpapa chief was thinking. Sitting Bull had said nothing after hearing what she had told Lemuel, nothing at all during the ride here.

The three of them were alone with the woman. Touch-the-Clouds apparently did not want others to hear of his wife's vision, at least not until Sitting Bull told him what it meant. Sitting Bull had strong medicine, and since Katia had seen him in her vision, he was the one who would have to interpret the vision for them; so Touch-the-Clouds had reasoned. Now his eyes shifted restlessly from his wife to Sitting Bull. It came to Lemuel that Touch-the-Clouds was afraid of what the other chief might tell him.

When Katia fell silent, the men said nothing. Lemuel could read no expression in Sitting Bull's impassive face. The fire in front of them was burning low; at last Lemuel reached for some kindling and fed the flames.

"I had a vision," Sitting Bull said at last, "before the battle with Long Hair and his Blue Coats. I saw the Wasichu falling into the Black Hills, and their heads were pointed at the ground. It is like the vision told to you by the Sitting Bull you saw."

"We had a victory," Touch-the-Clouds said. "Your vision told you that we would defeat the Blue Coats."

"And this woman's vision showed her another victory, one that cannot now come to pass," Sitting Bull said, "and she spoke of a defeat that would come after it, and of a world where the spirits will no longer speak. Perhaps her vision was of what will now happen to us."

Sitting Bull's face was impassive, but his eyes were fierce as he gazed steadily at Touch-the-Clouds. "This victory may be followed by defeat," he continued. "You do not fight as we were used to fighting. You do not let the young men win enough honor for themselves in battle. You make allies of men who are not like us, who do not understand our ways. You yourself are forgetting what it is to be a Lakota."

Touch-the-Clouds looked directly at Sitting Bull; only his eyes showed his anger. "I do what I must do so that my people will keep their land, so that they can live by hunting the buffalo."

"That is what you tell yourself," Sitting Bull said, "but I saw how you fought this battle. There was little glory in it for a warrior."

"The Wasichu are dead," Touch-the-Clouds said, "and they deserved to die for what they have done to our people in the past. They will not bring more of their miners and settlers to Paha Sapa. That is enough glory and honor for me."

"They may send more of their Blue Coats against us," Lemuel heard himself say.

He had not meant to speak. Sitting Bull slowly turned his head toward him.

"You rode with the blue-coated soldiers once, Orphan from the East," Sitting Bull said, "so you can see what they might do. But there is this. The woman spoke of things that cannot happen and of things that did not happen. We may still be able to avoid the defeat she said would come after the victory in her vision."

"I agree," Lemuel said, "but you cannot wait until more soldiers ride against us. I think that is what your wife's vision shows. You must prepare for your next action now."

"Are you so certain of that?" Touch-the-Clouds asked.

Katia looked at her husband. "The buffalo told me that the victory I saw in my vision would lead only to defeat and death. That was what I was shown in the end."

"Your vision showed you bodies lying in the snow," Sitting Bull said, "and Blue Coats pointing their firesticks at them. Perhaps the Wasichu mean to attack us in the winter. They can take us by surprise when we are most defenseless, huddled in our lodges against the cold."

"They will also have to bring their food, their wagons, cattle to feed themselves," Touch-the-Clouds said. "That will slow them down. We could defeat them by stealing their food."

Sitting Bull's eyes narrowed into slits. "Your wife's vision showed her people lying in the snow, women and children, all of them dead."

"They were killed because they were dancing and calling out to spirits for their power," Katia said, "and the soldiers were afraid of that."

Lemuel was suddenly certain that Sitting Bull had grasped the true meaning of Katia's vision. "I must speak," he said. "When the Blue Coats you killed don't return to their fort, others will start to wonder what happened to them. They'll be waiting for some word, for dispatches, for a scout to reach a fort with news. The Wasichu woman I found told me that reporters were with them, and miners, all of them writing dispatches to be sent back to newspapers—to talking papers, so that others would know what they found. Their wives will wonder what happened to the men. This Custer, this Long Hair, was not a man to do things in secret—he liked attention. The more time passes without any word, the more certain his commanders will be that Custer and his men met with disaster, and the more they will thirst for revenge against the Lakota and the Cheyenne. They may not wait until late spring or summer. They may decide to hunt you down during the Moon of Strong Cold."

"We would be at our weakest then," Sitting Bull said. "They could come at a camp with a force and kill the horses, drive the people into the cold. They would not even have to kill us themselves. The winter and the cold and the loss of our food and shelter and horses would take care of that."

Touch-the-Clouds was silent, but Lemuel could see that he was already turning things over in his mind, that his words and those of Sitting Bull had found their mark.

"You speak the truth," Touch-the-Clouds said at last. "We must strike again, and quickly, so that they will be afraid to come after us. We must show them our strength and their weakness." He looked at Sitting Bull. "This time, perhaps we can fight as we have in the past—draw them out into an ambush, strike and then disappear." He glanced at Lemuel. "I may need to send you among the Wasichu again."

Lemuel said nothing.

"There is the chief you know, the man called Clarke," Touch-the-Clouds continued in English. "You can find out what the Wasichu are thinking from him, and you can tell him things I would like for him to believe."

"I will advise you," Lemuel replied, "and I will do my best to see that you get what you want as quickly as possible, but I won't betray an old friend, and that's what you're asking me to do." He glimpsed a spark of anger in the other man's eyes, but Touch-the-Clouds was keeping his rage inside himself.

"I have advised you to strike," Lemuel continued, "to secure this victory with another. But fighting and winning will not be enough to get what you want. You will also have to know when it is time to stop fighting, to offer mercy and a treaty to an enemy who surrenders to you."

Sitting Bull said, "Speak in Lakota."

"We must meet with the other chiefs," Touch-the-Clouds said, "and decide where to strike first. That is what the Orphan was telling me. I think he has told me as much as he can. If I need any more advice from a man who knows the Wasichu, Yellow Hair Rubalev can give it to me."

Lemuel thought of Rubalev dancing with the scalp he had taken. He would not let any scruples influence his advice to the Lakota chiefs.

Touch-the-Clouds motioned to Katia. "You have told me what I needed to know," he told her. "Leave us now."

Katia slept restlessly. The others in the tepee were asleep, the chief with his wife, their two children near the entrance, and the woman Calamity Jane Cannary next to the fire. Sitting Bull had seen some of the truth of her vision, but not all of it. Even without being able to grasp all of what the vision meant herself, she knew that some of its meaning had escaped the great chief.

The battle she had seen in her vision could not happen, yet she felt that it was as real as anything that had come to pass in this world. The dead soldiers could not have been singing around their campfires on the Mountain Goat, and still she knew that what she had seen there was yet another truth.

At last she slipped quietly from under her blanket and went outside. The camping circle was quiet, the only sound that of a horse nickering, and then she saw a man walking toward her.

"My husband," she whispered as Touch-the-Clouds came up to her.

"I leave tomorrow," he said, "and every fighting man in this camp will ride with me."

She had expected that. She did not ask him where they intended to fight, or how. "I will pray for you," she said.

"I have something else to tell you," he went on. "You are free to leave me after I return."

"Again," she said.

"Yes. I do not need you as a wife, and you are not content as my wife, and you are useless as a wife. But I will not drive you away. Once again I am trying to save you from being shamed."

"And where am I to go?" she asked. "Who will look out for me? Grisha?" She wondered if her former guardian would want to keep her with him.

"No," Touch-the-Clouds replied. "I do not need you to tie Yellow Hair Rubalev more closely to me. I was thinking of Rowland, the Orphan. Surely you can see that he cares for you."

Perhaps Rowland did. Maybe that was why he had gone with her to the Greasy Grass River. If it was so, she should have seen it for herself.

"Yes, he would accept you as a wife, and both of you have glimpsed visions I have not. You also know how to live in the Wasichu world. It is right for you to be together."

It is useful to you, she thought, to have us together, that's what you are thinking. She kept her head down, not speaking until he finally stood up and walked away.

THIRTEEN

The Lakota and their allies had decided to make Fort Fetterman their first target. They would fight in the way White Eagle preferred to fight, in a way that Crazy Horse had used before with success: ride to the walls of the fort, draw the Blue Coats outside, lead them to where great numbers of warriors would be waiting to strike at them. Crazy Horse had seen that this was what they would have to do, and there would also be a chance for some glory and for counting coup. White Eagle could be pleased at the victory the Lakota had won for themselves in the Black Hills while still wishing that there had been more glory in it.

A vision had shown Crazy Horse how they would have to fight this time: draw the Blue Coats out, strike at their flanks where they were weakest, dart at them, and run away. The Blue Coats liked to fight in skirmish lines, from trenches, or from behind their walls and earthworks, and they could not be allowed to fight that way. Whenever Crazy Horse had a vision before a fight, he was protected from the enemy's weapons; no Wasichu bullets would be able to harm him.

Crazy Horse would lead one band of men to Fort Fetterman, while a smaller group went southeast of the fort to cut down the white man's talking wires. Touch-the-Clouds did not want the Wasichu to warn others of what was happening at Fort Fetterman during the attack, and draw other men into the fight.

White Eagle had no war bonnet, but he had white eagle feathers with which to decorate himself and strong war medicine in his pouch and his medicine pipe bundle. He tied the white eagle feathers to his long hair; with the medicine in his pouch, which held stones and some yellow nuggets from the Black Hills, was a piece of papery bark with inked symbols. The bit of bark was from one of the rocket-arrows used during the battle at the Mountain Goat, and it would, he hoped, protect him from Wasichu bullets. White Eagle painted rocket-arrows on his face and arms with blue and yellow clay; he would ride into battle wearing only his breechcloth and leggings. He had wanted to wear the blue jacket he had taken from a dead soldier, but Touch-the-Clouds had ordered all the men to leave all their trophies of battle with their wives and families. He did not want any of the Blue Coats at Fort Fetterman to wonder how they had found them.

Crazy Horse had prepared for battle as he always did, by painting his body with the white spots of hailstones and marking his face with a lightning bolt. This was to make himself look like the warrior he had seen in the vision sent to him when he was a boy, a warrior who rode on a horse that danced and changed colors in the vision that had given Crazy Horse his name. Crazy Horse tied a pebble behind one ear and wore a red-backed hawk in his hair, as the warrior in his vision had done. Some men, during the fight with Custer and his Blue Coats, claimed to have seen the hawk come to life on Crazy Horse's head as he galloped in a circle in front of one group of soldiers, firing at them with his Winchester and daring the Wasichu to kill him.

Crazy Horse's medicine would protect him from harm, whatever he did, but he did not want the men to circle any Blue Coats this time, taunting them and daring them to shoot at their attackers. Crazy Horse had another way of fighting, a way that he had used before and had taught to Touch-the-Clouds. They would attack and retreat in waves. If the Blue Coat chiefs sent more men out after them, the warriors would strike and then scatter in retreat, drawing the Blue Coats after them in smaller groups before striking again at their enemy with more men from a different direction.

Crazy Horse did not tell the men this himself. He had left that to Touch-the-Clouds, but all the men knew that Crazy Horse had come up with the plan for this battle. Indeed, White Eagle admitted to himself, he would have followed Crazy Horse into battle even if Touch-the-Clouds were not their war chief and the head of all the chiefs. Crazy Horse deserved his loyalty. Crazy Horse was a leader who could hold the men together and use them against the enemy. Crazy Horse was a man who had been touched by the spirits.

Crazy Horse had always been a man who rarely spoke, who was always wandering off from his camp to have his visions, who would often stare at even an old comrade as if he had never seen him before, but all of that was only a sign of how strong his medicine was. Crazy Horse lived in the world behind this one, the true world. Touch-the-Clouds might glimpse what was in the world of spirits and visions, but Crazy Horse would disappear into that world. There were times when White Eagle would look at the tall, imposing form of Touch-the-Clouds standing with the small and slight Crazy Horse and wonder which of the two chiefs was the greater man, the chief who moved into the true world easily or the one who only glimpsed that world.

He had been wondering about that when several of the chiefs had gathered for war talks, knowing that they would have to fight again before the onset of winter. White Eagle had been at the war council fire with his father Soaring Eagle, who had scowled when Sitting Bull told them about the vision that had convinced Touch-the-Clouds that they would have to fight. That vision had come to Graceful Swan, the second wife of Touch-the-Clouds, but Sitting Bull had been a part of her vision, and he had told them that if they did not fight, their victory in the Black Hills might be fleeting. A few of the men had been grumbling about women and visions and what the childless wife of Touch-the-Clouds could possibly know about war, but all of them had stopped their muttering when Sitting Bull called her vision a true one.

There the war council, except for more talk about how they would attack Fort Fetterman, might have ended, but then Crazy

Horse made a sign with one hand. All the men suddenly fell silent, seeing that he wanted to speak.

Crazy Horse said, "The spirits have spoken to me as well as to Sitting Bull. I saw myself being dragged into an iron cage of the Wasichu, with bars on its opening and cold metal sides. I ran from the cage and was struck down. Touch-the-Clouds was holding me as I died." He looked around at the other men with his strange pale eyes. "And then I saw another vision, of myself as an old man with many horses. I sat in front of my tepee and looked out over a land filled with buffalo and with no sign of talking wires and no trails for the Wasichu Iron Horse."

"Which was the true vision?" one of the younger men asked.

"I cannot say," Crazy Horse replied. "In each of them, I felt that I was in the real world. In each of them, I felt that I was seeing truth, but they cannot both be true visions. And there is this—when I sat by my tepee as an old man, I saw Wasichu, and also Wasichu Sapa, hunting the buffalo with our people."

Sitting Bull looked at Crazy Horse with his dark narrowed eyes. White Eagle could not tell what the Hunkpapa chief was thinking.

"Perhaps this means we will have peace with the Wasichu in time," Soaring Eagle murmured.

Sitting Bull glanced toward White Eagle and his father and said, "Perhaps this means that the Wasichu will take all of our lands and kill all the buffalo."

Crazy Horse lifted his war pipe. "I will know what the vision means," he said, "when this battle is over."

Fort Fetterman stood along a sharp bend in the North Platte River that offered the fort protection on its northern and eastern sides. White Eagle, along with most of the men, believed that the fort should have been abandoned by the Blue Coats some time ago. The fort was not far from the route the Wasichu called the Bozeman Trail, along which wagon trains bound for California and expeditions of miners heading west had moved. The Wasichu had promised to close the trail, and had abandoned other forts along the route, but had remained in this one.

That could mean only one thing. The Wasichu wanted to hold Fort Fetterman until the trail was again open and more whites moving along it had to be protected by the Blue Coats. That would violate their treaty with the Lakota and Cheyenne, but the Wasichu had already broken those promises by coming into the Black Hills.

In a way, White Eagle thought, it was just as well that the Wasichu had come into Paha Sapa. He had known that the whites would break their promises sooner or later, so it was good that they had done it in a way that had given the Lakota an excuse to attack them and win a victory. Now they would be able to force the Wasichu to keep their promises.

White Eagle had ridden ahead with three other scouts. Riding south, they sighted the walls of the fort at dusk. Other men would already be cutting the talking wires so that the Blue Coats could send no signals out to other places, and a war party was waiting along the Platte to the south, lest any soldiers try to flee the fort by boat. A craft heading downriver might escape the bullets of warriors, but it would not get past the rocket-arrows of Victorious Spirit and Glorious Spirit.

More warriors arrived after dark. Along with White Eagle and the other scouts, they camped a few miles to the west of Fort Fetterman. The men painted themselves some more and went through rituals in preparation for battle, smoking pipes and singing sacred songs and talking of their dreams.

In the morning, a small band led by Crazy Horse rode up to the fort's entrance. White Eagle was among them. Several Blue Coats were standing near the top of the wall. White Eagle lifted a hand and shouted to them, "I want to talk to your chief."

"You speak English?" one of the troopers shouted back.

It was a foolish question; had he not spoken to the man in Wasichu words? "I want to talk to your chief," White Eagle repeated.

"About what?"

"If you surrender this fort now," White Eagle said, "and ride away from it, we will not attack you. If you stay here, we will show no mercy—all of you will die."

White Eagle waited; his legs tightened around his horse. They would not surrender; he knew that. Crazy Horse knew it, and so did Touch-the-Clouds. They would have to prove that they meant what they said, and then the next band of Blue Coats they rode against would surrender and retreat without fighting.

They waited. Someone from inside the fort shouted up at the men on the wall, and then suddenly the Blue Coats were aiming their rifles at Crazy Horse and his men.

White Eagle flattened himself against his horse. Crazy Horse called out, "It is a good day to fight and a good day to die," and White Eagle took aim with his Winchester over his mount's head.

One of the Blue Coats toppled forward, caught by a Lakota bullet. Another staggered backward, clutching at his shoulder. By then, Crazy Horse was already galloping west along the river. Soon all of the warriors were riding after him. White Eagle could not tell if any of them had been wounded by a Blue Coat. Perhaps not; these Blue Coats, like the ones with Long Hair Custer, might be armed only with Springfields. The Lakota, thanks to Yellow Hair Rubalev, the gold he had been given, and the rifles and weaponmakers he had bought, had better firesticks than the soldiers.

White Eagle rode after the other warriors, urging his horse into a gallop, then glanced back over his shoulder. The walls of the fort were hidden around the river bend, and then a band of Blue Coats rounded the turn. White Eagle urged his horse on, toward the hills up ahead, where the rest of the warriors were waiting.

They dispatched the Blue Coats quickly, fighting the last of them with knives and clubs. As they had expected, another larger band of Blue Coats followed the first. The Lakota struck at them, fell back, separated into smaller bands to draw the enemy after them, then came together again to worry the flanks of the Blue Coats. The fighting was soon hand-to-hand; there were many chances to strike at the enemy and count coup. White Eagle, even in the midst of the fighting, knew that Crazy Horse and the men would sing of this battle for many days.

That night, Crazy Horse left most of his men to their kill songs and their tales of battle and went back to the fort with White Eagle and a few of the younger men. There they kept watch, knowing there was a chance that the men inside might try to flee downriver, toward Fort Laramie, but no Blue Coats left the fort. In the morning, they rode near the walls, trying to lure more Blue Coats outside. The wooden wall did not open.

"Their chief must be thinking hard now," Crazy Horse said. "He knows that if he comes after us, he will only lose more men, so he will try to wait us out." What they would have to do now was obvious, although there would be less glory for them. Crazy Horse sent two of the men downriver, with orders to return with the warriors waiting on the western side with the rocket-arrows.

The weapons made by Glorious Spirit and Victorious Spirit brought down part of the wall around Fort Fetterman and made small craters in the ground. The men inside held out for two days before holding up a white banner on a pole. White Eagle sat on his mount next to Crazy Horse as the Blue Coats filed out to surrender. Their chief, the man with an eagle on each of his shoulders, had brought only twenty men with him.

"Touch-the-Clouds said that we were to kill them all," White Eagle said, "if they did not leave their fort in the beginning." From what he had seen so far, the Lakota had lost ten men, possibly more, and others were injured. He was in no mood to show the Wasichu any mercy.

Crazy Horse shrugged. "They are leaving their fort now. They aren't going to fight us anymore." White Eagle knew by those words that Crazy Horse would let Touch-the-Clouds decide the fate of these men. "You speak their words, White Eagle," he went on. "Ask them some questions. Ask them why there were not more of them here inside their fort."

* * *

"It was Soaring Eagle come to me," Virgil Warrick said as he rode at Lemuel's side, "with that Laforte. Told me that if the soldiers saw me and some other darkies outside the fort with the Lakota, some of them might desert and come over to us."

That had been Rubalev's idea, and Denis Laforte's. Lemuel had not known that they had discussed the matter with Virgil.

"Said we might be mighty convincing," Virgil went on, "if'n the men who used to be soldiers put on their uniforms, wore 'em when we rode to the fort."

"What did you tell them?" Lemuel asked.

"Said we might just get the soldiers inside the fort angry instead of scared. Said they might just fight even harder against deserters. Said a lot of darkies might start thinkin' of changin' sides again if they had to watch what was happenin' to the troopers—I mean, some of 'em fought with Blue Coats once."

Lemuel's mouth twisted. "That's exactly what I told Rubalev."

"Not that I'd run away now," Virgil said. "Too late for that."

"Do you sometimes wish you hadn't come to Indian territory?" Lemuel asked.

"No, suh. I ain't sorry about that." But the black man sounded as though he had some regrets.

The Platte was low, the smell of autumn in the air. From behind the hill along the next bend in the river, a plume of pale smoke rose toward the sky. Lemuel and Virgil rounded the bend and spotted a small encampment of Lakota wickiups and shelters downriver.

White Eagle was among a group of men sitting around a fire, wearing a blue coat he had probably taken from a dead soldier. Lemuel dismounted as White Eagle slowly got to his feet.

"I greet you," White Eagle said in Lakota.

Lemuel nodded at him. "Maybe you can tell me why Touch-the-Clouds wants me here," he replied in English.

"To talk to the Blue Coats who surrendered to us," the Lakota replied. "To find out why there were not so many men inside their fort."

"Not many?"

"Few," White Eagle muttered, "not as many as we thought to be inside. I counted."

"You can talk to them almost as well as I can," Lemuel said.

"I talked." White Eagle frowned. "Their chief said that men were taken from him. He said after that the women left here and the children left with them to go to other forts. He said more men will be taken away and will go to other places. Touch-the-Clouds wants to know what this means."

"Where were these soldiers ordered to go?" Lemuel asked.

"Some back East, some to other places. I ask him to tell more, and he grows silent."

"Did you torture him?" Lemuel asked.

"No," White Eagle said. "Touch-the-Clouds did not want that."

Lemuel sighed, relieved. "I'll talk to him," he said, and motioned to Virgil to follow.

White Eagle led them toward two tents made of white cloth, army tents. The flaps of one of the tents were tied open. Inside, Lemuel could just make out the shadowy shapes of three men.

"Colonel Green," White Eagle called out. One of the men stood up and came to the opening. "Here is a man who will talk to you."

The officer stooped to come out of the tent. He was a tall man, as tall as White Eagle, almost as tall as Touch-the-Clouds. His uniform was covered with dust, his blue jacket torn at the shoulder seams. His brown beard was flecked with gray, his face set in a scowl.

"Told you before," the officer said, "that I have nothing to say." His eyes narrowed as he gazed at Lemuel and Virgil. "So they want me to talk to you. Don't know why I should want to talk to a couple of deserters." He cleared his throat and spat, just missing the toe of Lemuel's right boot.

"I'm not a deserter," Lemuel said, "and neither is the Negro. I fought during the War Between the States, and was mustered out after that. I lived in St. Louis for a time—that's where I met this man. When I left St. Louis, he came with me."

"To Indian territory," Colonel Green said. "Why?"

"I was to ask you the questions," Lemuel said.

The other man stared at him for a long time. At last Lemuel turned to White Eagle. "Leave us alone," he said in Lakota. "Get the others away from this tent. He may answer my questions then."

White Eagle motioned to the warriors sitting near the tent, then led them away. Virgil looked at Lemuel quizzically, his brow furrowed. "Go," Lemuel murmured. The black man wandered off toward the river.

"Can't see," Green said, "that there's anything I can tell you that'd do you any good—or do me any good, for that matter."

"I can help you," Lemuel said. "I'm not a deserter. I'm with these Indians because I was asked to find out more about what they might be doing." He took a breath, knowing what he would have to say. "Jeremiah Clarke—Colonel Jeremiah Clarke—asked me to learn what I could and report back to him. I fought with him during the war."

Green plucked at his beard. Lemuel could not tell whether the man believed him or not. "Come on inside," Green said.

Lemuel entered the tent. Green followed him, leaving the flap up to let in the light. The two men inside sat on blankets; he saw from the bars on the shoulders of their jackets that they were both lieutenants.

Green gestured at a blanket. "Have a seat," he said.

"I'll sit by the opening," Lemuel said, "where I can be seen."

"There's three of us and one of you. I think we could get our hands on that six-shooter of yours before those Indians could get here to help you. Might even pick one or two of them off."

"That wouldn't do you any good at all."

"I know." Green sighed. "These redskins—they don't fight like redskins. They don't fight the way they should. I've been thinking of that ever since we surrendered. Never thought I'd see something like those shooting rockets used by Indians. I have to wonder how they got them—they wouldn't have come up with that idea by themselves."

Lemuel said nothing as he sat down. He was here to find out what he could, not to give anything away. He glanced outside and saw that White Eagle and another man were watching the tent from a distance, rifles in their hands.

"The Indians who fought you expected to be fighting more men," Lemuel said.

Green sat down across from him. The other two men did not speak.

"The Lakota chiefs want to know why there weren't more men at Fort Fetterman," Lemuel continued. Already he was trying to figure out how he could help these men. Touch-the-Clouds could not let them go as long as the Lakota were fighting without losing the element of surprise; Green would surely report to his superiors about the new tactics and weapons the Indians had used against him. The best Lemuel could do was to try to convince Touch-the-Clouds to keep them as captives. It would not work, he told himself. Touch-the-Clouds would not waste food on captives, or keep men near them to guard them.

"You told one of the warriors here," Lemuel said, "that soldiers were taken from your command and sent to other posts."

"You must be talking about the one who knows English," Green said. "That redskin asked me why there weren't more men here. I told him they'd been posted somewhere else. Can't see as those Indians need to know anything more than that."

"Why were more men ordered away from here?" Lemuel asked.

"I don't see why I should tell you anything to pass along to those savages."

"They don't want to fight," Lemuel said. "If you had given up Fort Fetterman when they first arrived, they would have let you go. They don't want any more battles. All they want is a promise that they'll be left at peace in the lands given to them by treaty."

"And what if they don't get that kind of promise?"

"Then they will keep on fighting until they get it."

Green said, "They can't win."

"They can do a lot of damage, kill a lot of soldiers and settlers. If they don't get what they want, they'll have to keep fighting. They'll have no choice. They'd rather die fighting than live scratching out a living on a reservation."

Green glanced back at the two men sitting in the back of the tent.

Lemuel could not see much of their faces in the shadows, but they looked young, hardly more than boys. One of them had a wispy mustache, the kind of mustache a very young man might try to grow.

"Whatever we say," the young man without a mustache said, "they're going to kill us anyway, aren't they." There was an Irish lilt in his voice. Lemuel suddenly felt sorry for him, coming all the way across the ocean only to end up here.

"That depends on what you tell me," Lemuel said. "I can help you. Give me something to tell the Lakota chiefs that will convince them to let you go."

"Tell him," the other lieutenant muttered, "tell him we aren't the only fort that had men ordered away. If they don't know that already, they'll find out the next time another scout deserts and goes back to their side."

Green looked angry for a moment, and then his face sagged. "Sheridan's been ordered to pull men out," he said softly, "and send them south. Johnny Reb's getting rebellious again. There was some fighting in Florida, some in Mississippi. Not much, but can't tell how far it might go. Heard tell that they might even have to set up some defenses around Washington again. There won't be all that many soldiers posted along the frontier this winter."

Something leaped inside Lemuel. This was what the Lakota needed, an insurrection and rebellion that would force the government and the army to remove soldiers from these forts and station them elsewhere. It was also, he realized, a way to save the lives of Green and his men. Killing them was useless if Touch-the-Clouds could get what he wanted without more fighting. But he also felt sorrow and weariness at the news; perhaps he had fought in a war that would only have to be fought again.

"It's good you told me this," Lemuel said. "It means that both the United States and the Lakota can have a truce."

"A truce?" The young man with the mustache was speaking. "Seems to me they'd have more reason to attack if they know they won't be facing as many men."

"You're wrong," Lemuel said. "It means they can come to a truce and then prepare for the winter. There's no need for more fighting as long as the truce is kept." But again he was wondering if a lasting peace was what Touch-the-Clouds truly wanted.

"And what about us?" the Irishman asked.

"I will speak to the chiefs. I promise to do what I can to free you. I'll tell them that they can show their good faith by letting you go."

Green's mouth twisted. "Good faith," he muttered. "May the good Lord preserve us. I don't expect those savages to show us anything like that."

Lemuel found Touch-the-Clouds with a group of men sorting through jackets, sabers, rifles, and personal belongings that had belonged to the dead defenders of Fort Fetterman. They would leave most of the loot for the women who were trailing the warriors to sort through while the men rode on to Fort Laramie.

"I have something to tell you," Lemuel said to Touch-the-Clouds in English.

"Say it."

"Perhaps we can walk by the river," Lemuel muttered.

Touch-the-Clouds stood up and handed the saber he was holding to another man. The blue jacket of a captain was draped over his shoulders, and a rosary hung around his neck with other beads and ornaments. "Did the Blue Coats answer your questions?"

"Yes." Lemuel jerked his head toward the river. He wanted to speak to the Lakota chief alone, because he did not know how Touch-the-Clouds would react to what he was told. Better for him to show his anger only to Lemuel and then have time to compose himself before he held council with the other chiefs.

They left the other men and walked toward the Platte. "What did their chief tell you?" Touch-the-Clouds asked in Lakota.

"That the chiefs in Washington are withdrawing soldiers from the west and sending them south, that they may need more men to defend Washington. It means that they won't have as many here to fight you. You can have a treaty and be safe for the winter—the

Wasichu will have to keep it, at least for a while. Maybe for a long time, if another war starts." Lemuel felt a pang of sorrow as he considered that prospect.

"Then we have a better chance," Touch-the-Clouds said, "of taking Fort Laramie."

"You are still going to attack there?" Lemuel asked.

"Yes, and we will have to do it soon, before the end of the Drying Grass Moon."

"But you don't need to strike at Laramie now," Lemuel said. "Even with fewer soldiers there, you could lose many men trying to take it. My friend, I ask you to heed my words. Send a messenger to Fort Laramie under a flag of truce with this message—that you are willing to stop fighting. Offer to live at peace with the Wasichu as long as the Lakota and the Cheyenne and all of the people of the Plains are left the territories they were promised by treaty. Then hand over your captives, put your mark on the white man's talking paper, and ride with your men to your winter camps. The Blue Coats will not have the soldiers to come after you. They will need many of the men who might have come as settlers to these territories to serve in their armies if things get worse in the South."

Touch-the-Clouds halted on the bluff overlooking the river. The Platte was low; some of the trees had begun to shed their leaves.

"I think there's a good chance things will get worse for the Wasichu," Lemuel continued. "The English in Canada, the Grandmother Victoria's people, may see a chance to reclaim some of the land that was once theirs. If they do, the United States may have to fight in both the north and the south."

The Lakota chief was silent.

"You don't have to risk men trying to take Fort Laramie."

"My men are hungry for more battle honors. I have not given them enough." Touch-the-Clouds turned to face him, and Lemuel saw the fury in his face. "They want to count coup, they want their share of glory. We have our peace with the Kiowa and the Comanche and the Arikara and Crow, and with others we once fought. Once, we stole their horses and increased our wealth, we counted coup on their bodies. Now they are our allies, so the young men must win their honors against the Wasichu."

Touch-the-Clouds was admitting that he might not be able to hold his warriors back. "You are their chief," Lemuel said. "They will listen to you if you tell them the fighting is over for now. You would have to stop fighting now anyway, to prepare for the winter."

"After another victory."

"You will only lose men in a battle you don't have to fight."

Touch-the-Clouds took a step toward him, then halted. Lemuel kept his gaze fixed on the other man. "You did not want me to attack Long Hair Custer and his men," the Lakota man said. "You thought we could not win."

"I thought that, even if you won, your victory could be turned into a defeat. If soldiers weren't being ordered away from the forts to other places now, if the Departments of the Platte and Dakota didn't have other things to worry about, they would be already sending more cavalrymen after Custer. They have to be wondering why nothing has been heard from him. They must already have scouts following his trail in order to find out. There will be many who will want revenge for what happened to him."

Touch-the-Clouds was glowering at him. "Long Hair broke the treaty when he came into Paha Sapa."

"That is true."

"Exactly what do you advise, Orphan from the East?"

"I told you before—ask for peace. The Blue Coats won't have enough men to send any against your people and your allies this winter. If you are lucky, the trouble among the Wasichu will keep them busy for some time. You will be able to secure your territory and build up your strength with new alliances. If another battle comes later, you will be more ready to fight it."

"And the Blue Coats who surrendered to us?"

"Let them go after you have treated with the Wasichu."

"They were promised death if they did not surrender in the beginning."

"They gave themselves up in the end."

Touch-the-Clouds moved to the edge of the bluff and stared down at the river. "There is something to what you have told me," he said at last. "I will have to take counsel with the other chiefs."

"They will listen to you," Lemuel said. "They will be ready to stop fighting this season."

"And do you have any more advice?" Touch-the-Clouds asked, with a sharper edge to his voice.

"No, except that I am willing to be one of the men you send to Fort Laramie."

"I will consider what you have told me," the Lakota said, and Lemuel knew then that Touch-the-Clouds would accept his advice. "We will have to make graves for the dead, and put them under the ground as the Wasichu do. We will have to keep their talking papers and their personal medicine and holy things and give those things to the Wasichu who come to treat with us. I will tell them that their comrades refused to surrender and chose to fight us, but that we honored them in death. I will not have the Wasichu see me as a savage, an animal."

"Good," Lemuel said.

"But I won't have you go to Fort Laramie. I will send you north with Glorious Spirit and Victorious Spirit, since we won't need their rocket-arrows now. I think perhaps it would be well for you and the two brothers to pass the winter in the East, among the Wasichu. You can find out more about the Wasichu troubles for me, and the brothers can find other men of their kind to make more rocket-arrows and weapons for us."

Touch-the-Clouds turned away from the river. "You will leave tomorrow," he finished, and then walked back to his men.

The two Chinese men had learned to ride horses during their time among the Lakota, but had remained poor riders. Their uneasiness in the saddle and the necessity to haul what was left of their rocket-arrows in pony drags behind them made for a slow ride. Not, Lemuel told himself, that it mattered, since Touch-the-Clouds did not want them to ride too far, lest their weapons be needed again. They were to wait two days' ride up the Platte for a message about the results of the talks with the Wasichu.

Virgil Warrick rode at Lemuel's side. The black man had seemed relieved after being told that he could leave with Lemuel and the two brothers. Obviously Touch-the-Clouds did not want any negotiators to see that he had close comrades who were not Indians.

Virgil glanced back at the Chen brothers, then said, "I got a bad feeling about all this."

"About what?" Lemuel asked.

"Everything. See, here's how it is. I got to hope that things gets bad enough that more soldiers get sent south instead of west. That way, I'm safe. But if the South makes more trouble, it means more trouble for other darkies. Things could get a lot harder for them."

Lemuel could not deny that. He had spoken to Colonel Green before riding out, to tell him that he and his men would soon be free. Green had chuckled at that. "Free," he said, "we'll be free, all right, free to get orders to go fighting Rebs or go after niggers acting up." Green did not know very much of what was going on in the East, but the colonel had learned that some black men in the South had taken up arms, presumably to defend themselves. They would be convenient scapegoats for both the North and the South, hated in the North by men desperate for work who saw free Negroes as a threat, and in the South by those who wanted to return them to their former state as slaves. All that turmoil would serve the purposes of Touch-the-Clouds and his people, but it wouldn't help the blacks.

Behind him, Lemuel heard one of the Chen brothers mutter a few words in his own language. He looked back. "Stop now," the Chinese man said, kicking the sides of his horse with his heels. "We stop now." Lemuel still could not tell whether Glorious Spirit or Victorious Spirit was the speaker.

"Why?" Lemuel asked.

"Backside much hurt." The man mumbled something else and then dismounted awkwardly from his horse. Lemuel did not feel like arguing with a man valued so highly by Touch-the-Clouds. The mystery was why the two brothers had decided to throw in their lot with the Lakota.

Glorious Spirit and Victorious Spirit went through a series of stretches and bends, extending their arms and flexing their legs, then sat down near the pony drags. The horses nibbled at the grass. One of the Chen brothers opened his pack and took out a piece of dried meat.

"Ain't noontime yet," Virgil said to the Chinese man.

"Hungry now." The man gnawed at the meat. "Say we go to town," he continued. "Tall chief tell us that. He give us plenty gold for that." Maybe their decision to serve the Lakota was not so mysterious after all.

Even after finishing their food, the brothers did not seem anxious to leave. Lemuel unhitched the horses from the drags and led them down the steep slope to the river to drink. By the time he had rejoined the others, it was noontime and a wind was picking up.

Virgil was the first to spot the rider trotting toward them over the flatter land to the north. "Someone's coming," he said. "Ain't no Indian, neither."

The rider was Rubalev. His yellow hair streamed down from under his hat. He was alone, moving at a trot. He had ridden with the Lakota who were to attack Fort Fetterman, but like Lemuel and the others who were not Plains Indians, had been told to keep to the rear.

Lemuel started to walk in Rubalev's direction. Rubalev's horse slowed; when the blond man was closer, he lifted a hand in greeting. Lemuel did not move. Rubalev rode up to him, reined in his horse, and stared down at him from the saddle.

"You might look happier, Rowland," Rubalev said at last. "I am told that we have won another victory."

"Why are you here?" Lemuel managed to say.

"Touch-the-Clouds sent for me. He sent a rider to me with a message two days ago."

Touch-the-Clouds had asked Lemuel for advice and would consult with the other chiefs. There was no reason for him not to seek counsel from Rubalev as well. Perhaps the Alaskan man had regained the Lakota chief's confidence. Lemuel recalled how Rubalev had looked, dancing with the scalp of the Seventh's dead scout.

"The Lakota are going to seek a peace now," Lemuel said. "Touch-the-Clouds doesn't have to strike at another fort, or raid any settlements, because he can probably have the treaty he wants. The commanding officer at Fort Fetterman told me that the army is withdrawing men from the western forts and sending them south. He sounded as though he expects things to get worse for Washington."

"I was hoping for such events." Rubalev lifted a brow and regarded Lemuel for a moment. "I am of course sorry that they are also likely to cause more misery to some whom I once called friends." He dismounted and fed his horse a few oats from his saddlebags. He was riding a black horse, one of the Seventh's horses, not an Indian pony. The horse already looked ill-fed; Lemuel wondered how long the animal would last without grain, grazing on grass. Virgil watched Rubalev from a few paces away, saying nothing. The Chen brothers had finished eating and were playing some sort of game with dice.

Rubalev remounted his horse. "I must ride on," he said. He lashed his horse's neck lightly with his reins and rode away.

By evening, Lemuel estimated that they had traveled little more than twenty miles from Fort Fetterman. The Chen brothers had insisted on stopping to rest at frequent intervals, complaining first of sore backsides and aching muscles, and then about having to drag the rocket-arrows along in pony drags instead of in a wagon.

"Magic gunpowder and black and white powder can settle," one of the Chinese explained to him. "Maybe settle in tube so can no more make big noise. Cannot move rocket-arrows fast or get them all stirred up and then—boom! Blow us all to hell!"

There was, Lemuel told himself, no purpose in urging the two brothers along at a faster pace. It would be days, perhaps longer, before anyone arrived at Fort Fetterman to negotiate with Touch-the-Clouds and the other chiefs.

The four of them sat around the fire for a while after securing the horses and eating a supper of dried buffalo meat, hardtack, and coffee. The coffee, brewed by Virgil, had been taken, along with the hardtack, from the captured supplies at Fort Fetterman. The Chen brothers turned in first, crawling under their makeshift shelters of

tree limbs and canvas. Virgil offered to take the first watch. The fire
would keep animals away, but there was a chance, however slight,
that any wanderers who might be hunting or traveling along the
Platte would try to steal their horses.

Lemuel slept, dreaming that he was back in Tonawanda, trying
to explain who he was to the people he had known as a child. One
of the men kept saying that he could not be who he was, that he
had seen him with enemies of the Senecas, that he no longer
belonged among his people. The man had the voice of Ely Parker.
"The men among whom you live are not your only comrades," the
voice of Donehogawa murmured to him. "Others call out to you.
Soldiers call out to you." Lemuel woke up then and was suddenly
afraid.

He lay under his blanket, waiting until the fog lifted from his
mind, then crawled out from under his shelter. Virgil, standing
guard near the tethered horses, quickly turned toward him.

"I have to go back," Lemuel said softly.

"What?" the black man whispered.

He could not tell Virgil that a dream had come to him and that
he knew it to be a warning. "I have to ride back to Fort Fetterman,
tonight."

Virgil nodded, almost as if he understood somehow. "Told you
before I got a bad feeling," the Negro said, "and I ain't feeling no
better now."

"Wait here," Lemuel said as he began to saddle a horse. "I'll ride
back to you as soon as I can."

Lemuel kept his mount moving at a trot. The sky was clear, with a
nearly full moon to help light his way along the trail. Occasionally
he slowed, to let his horse rest or to move more slowly over stony
patches of ground, but something inside him was urging him on,
telling him not to stop, to ride at a faster pace, that he might already be too late.

Too late for what? he asked himself. He had been thinking about

Rubalev throughout his ride, and suddenly regretted that he had not ridden after him immediately, that he had not followed him back to Fort Fetterman. He thought of how Rubalev had chanted his kill songs after the battle in the Black Hills.

The breezes that had whispered through the night had died by morning. It was midmorning by the time Lemuel rounded a bend and saw the damaged wooden wall of Fort Fetterman up ahead. Warriors outside the wall were still digging graves for the dead; bodies stripped of their boots and uniforms lay nearby, already bloating. At least they had not been scalped. That must have taken every bit of authority Touch-the-Clouds possessed, to keep the men from taking those prizes; or perhaps it was simply that many of the dead had short or thin hair and that their scalps were therefore not worth taking.

Lemuel was closer before he recognized one of the bodies, a man whose brown beard had flecks of gray. Colonel Green lay among the dead. He was stripped of his jacket and shirt, but still wore his blue uniform trousers with the yellow stripe; he had been left that measure of dignity. There were no signs of wounds, of torture. Green had, it seemed, been shot in the back of the head; the bullet had come out through his left jaw. Lemuel did not look closely at the bodies lying near the colonel, certain that he would see the two lieutenants with them.

Rubalev rode toward him from the fort with two Lakota men. Lemuel felt his hand moving toward his Colt, then let it fall to his side again. He should have gone after Rubalev as soon as he saw him. He could have shot him at some point along the trail and left the body there.

"What are you doing here?" Rubalev called out in English.

"You killed them," Lemuel said.

"Of course we killed them," Rubalev replied.

"I told them they would live. I said there was no reason to kill them now."

"No reason?" Rubalev's eyes widened. "It was the order of Touch-the-Clouds. He saw that we could not let them go."

"I'm sure it was his order," Lemuel said softly. "I am equally certain that you're the one who advised him to do it."

"He did not want to let them go. He had promised to kill everyone who did not surrender right away." Rubalev leaned forward in his saddle. He held his reins with his left hand; his right arm rested near his holster. The two men with him were carrying their rifles. They wanted Lemuel to know that they were ready to gun him down as easily as they had their captives. "But then he wondered what would be of more use to him, keeping his promise or showing mercy. In the end, he did both. The Blue Coats here died, as he had promised they would, but their deaths were quick. One bullet in the back of the head—that was all it took for each. It was quick, Rowland. We did not waste bullets."

"Were you the executioner?" Lemuel asked.

"Touch-the-Clouds knew what was needed. It does not matter which hand held the gun." Rubalev's mouth twisted. "The men who will treat with us must know that when Touch-the-Clouds offers surrender or death, he means to keep that promise exactly. And there is this as well. He is to send you back among the Wasichu, is he not?"

Lemuel was silent. Touch-the-Clouds might have mentioned those plans to Rubalev; perhaps it had been Rubalev's idea in the first place.

"You can go back now, find out what you can, go to your old comrade Jeremiah Clarke. He will not know that you were with the Lakota in the Black Hills who fought Custer. He will not find out that you came here to Fort Fetterman. That makes you more useful to us than if he knew those things."

"I gave that man my word." Lemuel looked at Green's shattered dead face. "I told him that I would do everything I could to free him and his men."

"And so you did." Rubalev showed his teeth. "Do you not want the Lakota to keep their lands? Or have you changed your mind?"

"I haven't changed my mind."

"You know what the enemies of the Lakota want, and what they will do to get it. Think of that whenever your anger rises at the methods we have to use against them." Rubalev rested his hands on the horn of his saddle.

Lemuel's right hand hung at his side. He found himself gazing at the other man's hands, knowing that he could now draw on Rubalev and have a good chance of hitting him in the chest with one or two bullets before Rubalev could shoot back. The thought came to him in an instant and fled from him just as quickly. The two warriors with Rubalev would surely kill him in return. Rubalev already knew that he had nothing to fear from Lemuel.

"Leave us," Rubalev said. "Go back to where I met you. Let us do what we must do to have our treaty, and then you will see that we did only what was needed, what we had to do."

He had known what he was doing when he joined himself to the Lakota cause. They had done no worse to Green and his men than soldiers had done to their people in the past. Lemuel pulled lightly at his reins, turning his horse, and then rode away.

FOURTEEN

Jane groomed the dappled horse as Virgil Warrick spoke of his plans. The black man and Lemuel Rowland had been in this camp for almost a month now, until word had reached them about the new treaty, and now Virgil was talking of leaving again.

"Got a place north of here," Virgil said. "Ain't much more than a shack, but it suits me. Enough game, and plenty of fish. I can get enough pelts to trade at a post for anything else I need."

She had imagined that Virgil lived among another band of Lakota or Cheyenne, perhaps even had an Indian wife. Now it seemed that he was living more like a trapper or a mountain man.

"Got enough to get you through the winter?" she asked.

"I can get what I need, and I don't need much."

"You live out there all by your lonesome?"

"Mostly."

Jane finished brushing the dappled horse and moved on to a gray pony. It was one way she could make herself useful, taking care of some of the horses Touch-the-Clouds had left in this camp. The chief had a lot of horses, more than any other man here. She wondered if she could make herself useful enough for him to keep her here, to let her stay alive. Better to remain with his wife Graceful Swan, who was more civilized than most of these savages, than to be Rubalev's prisoner again. Winter was coming; there was frost on the ground in the mornings now, and an iciness in the air. It was easier for a body to die in the winter, especially if she was the prisoner of a man who did not especially care whether she stayed alive or not.

"I ain't always alone," Virgil went on. "There's a camp of Blackfeet up the river—I picked up some of their lingo. But being by myself suits me a lot of the time."

The pinto tethered next to the gray nickered and tossed its head as Jane walked toward it. Virgil steadied the horse, holding its head gently, as Jane began to brush its hide. The hides of the horses were getting hairier; another sign of winter.

Jane did not ask him if he was ever sorry that he had left civilization. She knew how foolish a question that was, given how civilization treated black men. The Indians might be savages, but they treated Virgil pretty much the same as they treated anyone else.

At the edge of the camp, some of the men who had ridden here with Sitting Bull mounted their horses, ready to ride to Sitting Bull's Hunkpapa camp. She noticed that Frank Grouard was with them, dressed in leather leggings and a long buckskin coat. She had taken him for one of the savages before Graceful Swan had revealed that he had been captured in a raid some years earlier. If the swarthy black-haired half-breed Grouard was indeed a captive, he surely seemed at ease in his captivity. Sitting Bull called him Sitting With Upraised Hands and considered him almost a brother, and she had often seen him roaming the encampment with Rubalev. But Graceful Swan seemed to go out of her way to avoid Grouard, and Jane had followed her example. Any man who was too friendly with that yellow-haired devil was someone she would rather keep at a distance.

She watched as Grouard rode off with the other braves. Virgil caught her eye. "They'll be riding to meet Touch-the-Clouds and maybe sing a few more war songs together," he said, "and then they'll be off to their own camps."

"Yeah." She was grateful to know that Grouard would not be here. She wondered if he ever longed for escape.

"Calamity," Virgil said then, "ever think about going back?"

Apparently his thoughts were running along the same trail as her own.

"Going back to what?" she asked. "Anyways, if I even tried to escape, the redskins'd kill me for sure."

"After some time goes by, it won't matter to them if you go back. Won't matter much what you say to anybody then. You might even get famous, bein' the last one left alive and all."

The last one left alive. That was why she could not go back, to people who would stare at her and whisper about her and know that a skinny no-good saddle tramp and mule skinner and wagon driver was all that was left of the lost companies of the Seventh. They would never forgive her for saving her skin by living with the redskins who had murdered her comrades instead of fighting on, for staying alive when all those brave men were dead, when glorious George Armstrong Iron Butt Long Hair Son of the Morning Star Custer was dead. That she was a woman would matter as little to most of them as it always had to her. They would think even less of her for that, for going off with the men and then not fighting with them. They would believe that the Indians had used her the same way some of the enlisted men had used her after giving her a few coins and some whiskey in return.

That was another reason for remaining with the Lakota. Whiskey had got the better of her too many times. Being sober all the time had made her ashamed of some of the things she had done. Better to stay in Indian territory, where whiskey was scarce and she wouldn't be tempted.

"I ain't going back," Jane said. "I can't go back. Ain't got nobody back there anyways." Her daughter, growing up as another family's child, did not count, and she had lost Bill Hickok's love long ago.

Lemuel Rowland was outside her tepee, calling to her. Katia left her fire and went to open the flap.

"White Eagle is here," he said. "He tells me that your husband will arrive here in two days. He'll want the camp to be ready to move by then."

She could not put off what she had to do any longer. "Are you coming with us?" she asked.

"Touch-the-Clouds wants to send me east again. He wants me to be his eyes and ears among the Wasichu."

She had suspected as much. "Then he will expect me to go with you," she said quickly.

"I don't understand."

"He told me some time ago that he would send me away. He doesn't want me as his wife anymore. It is the same as what he did before, when he let me go with Grisha to St. Louis. He would have told you himself, but you might as well hear it from me. He told me that I was to go away with you when the time came."

He was frowning. Maybe she was wrong about how he felt about her; maybe he did not want to have anything to do with her. The back of her neck burned; she looked away from him.

"I won't ask anything of you," she said. "You do not have to live with me as your wife. Touch-the-Clouds dosen't care how we live together as long as we are useful to him."

"Katia," he said, "I have only the highest regard for you."

She was about to say that she could not care for him, that she felt no more for him than a bit of gratitude for the kindness he had shown, but held back.

"When my husband is here," she murmured, "I will tell him in front of White Cow Sees that I am leaving him. He will tell me that I am free to go. And then we will leave, before the winter." Perhaps he would want to send Grisha east, too, to a place near her, where she might see him occasionally. Katia suppressed that thought.

"Katia—"

"It might be best if you speak to Touch-the-Clouds alone when he returns," she said, "and then he can tell you what he expects from us." She could bear this humiliation no longer. Katia turned around and crept inside her tent and lowered the flap behind her.

"We are to go to St. Joseph first, and then to Kansas City," Graceful Swan was saying. "I don't know where we will go after that."

Jane listened, trying to take it all in. Too much had happened all at once, what with Graceful Swan deciding to leave her husband and go off with Lem Rowland. Not that Jane truly believed things had happened quite that way. Maybe a lot of redskin men didn't think it was manly to make a woman stay if she wanted to go, but Touch-the-Clouds was not the sort of man who would let his wife walk out on him just because she wanted to, especially if she was leaving with another man.

"Well, I hope you'll be content," Jane said. Graceful Swan almost seemed sorry about going. The woman was used to white ways; she could not be that unhappy at leaving the hard life of a savage's woman behind, even if Touch-the-Clouds was forcing her to go.

"I was going to say—" The Indian woman gazed at the cooking pot made from a buffalo paunch that hung over the fire. The light from the burning wood and dried buffalo chips flickered across her face. "I will ask the chief if you may come with us."

Jane stared at the flat stones around the fire, then stretched her hands toward the warmth. "I can't go," she said at last. "He won't let me go."

"I can try to convince him that you won't say anything to anybody that would endanger our people. He knows that I want safety for us as much as he does. Rowland—Lemuel might convince him. Touch-the-Clouds might listen to him."

"That don't matter." Jane drew up her knees and rested her chin on them. "I hate the chief for what he did—ain't never going to forget that. But I wouldn't say nothing now anyway about what happened to the Seventh. It ain't so much that I care that much what respectable folks would think. They never thought much of me anyway. It's what the soldiers would think, and the wagon drivers, and the people like me. They'll think I was a coward, that I did wrong just to save my skin. They'll think I should have died with the rest of them."

"They won't know anything about it if you don't tell them," Graceful Swan said. "After some time goes by, it won't matter what you say. Eventually the whites will find out what happened in the Black Hills, but it will be over, it will become something that isn't worth a battle anymore, or a war, something that's past."

"Won't never be past for me," Jane said.

"What will you do?" the other woman asked.

"Now you know God damn well what I'll do, pardon my language," Jane replied. "The chief'll keep me around for whatever work I can do, or he'll turn me over to that Rubalev again." Either way, she probably would not get through the winter, which would end any worry over what tales she might tell if she ever got away.

She got up and left the tepee. The sky was still light, but the people in the camp were getting ready for the night. She went to the horses that were tethered behind Graceful Swan's tepee.

Virgil Warrick was with the horses. She watched as he finished brushing a chestnut mare. "You got a mighty grim look on your face," he said.

"Graceful Swan's leaving the chief and going off with Lem Rowland," Jane said.

"I know," Virgil said. "Lemuel Rowland asked me if I wanted to come along, said I might be helpful. Told him it didn't sound like things were getting any easier away from here for darkies."

"Then you ain't going," Jane said.

"No, I ain't." Virgil shook his head. "You jealous, Calamity? You worrying about Lemuel Rowland and that squaw now?"

"Hell, no." She forced herself to smile. "I ain't thinking of Lem and Graceful Swan. I'm worrying about what's going to happen to me."

Virgil stepped away from the horses. "If'n you got to stay in the territory, no reason you can't come along with me."

She gaped at him. "You mean that?"

"I don't mean for anything like what you might be thinking. There's a girl with the Blackfeet. I was courting her for a while, but she wouldn't leave her camp and I wouldn't go and live there. Ain't that I mind their ways, or how they treated me, it's just that I crave my time to myself."

Jane looked down and stared at the cracked leather of her boots for a while. "So if you like being on your lonesome so much, why're you asking me to come along with you?"

"I'll still be alone," he said. "Got a feeling there'll be lots of days when we don't got that much to say to each other, and when you won't feel like talking to me. And I'm thinking it won't hurt to have somebody near by who can shoot and ride and maybe be around to head out to the Blackfeet for help if'n something happens so's I need the help."

Jane felt the beginnings of a smile forming on her face. "What makes you think the chief'll let me leave?"

"You'd be a lot farther away from other white folks at my place. You can't ride out of there so easy, especially in winter. The cold and the snow'd be enough to kill you—even the Indians know to stay put in winter." He paused. "But maybe you ain't one to share a cabin with a black man, even if he got no designs on you."

She looked up. "I was out scouting with a black man when the Seventh was attacked. His name was Isaiah Dorman, and he was my friend, and a day don't pass that I don't think about him and feel sorry that he's dead."

Virgil was silent.

"He knew the Sioux," she went on. "He lived with them, and he knew their ways, and maybe he was kind of sorry when he went back to being a scout for the army, but he did his duty once he picked his side, and he died fighting."

"Should I talk to the chief?" he asked.

"Yeah. I'll go with you, Virgil."

"I'll talk to Rowland. He can tell me what I ought to say to Touch-the-Clouds."

"You do that. I'd be obliged." She was still trying to keep a long way ahead of death, even if it mean staying in Indian territory, hiding out in the middle of nowhere, possibly never seeing a white face again. She wondered whether that meant she was a coward or just somebody who saw things the way they were and knew when to move on, the way she had with Bill Hickok and her daughter.

Lemuel Rowland and his companions arrived in St. Joseph just as winter was setting in. They came there with greenbacks taken from the pockets of dead Blue Coats to spend on food and shelter and gold to trade with men whose names had been given to them by Rubalev's companion Denis Laforte and who could be trusted not to say where they got it.

The Chen brothers disappeared for a few days among the Chinese who had settled there, then showed up again early one morning. They had not found the kind of men that they had hoped to find in St. Joseph, only former railroad workers who owned laundries or eateries. They were looking for tougher men with different skills, and planned to go west on the Union Pacific, as far as San Francisco if necessary, returning east in the spring. Rubalev had promised to be in St. Joseph by then, and would see that Glorious Spirit and Victorious Spirit returned to the Black Hills.

Lemuel saw no reason to object. If Touch-the-Clouds had not trusted the Chinese brothers, he would have kept the two men closer to his side. The gold he had given them was one of the bonds that held them, but there was another bond that was even stronger. He had seen that after spending more time with Glorious Spirit and Victorious Spirit and watching how they smiled and their eyes darted with excitement as they spoke of their beloved rocket-arrows. Among the Lakota, they could practice their arts of weapon-making and create even more powerful rocket-arrows. They would never have been allowed to do that among whites, or even in their own country.

After the brothers left, he wrote short letters to Jeremiah Clarke and to Ely Parker and posted them. To Jeremiah, he wrote that he was in St. Joseph, telling him the name of his hotel; to Donehogawa, he said only that the territories of their friends on the Plains were safe for the next few seasons. Then he began finding out more about what had been going on while he was living among the Lakota. There had been an insurrection near Vicksburg in Mississippi, followed by an attack on a group of freedmen. Thirty Negroes had been killed before the revolt was put down by Union forces. There were Rebs hiding out in Florida's Everglades, emerging to hit at Union soldiers before disappearing again into the swamps. The hoped-for railroad that would link New Orleans and Texas with California was still only a dream, and would only have been sabotaged or used by die-hard Confederates if it had been built. There was a rumor that Robert E. Lee himself, ailing and close to death, had been summoned to Washington, to meet in secret with President Colfax to find ways to put down the insurrectionists without starting another war.

Lemuel wondered if Colfax, still mired in scandal, was up to the job of handling one possible war, let alone two conflicts. The newspapers were also full of reports of growing restiveness in Canada. There was talk of conscripting more troops.

A month after Lemuel had come to St. Joseph, a letter reached him from Ely Parker. There had been a small draft riot in New York City, and it was feared that worse violence was coming. In the wake of more bank failures, the city's poorest inhabitants, among them freedmen, recent immigrants, and other wretched folk, were competing with one another for whatever work they could find. The reformers among the Republicans had the unpalatable choice of turning a blind eye to the corruption in their party and among their elected officials in Washington, or of opposing the Republican president during a time when unity was more needed than ever. Much of this Lemuel had already gathered from the newspapers.

The Union for which he had fought, the toll that he and his comrades had paid in blood and pain and death, might have been for nothing. Had he been able to believe that the Lakota and the other red peoples to the West would keep their lands and their ways, he might have felt more at peace, more willing to accept what might come. Chaos in the East would ensure the safety of the Lakota for a time, but now he saw that what was happening might only endanger the Plains more in the end. Desperate people in the cities with nothing to lose might be drawn west, regardless of the dangers they would face. Financiers losing money might look again to constructing more railroads and to the fees they could extort from people and towns that would grow ever more dependent on their rails. Standing by while the Wasichu tore at one another might not win Touch-the-Clouds the permanent peace that his people needed to preserve their buffalo herds and their lives.

Touch-the-Clouds had to know that. If he had not come to this understanding by himself, surely Rubalev had seen it by now, and would already be advising the chief. Lemuel thought of when he had last spoken to Rubalev, outside Fort Fetterman, and felt his doubts biting at him again.

Dreams were troubling Katia once more. Her face was drawn and tense in the mornings from lack of rest; Lemuel often heard her cries through the wall as he lay in his own bed.

One morning, sitting across the small table in their sitting room, she finally spoke to him about her dreams.

"I keep seeing fires," she told him, "blazing from buildings, burning along the streets. I hear people screaming and calling for help. I'm running, trying to hide, and then I see soldiers in blue coats riding after me."

"You've been reading the newspapers," he said. "That might be affecting your dreams." There had been a story about Chicago a few days ago, about how the rebuilt city was thriving after the disastrous fire of 1871. The story had only hinted at the heavy burden of debt that rebuilding Chicago had cost. "The Chicago fire, and the fighting in the Black Hills—you may be confusing all of that in your mind."

She gazed directly at him then. "No," she said, "that is not what I'm dreaming about. These dreams have the power of my earlier visions for me—I can feel it. You know what I saw at Paha Sapa. You know what kind of vision came to me at the Greasy Grass. This dream of a fire is as real to me as those visions were."

He did not reply.

"I was dreaming of another place, not Chicago," she went on. "I was seeing what might come, not what is past. Much of what I saw wasn't clear, but that much I know. And there is something else. I saw you in these dreams. You were calling out to me, and I kept trying to reach you, but I could not find my way back to you."

She stood up and left the room. Again, she had barely eaten, had only sipped at her coffee.

She was staying here with him as Katia Rowland, and he had let the hotel's proprietor believe that they were recently married. A pair of newlyweds, people of means, who were returning from a journey to the West by stagecoach and by rail; he had hinted at all of this. That he had been sleeping on the sitting room's long couch ever since arriving here was not anything the proprietor had to know.

He thought of how Katia had looked at him on the day they had left the camp of Touch-the-Clouds. There had been pain on her face, and shame. A few Lakota men had ridden with them as far as the Missouri, leaving them to make the rest of their journey by themselves by horse and then by steamboat.

Katia had not spoken at all during their ride. As the Lakota men rode away, she had turned toward him and said, "I will never go back there, and I do not want to go back. I never want to go back. I can think of my people being free on the Plains and take some joy in any freedom they might win without having to live among them myself."

"Katia—" he started to say.

"I didn't want to leave with you," she said, and there was a bitterness in her voice that he had not heard before. "But even that is better than staying there, knowing that I will catch no more dreams on the Plains."

Her words had mystified him. "Why do you say that?"

"I know it, I feel it. No more dreams will come to me in the places where my people camp. Whatever happens now, I will have to seek my visions in another place. The Lakota lands are no longer a place for them."

She had said no more than that. Without her dreams, she was useless to her people. She was probably already thinking of herself as useless to him, as a woman who could not care for him. She did not bar her door to him at night; if he went to her, he was certain that she would not resist him. The thought of going to her that way repelled him.

Maybe it was better for her to believe that she could still have her visions, even if they were no more than bad dreams, to think that she still had some purpose. Maybe that was why she insisted that her dreams of fire were true visions.

Jeremiah Clarke did not send a letter to Lemuel. A Chinese boy came to Lemuel's room and handed him a note from the colonel saying that Clarke was in the saloon downstairs and wanted to speak to him.

Jeremiah was waiting for him at the bar. His beard was grayer, and he had grown leaner except for a belly under his buckskin jacket. He looked as though he had been drinking for a while. He nodded at Lemuel and said in a low voice, "Damn long time without a word from you."

"There wasn't any way for me to get a message out to you," Lemuel replied.

"When you didn't come back, I figured that either you were dead or you'd found yourself a squaw." Jeremiah picked up his glass and bottle and moved away from the bar to a table in one corner. Lemuel followed him. There had been enough time since writing his letter to think of what to say to Colonel Clarke.

"Looks like the Sioux and their friends got themselves another treaty," Jeremiah said as he sat down. "I don't suppose you had anything to do with that." His eyes peered at Lemuel from under the brim of his hat.

"The Sioux chiefs make their decisions without consulting me," Lemuel said.

"And I don't suppose you know anything about what happened to Custer. Oh, there are some who keep holding out hope that he's just camped out somewhere, or securing the services of some more Indian scouts, or that he's suddenly going to send out news about some monumental discovery he's keeping secret for a while, or at worst that he might have been captured and his officers are trying to figure out how to rescue him." Jeremiah poured some more whiskey from the bottle and drank it down quickly. "But if something like that was going on, that Barrows from the New York *Tri-*

bune would have dispatched a story about it by now with a rider. Hell, Custer would have been sending out his own stories by now if he could."

"All I know," Lemuel said carefully, "is that there were rumors of Army soldiers being seen near the Black Hills. Some of the young men in the camp where I was staying rode out to scout around. That was the last I heard before the Sioux and the Cheyenne were riding south to strike at Fort Fetterman."

"I'd think Custer was dead," Clarke said, "excepting I don't know how those Indians could have wiped out his whole command."

Lemuel thought of Jane Cannary, the last survivor. She had gone off with Virgil Warrick. Lemuel had not asked her why, although he doubted that Virgil had any amorous interest in the woman. It was just as well that she had gone with him. Rubalev, he was certain, would have killed her as soon as he had the chance.

Jeremiah's eyes were on Lemuel again. "What made you come back?"

"With the new treaty, there was no more reason for me to stay among the Sioux. The Oglala chief called Touch-the-Clouds counts me as a friend of a kind, although I'm not sure how much he trusts me. There was no reason for me to stay, since I had found out as much as I could, and that was little enough. The Sioux didn't stop me from leaving."

"As far as I can tell, you didn't find out much of anything, even after being gone a while." Jeremiah sighed. "Not that it matters now. We couldn't fight any kind of Indian war with all that's going on now. The army's got other things to worry about. Crook's around, but I don't know what Sheridan thinks he can do."

Lemuel tensed. "General Crook's here?"

"Not here in St. Joseph, up in Omaha. They put him in command of the Department of the Platte. Nobody's talking about that much—it isn't exactly a secret, but nobody's sending out a lot of reports about it, either. Crook might have been leading his troops in action against the Sioux by now if it weren't for that treaty."

Lemuel considered that information. The Gray Wolf—that was

what the Apache in the Southwest had called General George Crook when he was going after them some years back. He would be a formidable opponent if he was ordered into action. Crook had fought Indians in winter before; Lemuel doubted that he would have been ordered to Omaha unless his superiors were considering an attack. He did not like the idea of the Gray Wolf being so close to Lakota territory.

The colonel poured himself another drink. Lemuel sat back, knowing that the liquor would make Jeremiah more talkative.

"I'll tell you this." Jeremiah's voice was low. "A lot of the men wouldn't go Indian-fighting now even if they sent us plenty of cavalry and infantry along with wagon trains of Gatling guns and Winchesters, and Sheridan and Sherman came along as our field commanders. It's one thing to be protecting miners and settlers and keeping them and the Indians apart. It's another to be keeping the rails safe for some swells back East who think of nothing except filling their own pockets. I fought for the Union. They're busy buying it up for themselves. If old Ulysses S. Grant was still around, he'd clean out that nest of vipers in Washington."

Lemuel was silent.

"What are you going to do now?" Jeremiah asked.

"Maybe go back to St. Louis," Lemuel replied, "or even back to New York. There ought to be some work for me in one place or the other."

Jeremiah leaned forward and rested his arms on the table. "Take my advice," he said. "Go west to California if you want to stay out of any battles. I heard talk that they're thinking about becoming a republic again. And Texas—" His voice trailed off.

"It's probably just talk," Lemuel said.

"Yeah, just talk. Just talk for now, anyway."

Lemuel sat back. Except for the news about General Crook, Jeremiah Clarke had told him little more than he had already gathered from newspapers and overheard conversations in this saloon, and he no longer seemed interested in any information Lemuel had about the Sioux. That in itself was good to know. It was more confirmation that the Plains were safe for now.

* * *

She had known while riding away from the camp of Touch-the-Clouds that no more visions would come to her on the Plains. There would be no more dreams to tell Touch-the-Clouds how his battles would go or how they might have gone in some other world. Perhaps he had sensed that; maybe that was why he had sent her away with Lemuel Rowland.

Then dreams had begun to come to Katia again in St. Joseph, frightening dreams of fires and people running through streets, of Blue Coats firing at Wasichu and Lakota alike. Other visions were of Blue Coats and Lakota riding through other streets, and still others showed her grassy hills black with herds of grazing buffalo. Soon the dreams were coming to her even when she was awake. At first, she would glimpse the burning buildings from the corner of her eye, or hear the cries of terrified people as if from a distance. Then they would be all around her, blotting out the walls of her room; the sounds of screams would grow louder until she could no longer hear the sounds of horses and wagons in the street below.

The visions carried the force of those that had come to her before. That could mean they carried strong medicine and were showing her a world that was as real and as true as the one in which she lived, or else that they were signs of madness.

She was living in the Wasichu world now. The white people had driven off the spirits that had once inhabited this land. Those spirits could no longer speak to her or reveal the true world behind this one to her. That had to mean that her visions were false ones, that she was indeed mad.

She could not remember the journey from St. Joseph to Kansas City, only that the cries of doomed people would come to her suddenly, without warning, drowning out the sound of the train's wheels against the track. Rowland had called for the conductor once; she had murmured something about a headache. Once she had seen flames leaping from the floors and seats of their car, and had thought that their train was ablaze before seeing that the other passengers still sat calmly in their seats. Often she had to hang on to Rowland's arm to steady herself while she closed her eyes to her visions.

"What is wrong?" he had asked her when they were in their hotel room in Kansas City. "Is it a fever?" He put his hand to her forehead.

"It's nothing."

"You are ill."

"I am seeing visions. I can't be seeing them here, I know that. They can't be true, not here."

He had not asked her anything after that.

Not long after their arrival, Rowland found them a flat in a house along a quiet street. Sometimes she glimpsed flames above the roofs of houses or the river beyond, or saw blue-coated riders riding below in the streets, but no people rushed out to fight the fires and the riders would vanish as suddenly as they had appeared. At night, she slept without dreaming.

A day came when Katia awoke and saw no flames and heard no cries of fear. She dressed and went into the sitting room, where Rowland was already awake and drinking coffee. She sat down across from him at the table.

"You look better," he said as he poured coffee into a second cup.

"I feel better." It was coming back to her now, how he had brought food to her, held her head while she drank water from a glass, and had poured heated water into a basin when she was strong enough to wash herself. He had even emptied the chamber pot under her bed on those mornings when she was too weak to empty it herself.

"I thought of fetching a doctor," he said, "but I didn't know which of them here I could trust, and I suspected your visions were troubling you. No physician would have known how to treat that." He paused. "Katia, what were you seeing?"

"More fires. Soldiers riding and shooting at Wasichu."

"Wasichu soldiers shooting other whites?" he asked.

"Yes, and Blue Coats riding with the Lakota, as if—almost as if they were riding off to fight together. None of it made any sense." She sipped some coffee. "I thought I was going mad."

"And now?"

"They are gone. My visions have left me. I hope that it is for good." Katia tilted her head, hearing a voice calling out something about a fire, and then realized that she had heard someone outside, in the street. The room was cold; she shivered.

"How long has it been since we came here?" she asked.

"Two months," he said, "nearly three. The Chen brothers are already in St. Joseph—at least they were some time ago. They may be riding back to Lakota territory by now."

"How do you know?"

"Rubalev sent a letter to me. The man he sent it to brought it to me last night. Rubalev went to St. Joseph to meet the Chinese and to see that they get back to the Plains. He has hopes that other men will be with them."

"Is that all he said?" Katia asked.

"Yes."

Perhaps Grisha would come here. She might be able to persuade him to take her with him, wherever he was going. Then she thought of how Rowland had taken care of her, and felt shame.

"Katia," Rowland continued, "there's something I must say. I had better say it now, while you look untroubled and I've summoned up enough courage to ask this of you."

She lifted her head and made herself look at him, knowing what he was about to ask.

"I want you to be my wife," he said, "and not only in name."

She said, "You want me to share your bed."

"I didn't mean that." He looked away. "I did not mean only that, Katia. I was thinking of marrying you. I can find someone to marry us here, and maybe that would make it easier for you if I came to you, if we—" He straightened. "I am not much used to expressing feelings of love for a woman."

His admission of that, and his awkwardness, touched her. Katia thought of the indifference of Touch-the-Clouds, and of Grisha's coldness, and wished that she had more feeling for Rowland.

"I must think about it," she said. "I do not know how to answer you now."

His face brightened with hope. He was happy, she saw, because she had not refused him outright. Surely he knew that, if she had nowhere else to go, she would have to accept him in the end. She suddenly felt sorry for him, and also pitied herself for being unable to love him.

Rubalev arrived in Kansas City without warning. Lemuel caught a glimpse of him outside a hotel as he climbed into a carriage. Two days passed without a word from the man, and Lemuel decided not to seek him out. Rubalev would find him.

Three days after he had seen Rubalev, the Alaskan came to his flat. Katia was better by then, able to brew some coffee and to serve it with some cold meat and bread baked in their small wood stove.

"You are looking well, Rowland," Rubalev said as he poured himself coffee, "but Katia has grown too thin."

"I was ill this winter," Katia said, keeping her head bowed.

"It was nothing serious, I hope."

She looked up. For a moment, Lemuel glimpsed longing in her dark eyes, and then she looked away. She had still not given him an answer to his proposal of marriage. That she might still care deeply for the man who had been her guardian did not surprise him.

"I was troubled by nightmares for a while," Katia said. "They kept me from sleeping, and I grew much weaker, but that has passed. Now I hardly dream at all."

"The Chen brothers rode back to the Plains with Denis Laforte," Rubalev said, "and they have found ten more Chinese men to aid them in their work. Now I must procure supplies for them, and men to haul them whose silence can be bought. And what have you learned during your sojourn here?"

"Probably little that you couldn't find out for yourself," Lemuel replied. "Vice President Henry Wilson is ailing, and hasn't been seen presiding over the Senate recently."

Rubalev shrugged. "The fate of a vice president will make no difference to us."

"Union troops are occupying Florida and part of Alabama."

"I know that as well, and also that Canada made forays against Detroit and Maine."

"The British forces were repelled by the Army," Lemuel said.

"For now."

"There were two newspaper reports that the long-missing George Armstrong Custer was spotted this winter on the Plains, in a Sioux camp. It's said that some of his men were seen with him, and that they have decided to remain there for now, living among the Indians and seeing that treaties are kept. His wife Elizabeth is stoutly denying such rumors, claiming that her husband has been slandered as a deserter. I don't suppose you would know anything about that."

Rubalev showed his teeth. Lemuel had suspected a possible origin for the reports ever since reading them. From a distance, and even at closer range, the blond Alaskan, in a blue officer's coat or buckskin jacket, might be mistaken for Custer. One of the few adventurous reporters out on the Plains, looking for a story among the Indians, might have embellished such a report.

"Let his wife say what she likes," Rubalev murmured. "She can hardly admit that he might again have found the charms of Mon-ahseetah, Young Spring Grass, more to his liking than her own."

"No one will believe that for long," Lemuel said, "especially since there's been no word from anyone traveling with the Seventh."

"It does not matter if they stop believing it later," Rubalev said, "as long as it is believed for now." He took a bite of the meat and bread, then drained his coffee.

Lemuel was about to mention what Jeremiah Clarke had told him about General Crook, but hesitated. It was possible Rubalev knew about Crook's new posting, although it was unlike him not to have mentioned that by now, since it was the sort of information the man would have easily shared with him.

Rubalev's eyes narrowed as he gazed across the table. "Where did you go before you came here?" Lemuel asked.

"I returned to St. Joseph from the West, by train. I spent some time among the Mormons in their clean and most attractive but exceedingly dull city. The Prophet Brigham Young is somewhat apprehensive about the Union, given his recent confrontation with the governor Washington tried to impose on Utah. We may win ourselves an ally there, or at least keep the Mormons from becoming our enemy. They believe that the Lakota might be a Lost Tribe of Israel. I assured the Prophet that his missionaries might even be welcomed by Touch-the-Clouds in time."

Lemuel kept his face still, trying to imagine Rubalev in the New Zion of the Mormons, passing himself off as a sober and respectable sympathizer. "In what capacity," he asked, "did you offer your assurances to Young?"

"As a representative of the Lakota—an ambassador, you might say, a mediator between Touch-the-Clouds and any of the chiefs among the Wasichu. Touch-the-Clouds will need other such ambassadors."

"I know that," Lemuel said.

"You do not seem to have been doing very much in Kansas City," Rubalev said. "Perhaps it was useless for you to have come here."

"I would have been more useless poking around and arousing suspicion. There are many in Missouri who would support the recent rebellions in the South, if they thought they might be successful. This is a state where many still have divided loyalties."

"I am aware of that."

"I think Katia would be safer away from here."

She was looking at Rubalev. Her face was impassive, but he saw the hope in her eyes.

"Exactly how much use do you think you can be somewhere else?" Rubalev asked.

"I was speaking of Katia, not myself." He would settle this matter of Katia one way or another. If she chose to leave with Rubalev, he would not stop her.

"She cannot come with me." Rubalev kept his gaze on Lemuel. "I will be traveling quite a bit. It would be very hard on her. You also forget that Touch-the-Clouds allowed her to leave with you. Had he wanted me to have her, he would have arranged for that."

The man was talking about her as though she were a horse to be traded, but that was probably how both he and Touch-the-Clouds regarded her. Lemuel glanced at the woman briefly; her face was as expressionless as before.

"I can endure hardship," Katia said suddenly, "as you should know by now, Grisha." She glanced at Lemuel. "And I do not worry about my safety. I am content to remain with you." He saw that she was saying that out of pride, and both pitied and respected her for it.

Her former guardian looked away from her. "Do you have any messages for Touch-the-Clouds and the other chiefs, Rowland?" Rubalev raised his brows and smiled. "I mean of course information other than the unimportant intelligence you have already gathered."

"Are you returning to Lakota territory?"

Rubalev's eyes shifted. "No, but I can get a message to Touch-the-Clouds."

"Then you should tell him, if he doesn't already know, that General George Crook is commander of the Department of the Platte—has been since this winter, in fact."

Rubalev was very still, but his eyes shifted again, and Lemuel was sure that he had surprised him with the news.

"My guess is that he'll be looking for Custer and the Seventh before long, if he hasn't sent out scouts already," Lemuel continued. "He might risk violating the treaty to do that. It wouldn't take him long to find out what happened, and then he will have an excuse to attack the Lakota."

"For Crook to find out anything," Rubalev murmured, "someone will have to talk. The warriors who fought the Seventh know enough not to say anything to strangers."

"Men can grow careless. A scout can find something that was overlooked. And Crook knows that he will need some Indians on his side in order to fight Indians. There are probably still a few Arikara and Crow who may prefer to join the Gray Wolf's forces as scouts if they think he has a chance of defeating the Lakota in battle."

"That is so," Rubalev said, frowning with annoyance at having to admit it. "Crook is not the impetuous fool that Custer was."

"I would have left Katia here and ridden to Touch-the-Clouds myself to tell him this," Lemuel said, "but it was clear that Crook wouldn't fight this winter. The men under his command suffer from a lack of morale. They have a government they distrust and a chance of being sent to fight other battles in the northeast or the south. Crook won't fight this spring or summer, not without enough men and with orders to keep the peace. But if he can find an excuse to fight, to break the treaty, be sure that Sherman and Sheridan will be happy to let him take it."

Rubalev scowled.

"But I can try to prevent that," Lemuel finished.

"How?" Rubalev asked.

Lemuel had been considering what he was about to say ever since hearing about Crook's new command. "I'll go to Omaha," he said. "I can get a letter of introduction from Jeremiah Clarke. When General Crook learns of my past service with Grant and my time among the Lakota, I think he will see me."

"And what can you do even if he does agree to see you?" Rubalev asked.

Lemuel rested his arms on the table. "Volunteer my services as a scout, of course."

Rubalev gazed at him in silence for a while, then smiled. "You shame me, Rowland. I should have thought of this myself."

FIFTEEN

"I have no doubt that you could be of service to the army, Rowland," the general said, "but at present, I will not send any scouts into the lands the Sioux are claiming as their territory."

Lemuel sat in front of George Crook, in a high-backed wooden chair on the other side of the general's desk. During the course of their conversation, General Crook had insisted on referring to the Lakota territory as "what is now the Sioux reservation," or "the territory the Sioux are claiming as their own," as though the treaty now in effect were only a temporary one and the territory would eventually become the system of agencies and allotted lands the white man had intended it to be, as though the Lakota would eventually be forced from their hunting grounds in the Wyoming and Montana territories and confined at last in the small space of a Dakota reservation.

Yet Crook did not strike him as a man itching for a war on the Plains. The general had spoken briefly of his campaign against the Modoc people in California and his battles with the Apache almost as though he was sorry to have had to fight such worthy opponents. His pale eyes had grown warmer as he mentioned the red men and the two Modoc women who had served him as scouts in California, who had come to believe that their people were doomed to defeat and that their only proper course of action was to serve the white chief in the blue coat and thus end the fighting quickly. Crook had praised the Apache for their tactics and for their ability to strike suddenly in small bands and then quickly vanish into their barren desert lands.

"I cannot violate the treaty at the moment without risking a court-martial," Crook continued, and there was a hint of weariness in his voice. His thick curly forked blond beard and closely clipped short blond hair were sprinkled with gray; it would not be many more years before the name the Apache had given him, the Gray Wolf, fit.

"Ordering scouts into Sioux territory might be a treaty violation," Lemuel said, "but scouts without a direct order from you would be another matter. The Sioux will allow others to enter their lands as friends. They would not have to know that they were scouts reporting to you."

Crook's mouth twitched. "Ely Parker's letter tells me that you were educated as an engineer, but you now sound more like a practicing member of the bar." His gaze grew more distant. "Without the service of my scouts in the Southwest, my scalp most likely would have decorated an Apache lodge by now. Without my Indian scouts in particular, I could not have learned enough to know how to fight their red brothers. And I couldn't fight the Apache easily now even if they broke their treaties, because not a single one would dare to be my scout against his own people."

The general did not have to explain why. The story had spread northward to the Lakota encampments. The Chiricahua Apache chief Cochise had been the first to reach an agreement, and then, after a prolonged search and a battle with Crook's soldiers, the Tonto Apaches and their chief Delshay had won what they demanded, the pieces of paper that would allow them to move around their lands as the white men did. It was widely believed among the Lakota that Three Star Crook and his Blue Coats might have defeated the Apache and forced them onto reservations if, for mysterious reasons, Three Star had not suddenly decided to sue for peace.

To Lemuel, the reasons for giving the Apache what they wanted were no longer so mysterious. The growing rebellions in the former Confederacy provided enough reason for coming to terms with the Apache. Better to have the Texans worry about guarding themselves against Apache raids from the west than to have them tempted to become part of a wider revolt against the Union. That the Apache had so far refrained from any raids against Texas had not made settlers near their territory less fearful of their former red foes. In any event, Texans were increasingly distrustful of the Mexicans to their south, and also of the Kiowa who roamed the southern plains with their cattle herds whenever they were not hunting what buffalo were left in their lands. There were also the Comanche and Quanah Parker, their feared leader, to worry about. None of those people, whose war chiefs had smoked pipes of peace with the Lakota, were likely to attack their former enemies without provocation, as long as the treaties were kept. The precarious peace would hold as long as the possibility of war in the east, north, or south threatened.

As for the army's Indian scouts, those who had been too slow to return to their own people had suffered for it. The Apaches in particular had visited the same cruel tortures on traitors as they had on the unfortunate settlers they had attacked earlier. Any Indian who scouted for the white man now would be shown no mercy if ever he were captured. Lemuel had heard of a few former scouts who had volunteered to fight the recalcitrant rebels in the South rather than remain near the Plains and risk capture by their own people. It was said that almost all of those scouts had died in the worst of the fighting, that some had seemed to rush to their deaths. There had been little for them to lose.

That was one circumstance that made the game that Lemuel was playing now especially dangerous. He had to trust that Rubalev would somehow be able to assure Touch-the-Clouds that, whatever he might hear about the Orphan later on, Lemuel's loyalties still lay with the Lakota. He had no reason to doubt Rubalev, but memories still sometimes came to him, usually in the night after he woke from a restless sleep, of Rubalev dancing with the dead scout's scalp or standing by the bodies of the executed Blue Coats at Fort Fetterman. Rubalev, he knew now, would discard him quickly if he found it necessary.

Crook, whatever respect he had for his red foes, must have sued for peace with them only with great reluctance. Sheridan had probably sent him the order to withdraw, and Lemuel knew enough about General Sheridan to know how much he must have hated giving such a order.

"So you are telling me," Lemuel said, "that you do not need my services."

Crook sighed. "You are wrong there. What I learned fighting Apaches isn't going to help me on the Plains against the Sioux. I need whatever information you can give me. What you can tell me about the Sioux, their movements, their chiefs, their past battles—any such information might be useful to me later."

Lemuel had come to Omaha knowing that Crook might well have no use for him as a scout. In a way, he was relieved; the important thing was to keep Three Star from learning too much, and Lemuel could perhaps accomplish that more easily with misinformation than by trying to mislead Crook's scouts. He wondered now what he should tell the man, what kinds of tales might keep the general from considering an incursion into Lakota territory.

Perhaps nothing he could say would make any difference. If the situation in the East worsened, Crook would lack the means to attack, might even be ordered to a command elsewhere. But if the rebellions were put down for good, the recent treaty would soon be forgotten, as so many others had been. And there was still the chance that conflict and hard times in the eastern states would drive more people to seek their fortunes elsewhere, perhaps in the Dakota, Wyoming, and Montana territories. The only way to protect those settlers and open the land up to Eastern investment—looting might be a better term for it—would be to force the Lakota onto reservations once more.

"I don't suppose," Crook continued, "that you know anything, or have heard any rumors, of what might have happened to the companies of the Seventh Cavalry led by George Armstrong Custer."

Lemuel hesitated. He had expected the question, and had been prepared to tell Crook the same story he had told to Jeremiah Clarke.

"His wife has been pressing hard," Crook went on. "She has written letters to several officers demanding an investigation." The Gray Wolf regarded him steadily with his pale eyes. This man would not be convinced by the story Clarke had heard. He would certainly not believe it coming from a man who had claimed only a few moments ago to be a friend of some of the Lakota chiefs, and thus presumably privy to some information about Custer's fate.

"He was on an expedition," Crook said. "He was to explore the Black Hills territory, but not to go after any Indians or attack them— so I was informed, at any rate. But Custer was always impetuous."

Another story was suggesting itself to Lemuel, one that would be closer to the truth and thus have a hope of convincing the general. "I do not know what happened to Custer," he said carefully, "but I can make a guess."

Crook folded his hands.

"There were rumors in the camp where I was staying about an attack on one encampment, one which supposedly claimed the lives of several women and children as well as men. Several of the young warriors grew angry and rode out to find out if this was true. The Sioux were on the move then, following the buffalo as they always do during the summer, and soon a great many encampments were gathering south of the Belle Fourche River, near the Black Hills, where Custer and his men had apparently been sighted."

Crook drew his brows together.

"There might have been as many as two thousand Sioux and Cheyenne warriors in that one place, perhaps more. I can't be certain, since the Lakota with whom I was traveling were riding well behind the others, making certain that their women and children were safe, and did not reach their comrades until the fighting was over. Custer divided his forces and sent some of his men to attack, but they were driven back. At least that is what I was told."

Crook looked as though he believed him for the moment. Lemuel thought of Custer's exploits during the War Between the States, how he charged into the thick of things, heedless of his safety or that of his men. Custer's Luck, they had called his good fortune, his way of surviving the most reckless of charges. Crook would find it easy enough to believe that he would do something as ill-considered as rushing to fight an Indian force that outnumbered his own.

"He had scouts with him," Crook said. "He couldn't have been employing them very well if he did anything that foolish. Of course, with Custer—" He shrugged and fell silent.

"One cannot fault General Custer's courage," Lemuel said.

"No, one cannot fault that." Crook sighed. "Go on with your story, Rowland."

"I was told that the Seventh sustained heavy casualties, and that Custer finally surrendered. Given that he had violated the treaty with the Lakota chiefs by coming into the Black Hills, and had also attacked an Indian camp, one could argue that the Lakota would have been justified in killing him. Apparently they settled for making a captive of him instead. If he's still alive, he would have no way of letting his wife know what happened. He can only hope that she'll wait for him."

Crook was looking doubtful again. "And would they also have made captives of the hundreds of men with him? I am assuming that most of them or a goodly portion of them survived, even after the fighting. The Sioux couldn't have killed them all."

Lemuel nodded. "From what some of the Lakota men told me afterwards, many took the opportunity to desert. Some apparently went west—exactly where, I do not know. It was after this that the Indians decided to attack Fort Fetterman. Once they had their victory there and had secured what they wanted by treaty, there was no reason for me to remain among them. I returned to St. Joseph and reported to Colonel Clarke there."

"There was also no cause for you to remain in the West." Crook's pale eyes seemed almost too piercing. "I know something of your past, Rowland. You might have gone back to live among your own people in Tonawanda. You might have gone to New York and taken advantage of some of Ely Parker's connections. He has done well for himself since his disgrace in Washington. I hear that he is even involving himself again in politics these days."

"So I have heard." Lemuel knew only a little about Donehogawa's political activities. The martyred Lincoln, the prematurely dead President Grant—they had become the symbols of those Republicans who were hoping for reform. The problem was that the more corrupt wing of the party, the one that clung to President Colfax and had rallied around James G. Blaine, the Speaker of the House, could also claim a connection to them. And the two wings of the party were still bound together in these troubled times. It was known that some in the South hoped that a Democratic president might be more sympathetic to the rebels, and that disunity among Republicans might give the presidency to a Democrat.

"To put it another way," Crook said, "I fail to understand why you thought of coming to me. I know what you would risk if you go scouting in Indian territory and the Sioux find out that I sent you, which makes me wonder why you offer to do so. I fail to see why you are so willing to help in preparing me for war against the Sioux."

"I am not interested in preparing you for war," Lemuel said, "but for peace."

The general frowned.

"If the Union is preserved," Lemuel continued, "the men who have been filling the pockets of many in Washington will look to the West again. They'll want to build more railroads and more settlements. They will be more able and willing to send more soldiers to serve under your command. They may try to bargain with the Sioux for their lands first, but the Sioux won't be willing to give them up now, and that would mean war. Their territory would have to be taken by force. I don't have to tell you how long and bloody a battle that would be, with so many alliances among the Sioux and other red men. The army wouldn't just be fighting here, but along the southern Plains as well."

Crook's expression was grim.

"The army would win in the end, of course. The Sioux are greatly outnumbered and the army could be supplied with better weapons than any the Indians could hope to get. You would break the power of the Sioux chiefs. The hoped-for Northern Pacific Railroad could finally be completed."

Lemuel caught a glint of anger in Crook's eyes; he had sensed that the general might already be repulsed by the thought of preparing the way for more greedy adventurers. "It would be better not to fight such a war," Lemuel concluded.

"Of course it would be better not to fight it," Crook said. "I'm in agreement with you there. But if I am ordered to fight, I will do so, even if it means breaking the treaty. The Lakota won't remain at peace with us for ever. If they cannot fight their old red enemies, they will have to find new enemies. They are warriors, Rowland. You have lived among them—you know that even better than I. It would not surprise me if they broke the treaty first." The general was silent for a moment. "I am curious as to why, now that you have left their territory, you are still so concerned about them."

"Perhaps it is because when I left them, I brought a Sioux wife with me. If her people are forced to fight a war, I would rather it were over quickly, with as few deaths as possible."

"I see." Crook got to his feet, and Lemuel knew that their meeting was over. "I may have a use for you later, Rowland, but you would be a wiser man if you went back to your own tribe and lands with your wife. Your people learned how to live as civilized men, the Cherokee and the other civilized tribes have learned that, and the Sioux will eventually have to learn it as well or risk extermination." But again the general sounded as though he hoped that war would not come.

Lemuel was about to enter the hotel room he was sharing with Katia when the door suddenly opened. Katia stood there, in a plain blue cotton dress, her lips pressed together in a straight line.

"I saw Grouard," she said, and then drew him inside before closing the door behind him.

"What are you talking about?"

"Frank Grouard, Sitting With Upraised Hands. He is here, in Omaha. When you left to go the headquarters of Three Star Crook, I followed you."

She let go of him and sat down in a chair near a small round table in the corner. An oil lamp flickered on the table, casting a pattern of light and shadow on her face.

"Tell me this again," Lemuel said, "and slowly," and then seated himself on the small sofa near her.

"I followed you. I was thinking that, if anything happened, if General Crook grew suspicious and kept you there, I might see what I could do to help you, to get word to Grisha if need be."

Only a fortnight ago, he might have laughed at the notion of Katia getting him out of any kind of trouble, but something had changed in her after their meeting with Rubalev in Kansas City. She had gone out the next morning and returned with food for them, and then she had taken some of their gold to Rubalev to trade for more greenbacks. Her timidity and nervousness had seemingly vanished.

He thought of their last night in Kansas City, before they had left on a riverboat for Omaha. He had asked her again if she would become his wife in truth.

"I will be your wife, Lemuel," she had told him in Lakota, staring directly into his eyes before he lowered his head, embarrassed. "But I do not need a Wasichu medicine man to chant of Jesus, or to draw my mark on a talking paper in order to make me your wife." She had taken him by the hand then, and led him to her room.

There had been little joy in it for her. He had felt that as he held her, that she was only enduring him as a prostitute might, as the soiled doves he had sought out from time to time during the war had endured him. His distaste for the weakness in himself had grown so great after war's end that he had sworn never to go to a woman in that way again, and he had nearly withdrawn from Katia when he felt her hands gently touch his back and the nape of his neck. She had whispered his name, and he had felt that some love for him might at last be flowering inside her.

"I waited outside, in the street," Katia went on, her voice trembling. There was fear in her face, but also concern for him. "I saw Grouard with some other men, all of them talking and laughing. I could not hear what they were saying, but Grouard looked as though he belonged there, as though he knew them well."

How long had Grouard been in Omaha? Lemuel struggled to quell the turmoil in his mind as he considered the possibilities. Grouard might have come on his own, to gather intelligence for his good friend and sworn brother Sitting Bull. He might have decided to leave the Sioux and throw in his lot with the Wasichu, possibly for personal gain; the rumor was that Frank Grouard had resented not being able to do some mining of his own in the Black Hills. He might have had a falling out with Sitting Bull. Rubalev, who had become friendlier with Grouard, might have sent him to General Crook, but that would mean that the Alaskan did not entirely trust Lemuel.

"Grisha might have sent him," Katia said. She might almost have been reading his mind, but then he saw the tautness in her face and realized that she was only trying to reassure herself.

"No," Lemuel said, "I don't believe it. Rubalev knows one thing about me. Once I give my word, my loyalty if you will, I keep it. When I promised to be a friend and ally of the Lakota people, he knew that I would keep that promise, even if there are times when I wish that I hadn't made such a pledge." Rubalev had seen that in him after the battle in the Black Hills, after the attack on Fort Fetterman. He had seen that Lemuel would not go back on his promise even if what his allies did was abhorrent to him. It had been the same for him during the war to preserve the Union. He had given his promise to fight for the Union and had kept it, even during the worst of the slaughter, even when he had come to doubt that any Union was worth such bloodshed. It was what whites called honorable, living in such a way, keeping one's promises, even when so many of the Wasichu failed to live that way themselves.

"Lemuel," Katia said softly, and then fell silent.

"No," he continued, "Rubalev couldn't have sent him. I wish I could believe that he had, but I can't. If Grouard has been here for some time, Rubalev would have told me that he was here, might have told me to contact him. It would have been foolish for him to send us both here and have us being suspicious of each other. If he sent him after I decided to come to Omaha, then Grouard may seek me out. It should be easy for me to find out how long he has been here if he does."

Katia looked away from him. "I think it has been for a while," she said. "He talked to those men as if he was very familiar with them. You came among the Lakota willingly. Grouard was taken as a captive. However close he might have grown to some of the men, perhaps that was always in the back of his mind, that one day he would be free and would have his revenge on the Lakota for his captivity."

Grouard might have been at Crook's headquarters on the same mission as Lemuel, to offer his services as a scout. He might be enlisted as an army scout already; perhaps that was another reason the general had sent Lemuel away. There were other possibilities; Grouard could have told Crook much about the movements of the Lakota, the councils of the chiefs, the presence of gold in the Black Hills, Custer's defeat, even about the Chen brothers and their rocket-arrows. Lemuel wondered how much Grouard might already have told him.

Katia said, "Grouard may know almost as much as you do."

"And he can guess at anything he doesn't know." Maybe the half-breed had come here only to find out what he could before carrying the knowledge back to the Lakota, but Lemuel's instincts were warning him against accepting that comforting possibility. Until he knew for certain why Grouard had come to Omaha, he had to regard him as a danger and a possible enemy.

Lemuel might have sent word to Rubalev, or sent Katia to join her former guardian in Kansas City. The Alaskan had said that he would be in Kansas City for much of the summer before leaving for Chicago and the East. Instead, Lemuel moved around Omaha, making himself as inconspicuous as possible, trying to find out what he could about Frank Grouard's presence here. He would send Katia away once he learned more about Grouard.

Within three days, he had found out that Grouard had come there last winter and had gone to General Crook to volunteer as a scout. Grouard had been drawing army pay ever since.

Lemuel considered what to do as he walked back along the tree-lined street that led to his hotel. There had been no trees here before the settlers came, but the people of Omaha had begun to plant them in every available space, as if to shield themselves from the flat windswept land that lay beyond the city.

Katia was in their room, resting on the bed. She had been keeping to their room ever since she had sighted Grouard. She sat up as he closed the door. "Are you ill?" he asked, concerned for her.

She shook her head. "No, only bored." She smoothed down her skirt. "Hiding can be quite tedious."

"We're not going to hide from Frank Grouard any more."

Her eyes widened.

"Trying to keep ourselves hidden will only make him more suspicious of us if he does find out we're here. He may already know I'm in Omaha. He's a scout for Crook. I found that out today while listening to a couple of cavalrymen at a saloon. He might know that I went to see the general."

Katia shook her head. "But—"

"If he came here to spy for the Lakota, we have nothing to fear, and if he came here to work against them, I had better find that out. We don't know what he might have told General Crook already."

She gazed at him in silence. "What are you going to do?"

"Escort you downstairs and order some supper." He smiled, trying to conceal his worry from her.

There had been little contact between Lemuel and Grouard among the Lakota. They had spoken to each other only a couple of times in the camp of Touch-the-Clouds. Lemuel went to the stable where he was keeping the horses he had bought for himself and Katia and rode toward the stockade that surrounded the headquarters of the Department of the Platte.

Frank Grouard was loitering outside the corral with two other men, both with long black hair and hats adorned with eagle feathers. Lemuel slowed his horse, thinking for a moment that Grouard might not recognize him as he rode by, and then the half-breed beckoned to him.

"You," Grouard shouted, "I know you. What is it they called you?"

Lemuel dismounted. "Poyeshao," he replied, and then in Lakota, "the Orphan from the East."

"Hah." Grouard bared his white teeth in an attempt at a smile. "An old comrade," he said to the other two men. Their eyes narrowed as they stared coldly at Lemuel. "A blood brother of the great chief Touch-the-Clouds, so they say."

"You are mistaken there," Lemuel said. "We swore no such oath."

"Then Tatanka Wotanka—Sitting Bull—paid me more respect than did your Lakota comrade to you." Grouard turned toward his companions and jerked his head; the two men left them.

"Now I can ask you," Grouard said in a low voice, "what you are doing here."

"I came to offer myself to Three Star Crook as a scout," Lemuel said.

"Had he taken you on as one, I would know," Grouard said, "so he must have sent you away."

"He did. There is a chance he may need me to scout for him later." Lemuel kept his eyes on Grouard. The man had told Rubalev that he was not an Indian half-breed as most of the Lakota thought, that he had been born in the South Seas, a story Lemuel doubted.

"Who sent you here?" Grouard asked. "Yellow Hair Rubalev? Touch-the-Clouds?"

"No one sent me." Lemuel led his horse to a hitching post. "I left with Graceful Swan, the second wife of Touch-the-Clouds. He didn't try to stop her from leaving him, but we could not have lived easily in his camp after that."

Grouard laughed. "I heard about that. I forget who told the story to me. If it had been any man but Touch-the-Clouds, many would have mocked him for giving away a wife so easily, but since she gave him no sons and went around seeking visions like a man, per- haps he thinks he is well rid of her. And of course no one will dare to mock Touch-the-Clouds, even in a whisper." Grouard laughed again. "No, he may be sitting with his braves now, mocking you for accepting her."

Lemuel tensed with anger. Grouard's smile grew broader. His anger faded; it did not matter what he said, what he thought, about Katia. Better for Grouard to think that Lemuel's ties of friendship with the Lakota were broken.

"Maybe you should not be so quick to scout for Three Star," Grouard said. "If you were caught by the Lakota—"

"My fate would not be any worse than yours at their hands."

Grouard's black eyes shifted. "You must need money." Lemuel did not deny it. "Three Star would not pay you much, but even army pay is better than nothing. I will see what I can do. Come back here tomorrow or the day after."

"Thanks," Lemuel said.

"Do not be too quick to thank me, Orphan." Grouard turned and strode away from him.

Lemuel spent the rest of the day with some of Crook's scouts and drivers, saying as little as possible, letting them assume that he was another one like Grouard, who was thinking that it might be to his advantage to change sides. He rode back to the stable at dusk and walked to his hotel brooding about what Grouard might already have revealed to Crook. Maybe he had not given away as much as Lemuel feared. Grouard might be waiting to see what Crook would do, what intentions he had, before committing himself completely. A man who had changed sides once might change sides again.

Inside the hotel, two men were drinking at the bar in the down- stairs saloon; a couple sat at one table eating their supper. At another table, near the stairs, Katia sat with Frank Grouard.

Lemuel walked toward them slowly. Grouard had a bottle and a glass in front of him. Katia's face was impassive, but her right hand trembled slightly as she rested it on the table next to her own empty glass. Grouard leaned back in his chair and smiled briefly.

"What are you doing here?" Lemuel said as he sat down across from them.

Grouard shrugged. "I saw Graceful Swan when I was riding past here this evening, and decided to call on her."

Lemuel glanced at Katia. She might have been outside for only a moment, taking a walk, escaping the confines of their room for a little while.

"I was most surprised to see Sitting Bull's old comrade here," Katia murmured, surprising him with the calmness of her speech. "I knew that you would be back soon, so I invited Mr. Grouard to sit with me here while waiting for you. I was certain that you would have much to talk about."

Grouard kept his eyes on Katia. "We do. It is between us. So you may leave us now."

She got to her feet and came around the table. Grouard watched her as she went toward the stairway. "She was never like the other squaws," Grouard said under his breath, "but I did not think she could be so—" He motioned with one hand. "She could make some money here. There are houses that would have her."

Lemuel forced himself to ignore that slight to her honor. "What do you have to say to me?" he asked.

"We are here for the same thing, are we not?" Grouard poured himself a glass of whiskey, drank it down, then rested his arms on the table top. "The Lakota will hunt this summer. They will not think of war. They will not be thinking of the Wasichu. But Three Star Crook will be thinking of them, and of what will happen later. The Lakota will not stay at peace—they will begin to think of counting coup again."

It was what Crook had said to him, that the Lakota were warriors. Another war would come; all that he could hope to do was to post-pone it until the Lakota and their allies were prepared to fight it.

"I have my honor," Grouard continued, "and so I do not look at you and say, 'Here is another one who has turned against his old friends.' Instead I say, 'Here is another man who knows that the only way he can help his red brothers is to go to Three Star.' This is the time for Three Star to be given what we know, and then he will wait until those on the Plains fall out among themselves again. That will be the time to strike."

Grouard poured himself another drink, then pushed the bottle across the table. Lemuel poured some of the whiskey in Katia's unused glass and lifted it to his lips, feigning a sip.

"I wonder which old enemy the Lakota will turn against first," Grouard said, "the Crow or the Arikara. Or maybe it will be the other way around, and the Crow will break the peace first."

Lemuel did not have to listen to any more. He could imagine what Grouard was thinking: If the Lakota and their allies fell out, there would be more red men willing to scout for the Blue Coats. By exploiting the divisions among the red men of the Plains, Crook would have the advantage. If Grouard helped the general win his victory, he could hope for a claim of his own in the Black Hills, and perhaps a lucrative post at one of the agencies where the Indians, once they were confined to reservations, would be forced to trade for whatever goods they needed. And Grouard would tell himself that he would do whatever he could to help his defeated Lakota friends.

"Sitting Bull should have been the chief of all the Lakota," Grouard said. "He would have been if not for Touch-the-Clouds." Lemuel could imagine Sitting Bull harboring such thoughts, even saying them aloud to Grouard. Sitting Bull had hoped only that his people be left alone with their hunting grounds and their buffalo, to live as they had; he had not wanted to fight them as had Touch-the-Clouds, with rocket-arrows and Rubalev's network of spies and traders and gold taken from their sacred Black Hills. But Sitting Bull would not turn against a chief to whom he had pledged himself—at least, Lemuel told himself, not until that chief had shown himself unworthy of his trust. Grouard might be hoping to bring about such a breach.

"And some say that Crazy Horse is a greater chief than either of them," Lemuel said.

"Hah." Grouard ran his hands through his thick black hair. "Yes, you were wise to leave Touch-the-Clouds when you did." He grinned. "I have not told Three Star most of what I know. I wanted to find out what he knew first, what kind of man he was."

You wanted to be sure you had picked the right side, Lemuel thought, in case you decided to change sides again. You wanted to be sure that, when you revealed what you know, you got the most possible profit for it.

"Too bad I didn't know that when I went to see Crook," Lemuel said. "I might have had a handsome price for what I could have told him and then there would have been less information for you to sell him."

Grouard laughed. Lemuel did not know if the other man was beginning to trust him more, or if he was simply playing along, but it did not matter. Grouard was a threat to him and to the Lakota.

"Have another drink," he said to Grouard, pouring from the bottle into the other man's glass and then topping off his own. Grouard gulped his drink down; Lemuel forced himself to swallow some of the whiskey and felt it burn his throat.

"There is something you should know," Lemuel continued in a softer voice.

Grouard lifted his thick brows.

"I can't tell you about it here."

Grouard looked around the room. "There is no one here to listen to us."

"Even so—" Lemuel looked toward the men at the bar. "It might be better to speak of this somewhere else. We are not the only two former friends of the Lakota chiefs who are here in Omaha. Yellow Hair Rubalev has arrived here, too, and he's keeping himself well hidden. If I hadn't accidentally seen him—"

Grouard had tensed at the name. Now he looked both angry and frightened. Good, Lemuel thought; now he could be sure that Rubalev had not sent the other man here.

"That man—" Grouard's eyes shifted. "What can he want?"

"Once Touch-the-Clouds listened more to his counsel. Maybe Rubalev is also thinking of changing sides." Lemuel stood up, feeling his stomach knotting; he did not want to think of what he would have to do.

Grouard shook himself. "He might change sides. I do not know what he wants, what he is trying to do. Where did you see him?"

Lemuel jerked his head toward the doorway, then stood up. Grouard came around the table; Lemuel saw that the other man was unsteady on his feet. There were only three men at the bar, along with the barkeep, and they were talking in low voices among themselves.

They went outside. It had grown dark; a carriage rattled past them. The street was quiet enough for Lemuel to hear a train whistle from the station at the other end of town.

"Where did you see him?" Grouard asked again.

"Slipping into a rooming house by the kitchen door," Lemuel improvised.

"A rooming house. Doesn't sound like Yellow Hair."

Lemuel had known that a moment after telling the lie. "No, it doesn't, which makes me even more suspicious. The place isn't far from here."

"You want to go there?" Grouard's face was hidden in the darkness. "I do not want to know why he might be here. I am thinking now that maybe I should not have come to Omaha."

Perhaps he could be persuaded to leave. Lemuel would be rid of any danger Grouard might pose. That faint hope quickly faded. Grouard might be fearful for a while, but he might have second thoughts about leaving Omaha once he was sober. He would also have a chance to find out that Lemuel had lied to him.

Lemuel moved along the wooden sidewalk. Grouard stayed at his side. "Maybe he is only on his way to another city," Grouard muttered.

"Possibly. But don't you think we'd better find that out?"

"Yes." Grouard sounded even more drunk. "Maybe you are right. But—"

"We'll go through here." Lemuel led him toward an alley between the hotel and a general store. "A shorter way to get there, and it's better than taking a chance on having him see us coming to the front of the house."

They entered the darkened alley. There were a few old barrels behind the store, where something could stay hidden for a while. The two had reached the middle of the alleyway when Grouard suddenly halted.

"Eh," the half-breed said, his voice filled with suspicion, "maybe you—"

Lemuel had his Colt out by then. He brought it down on the back of Grouard's head and heard the other man grunt. Grouard was still on his feet. Lemuel hit him again and heard him fall forward. He bent over the prone man and struck a third time, and then heard a rustling sound behind him.

Someone had followed him into the alley. He clenched his teeth and spun around quickly, his gun still in his hand, to face a shadowed figure.

"Lemuel." That was Katia's voice.

"What are you doing here?" he whispered.

"I saw you leave with him. I was watching from our room. I had the door open just a little and I saw you walk out with him. I didn't like it."

He leaned over Grouard. The man was still. "He is still breathing," Katia said. "Hit him again."

He hesitated.

"It's why you came out here with him, isn't it?" she said. "To be rid of him."

He had killed before, during the war. He had done it without thinking. Death had been all around him and he had thought himself hardened to it. He was still at war, and Grouard was an enemy.

Katia grabbed his gun by the cylinder, twisting it out of his hand. She crouched down and then swung at the back of Grouard's head. Lemuel heard the sound of bone cracking. She hit the half-breed two more times on the back of his head, then stood up.

"We can't leave him here," she said softly.

"I know where we can hide him," he said numbly.

"Be careful. There is blood—you don't want it showing on your clothing."

He knelt and slipped an arm around Grouard's chest. The man

did not seem to be breathing now. He began to drag him toward the barrels, with Katia holding the man up from the other side. They stretched the body out against a back wall and pulled the barrels in front of it.

It might be a day or two, perhaps longer, before Grouard's body was found. Lemuel did not think the man would have told others where he was going and why, but could not be certain of that.

He might be at war, but this felt like murder.

"Come on," Katia said. "We must go back to our room."

Lemuel could not sleep. Katia lay beside him, breathing evenly, but somehow he sensed that she was feigning sleep. He had wanted to leave this place immediately, find somewhere else to stay, even while knowing that this might endanger him even more. The body might be found quickly. The men at the bar might recall seeing him leave with Grouard. If he fled, the army might be after him if General Crook's suspicions were aroused.

"We'll have to stay here for a few more days," he had told Katia, and she had nodded, agreeing silently with him.

In the morning, he and Katia went downstairs and sat at a table, ordering breakfast as they usually did. He kept expecting someone to run into the hotel shouting that a body had been found. They finished their food and went back to their room. Katia moved around the room restlessly or sat in a chair, staring silently out the window. He thought of how she had followed him, of how she had hit Grouard with the butt of his Colt.

In late afternoon, shouts from the hallway and the saloon downstairs told him that Grouard's body had been found. There would be a knock on his door soon. He would open it to see a marshal, or perhaps an army officer.

The voices soon faded. The hotel was suddenly so quiet that it seemed empty, as if everyone in it had decamped to other lodgings.

"Katia," he said at last. His voice sounded strange to him in the silence. "We'll have to go downstairs and have some supper."

She did not reply.

"I've been thinking," he went on. "If nothing happens, if everything goes as it should—" He paused. "Crook may take me on as a scout after all. I'll have to see what I can do to find out what kind of campaign he might plan. You would be safer away from here."

She looked toward him, but remained silent.

"I think that you should go to New York. I shall write to Ely Parker and ask him to take you in until I can join you there."

"Very well," she said softly.

He stood up and held out his arm to her. She rose and walked over to him. "You could not have killed him without me," she whispered. "You would have stood there, shocked at yourself for doing what you did, and he would have come to his senses, and you would have been caught."

"I know."

They left the room. Downstairs, the saloon had grown noisier; a group of men hurried in to join others at the bar.

"Just heard it from a reporter for the *Republican*," one man in the group called out. "Crook's been ordered to Missouri. Fighting's broken out on the border with Arkansas."

"When are they going to stop calling it skirmishes and start calling it a war?" another man said.

"Maybe when British warships show up in our harbors. From what I heard, that could happen almost any time."

Lemuel led Katia to a table, listening for some word about Grouard's body and its disposition, but the talk was of battles and the threat of war and General Crook's new orders. Not all of the soldiers here were being sent; some would remain in Omaha. But there would be no scouting of the Plains, no forays into Indian territory.

Katia leaned toward him. "You don't have to stay here now," she said. He could barely hear her over the sound of the men at the bar.

He said, "I know."

"What will we do, then?"

"I was going to send you to New York. We'll go there together." He touched her hand lightly and listened as the men in the saloon spoke of the uprising in Arkansas and the fighting that was likely to come.

SIXTEEN

John Finerty descended the wide staircase to the hotel's lobby. Evening was coming on, time for a libation and perhaps some company, depending on who was in the bar at this hour. Finerty had arrived in Cincinnati only that morning, but already he was growing restless, ready to move on.

He had left the city immediately after the end of the Republican convention, hot on the trail of a rumored skirmish between rebel forces and Ohio farmers farther down the Ohio River. By the time he arrived on the scene, the rebel gunboat that was supposedly firing upon the Ohio side of the river had turned out to be no more than a party of steamboat passengers having some drunken fun with firearms.

Still, Finerty told himself, it could easily have been otherwise. That so many had panicked and been so quick to assume that war might be breaking out along the Ohio showed how edgy and worried people were. No sooner had one rebellion been put down than another seemed to break out elsewhere. Negroes had been lynched or burned out of their homes in at least four states of the former

Confederacy, and among the soldiers sent in to protect the blacks were recent immigrants who deeply resented having to protect the freedmen who would now be competing with them for work.

Finerty could understand such hard feelings, reprehensible as they undoubtedly were; life had become harder here for many of his countrymen. He had left Ireland himself to come to this country twelve years earlier. As a youth of eighteen, he had been full of optimism then, ready to begin a new life. That the United States were still at war with the Confederacy had not deterred him; he had willingly joined up with the Ninety-fourth New York Regiment. Since war's end, he had been considerably more fortunate than many of his Irish brethren in the United States, rising to become one of the better-paid correspondents for the Chicago *Times*, and yet his dreams could still taste sour in his mouth.

He had traveled back East that May to cover the Centennial Exposition of 1876 in Philadelphia just after its opening, which had featured appearances by President Colfax and the emperor of Brazil. Among the displays were Alexander Graham Bell's improved telephone, a writing machine with keys called a typewriter, and a contraption built by a fellow named Edison that was called a mimeograph. To Finerty's eyes, the exhibition of such wonders had seemed a presentation of technological promises likely never to be fulfilled.

Thomas Edison, with whom he had conducted a brief interview, had agreed with him. "Lost my job not long ago," Edison had told him; the shabbily-dressed man had been working for the Gold and Stock Telegraph Company in New York until it was taken over by Western Union. "Did a lot to improve their machines, but they aren't going to need 'em until things get a lot better than they are. Been trying to sell my inventions to raise some money for my own laboratory, but I can't find any buyers." Finerty had pitied the unfortunate man who seemed to have the talent of a Daedalus for creating new wonders, but who lacked the backing needed to bring his inventions into existence.

Now the Union Finerty had fought to preserve and that the Centennial Exposition was meant to celebrate was again endangered, and the homeland he had been forced to flee was still in the grip of the British. The bloody British, he thought bitterly. If the damned British started making more trouble on the Canadian border, he might even consider enlisting in the army again, just to fight them.

The Gibson House, although even more stifling in July than it had been in June, was a somewhat more congenial establishment in the absence of politicians. Finerty, who had arrived there only this morning, preferred to await word of his next assignment for the *Times* in some comfort. Maybe he would be sent west, now that George Crook was going back to Nebraska, although his editor Clinton Snowden was hinting that he might decide to send Finerty to Washington instead.

Finerty had been in Omaha a year ago, to cover General Crook's activities there, just before the outbreak of hostilities along the Missouri–Arkansas border. He had gone expecting and hoping to see more of the Plains, possibly in the company of some of Crook's scouts. A scout named Frank Grouard had hinted that Crook was only waiting for a pretext to send scouts into Sioux territory. Grouard claimed to be a friend of Touch-the-Clouds, an adopted son of Sitting Bull, and a blood brother to Crazy Horse, but such stories might be as fantastic as Grouard's claim that his mother had been a native princess in the South Seas. Still, the fact that Grouard had been willing to join up with Crook against his old friends was a sign that the power of the Sioux might be waning. Others might follow his example.

Others would have to, Finerty reminded himself, if Crook were to acquire any more scouts like Grouard, men who were intimately familiar with the ways of the red men of the Plains. Grouard had died suddenly, and rather mysteriously, just before Crook had received his orders to muster his men and head south. Most thought the scout had been drinking and afterwards had gotten into a fight in the alley where his body was found; Grouard could not hold his liquor and had been in fights before. Several blows to the head had killed him, and apparently his antagonist had dragged the body behind some barrels, perhaps hoping that Grouard was not too badly hurt and would sleep it off, perhaps knowing that the man was close to death.

There had been no chance for Finerty to investigate the whole business—a story about the scout's earlier, perhaps apocryphal, adventures and his untimely end might have been of interest to readers of the Chicago *Times*—because he had followed Crook to southern Missouri, to observe the army's summer campaign against Arkansan guerrillas. Little had been accomplished in that campaign, except for drawing the commander of the Department of the Platte and most of his forces south. The rebels, as Crook had put it, possessed the talent of the Apaches for disappearing. The general had even wondered if a few of the Apaches' Kiowa brethren might have sneaked eastward to aid the rebels, a possibility that would have sounded farfetched coming from another man, but Crook had dealt with Apaches and Kiowas before.

For Finerty, the campaign in northern Arkansas had yielded little more than stories about the frustrations of Crook in dealing with the guerrillas and the boredom of the men under his command. Resentment among Crook's men had thickened the air with rebellious talk. Let the rebels have their damned second Confederacy; let the niggers move to the small towns and farms springing up along the borders of Indian territory where at least they would not be taking work away from honest white men; let Texas and California call themselves autonomous republics and make whatever agreements they wanted with Mexico to keep Díaz's troops out of their lands; discharge the soldiers and let them get on with their lives in the Eastern cities, in California, or anywhere else they might want to go.

Finerty had heard a good deal of such talk. Lately, he was beginning to have more sympathy for such sentiments himself.

He came into the saloon and surveyed the large room. Few people were there at this hour, but a glance toward a table near the bar revealed two potential sources of both interviews and a diverting evening, should those two illustrious parties be amenable to granting him an audience. William Cody, whom Finerty had last seen treading the boards in a touring production of a stage epic entitled "Scouts of the Prairie," was one of the two men sitting at the table, looking quite splendid in a white Stetson and fringed buckskin, with his hair flowing over his shoulders. The thick bushy hair and mustache of the man in the white suit sitting with him were instantly recognizable.

As Finerty walked toward them, Cody caught sight of him, stood up, and beckoned to him with one arm. "Irish John!" Cody bellowed. "Come on over here, you ink-stained wretch. I'm already two drinks ahead of you."

If that was the case, Buffalo Bill Cody was being more abstemious than usual. "Ink-stained wretch, eh," the other man said as Finerty came to the table. "I used to be one such slave of the press myself, out in Nevada and later for the San Francisco *Morning Call*."

Finerty held out his hand as the man in the white suit got to his feet. "John F. Finerty, of the Chicago *Times*, and I am most grateful for the pleasure of finally meeting you, Mr. Clemens."

Samuel L. Clemens shook his hand vigorously. "The *Times*, eh? Then you have a far better berth than I did in my former position at the *Morning Call*. I was the only reporter there when I started, with no one to share my shame. Had I been more lofty and heroic, I would have thrown up my position and starved, like any other hero, but I lacked experience with heroism and didn't know how to go about being so principled."

The three men sat down. Clemens tapped some more tobacco into his pipe and lit it. Finerty had last seen the man who wrote under the name of Mark Twain at a lecture in Chicago. There had not been an empty seat in the house; the writer was doing well for himself.

"What the hell are you doing in Cincinnati, Irish John?" Bill Cody asked.

"I just got back this morning. There were reports of a Confederate gunboat firing on Union territory farther down the Ohio. Turned out to be some drunken patriots on a steamship shooting at their own soil." Finerty leaned back in his chair. "Before that little adventure, I was here to cover the Republican convention."

"Perhaps I should have appreciated my position at the *Morning Call* more," Clemens muttered, "since one of my more amenable duties was to show up at the police court and report on the disposition of squabbles and assaults among feuding Chinamen. You, on the other hand, had to report on some of our foremost grafters."

"That may be the truth about most of the delegates and their candidates, Mr. Clemens," Finerty said, "but there were a few notable exceptions. The upright Mr. Roosevelt of New York gave a fine speech attacking Senator Conkling from a balcony of this very establishment."

"Senator Conkling." Clemens snorted. "To quote Congressman Blaine, that particular senator presents a most excellent example of manhood, especially with his grandiloquent swell, his majestic, super-eminent, overpowering, turkey-gobbler strut." Clemens took a puff from his pipe. "Those have to be both the wittiest and most accurate words our next president ever spoke on the House floor."

Finerty did not contest Clemens's prediction. That James G. Blaine, Speaker of the House, would be elected president had been almost a foregone conclusion ever since the Republican delegates had left Cincinnati. President Colfax, with his pockets full of bribes in the form of Union Pacific stock, could not run again and have a prayer of winning, while Blaine was popular, congenial, and had engaged in a minimum of larceny. Were his Democratic opponent, the reform-minded Governor Samuel Tilden of New York, to be victorious in the elections, Finerty might hold out some hope for the Republic, but Tilden would need the votes of Democrats in the South to win, men who had already lost the vote for revealing themselves to be unreconstructed rebels, or else because they resided in counties now occupied once more by Federal troops.

"I will say this," Finerty said. "Blaine as president is surely preferable to having that rooster Conkling occupy that high office."

"Or that windbag Colfax," Cody said. "I suppose, now that his Union Pacific stock is nearly worthless, he'll be forced to make an honest living."

"Or a dishonest one," Clemens said. "The president could do quite well on the lecture circuit, I think, being the windbag that he is, especially now that the house-emptiers so greatly outnumber the house-fillers."

President Colfax had not been much in evidence at the convention either physically or inspirationally. No one there had mentioned his name, or had even offered a eulogy to the late vice president, Henry Wilson, who had passed away last autumn. Indeed, Finerty reflected, an uninformed observer listening to the speeches at Exposition Hall might not even have known that Colfax had been the Republican president during the past few years. The dominating presence at the convention had been the ghost of President Grant. Soldier, commander of the Union forces, general, statesman—many seemed to have forgotten that several of those in Grant's administration had begun to grease their palms while Grant was still alive. Many preferred to believe that Grant, had he not fallen victim to an accident, if he had been given more time, would have become the Hercules who would sweep the Augean stables of Washington clean.

Clemens signaled to a waiter. "Gentlemen," he said, "I am going to order the most worthwhile of the gifts the politicians have bestowed upon us in recent years. It's a libation called the mint julep, and I last enjoyed one at the Willard Hotel in Washington."

Finerty grinned. "I'm familiar with the drink. It's said that it was invented for the pleasure of the lobbyists who come there to importune our elected representatives, and the bartender here knows how to make one."

A waiter came and took their order; soon three juleps crowned with sprigs of mint leaves sat on the table. Bill Cody was talking about his reasons for coming to Cincinnati; he had heard stories about a young sharpshooter in the region, and had already seen her demonstrate her skills. "Annie Oakley Moses is her name," he said. "Just a slip of a girl, but the stories about her weren't tall tales. That little gal might make an interesting attraction in my next show."

"A new production?" Finerty asked.

"Oh, I could have gone on increasing my store of filthy lucre with 'Scouts of the Prairie,' but I'm planning to move beyond the stage and theaters," Buffalo Bill replied. "I'm putting together something more like a circus, a truly spectacular wonder, a show that no one will want to miss." He looked around the table, obviously waiting for Clemens or Finerty to prompt him with a question.

"And what is this wonder to be?" Clemens asked.

Cody's chest swelled. "A kind of Wild West show." He signaled to the waiter for another drink, then leaned forward and said, "Custer among the Indians."

"What was that again?" Finerty said.

"That is the title of the production I am planning to mount," Cody said. "'Custer Among the Indians.'" In a lower voice, he continued, "I'm going to stage it outdoors, with the audience seated around a wide open space in a big circle. Custer and the Seventh ride into the circle. Suddenly they're surrounded by Sioux. A tremendous battle ensues—looks like Custer and his men are finished. But then—"

The waiter arrived with Cody's drink. He gulped down half of the julep, then leaned back. "The Injuns suddenly raise a white flag. Seems they want to talk. They parley, smoke the peace pipe, and then they tell Custer how much they admire his courage. They admire it so much that they offer to make him a blood brother, and a most thrilling and authentic demonstration of Injun ceremonies and wild dances follows in the next scene."

Clemens's mustache twitched. Finerty repressed a smile. "No one knows if that's what really happened to that rather impetuous cavalry officer," Clemens said.

"Exactly," Cody said, "but it could have happened. Probably didn't, but it's the kind of thing people would like to believe. We see Custer and the Injuns ride off together to hunt buffalo. I'll have some real buffalo for that scene, of course. And then—"

Finerty waited.

"An attack," Cody said in portentous tones, "by some old Injun enemies of the Sioux. And Custer and his red brothers whip 'em together. The spectacle ends with a victory dance by the Sioux and the Seventh before they all mount their horses and ride into the sunset."

"An edifying ending," Clemens said. "Why, I don't think even the bereft and still grief-stricken Mrs. Elizabeth Custer could take offense at that."

"Especially since you are apparently going to avoid any mention of Custer's rumored dalliance with a Cheyenne squaw," Finerty added.

"Oh, I considered touching on that subject," Cody said, "but that would slow down the action somewhat, and I've got other ideas for a love story."

"Such as?" Finerty said.

"Well, you know that Calamity Jane Cannary rode out with the Seventh when they disappeared," Cody said. "I'm thinking that if this little sharpshooter Annie Oakley Moses has real potential as a performer, I might cast her in the part of Calamity. I could try her out in 'Custer Among the Indians' first, see how she works out. If she's good enough in a small part there, I might write the love story around her." Buffalo Bill downed the rest of his julep and beckoned to the waiter again.

"And what is the title of this love story to be?" Finerty asked.

Cody brought his hands together and looked solemn. "'Calamity Jane, Squaw Woman,'" he said. "She's captured by the Sioux, along with Custer and the Seventh. There she is, the lone white woman among all those redskins, and then a handsome young redskin Lochinvar appears. He's fallen in love with Calamity at first sight—he wants to marry her. He enters on horseback, doing some trick riding, showing off his prowess at shooting and buffalo hunting in his effort to win her affections. Maybe he and Calamity have some shooting contests, and do some trick riding together during the courtship. And then—"

"—a band of enemy Injuns suddenly attacks," Clemens murmured.

"You have been reading my mind, Clemens. Hell, maybe I ought to hire you to write some of my Wild West shows."

Clemens lifted his eyebrows. "Sir, I doubt that my talents would be the equal of your imagination."

Cody smiled before continuing. "Calamity's red suitor rescues her, and then we discover that he's not really a redskin at all, but a white man captured by the Sioux as a boy—there's no point in offending people's sensibilities here. I mean, I did some scouting with Calamity, and she wasn't exactly a respectable woman, but even she'd draw the line somewhere, and I wouldn't want Wild Bill Hickok upset, even if he and Jane did part company." Cody paused. "Might almost be worth it to cast him in the part of the brave, but he's not much good at memorizing lines. Then again, I wouldn't have to give him many lines for a part like that." The waiter set down his next mint julep; Cody lifted the glass, as if about to make a toast. "And the whole show ends with a grand Injun wedding ceremony for Calamity Jane and her brave."

"Buffalo Bill," Finerty said, "I think you're on your way to making even more filthy lucre than you did with 'Scouts of the Prairie.'"

"I'll be looking over that sharpshooter gal again tomorrow," Cody said, "and after that, I've got to find myself some Indians to hire for the show. I want some real authenticity for this spectacle."

"You want to hire some Indians?" Clemens arched his brows. "Why, given the way your productions are likely to burnish their reputation, maybe Chief Touch-the-Clouds and Chief Sitting Bull ought to be paying you and providing some of their braves as performers for free."

"Lo, the poor Indian, the noble savage," Finerty said. "Used to be a man only heard such sentiments in the East. The further the distance from them, the more noble the savages seem—or so it was once. Now you can hear a lot of sympathetic talk in the West. Even men who were fighting the redskins hand to hand a few years ago are admitting that the Indian might have some virtues."

Clemens leaned back in his chair. "True enough. Had I known how the red man's virtues would grow in the public's estimation, I might have made a few changes in my tale of Tom Sawyer. Obviously my imagination failed me there as to what the public would want. Perhaps Injun Joe should have been portrayed as one of the upstanding citizens of St. Petersburg, and gone to rescue Tom and Becky from the caverns." His pipe had gone out; he tapped some more tobacco into it and fired the pipe up again.

"Might be you should write about some of the Sioux chiefs, Irish

John," Cody said. "Might even get yourself an interview with Sitting Bull or Touch-the-Clouds—although you'd probably get better pay writing dime novels about them." He sighed. "When I was hunting buffalo for the workers on the Kansas Pacific, I never thought I'd see the day when the Indians would pretty much decide where the railroads were going to go."

"The railroad magnates aren't doing very well at whipping up terror of an Indian threat so as to wring some profit from their Western ventures," Clemens said. "They badly need an excuse to send in the army to protect their interests, but the savages refuse to cooperate with them by behaving in an appropriately bloodthirsty manner."

"Given the behavior of some of our more prominent citizens in the East," Cody said, "it wouldn't take much for a redskin to look like a model of virtue by comparison."

The waiter returned with another round of mint juleps, the second drink for Finerty and for Clemens. Finerty had lost track of Buffalo Bill's consumption, although the only obvious effect of the liquor on the showman was to make him sound more subdued.

"I recently saw one such model of Indian virtue in New York," Clemens said, "giving a lecture at the Cooper Union. The fellow has only been on the circuit for a few months, and already he's drawing a good crowd with his tales of his adventures among the Sioux."

"He's a Sioux?" Cody asked.

"No, an Iroquois by the name of Rowland, but he knows the Sioux well and he lived among them for some time, and his wife is Sioux. She was sitting up in the front row during his lecture, looking appropriately attentive and as respectable as any swell New York matron. Perhaps I should have used someone like Rowland as a model for my character Injun Joe. He tells quite a tale, beginning with his days in the army as one of the officers on the staff of General Grant, serving with the general's aide, Ely Parker."

Finerty lifted his brows. "The disgraced former commissioner of Indian Affairs?"

"The commissioner who is now a most prosperous New York

businessman," Clemens replied. "Parker has worked hard to make up for the mistake his ancestors made in selling the island of Manhattan so cheaply. He's bought up land there and then sold it at quite a handsome profit. He apparently arranged for the first lectures by his red colleague Rowland—perhaps as a favor to his friend, perhaps as a way of winning more public justification of his earlier policies as commissioner. Parker must have the touch of a Midas, because the lectures are bringing in more than anyone expected."

"Parker was right, I suppose," Cody said. "He wanted peace with the Indians, and now we have it."

"Not because of anything Parker did while in office," Finerty said, "only because the army is needed elsewhere, and the Indians are somehow managing to maintain their alliance and to keep from fighting among themselves. Otherwise, there would surely have been war on the Plains by now."

"I'll tell you one thing," Cody muttered. "I'm surprised the Sioux haven't gone looking for a fight with somebody by now, with the Crow or the Arikara if there's nobody else to fight. It isn't like them."

"Then perhaps our current peace is no more than a temporary truce," Clemens said, "a brief interlude in the affairs of the nation until the new secessionists are forced back into the fold, the Indians revert to their customary savage ways, and the many apostates in the West have their faith in our manifest destiny rekindled."

Finerty was thinking of what Crook had told him. The general was hoping that war with the Sioux would not come, but he was prepared to fight if it did.

"War will come," Crook had said, and he had meant more than the skirmishes with rebel guerrillas. He had finished, "But I cannot tell who it is my men and I will be fighting."

A crowd had gathered on 77th Street, on the west side of Central Park and across from the stone walls that marked the still-unfinished

Museum of Natural History. The speaker addressing the assemblage from a makeshift wooden platform was a compact man with a broad freckled face and an Irish brogue.

"They're drafting us to fight the bloody British here when we should be fighting them in our homeland!" The man waved his arms. "They're drafting us to fight rebels in the South so the bloody free blacks can take work away from honest white working men!" He lifted one arm and pointed over the crowd at one wall of the hoped for and possibly never to be completed museum. "They're sinking money into that building while our families starve! And I can tell you this, boyos—none of the rich will be doing the fighting, or sending their own sons to fight. They'll buy their way out of it and send their substitutes to fight in their place, just like they did during the last war!"

Lemuel Rowland stood on the edge of the crowd. What the speaker lacked in eloquence, he made up for in conviction. Several people near the speaker cheered; another group of men streamed from a side street toward the crowd.

"From each man according to his abilities," a man next to the platform shouted. "To each man according to his needs." More people were joining the crowd, a few of them waving red flags.

Lemuel saw that there was little chance now of finding a carriage and driver to take him downtown, back to Ely Parker's house. This crowd would soon be a mob. There had been a riot in New York earlier that autumn, one that had gone on for two days and nearly turned into a revolt. By the end of the rioting, five black men were hanging from lampposts, a block of tenements had been burned to the ground, and windows had been shattered all over Manhattan. There had never been a final and complete reckoning of the number of deaths and injuries suffered by the rioters, their victims, and the policemen who had eventually restored order to the city.

Lemuel had thought that another riot might be brewing after the recent elections. Blaine and his running mate, Governor Rutherford B. Hayes of Ohio, had won a narrow victory, but there were many who believed that the election had been stolen from Tilden. Had the voters in the occupied states of the South been allowed to cast their ballots, Lemuel had little doubt that Tilden would have been inaugurated as president that coming March, but whether a President Tilden would have kept the peace on the Plains was open to question. Tilden might have restored peace to the South, and he would also not have been open to the charges of corruption that were already being leveled against Blaine in the wake of his victory. With peace restored to the South, Tilden might then have turned his attention to quelling the growing separatist sentiments in the West, a course that would have been urged upon him by Generals Sherman and Sheridan. Blaine of course would have his own reasons for looking westward now, for wanting to serve the interests of the financiers and railroad men who had helped him line his pockets.

Lemuel looked around at the people near him. They were clearly not thinking of either Blaine or Tilden. Another man was speaking now.

"I fought for the Union," this speaker was saying. "I saw my best friend die when a minié ball shattered his face. What was I fighting for? The Union? There ain't no Union now except in name."

The size of the crowd was increasing. The gray sky was growing darker. As Lemuel was about to slip away, he saw two policemen moving toward the fringes of the group. He watched them, wondering why only two had been sent, and then one of the policemen raised his arm.

"We're with you, boys!" the policeman called out. The crowd cheered. Lemuel felt a dizzying disorienting feeling that he had not felt for some time, the sense that the situation in which he now found himself was not quite real, that the mob would melt away.

"Look!" someone else shouted in a high-pitched voice. "Saw him at the Cooper Union, going in to give a speech." A newsboy in a ragged coat with a pile of newspapers under his arm was speaking. He lifted an arm and pointed at Lemuel. "Right over there."

Lemuel had a sudden impulse to flee. Had it been later in the day, he might have been able to lose himself in the park. Had it been darker, the sharp-eyed boy might not have recognized him.

"Come out and talked to a few of us afterwards, he did," the boy said. Lemuel had given several lectures at the Cooper Union that autumn, and had spent time after leaving the hall with some of those outside who could not afford the cost of a ticket, the newsboys and street vendors and others who were loitering outside. He had been the civilized red man willing to share his tales of the Indians of the West with even the poorest of the city's inhabitants, as Ely Parker had advised him to be.

Other people were turning to look at him. He swallowed his fear. "He's an Indian," the boy said, "from out West. Lived with a bunch of wild Indians there, he did."

This crowd could turn on him. The respectable and more prosperous citizens of New York might be sympathetic to his stories of honorable Sioux and noble Indians who wanted only to keep their land, Indians who were already making allies among many living in the regions bordering their territory, but the poor could be less understanding. Some of them had been among the audiences at his lectures, standing in the back of the hall. Often they asked more pointed and difficult questions of him than did the wealthier members of the assemblage: Why did the redskins need so much land for themselves? Wasn't it true that the railroad owners were once willing to give a poor man some land as long as he was willing to go out West to claim it and farm it? Was it true that there was gold to be mined out there, gold that might have made a lot of poor men rich if they could only get to it to mine it? Might not the Indians make war on the settlers again?

"Is that true?" a young man with a broad Slavic face asked. "You an Indian?"

"Yes, but I am not a Sioux."

"Did you really live with those wild redskins?"

"Yes," Lemuel replied.

"Thought I might go out there once," the man said, "have my own spread, but there's no chance of that now."

"The men who wanted more railroads crossing the Plains weren't being honest with people like you," Lemuel said, "when they spoke about free land. They didn't tell you how hard much of the land out there is to farm. All they think about is moving people into those territories so that they can lay down more track to connect them, to bring the farmers' grain and cattle to market. You would have been completely dependent on their trains and their tracks, and once you were there, they could have charged you whatever they wanted to in payment. You would have had no choice but to pay it. And they wouldn't have done anything for any farmers who might be ruined, who might have been lured west by false promises and then failed."

It was the same sort of answer he had given to such questions before. He looked around at the faces near him, and his fear faded; they were listening to him for the moment.

"But this doesn't mean that there isn't room in the West for you," Lemuel continued, "and places for people like you. The towns near the Indian territories need skilled workers, there are even two ironworks being built along the Bozeman Trail where some of the army's forts once stood. The Lakota—the Sioux and the Cheyenne and the others who live on the Plains—will welcome those who come to them in peace. All they ask is that their own hunting grounds be left to them and the buffalo, hunting grounds that would be useless to farmers. All they ask is that they be treated as friends, not as enemies, not as people to be herded into small plots of land while their territories are stolen from them."

The knots of people, even those farthest from him who probably could not hear him well, were silent and attentive. Lemuel had gone over his lectures with Ely Parker, writing them down, practicing his elocution and timing, deciding which stories would cast the Lakota in the best light, but it was not until he gave his first lecture to a small gathering that his gift had manifested itself. He had caught the attention of the listeners immediately, and held it, and had seen them moved by his words, and had not known afterward how it had happened. Practicing his speeches with Donehogawa, deciding on what to say, learning how to vary the tone and pitch of his voice—none of that by itself could have given him a power that seemed to come from outside himself. Sometimes he heard his own voice as if it were coming from someone else, as if someone or something else was using him to speak. The ghost of a Seneca sachem, perhaps, of a chief who had been able to move his people in council long ago—or perhaps it was simply a gift Lemuel had not known before that he possessed.

"I heard," a man shouted from the back, "that a black man's as good as a white man out there, a red man the same as a white man—maybe even a little better. What kind of place is it where a man can't live with his own and not have some nigger or redskin acting like—like—"

"Would you rather be conscripted into the army," Lemuel interrupted, "and forced to protect black men from white men, or white men from red men, at risk to your own lives?" There was a murmur from some in the crowd. "Would you rather have the wealthy and powerful protecting their own interests by using you to do their fighting for them? No one in the West is forced to live among people he finds disagreeable. That happens here, in the Eastern cities, in the tenements."

He was aware that if he had been delivering these lines in an auditorium, the speech would rank among his worst, yet these people were listening, were clearly willing to believe what he said. His words, and the gift he had for making others believe them, had silenced even the angriest of the crowd.

The words he needed flowed into him. In the West, there would be no conscription, because the people, whatever their differences, were at peace. Men had fought and died for a Union that had become a multitude of bankers and magnates and their paid-for officials in Washington grasping for ever more wealth and power; it was no wonder others besides rebellious and unreconstructed Southerners dreamed of governing themselves. He had said it all many times, in different ways, in all of his lectures, and there was enough truth in what he said to sway those who listened.

A roar went up from the crowd, a cry of rage. For an instant, Lemuel thought that he had lost them after all, and then saw what had provoked their anger. Blue-coated men were riding up 77th Street on horseback. It was the army, not the police, who would disperse this crowd.

"Get them!" a man near Lemuel cried. He had lost them; Lemuel backed away, not knowing what to do now. Others were shouting; people turned away from him to look at the soldiers.

Suddenly the crowd surged toward the mounted men. Lemuel watched as the uniformed men aimed their rifles, then threw himself to the ground. He heard the sound of rifle shots and then screams.

He looked up and saw several men dragging one of the mounted men from his horse. More shots rang out. Lemuel struggled to his feet.

"Let's get out of here," a voice said near him. He turned to see a small woman in a loose brown coat. She pulled at his sleeve. "Come on," she said, "what are you waiting for? Do you want to get arrested for inciting to riot?"

She let go of him and ran toward the park; he followed her.

The riots had swept through the city for two days. Katia stood by one of the third-story windows, listening to the ringing of alarms, the tolling of bells and a faint shrieking that rose and fell, that might be either the wind or the cries of the dying. Streams of smoke and intermittent flashes of light were visible in the northwest. Parts of the city were burning.

Grisha pulled her away from the window. "It is not safe for you there," he said.

"My husband is still missing," she said.

"You will not bring Rowland to safety any sooner by standing where a stray bullet might hit you."

Grisha was exaggerating. The downtown areas south and east of the Fifties were still untouched. The rioters had attacked the great houses farther uptown first.

"He must be waiting it out somewhere," she murmured.

"Yes. He would do that, he would find a place to wait it out. Now come away."

She let him lead her to her room. Grisha had come there, to Ely Parker's brownstone on East 21st Street, the night the rioting had started, appearing suddenly with no warning. Apparently Parker was used to such unannounced visits, and the two men had retired to Parker's study. Katia had found out the next morning that Lemuel had never returned to the house and that the rioting and looting had spread to Fifth Avenue.

Grisha opened the door to her room. "I hope he is safe," she whispered, surprising herself with her concern for Lemuel.

"He knows how to look out for himself." Grisha paused. "I spoke to Donehogawa about taking you to Washington."

"And my husband?" she asked.

"Of course. He can give some of his speeches there."

Not long ago, she would have welcomed being with Grisha again, going to Washington, staying in his house. She would not have been fearing for Lemuel Rowland, or thinking about him at all.

"I don't want to go back to Washington," she said.

"It will be better for you there, Katia. I will buy you some new dresses—there will be parties, people to see, people who will want to see you."

"I do not want to go there."

"And where would you go instead of to Washington?"

She did not know how to tell him. To St. Louis, perhaps, then on to St. Joseph, or to one of the other places where those of her people who had learned Wasichu ways sometimes came, to trade with the whites and to prove that they were no threat as long as the treaty was kept. Katia thought of how Lemuel spoke of those places, the towns and settlements bordering the Lakota lands. There, she would not be a Lakota woman who had lived too long among the Wasichu, an outsider among both her own people and the whites. There would be others like herself, people who were learning to move between those two worlds.

"Where would you go?" Grisha asked again.

She swayed and put a hand against the wall to steady herself. The hallway was suddenly lighter, the gaslights too bright. Sparks of light danced in front of her eyes.

"Good night, Grisha." She went into her room quickly and closed the door behind her, then crossed the room to the window and flung it open.

Cold air stung her face. She looked toward the west, but could not see any signs of the rioters. The bells had stopped ringing, the city was silent. The left side of her head throbbed with pain. She sank to the window seat and looked down.

Lakota warriors were in the street below, riding past on horseback, as if in a triumphal procession. Crazy Horse was among them, wearing his war paint of lightning bolts and white hailstones with his long hair streaming behind him. Walking Blanket Woman, with her dead brother's coup stick clutched in her right hand, rode with the warriors, just behind Sitting Bull, who wore his bonnet of eagle feathers. There were bare-chested warriors in war paint and others in Wasichu clothing, and in the midst of the procession a tepee, painted with red and white stripes and stars on a blue background, had been pitched on top of a flat wagon. Four horses pulled the wagon; a man sat in front of the tepee. He turned his face toward her and she recognized Touch-the-Clouds.

She looked up and the familiar skyline of New York was gone. The city had vanished.

The dizziness caught her then. Katia managed to close the window before stumbling to her bed.

She lay there in the dark for a long time, unable even to get up to take off her clothing and prepare herself for sleep. The eerie silence persisted; she could not even hear the sounds of the house, the footsteps on the stairs, the murmur of voices in other rooms.

At last she heard a tap on the door, and then it opened. "Mrs. Rowland." That was Bridget, one of the two maids. "Och, you poor thing—are you ill?"

"No," Katia said, "I'm all right," and opened her eyes. The gray light outside the windowpanes told her that it was morning.

"You're sure?" Bridget helped her sit up and plumped up the pillows behind her. "You gave me a fright, Mrs. Rowland, lying there like that in your dress. I feared it might be the typhus."

"What is happening outside now?" Katia asked. "Have you heard anything?"

"A gentleman's downstairs, Mr. Roosevelt, with his wife and some of his family. Come here in the middle of the night, and told us some of what was going on. Mob of people burned down his new house on the West Side, and some others round it, up on Fifty-seventh Street. Better if they had burned out the filthy tenements downtown." Bridget slipped off Katia's shoes and then covered her with a blanket. "There's a lot of people like Mr. Roosevelt staying in other houses on this street, but the rioting's almost over. That's what I heard when the gentlemen were talking this morning. Had to bring in more soldiers to stop it—some of the police were rioting, too. They say at least three hundred people are dead."

"Bridget." Grisha was standing at the door, in the same black suit he had been wearing last night, looking as though he had not slept. "Go downstairs and see what you can do to aid Mrs. Roosevelt and her daughters. I will look after Mrs. Rowland."

Bridget hurried from the room, but left the door open. "Rowland is back," Grisha said.

Katia stiffened and clasped her hands together. "Is he—"

"He is downstairs, fortunately with only a few bruises, from which he will quickly recover. He says a woman got him away from one crowd before it began to riot. He managed to get her to her flat safely, and then had to hide there when the rioting reached her street. A man was hanged there, Rowland said, a man in evening clothes. The mob pulled him out of a passing carriage."

Katia sighed, unable to speak.

"Rowland was wise to stay hidden. Communists, socialists, discontented veterans of the war to preserve the Union, the wretched poor—no one knows who started it, not that it matters now. They probably all had a hand in it." He came toward her and stood over the bed. "It is almost over. Martial law has been declared here. When it is quiet enough, when I can get the permissions, we will go to Washington, you and Rowland and I."

"I told you before that I didn't want to go there."

"You will be safer in Washington," Grisha said.

She heard footsteps outside, in the hallway. Lemuel appeared at her door. Katia restrained herself from getting out of bed and running to him, from showing how much she felt for him in front of Grisha.

"What is this talk about Washington?" Lemuel asked.

Grisha turned around. "I was suggesting to Katia that it would be to her benefit, and to yours, to come to Washington with me."

"I don't want to go," Katia said softly.

"You will be safer there," Grisha said.

"You're mistaken, Rubalev," Lemuel said. "I've been through enough during the past three days to convince me that this won't be the last such riot. The same thing could happen in Washington."

"The government will not let it happen there. They will take this as a warning. They will take steps."

"They'll have to keep more troops in New York now," Lemuel said. "They'll have to conscript more men to have enough soldiers to keep the peace here, and in the south, and in Boston and any other Eastern harbors where British ships aren't more than a few miles offshore. I don't know how the government in Washington will be able to do that very easily, given that widespread bitterness about conscription is one of the things that kindled this uprising."

Lemuel came to the bed. "Where do you want to go, Katia? Or is that you prefer to stay here?"

She shook her head. "I can't stay here. Donehogawa has been kind, but I have stayed here long enough. I want to go west again. I can't live among my people any more, I know that—too much has changed in me. But I want to live near them."

"You are making a mistake, Katia," Grisha said.

Lemuel turned toward Grisha. "A mistake? I think not. My wife would be safer out there than here. There is peace out West, and given the troubles Washington faces now, that peace is likely to endure for some time."

Grisha's eyes narrowed. "This sounds like something that you would say in one of your lectures."

"My lectures weren't lies, Rubalev. I didn't give my talks simply to feed the discontent of people, or to win their sympathy for our Lakota brethren. When I began, I had my doubts that people would listen, that what I dreamed of could ever come about. But now I know that it can. The longer there is peace on the Plains, the greater the chance that war will never come."

"That will not stop the Lakota from preparing for war."

"Of course they must prepare for it," Lemuel said, "if only to keep their former enemies from attacking them. A stalemate can serve the Lakota as well as any war."

Grisha was silent. Katia thought of her vision, of the procession she had seen only a few hours ago. Lemuel was wrong; war would come. That was what the vision meant; she was certain of that now, and she would not have had such a vision here, among the Wasichu, unless it meant that the Wasichu would be defeated. The Lakota were warriors; sooner or later, they would fight.

"In any case," Lemuel continued, "Katia is able to decide for herself where she wants to live."

Grisha opened his mouth, about to speak. She shot him a glance. "Yes," she said, "I am, and I will not go to Washington."

"And where do you wish to go?" She heard the suppressed anger in Grisha's voice. He could not care about her so much; he did not need her anymore to further his ends, whatever they might be now. Perhaps he was simply angry that she no longer needed him.

"I want to go West," she said, "with my husband. I will leave it to him to decide where we will go."

SEVENTEEN

White Eagle sat outside his tepee with a drum, softly tapping out signals in the talking wire code. His camp was in Dakota Territory, a day's ride to the west of Fort Abraham Lincoln. White Eagle still thought of the circle of pitched tepees as a camp, although the Lakota there were living in ways that his grandfather would have found strange.

Three of the men in the camp, among them Denis Laforte, were Wasichu Sapa, black men, who had taken Lakota, Cheyenne, or Arikara wives. There was also, at the edge of the camp circle, a tepee that stood near a pole from which a talking wire had been strung. Through the talking wire, using one of the signalling devices inside the tepee, White Eagle could send signals to Bismarck, the town across the Missouri River from Fort Lincoln, to the Wasichu medicine man who worked there with his assistants, and from Bismarck to places that were far away. A few of the young men were inside the tepee practicing their telegraphy.

Telegraphy—that was what the Wasichu called the tapping that sent words and messages through the talking wires. White Eagle had quickly learned how to do the tapping in the white man's language, but for the past months he had been devising a Lakota code for the sounds. Morse code was what Talking Wire Man Edison, the Wasichu medicine man in Bismarck, called the telegraph signals. Spirits inside the wires flew with those signals to far places, where other men could listen to them and know what the spirits were trying to tell them.

If war came, the Lakota would need to know how to use this telegraphy, this Wasichu medicine that could send their signals over great distances. So Touch-the-Clouds believed, which was why White Eagle had learned how to tap out the messages and had taught the skill to others and was now practicing the signals in a Lakota-based code. The Eastern Orphan Rowland had told Touch-the-Clouds about how useful the talking wires and the messages carried over them had been during the great war between the Blue Coats and the Gray Coats. Four Star Grant, the chief who had later become the Great Father in Washington, had been able to send commands to chiefs and warriors who were far away from him, and find out where men at a distance were moving and what battles they had recently fought.

Touch-the-Clouds had smiled while speaking of the talking wires. Cut the wires, and an enemy could be cut off from knowing about the movements of both his own men and his foes—although the Orphan claimed that there were some men who had mastered the signals so well that they could place cut wires against their tongues and capture the signals being carried by the wire spirits. Cutting the wires to keep an enemy in the dark about distant events was one good tactic, but Touch-the-Clouds had seen that knowing the medicine of the talking wires could also be useful in warfare in many ways.

War, White Eagle thought. War would come, sooner or later, whatever some of those who lived among and traded with the Lakota and their allies preferred to believe. Even the older men, those who had counted coup in battles long ago, had seen that they had to be ready for war, even if the peace they had now lasted for several more years. The Wasichu would grow greedy once again, and they had broken treaties before. Touch-the-Clouds had seen that the Lakota would have to find new ways to fight.

Denis Laforte came out of the tepee where the telegraph was kept, followed by two children. One was White Eagle's daughter, Dancing Girl, his only child and now nearly twelve summers old. The other was Yellow Bird, the son of Young Spring Grass and Long Hair Custer; the boy was close to Dancing Girl's age.

"The children are learning fast," Laforte said in the Wasichu tongue as he walked toward White Eagle. "They can send and receive messages nearly as well as the men now."

"Better," Dancing Girl said, using the Wasichu word. "The wire sings to me." She wore a long deerskin tunic and denim leggings; her black hair hung down to her waist. Her face was already much like her mother's, with the same large brown eyes and slightly crooked smile.

White Eagle frowned at his daughter, who passed too many of her days among the wire warriors instead of doing women's tasks or playing with the other girls, then smiled. When Brown Bear Woman had died, only four years after the birth of their daughter, White Eagle's grief was so large and crushing that he had thought that he might never take another wife. His mother, White Buffalo Woman, had taken in Dancing Girl, and he had not needed a wife in the camp of Glorious Spirit and Victorious Spirit. Since the signing of the treaty at Fort Fetterman almost four years ago, he had spent as much time in the Wasichu towns bordering Lakota territory, in Bismarck and Deadwood and Red Cloud, as among his own people. He had felt how unlike his father, how unlike most of his people, he had become after arriving at this camp a year ago to teach younger men some of the Wasichu ways and to learn the language of the talking wires from Edison, the Wasichu in Bismarck.

Dancing Girl sat down next to him. "Send me a message," she said.

White Eagle tapped out a few signals.

"The message is in English," Yellow Bird said.

Dancing Girl made a face at him. "Anyone can hear that it's in

English. Let Father send the rest of the message."

White Eagle beat out a stream of signals.

"The Great Father Blaine in Washington has agreed to treaties with the Little Fathers of Texas and California," his daughter said. "Is that true?"

"It is," Laforte replied. "Talking Wire Man Edison read it in a Bismarck talking paper yesterday. Your father received the message this morning."

"Speak in Lakota," White Eagle said. He was beginning to worry that Dancing Girl spoke more easily in the Wasichu tongue than her own, while Yellow Bird rarely used his mother's Cheyenne tongue. They might have to know the white man's speech, but he did not want them to lose their own. Words shaped the world. He had found that out after learning the Wasichu tongue. The world he had known as a child, the world of wakan beings and visions and *pte*, Uncle Buffalo, became a place of things to be parceled out, looked at, examined, and taken apart. The Wasichu tongue could blind a man to the spirits that lived in all things and make him see the hills and plains and mountains as soulless places.

"Send me another message," Dancing Girl said.

White Eagle tapped on the drum.

"A day's ride west of our camp, a young Wasichu man who wears small glass shields in front of his eyes has come to camp on the Little Missouri River," Dancing Girl said in Lakota, and then in English, "Father, that's silly. Why would a man wear shields over his eyes?"

"It is another message from Talking Wire Man Edison," Laforte said. "This Wasichu man is so shortsighted that he must wear lenses in metal frames—they are called spectacles—in order to see anything at a distance." He spoke the words in English, and White Eagle did not object, because there were no words for "spectacles" or "lenses" in Lakota.

Dancing Girl leaned against her father. "When I am older," she said in Lakota, "I will go to war."

"You cannot," Yellow Bird said. "You are a girl."

"Walking Blanket Woman went to war. She fought in the Black

Hills. She was at Fort Fetterman, counting coup with the men."

"Walking Blanket Woman had no brothers and no husband," White Eagle said. "It was proper for her to fight in their place and take vengeance against the Wasichu for their deaths."

"I have no brothers and no husband," Dancing Girl said. "Buffalo Calf Road Woman talks of going to war." She shot a look at Yellow Bird. "And your mother went to war in the Black Hills against—"

"That is enough," a woman's voice said behind them. "You should not speak of what happened in the Black Hills, not in a place near so many Wasichu, and I hope you will never have to go to war."

White Eagle looked up and saw his wife, Young Spring Grass, standing by the opening of their tepee. There was another thing his grandfather would not have understood, how he could take a woman as a wife who had been used by Long Hair Custer, who had given the Blue Coat chief a son and then been discarded by him, whom no man among the Tsistsistas, her own Cheyenne people, would have had as a wife. But White Eagle had wanted a wife who knew something of Wasichu ways, who would not shake her head at him and make signs against evil spirits with her hands when he spoke of rocket-arrows, talking wires, exploding balls, and other Wasichu medicine.

"Everyone knows what happened in the Black Hills," Dancing Girl said.

"We know," Young Spring Grass murmured, "and the Wasichu have their suspicions about what took place there." She gazed at her light-haired son. "But it is better if we do not talk of it, especially while the Wasichu are at peace with us."

His wife, White Eagle thought, was wise about that. Many Wasichu knew, or had guessed, that Custer and his men had all died, one way or another, but by now, after over four years, many of the whites had come to believe that Long Hair must have brought his fate upon himself. Perhaps his Blue Coats had attacked a Lakota camp and been punished in return. Perhaps they had surrendered, and then decided to desert from the army. Perhaps Long Hair and his men were hiding in Texas or California, waiting for war to come again, so that they could rejoin the battle against the red man. The Wasichu could believe whatever they liked, as long as the treaty was kept.

The sheer white cliffs and grassy valleys of the Badlands were behind him. Lemuel had ridden one day's ride from the Easterner's cabin on the Little Missouri with two of that young settler's hands. Those two men had left him to camp by himself for the night, and the next day, after a slow ride, Lemuel had followed a trail to a small Arikara encampment. The Arikara chief there had known little Lakota and almost no English; Lemuel had not been able to ask what he and his people might have heard about the young man who had come to live along the Little Missouri.

Lemuel had not told the young man that he had met his father, Theodore Roosevelt, in New York. He would have had to say then that he had last spoken to him during that dreadful November of 1876, when riots had convulsed the city, and he had sensed that young Roosevelt might not welcome any discussion of the evening that had marked such an abrupt change in his family's fortunes.

The young man bore his father's name, Theodore, but his men called him Four Eyes behind his back. With his thick glasses and prominent teeth, he did not look much like his handsome and impressive father; his shrill high voice and pompous manner of speech were, Lemuel had noticed, another source of private amusement for Roosevelt's hired hands. But the young man, only twenty years of age, had spirit. The life of wealth and privilege he had known in New York had vanished in the wake of the riots and more bank and business failures. He had left Harvard after his father's death earlier that year to settle his family's affairs and to see his mother and sisters off to England. They would be safer there, his mother had a brother in England, and so young Theodore felt it wiser to overlook the uneasy state of relations between England and the United States. As for himself, he had come West, he claimed, largely out of curiosity.

Lemuel had his doubts about that. Young Roosevelt had clearly retained some of his considerable wealth to be able to afford his silver spurs, silver belt buckle, and his perfectly tailored buckskins. He still had connections among the wealthy families of New York, people who might be interested in profiting from the West in time. Roosevelt might be hoping to go in on some venture with them, if the peace endured and any opportunities presented themselves. In the meantime, judging by the bear and buffalo heads Roosevelt had already mounted on the inside walls of his unfinished cabin, he was keeping himself well occupied by hunting.

"By Godfrey," Roosevelt had told him, "the hunting's good out here. A gentleman can live the way a gentleman should." Lemuel had refrained from mentioning that few gentlemen could be found in these parts, and that the Indians would not take kindly to the extravagant slaughter of buffalo. The young man was intelligent; he would soon find that out for himself. He did not need to hear it from Lemuel; as a red man, whatever his accomplishments, he was definitely not a man whom Theodore Roosevelt, Jr. would think of as a gentleman.

Lemuel rode away from the Arikara camp just after dawn, so impatient now to reach the ferry to Bismarck that he decided to skirt the camp of White Eagle instead of stopping there. Katia would be waiting for him in Bismarck, and Touch-the-Clouds would be expecting a report from him eventually on whatever wonders Edison might be concocting in his laboratory. Lately, the inventor was working on a new source of illumination, a lamp he called an incandescent light, although such a device was not likely to be of much use to the Lakota and their allies. Edison did not seem to care; he worked on whatever interested him and knew that Touch-the-Clouds valued him too much to object to that. The man reminded Lemuel of Crazy Horse in the way he seemed to live in a world of his own, apart from this one.

Rubalev had brought Edison and several assistants out here. Edison wanted his laboratory, and whether he built it in the East or in Lakota territory had made no difference to him. He had come up the turbulent Missouri in a steamboat filled with equipment and supplies, and more shipments had continued to arrive afterward by train from Duluth to the outpost of Seward and from there by wagon to Bismarck. Rubalev had stayed long enough to get Edison and his wife settled, and then had left Bismarck.

Lemuel did not want to know where the Alaskan had gone. To Washington, perhaps, to see that those diplomats whose governments preferred the present state of affairs in North America continued to remain neutral. Perhaps Rubalev was trying to interest the Russians in buying back Alaska and appointing him as its governor. That, to Lemuel, would be a welcome development. He found his insides eased at the thought of never seeing Rubalev again.

"Listen carefully," Mary Stilwell Edison said to the small group of women who had come to her husband's laboratory. "Mr. Edison's new machine is quite remarkable."

Katia had never seen the inside rooms of the laboratory before, but Thomas Edison was, according to his wife, so pleased with his new invention that he had allowed her to invite the wives of his assistants to come and look at it. Mrs. Edison had invited Katia as well. Lemuel was not one of Edison's assistants, but was in the laboratory often enough almost to be considered one.

The goodhearted Mrs. Edison had not invited Mrs. Miles, the wife of Fort Abraham Lincoln's commanding officer, or any of the other officers' wives, which was just as well. They probably would not have accepted the invitation anyway given that accepting it would have required being ferried across the treacherous waters of the Missouri. Except for occasional forays outside the fort on horseback, the military wives kept to their residences there and had little to do with the townsfolk upriver, and avoiding a crossing of the Missouri provided a good excuse. They, or their husbands, apparently did not want to grow too friendly with the citizens of Bismarck, perhaps because there were a few others like Katia who lived there, Lakota and other Indians who seemed to think themselves the equals of whites.

Edison's new invention sat on a table in front of them. John Kreusi, one of the inventor's assistants, was fitting a shiny cylinder to the device, which had a handle at one end and a flywheel at the other. A gadget that held a needle was poised above the cylinder.

Edison took hold of the handle and turned it; the cylinder rotated as the needle etched a grove. Edison leaned over the machine and shouted, "Mary had a little lamb, its fleece was white as snow." A smile crossed his wide, pale unbearded face; he looked up at his wife. "Now you say something, Mary."

"Oh, dear." Mary Edison giggled. "I wouldn't know what to say."

Edison stopped turning the handle, moved the needle back to where it had started, and turned the handle again. He cupped an ear with his free hand. Katia had at first thought of him as a man with no interest in hearing what others had to say. In fact, she had soon learned, he was hard of hearing.

"Mary had a little lamb," the machine said in a faint voice, but one that Katia easily recognized as Edison's. "Its fleece was white as snow." Then, more faintly, "Now you say something, Mary."

"Oh, dear," Mrs. Edison's voice replied, "I wouldn't know what to say."

"Land sakes," Mary Edison said. The women fluttered around the device, marveling at it.

"Been working on it a while," Edison said. "Tried paper covered in wax. Tried some other things, but the foil's what worked best. I call it a phonograph."

"Won't be much use to the Injuns," another assistant, a man named Polk, muttered, "and they and their friend Rubalev's payin' our bills."

"You are mistaken, Mr. Polk," Katia said quickly. "To be able to hear the voice of a medicine man who is far away, to preserve our chants and sacred songs—our chiefs would be most grateful for such a machine."

The others smiled at her, with the friendly but wary expressions to which she had accustomed herself.

The Wasichu inventor allowed them to admire the phonograph for a while before another assistant gently herded them out of the room and down the wooden stairs. Katia thanked Mrs. Edison for the tea and cakes that had been served to the ladies earlier, then went to her horse. The Wasichu women from the East had grown used to seeing her astride on horseback, although most of them preferred their landaus and wagons.

The house she shared with her husband was a rented shack only two miles from Edison's laboratory, on land with a small barn, chicken coop, and some grazing land and a corral for their few horses. Lemuel's pinto was in the corral. She took the saddle off her horse, rubbed it down, then led all three of the horses into the barn.

She had been happy here, and held that happiness as close to herself as the small medicine pouch of amulets that hung around her neck, but soon Anton Hobel, the owner, would be back with his new wife from Kansas City. Lemuel and she would have to leave this house then, but they could find rooms in Bismarck, perhaps in its renovated but still shabby hotel. She did not care where they went, as long as they were together.

Katia left the barn and went inside to greet her husband.

Katia had cooked a chicken for his supper. Lemuel ate the food with relish, but would have been as happy with beans or salt pork and bread. They went to bed early and again Katia showed him the joy she took with him.

Once he had realized that she had come to care for him, he had hoped that there might at last be a child for them, but no child had come. Lemuel had gradually discovered that he did not care about that, either. How strange they both were, he thought, to be content that way; how different their world had become from that of the people around them.

He held her for a while, knowing that she would not fall asleep right away. He would have to tell her what he planned to do.

"I had a letter from Donehogawa today," he said at last. "He is asking—he wants me to go to St. Joseph."

"Why?"

"Because from there I can easily get to Fort Leavenworth and talk to Jeremiah Clarke."

She was not asking him why he had to see Jeremiah Clarke. She had probably guessed at the reason; Clarke's most recent letters had revealed his growing disaffection with the army's commanders in Washington. Lemuel would have to find out anything he could about what the army might be planning. He would not learn much from Colonel Nelson A. Miles, who was now in command at Fort Abraham Lincoln, on the other side of the Missouri from Bismarck, where the Fifth Infantry was now stationed with new recruits for the Seventh Cavalry. Miles was congenial, intelligent, and revealed nothing of what the officers above him might be thinking. There was no doubt that he had at least an inkling of any moves they might be planning.

"My wife is the niece of General Sherman," Nelson Miles had told the delegation from Bismarck that had welcomed him to the territory. His cold eyes had told Lemuel that he was not especially happy to see someone like White Eagle, in his feathered bonnet, among the delegation. "And another uncle is Senator John Sherman of Ohio." Miles had wanted to make certain everyone knew about his connections at the outset, and it was rumored that he routinely ignored the chain of command and took his orders directly from Sherman.

In the months since Miles had come to Fort Lincoln, relations between the soldiers and the Lakota and Arikara who camped below the bluffs that overlooked the fort during the winter had grown more uneasy. Miles could not violate the treaty and his orders, but he could delay deliveries of promised food to the Lakota and Arikara, food they had already paid for with hides, pelts, and small bags of gold. He could make it clear that he disapproved of whites who were overly friendly with the savages, and that he especially disliked any who, like Edison, did not seem to mind benefitting the red man in some way as long as they got what they wanted. Miles let other whites know where their true loyalties had to be in the end.

It was, Lemuel supposed, almost a miracle, given the hostility of Miles, that the peace had not already been broken. If I were thinking of starting another war, he thought, Miles is just the sort of commander I would send out here.

In the darkness, Katia murmured, "If you are going to St. Joseph, then I will go with you."

"You don't have to come along, Katia. I'll be back here by autumn, probably sooner."

"I want to come along," she said. "I will miss you if I stay here."

It warmed him to hear her admit that. Perhaps she would also be safer away from Bismarck. Miles might take some kind of action, perhaps sending out a few scouts or a small expedition, that would strain the treaty without actually breaking it. He might even do something bolder, just to provoke the Lakota, to have some excuse to fight.

"We'll leave here together," he said.

"Good." Her arms were around him once more.

June had come, Congress was still in session and soon to adjourn for the summer, yet the lobby of the Willard Hotel was almost completely empty. John Finerty was immediately wary, wondering what was going on. Normally the lobby was filled with what could only be called a motley crowd of elected officials, office-seekers, correspondents, diplomats, representatives of the Autonomous Republics of Texas and California, and an assortment of ambiguous-looking men looking for favors of some sort. There were only a few men in the hotel lobby today, and all of them were standing by the entrance.

Finerty crossed the lobby. There were two Negro men among the group in front of the door. One was Frederick Douglass, the noted lecturer and newspaper editor; the other was James Wormley, the owner of the Wormley Hotel on 15th and H Streets. Douglass was often here, importuning any officials who might be able to help with the growing number of colored refugees who had come to Washington from the South. A number of Negroes had been forced to flee the less frequent but still vicious violence directed against them there.

Not that they were exactly welcomed here by the city's white citizens, Finerty thought. The government of the United States might claim that the South, at last, was back in the Union fold, but it was kept there only by the forces of occupation. President Blaine, according to one of Finerty's informants inside the White House, had been consulting in secret with Edwin Stanton, Chief Justice of the Supreme

Court, which might account for the increasingly harsh treatment being meted out to the South. The older Stanton got, Finerty mused, the more radical he became; he would see the South punished in the way he thought it should have been in the years following the Confederacy's surrender. Stanton had won some sympathy even among the many Washington residents who had ties to the South; if the Negroes were better protected in the South by Federal troops, then they might stop migrating to Washington.

"How do you do, Mr. Finerty," Frederick Douglass said to him. The Negro was a small man with thick graying hair and a deep, resonant voice. "Mr. Wormley and I had an appointment to meet a Mr. Grigory Rubalev here, but apparently he has not yet arrived."

"Top of the morning to you both," Finerty murmured. "Coincidentally, I was supposed to meet Mr. Rubalev here this morning myself." He nodded at James Wormley, who was taller and lighter-skinned than Douglass. "I am a little bemused to see you here in a competitor's lobby, Mr. Wormley."

The hotel proprietor looked solemn. "Our business with Mr. Rubalev is important enough for me to have agreed to meet him in Hades, had he wished to do so."

Finerty went to the door and looked outside. Now he saw what had drawn the attention of the men standing near him. Soldiers were outside, setting up a barricade of wagons and Gatling guns across Pennsylvania Avenue. He stepped outside for a moment and peered up the avenue at the gate fronting the White House grounds. More soldiers were there, standing outside the gate. An officer with a colonel's insignia on his shoulders glanced toward the Willard's entrance.

Finerty quickly retreated inside. "Saw them marching and riding out this morning," one of the men inside muttered. "There were soldiers on Capitol Hill not long after dawn. I was on my way over here when I saw more of them going to the White House."

"What's going on?" Finerty asked.

"Damned if I know."

Douglass and Wormley had abandoned their station at the entrance for two chairs near one corner. Finerty walked toward them, wondering what the pair wanted with Grigory Rubalev. Residents of Washington from all walks of life seemed to be acquainted with Rubalev or to have some sort of business connection with him. Finerty had been in the city as the Washington correspondent for the Chicago *Times* for a little over a year now, arriving just after Blaine's inauguration in March of 1877, and had begun to pick up bits of intelligence about the somewhat mysterious Grigory Rubalev not long after that. The man had been seen in Washington at intervals ever since the War Between the States. He numbered among his acquaintances some of President Grant's former officials, various members of Washington's most respectable families, and several foreign envoys, but he had also been seen with less reputable sorts. From time to time over the last decade and a half, Rubalev had closed up his house on 11th Street and disappeared—to see to certain interests he had in the West, although no one seemed to know exactly what those interests were. Lately, he seemed to be an unofficial ambassador of the Plains territories, bringing any complaints the Indians out there might have to the attention of the government. The officials at the Interior Department and the Bureau of Indian Affairs tolerated that particular thorn in their side mostly because there was no choice. Until more regiments of cavalry and infantry could be freed to serve in the West, the government would have to abide by their treaties with the Indians, and have the consolation of knowing that the people of the Western territories still regarded themselves as citizens of the United States. Indeed, to hear Rubalev tell it, they were almost more fervent in their support of the Republic and its institutions than many in the East.

An adventurer, a seller of weapons, a blockade runner during the Civil War, the former guardian of a beautiful young Indian woman with whom he had once had an ambiguous relationship, a spy for a foreign power, a friend of Indian chiefs—those were a few of the rumors Finerty had heard about Rubalev. Whatever the man was, he knew a great many people who knew, in the end, very little about him. Finerty had been forming his own ideas about the man, after corresponding with colleagues at the New York *Herald*, the Bismarck *Tribune*, the San Francisco *Chronicle*, and the *Rocky Mountain News*.

Their letters had told him of a man who would appear in their communities with a seemingly inexhaustible amount of money to spend and a number of friends to visit before he vanished once again into the farthest reaches of the Plains.

Rubalev, Finerty had concluded, was at the center of a conspiracy, one that might involve a fair number of people at this point, and which somehow involved events on the Plains. The problem was that he had precious little evidence for his suspicions, and no notion of what the purpose of such a conspiracy might be. Impetuously, he had dashed off a note to Rubalev, telling the man that he had spent some time in Omaha at the headquarters of General Crook and inviting him to join Finerty for coffee or a drink at the Willard Hotel. Maybe if he got Rubalev talking, some clues about the fellow might slip out. To Finerty's surprise, Rubalev had taken him up on the invitation.

Frederick Douglass looked toward him as Finerty sat down. "Are you perhaps planning to interview Mr. Rubalev?" Douglass asked.

"Maybe. It seems the gentleman confused his dates by making appointments with the three of us at the same time."

"Our business with him will not take long," Douglass said. "Mr. Rubalev indicated that he would be willing to escort several Negro families to new homes in the West. We came here only to make the final arrangements, and to ask if it might be possible for him to take a few more."

Finerty added another item to his mental list of Rubalev's pursuits: a Moses to those colored people who were seeking a new life in the regions bordering the Plains, where the red man, the white man, and the black man had apparently begun to aspire to a kind of Promised Land.

"Of course," Finerty said, "given the signs of military activity in the city, Mr. Rubalev may be delayed in making his way here." He paused. "You haven't heard anything about why the army might have been called out, have you?" He had learned during his time in Washington that the blacks who lived here often found out about certain events in advance of many whites, perhaps because their lives here were always more precarious. Preserving their safety required constant vigilance.

"I have heard nothing," Douglass replied, and Finerty did not know if the Negro was telling the truth or not. It annoyed him as a newspaperman that he had had no inkling of why the troops were in the city streets, that the reasons for their actions were completely mysterious to him. Perhaps some desperate Southerners had entered Washington hoping to commit an act of sabotage.

"Well, I'll be," one of the men over at the doorway said. His voice echoed through the empty lobby. "There's a stream of carriages coming out through the White House gate. Almost looks like a funeral procession."

Assassins, Finerty thought, and quickly got to his feet. He could not sit here any longer without trying to find out what was going on. He hurried to the entrance and went outside, not looking to see whether Douglass or Wormley were following him.

The air had grown warmer and more humid, a precursor of the summer heat that drove everyone who could afford to leave town out of the city. Five carriages were heading up Pennsylvania Avenue, away from him. Finerty turned in the direction of the Capitol and saw more blue-uniformed men on horseback. A few of the soldiers manning the barricade blocking the avenue turned to look at him. The colonel was several feet away, talking to another officer.

"What's going on?" Finerty asked.

A freckled lad squinted at him. "All I know is we were ordered—" The colonel turned around and shot him a glance. The young soldier looked away and quickly stood at attention.

"I am a correspondent for the Chicago *Times*," Finerty called out.

The colonel came toward him and said, "Then don't go running off to Western Union hoping you can get a story out. Nothing goes out, nothing comes in. Washington City's under martial law now."

Finerty backed away and walked back to the Willard. Rubalev was there, standing at the top of the steps leading to the entrance. He wore a plain brown suit, a bit on the shabby side, which seemed unlike him; the few times Finerty had seen him at receptions or in restaurants, he had always been impeccably and expensively dressed.

"Mr. Rubalev," Finerty said as he ascended the steps, "I am John Finerty." He looked back at the barricade. "That officer told me that the city's under martial law."

Rubalev nodded. "I know," he said. "I found that out earlier this morning. I had to slip out of my house by the back door and enter the Willard by the service entrance."

"You did not have to go to all that trouble on my account."

Rubalev smiled. The smile held no trace of joy or warmth. "I came here on Mr. Douglass's account, Mr. Finerty," he replied.

"Och—of course. I was speaking to him and Mr. Wormley inside."

"Unfortunately, it now looks as though there's very little I can do for them." Rubalev turned and went inside.

Finerty followed him into the lobby. "I have failed as a newspaperman," he said. "These events have taken me completely by surprise."

"They have taken everyone by surprise, Mr. Finerty. I do not know what business it is you have with me, but you will please excuse me while I speak to Mr. Douglass and Mr. Wormley. If you are still here later, perhaps I can give you a few moments."

The tall blond man strode away. Finerty remained by the entrance. It was time, he thought, to nose around more, to sneak outside somehow and see what he could find out. It was unlikely that Southern forces were now threatening the city, as they had during the War Between the States; there were enough occupying forces in northern Virginia to prevent that.

The thought of assassination came back to him. An assassin had robbed Abe Lincoln of his life, Andrew Johnson had nearly been thrown out of office, President Grant had died suddenly in what was assumed to be an accident but might not have been, Colfax had been caught with stock holdings that could only have been bribes—it was enough to make Finerty worry about the welfare of President Blaine. He thought of the rumors he had heard for some time, that still circulated in some Washington circles, of a post-war conspiracy designed to remove Lincoln and Secretary of State Seward and other members of the government from power in order to replace them with more radical Republicans, men who would punish the South and tighten their grip on the rest of the Union. Occasionally, even now, the name of Edwin M. Stanton would be whispered in connection with such rumors. The chief justice, it was said by any who were brave enough or reckless enough to voice such thoughts, was so fervent in his devotion to the Union, and in his hatred of those who had tried to tear it asunder, that he would destroy the Constitution itself in order to preserve the Union. Blaine had been meeting in secret with Stanton. Finerty wondered if that had bought the president the chief justice's favor, or had only sealed his fate.

Wild suppositions, perhaps—but Finerty was beginning to feel that his reporter's instincts were now at work again. He would see what he could find out. He would have to be careful not to give anyone an excuse to use martial law to clap him in jail. He moved toward the entrance and realized that he should also start giving some thought as to how, if it should prove necessary, he could get out of the city.

In the few years since the Treaty of Fort Fetterman, a town had sprung up at the northeastern end of Kansas, across the river from St. Joseph, Missouri. The white and black inhabitants of the town called it Elysium, Kansas. The Kiowa who came there to trade, the few Cherokee who made their homes there, and the bands of Lakota and Cheyenne who set up their camps there during the winter months called the town a variety of other names.

Lemuel Rowland, riding across the grassy hills toward the outskirts of Elysium, again felt astonishment that such a place could exist. Well-traveled trails led from the circles of tepees toward the wooden structures of the town. Farms owned by blacks, whites, and Cherokees were within a day's ride of the town; there were two blacksmiths now, a telegraph line that connected the town to Atchison and Fort Leavenworth, and a ferry that carried passengers across the Missouri between Elysium and St. Joseph.

Lemuel rode past a small Cheyenne camping circle of ten tepees. Three small children were helping two women tie bundles of belongings to a travois. The Cheyenne and the Lakota who were camped here would soon be taking down their tepees and moving out to the Plains to hunt the buffalo and to gather for their annual Sun Dance. Rubalev had persuaded, or bribed, several engineers from Britain and a few gunmakers from New York to come to the town of Deadwood not long after bringing Edison to Bismarck. There was a small ironworks in Deadwood now, and the Lakota were now making some of their own firearms. The Wasichu engineers were not allowed into the Black Hills themselves, and the Chen brothers now made their ever larger and more destructive rocket-arrows in a settlement two days' ride south of Bismarck. The Black Hills, the Center of the World, would remain sacred, untouched by outsiders, if not by the Lakota themselves. They had to go into Paha Sapa to mine the gold that had been given to them by the Great Spirit, the gold that could buy the Wasichu medicine men and the white man's magic that would give them the power to hold and keep their land.

Lemuel thought of Katia. They had been in Elysium only a day before he had ridden south to Leavenworth to speak to Jeremiah Clarke. The colonel had surprised him with both a newfound sobriety and stories about dissension among the commanding officers above him. Sheridan had been called to Washington over two weeks ago, and there had not been a word from him since then, or from General Sherman, for that matter. General George Crook was sitting up in Omaha, waiting for orders that had not yet come, as was General Alfred Terry in St. Paul, Minnesota. Clarke had been put in temporary command at Fort Leavenworth, with no word of when the next commanding officer would arrive, or who he might be.

Lemuel had found out about the confusion and disaffection in the army only after Jeremiah had told him the most recent news out of Washington. "Came by telegraph a day ago," Clarke had told him moments after Lemuel had entered the fort and then his office. "Three Rebs somehow managed to get into the ranks of the White House guards. President Blaine was at a meeting with the vice president and some members of the Cabinet when they burst into the room. One God damn Reb killed Vice President Hayes straight off and wounded Blaine, and then some other guards rushed in and shot the assassins. That's about all I know. There's martial law in Washington now, and nothing's getting out."

Clarke had stared thoughtfully at Lemuel for a long time before continuing. "I've been out here a long time now," he said. "Thought when I first came that we'd be fighting the Indians before too long. The longer I wait, the more I wonder about what we're doing here. I'll be honest with you, Lemuel. I don't want to fight Indians. Hell, I gave up drinking because I got sick and tired of court-martialing enlisted men for trading liquor to the redskins and figured I had better set them an example."

Clarke fell silent again, then said, "You can tell Touch-the-Clouds and Sitting Bull and the other chiefs that I'm not their enemy."

Lemuel considered what Jeremiah had told him as he followed the trail toward the dirt road that led to Elysium and to Katia. Ahead lay the tree-lined road that would take him to the center of town. A few of the willows and elms were little more than saplings, having been planted only a year ago; some of the dwellings were barely more than shacks.

He swayed in his saddle, suddenly feeling the odd disorientation he had felt when he and Katia had first arrived. The cluster of buildings he had seen on the bluffs above him as he stepped from the steamboat ramp onto the wooden dock had almost looked like a mirage. Now he felt that way again, as if this community south of the Lakota lands might disappear forever, as insubstantial as the shared dream that had created it.

How they must hate this place and the others like it, he thought then, thinking of the bankers and railroad men he had seen in the East. Again he felt how precarious the existence of Elysium was.

There were no fences around the plots of the houses that lined the road. Children and a few women stood near the road, making no sign to Lemuel, watching in silence as he passed them. He was near the stable before noticing that a large crowd had gathered in front of the telegraph office next to the town's general store, across the road from the stagecoach stop around which the town had grown.

He left his horse at the stable and hurried toward the crowd.

Garry Toland, one of Elysium's two telegraphers, stood on the wooden walkway, speaking to the townsfolk. Katia stood near Toland. She caught sight of Lemuel and went to him, took him by the arm and drew him away from the crowd.

"President Blaine is dead," she said to him in a low voice. Lemuel could hear Toland shouting something about a Supreme Court ruling and an emergency council. "The vice president is dead, too. They were shot by assassins, and apparently several Cabinet secretaries were wounded. Washington will be under martial law for at least the next few months, until the council is certain that they've found all of the conspirators." Her hand shook as she gripped his arm more tightly.

"Wait here, Katia." Lemuel pushed his way through the crowd until he was standing just below Toland. "I just got here," he said. "What's going on?"

Toland turned toward him. "There's a state of emergency been declared," the telegrapher said in his flat voice. "Martial law in Washington and at least two other Eastern cities. In the absence of a successor to the president who is able to assume his duties, an emergency council will govern until the emergency is past."

"Who are the members of this emergency council?" Lemuel asked.

"Got that written down." Toland pulled out a piece of paper from his pants pocket. "General George B. McClellan, General Nathaniel Pope, General Ambrose E. Burnside, General William Tecumseh Sherman."

"General McClellan?" a man shouted from the crowd. "Thought he were a senator."

"Been recommissioned as a general, it says," Toland replied.

McClellan, Lemuel thought, an incompetent that President Lincoln had removed from command during the Civil War. Had McClellan gone mad? Were he and Pope and Burnside even capable of seizing power in this way? Why had he thrown in his lot with Stanton, who had done his best to ruin him in Washington years ago? And Sherman—somehow he found it hard to believe that Sherman could be a part of this revolt.

"Oh, one more thing," Toland said. "It's Justice Stanton who ruled that they could suspend the government and form this here council."

Stanton, Lemuel thought, the man who had precipitated the crisis that had led to President Johnson's impeachment. The man had to have been weaving his web ever since being forced out as Secretary of War in 1867. There had been plenty of Washington rumors about Stanton a decade ago, but he had campaigned for Grant for president and been rewarded with a seat on the Supreme Court.

Lemuel was abruptly convinced that this seizure of power was mostly Stanton's doing, and that McClellan and the other generals were merely his tools. McClellan might have become a part of the scheme in hope of reining in Stanton's harsher actions against the South. He thought then of Sherman and Sheridan. Sherman had always distrusted Stanton; now Lemuel was convinced that the general could have had nothing to do with the coup. The conspirators might only be using Sherman's name, possibly to convince other officers that Sherman was still in command of the army, that he and Sheridan would finally move against the Lakota. Lemuel wondered if Sherman, and perhaps Sheridan, were under house arrest, being held in a prison somewhere, or were already dead.

"What does it mean?" a colored man in the crowd asked, looking from Toland to Lemuel.

"I don't know," Lemuel said. "Stanton wanted to punish the South after the war. Given all the uprisings there, and now the assassinations of the president and vice president, he can probably claim that he was right all along about that."

"But what does it mean for us?" another man asked.

"I don't know that, either," Lemuel replied, then began to make his way through the crowd to Katia. People parted to let him pass.

Katia still stood where he had left her. She stared past him as if she did not see him.

He said, "We had better go home."

Her fingers closed around his wrist. "No." She was speaking in Lakota now. "I want to stay. We have to send a message."

"A message about what?"

She swayed a little, then steadied herself. "To Touch-the-Clouds. He has to know that war will come."

"Touch-the-Clouds will have moved his camp to the Yellowstone River by now, to wait for others to join him for the hunt."

"Send a message to Bismarck," Katia said, "and to White Eagle's camp. White Eagle will find a way to get it to Touch-the-Clouds. War will come. Touch-the-Clouds has to be told." She was speaking in a whisper now, so softly that he could hardly hear her.

He slipped an arm around her shoulders. "Stop it, Katia. What's happening is frightening, it's almost impossible to believe. But it's the South that's more likely to suffer now than the West. Stanton is—"

"Do not speak to me of that. A vision has come to me, Lemuel. I am seeing it now—flames and Blue Coats all around us and people screaming and a war in which the Lakota will have to fight. I hear them fighting all around me, I hear them singing their war songs. They are as real as the spirits I saw in the Black Hills and at the Greasy Grass, as real as the warriors I saw riding in the street in New York."

She had never told him about any vision in New York. Her face contorted; he saw her struggling to contain herself. "The war will be carried here," she said, "if Touch-the-Clouds does not act. Promise me, promise me that you will have this message sent."

"I promise," Lemuel said. He could grant her that much, and leave it to White Eagle as to what to do with her message. "What do you want to tell him?"

"War is coming, my former husband," she said. "This vision is as true as the vision of Sitting Bull and Custer at the Greasy Grass. You married me for my visions and now I have seen the vision you must follow. You must prepare to fight, and you will need every comrade you can find to fight with you. Do not wait. Prepare yourself, and tell all of your allies to prepare for war."

"The treaty—"

She looked at him and he saw terror in her eyes. "The treaty will be broken. You must know that, even if you pretend it isn't so."

He thought of how immaterial the town of Elysium had looked as he was riding toward it.

"I see flames," Katia said, "burning around me."

"I'll have the message sent for you," he said, trying to console her. "Your vision is only a warning, Katia. It doesn't have to come to pass."

The crowd was dispersing. Toland had gone back inside, perhaps to receive another message. "Come with me," Lemuel said as he led her toward the telegraph office.

Dancing Girl saw the dust cloud in the distance as she sat outside the talking wire tepee. She and Yellow Bird had been listening with the men to the messages from Bismarck the day before, and then the messages had stopped.

She had known what the talking wire was telling them before the men translated the messages aloud. The Great Father was dead, and now the chiefs of the Wasichu in Washington were three Blue Coats. A fourth chief, Four Star Sherman, had been found dead at his home, with a Wasichu medicine man saying that the evil spirit that had killed him had struck at his heart, and now Three Star Sheridan had been relieved of command. Many men, more than could be easily counted, had also been hanged in many places in the South. More men in the Eastern cities were being summoned to put on the blue coats of the army and fight. The men in White Eagle's camp had been hearing such messages for nearly a week now, and then the spirits in the talking wire had suddenly stopped speaking to them.

The silence disturbed the men. Why would the wire to Bismarck fall silent? A fierce wind had torn across the land the other day, from behind the rise to the west that sheltered the camp. Maybe the wind had brought down the talking wire. The talking wire was often silent in winter, usually for moons, when the snow came and tore the wires from their poles. But the wire was not often silent in summer.

Dancing Girl's father White Eagle had listened to the silence for a time, then told Denis Laforte that morning to ride east and scout around Fort Lincoln. Four days ago, a message had come telling her father that the former wife of Touch-the-Clouds, Graceful Swan, was having visions of war and warning the chiefs to prepare for battle. White Eagle had sent a rider to an Arikara camp a day's ride west, telling him to relay the message of war to Touch-the-Clouds.

Her father might be thinking of that vision now, Dancing Girl thought.

To the north, a black cloud had formed on the horizon. A storm might suddenly come upon them; storms could come almost without warning on this flat, empty land. A gentle breeze was still blowing. She sniffed at the air, then guessed that the storm would not reach them until night and might miss them altogether.

Looking east, she cupped a hand over her eyes and stared at the dust cloud. She could make out the form of Denis Laforte; that was the way the Wasichu Sapa sat in the saddle, and he was riding awfully fast, at a full gallop. Far behind him, almost at the eastern horizon, she saw another dust cloud, a much larger one.

"Someone's coming," Yellow Bird said to her, "a lot of people."

Her father was standing with some of the wire warriors near the talking wire pole, having a palaver about the coming buffalo hunt. White Eagle gazed in the direction of the dust cloud and watched it for a while, then let out a cry.

"Aieeee!"

Another man took up the cry. "Aieeee!"

"Fuck," White Eagle said in English, "son of a bitch," and then in Lakota, "It is a good day to die." He spun around and waved his arms at Dancing Girl and Yellow Bird. "Tell the women to take what they can and get away from here."

Dancing Girl ran toward the tepee of Young Spring Grass, then turned to look back. Laforte was still far ahead of the second dust cloud, but she could now see bits of blue color amid the brown and yellow of the dust and the red and white of a Wasichu flag. Blue Coats were riding here. Soldiers were not supposed to be in this land, not this far west of Bismarck. They were breaking the treaty by riding here without warning, without first asking if they could come here.

"Go on, Dancing Girl!" Yellow Bird screamed at her. "I will get the horses!"

"The Blue Coats are coming!" Dancing Girl shouted as she ran toward the circle of tepees. It came to her suddenly that she had shouted the words in the white man's tongue. "The Blue Coats are coming!" she shouted in Lakota. Two women darted out of their tepees, one with a child in her arms. "Get away from here as fast as you can!" She could hear Laforte's cries, carried to her by a wind that was starting to pick up. He was warning them to run for cover on the rise and make their stand there.

"It is a good day to die!" a warrior shouted in the distance.

Lemuel had ridden out with Dives Backward to keep watch along the river. The prevailing mood in the town of Elysium, and in St. Joseph across the Missouri River, was one of fear and apprehension. The memory of Quantrill and his guerrillas, who had slaughtered so many in the name of the Confederacy during the Civil War, was still fresh in this region. Another band of cutthroats might form to take vengeance against any whose allegiance was to the Union.

The Union, Lemuel thought, wondering if anything still existed that could even be called the Union, if three generals with the sanction of the chief justice of the Supreme Court could be considered a legitimate government. He also worried about how long the peace of the Plains territories would endure. The sooner the cabal in Washington managed to crush the Southern resistance completely, the sooner they could turn their attention to the West. The railroad men and the bankers had probably already slipped some of their stocks and bonds to the cabal, knowing that the stocks would become more valuable only after the Plains were open to development.

Stanton was another matter. Stanton was a stern, unyielding zealot, which probably meant that he was even more dangerous than someone who was merely greedy.

Dives Backward reined in his horse. "Maybe go back," the Cheyenne said in English. A half-breed Kansan had ridden into town two days ago claiming that he had seen at least two hundred men, all armed and many in the blue coats of soldiers, less than a half-day's ride south of Elysium, not far from the river. Since then, the Indians camped there had sent out a few scouts and other men were taking turns keeping watch along the roads that led to the town.

"Maybe go back," Dives Backward said again. His English was not fluent, but his Lakota was even worse.

"We might as well," Lemuel said. Except for a stagecoach heading toward Atchison, there had been little activity along the road that followed the Missouri south along the low bluffs overlooking the river. The half-breed had been quite agitated about seeing men in the blue coats of soldiers, but a band of guerrillas fighting for the South might want to disguise themselves.

They rode north. Dives Backward began to sing in Cheyenne; Lemuel understood enough to make out his words. "We fought the White Chief with Yellow Hair," Dives Backward sang, "we fought the one called the Son of the Morning Star. Now his spirit rides over the Plains, now God has made his spirit watch over us and protect us so that the treaty is not broken again." Dives Backward had not been at the Battle of the Black Hills, but Lemuel had heard other Indians sing of Custer; they had made him into a legend.

"His spirit must watch over us," Dives Backward sang, and Lemuel recalled the vainglorious man who had been so quick to rush into battle.

The dream had come to her before, and now she knew that she would not escape her dream this time. The fire was all around her, and people were screaming.

Katia let out a cry and was suddenly awake. Someone called out in the night; the bell in the nearby church was ringing.

"Fire!" a man's voice cried out. "Fire!"

Katia rolled out of bed and ran to her window. Across the road, the small wooden church that had been put up by a group of Elysium's Negroes was burning. She looked up the street and saw more flames leaping from the roofs of other buildings.

She slipped into her deerskin boots, grabbed a short cape from a hook on the wall, and hurried to her door. She yanked at the knob, pulling the door open, and ran into the sitting room.

The room was filled with smoke. Jenny Catcher, the Cherokee woman who had rented Katia and Lemuel a bedroom in her house, had her face covered with a cloth. Katia stumbled toward the other woman and took her by the arm. The smoke was so thick and the room so dark that she could barely see the door.

The church bell across the way had stopped ringing. Katia let Jenny lead her to the front door. As they made their way outside, she saw that a bucket brigade had formed down the road to fight the fire, in front of the general store. The telegraph office was burning, and there were other fires; she saw fires and the billowing pale smoke rising from the flames to the night sky. Much of the town was on fire, she realized. How could the flames have spread so fast? She gulped air, nearly choking on the smoke.

People ran from the nearby buildings. "We've lost it!" a man with a bucket shouted as a blackened wall of the church collapsed. More people were running into the street, some carrying bundles of belongings.

Katia was still hanging on to Jenny Catcher's arm. The Cherokee woman turned to watch the flames dancing on the roof of her small house. "It's all going to burn," Jenny muttered. Her voice was steady for a woman who would lose everything, who would be left with nothing but the nightgown she was wearing.

The roof of the telegraph office suddenly caved in, sending showers of sparks and pieces of burning wood over the men fighting the fire. "Come on," Katia said to Jenny. "We aren't safe here."

A wagon rattled past them. They followed the stream of people heading away from the center of the town. She felt as though she was still in her dream. She opened her mouth, but no sound came out; inside her head, a part of her was screaming. The crowd had reached the livery stable when, in the distance, Katia heard the short, sharp sounds of gunfire.

The stable was on fire. She heard the shrieks of the horses inside. Two men led two horses through the open stable door; the horses reared.

Men rode toward them out of the darkness. In the light of the burning stable, Katia saw their blue coats and the yellow stripes on the sides of their trousers. She watched numbly as a man aimed his rifle into the crowd; others were shooting at people with revolvers.

The crowd surged toward her. Katia lost her grip on Jenny and nearly fell to the ground. She stumbled toward the side of the road just as a rider bore down on her. His horse reared; she saw him take aim. She leaped toward him; the gun barrel caught her on the side of the head.

Katia was lying on the ground. She managed to sit up. There were three of them around her now, all in blue coats, all with their rifles and revolvers trained on her. Everything seemed to be happening very slowly. She had known that war would come again, and had feared it, but she was no longer afraid. The spirits had spoken truly to her in her dreams and visions, and she had served their purpose. She thought of the vision of victorious warriors she had seen in New York and knew then that this war had to come.

"Hoka hey," she said to the men who would bring death to her, "It is a good day to die," and then a bullet caught her in the chest.

The people of White Eagle's camp had made it to the rise before the Blue Coats were within range. The women had led the way through the trails among the rocks, then concealed themselves behind boulders. The men followed, taking up positions on the slope of the rocky rise. Three of the younger boys herded the horses into a small clearing sheltered by a rock outcropping. The horses were growing skittish. The boys tethered them and moved among them, rubbing them down and soothing them.

Dancing Girl was behind a rocky boulder with Young Spring Grass and Yellow Bird. She peered over the rock. There had been barely enough time to ride here, to reach safety and secure the horses, and to have a place from which to fight.

"This is good," Young Spring Grass murmured beside her. "We have the higher ground, and the men have many weapons." So did several of the women; Young Spring Grass had brought her Winchester rifle, while a few of the other women were armed with

Springfields. If the Wasichu woman Unlucky Jane could use such weapons and go into battle with men, perhaps other women should learn how to use the white man's firesticks. So Young Spring Grass had reasoned, and Lakota and Cheyenne warriors could now make or acquire enough firesticks of their own to allow the women a few.

Dancing Girl stood on her toes and peered over the rock ledge. The sky was growing darker, and not only from the sun setting behind them; the black clouds to the north were thickening. She still could not tell if the storm would reach them or miss them.

Out on the plain to the east, where the camp had been, the Blue Coats had chased off the rest of their horses, smashed up the telegraph, and set the tepees on fire. A plume of black smoke rose from what had been Dancing Girl's home, but the tepee did not matter. What mattered was that the women had only what food and water they had hastily grabbed, and the men had almost none, while the Blue Coats probably had enough to last for some time. There had to be nearly forty of the soldiers; not so many, but there were only fifty people with White Eagle, and that number included the women and children.

What also mattered, Dancing Girl thought, was that the Blue Coats would have more firesticks and more bullets for their weapons. They would try to get the people they had driven to the rise to waste their ammunition.

"Bastards," Young Spring Grass said in English. "Big ugly Wasichu sonabitches." She had learned some words in English during her time as Long Hair Custer's woman. "They must have meant to attack us in the night, or maybe just before dawn," she continued in Lakota. "That is how they fight. They would have crept up on us and started to kill us before we were hardly awake, when we would not be able to defend ourselves or escape. If Buffalo Man Laforte had not seen them . . ." She let out a sigh.

Denis Laforte was farther down the slope, behind a rock with White Eagle. Goose Beak, who was crouched with her daughter behind a rock just below them, was whispering to another woman.

She turned and looked up at Young Spring Grass. "Red Fox Woman tells me that the Wasichu Sapa Laforte saw the Blue Coats before they saw him," Goose Beak said. "He says that the Blue Coats must have cut the talking wire, so that we could not send signals to Bismarck."

"Of course they would have cut the talking wire," Young Spring Grass muttered. "They must have severed it before they rode out from Fort Lincoln, so that no one could warn us."

The Blue Coats were galloping toward the rise now. "They must be very angry," Yellow Bird said. "They expected to surprise us. Now they will have to wait out of range of our firesticks and see what happens."

"They could try to take the rise," Dancing Girl said.

The boy shook his head. "They would lose a lot of men that way."

"But they could also make us spend many of our bullets that way, and the medicine powers in our firesticks would have to be at their strongest for our bullets to hit all of the men our warriors aim at, or even to hit most of them. The soldiers will be furious, because trying to surprise us didn't work. They'll be so angry that they will want to kill us all."

"Be quiet," Young Spring Grass said.

Some of the soldiers had hitched abandoned pony drags to their horses. Perhaps they would use the poles of the drags to help shield themselves, Dancing Girl thought, when they were closer.

Red Fox Woman was chanting. Dancing Girl realized that she was calling to the wakinyan, the thunder beings. Red Fox Woman was trying to call down the storm. Dancing Girl shivered; even for a medicine man of much power, calling down a storm was a dangerous business.

"Red Fox Woman has strong medicine," Yellow Bird whispered. Dancing Girl had heard such rumors about the older woman, although she had never seen signs of any such medicine.

"Red Fox Woman is crazy," Young Spring Grass muttered as the chants grew louder. "She can't call the storm down on the Blue Coats without calling it down on us, too."

By evening, it was clear that the wakinyan were not listening to

Red Fox Woman. The black clouds had moved east by the time night came, and the Blue Coats still waited below, keeping watch so that none of the people trapped on the rise would try to get away. Dancing Girl stretched out behind the rock, trying to sleep.

White Eagle slept while a few of the men kept watch. A hand gripped his shoulder, waking him. He opened his eyes and saw that it was still dark. The night was still; the silence pressed in around him. He sniffed at the air and looked up at the sky, but saw no stars.

"The Blue Coats are closer to us," Gray Horse, one of the wire warriors, whispered to him. "They have dug trenches in the ground for themselves, and they have made a wall of the poles and hides they stole from us. They are close enough now for us to hit them with our firesticks, but they can duck down into their ditches, where it is hard to take aim at them from here."

The men were already itching to fight; White Eagle could feel it. Some of them would want to rush the Blue Coats, draw their fire, and then retreat to the rise. If they were lucky, they might pick off a soldier or two, maybe more. If they were unlucky, White Eagle would have even fewer fighting men.

"A storm is coming," he said.

"It is racing upon us," Gray Horse said, and suddenly White Eagle felt the back of his neck prickle.

He flattened himself against the ground; Gray Horse threw himself down next to White Eagle. At that moment, the air was ablaze with light, the bolt of lightning so near that he could smell it. White Eagle was afraid that the lightning had struck somewhere on the rise, and then the sharp crack of thunder nearly deafened him.

The wind shrieked; hail suddenly pelted his back. He pressed closer to the rock, trying to shelter himself. The wind was rising. He had seen many storms in his life; the thunder spirits, like all spirits, were capricious and would often send storms against the land and the people on it with little or no warning. But the howling and power of the wind, and the painful pounding of the hail against his back, told him that this storm would be stronger than most.

He should not have humored Red Fox Woman, he thought. Having seen no sign that she possessed any medicine, he had not stopped her from trying to summon the wakinyan after hearing her cry out her chants from the rocks above him. I should have forbidden it, he thought. I should have sent a man up there to stop her, and if I live through this, she will never call on any spirits again. He dug his fingers into the ground. This was a wind that could blow a man from a mountain, or from the slope of a rise. That would give the thunder spirits a good laugh, seeing people being blown about like sagebrush and scattered across the land by the wind, and then he almost laughed aloud.

The Blue Coats below would have even less to shelter them than did the people on the rise, and their trenches would be filling with hailstones. White Eagle lay still. Icy needles were thick around him; the hail was turning into sleet. He clenched his teeth, feeling the air grow cold, and sent up a silent appeal to Wakan Tanka to let him and his people live.

The lightning was so bright that he could see it through closed eyes; the thunder clapped again. The wind shrieked and a long time passed before he felt the sleet become rain. The wind was dying, the darkness lifting. The rain was still falling steadily as White Eagle got to his feet and looked around himself.

His cloth shirt and leather leggings were soaked through, and his long hair dripped with water. He shivered violently. A baby wailed from the rocks above. Gray Horse and the other men near him were also dripping with water, but seemed unharmed.

White Eagle steadied himself, peered over the rock, and looked down. "Hie!" he called out.

The wind had scattered the poles and hides the Blue Coats had been using as shields. Through the gray sheets of rain, he could make out the shadowy forms of soldiers hunkered down in their ditches or stretched out on the ground. A few of the Blue Coats were standing, hanging on to the reins of their horses as the animals bucked and reared.

White Eagle saw his chance and picked up his Winchester. "Attack!" he shouted to the men. "Crooked Horn, you and your brothers cover us! It is a good day to die!" He pulled back the lever of his rifle, aimed the weapon, and fired as he ran down the narrow path that wound among the rocks.

Dancing Girl watched the men fight from her place behind the rock. A few of the men, led by her father, had run down the slope, darting from side to side while shooting at the Blue Coats. Three of the soldiers had taken up position, kneeling and firing at White Eagle's men as they rushed to attack, but others had tried to flee on foot, having lost their horses.

When other men followed White Eagle down the hill with some of the horses, leaping onto their backs before riding at the Blue Coats, two of the Blue Coats who still had horses mounted them and began to gallop away. A few soldiers on foot were running after them, crying out to them, when they were cut down by gun-fire. One soldier fired at Gray Horse and missed. Gray Horse flung himself at the man, struck him with a coup stick, then jammed his Colt against the Blue Coat's chest and fired. Three warriors rode after the two Blue Coats who were trying to escape.

The soldiers had brought their deaths upon themselves. They would have shown her people no mercy; her father and his men would count many coup.

Young Spring Grass let out a high-pitched war cry, then ran down the slope with her rifle. By then, the rain had nearly stopped, and most of the soldiers were dead. Good, Dancing Girl thought; they came after us, they broke the treaty, they deserve to die.

By the time the rain stopped, the battle was over. The men took a few scalps, but most of the dead had hair too short to be worth taking as a trophy. Young Spring Grass and the other women began to strip the bodies of clothing.

"See," Young Spring Grass called out as Dancing Girl went to her side to help her undress one of the dead. Young Spring Grass held up a chain from which dangled a golden cross. "His personal war medicine. Take it." She handed the chain to Dancing Girl. "Maybe it will bring you luck."

Dancing Girl gazed at the dead soldier. "It didn't bring him much luck."

"The wakan spirits listened to me," Red Fox Woman was saying as she pulled the boots off of one dead soldier. "No one will ever accuse me of being crazy and having no medicine again."

Some of the men were singing kill songs. "Our enemy cut the singing wire," one man chanted, "so the spirits of the wire could no longer sing to us and warn us, but now we will sing over the bodies of our enemies."

Dancing Girl's gorge rose in her throat. She had dreamed of going to war, but the sight of all this death suddenly sickened her. Her people had been at peace too long; she was not used to the sight of killing. But she would grow harder when they were fighting once more, she would grow up to be like Walking Blanket Woman and Young Spring Grass. War was coming now; that was certain.

She stood up and went to her father. He sat with Denis Laforte, watching the women at their work and listening to the kill songs. He looked up at her.

"Father," she said, "are we going back to where we had our camp?"

"No. We have no talking wire now. We cannot know what is going on in Bismarck. When these men don't return to their fort, others may come after us." He took her by the arms. "We will go to the camp of Touch-the-Clouds. We will tell him that the Blue Coats broke the treaty. And then we will go to war."

Some more men had crossed the river from the Missouri side to help with burying the dead. The few survivors of the massacre in Elysium were taking a bit of solace from that. They would not have to fear that other people living near them would now turn against them.

Lemuel and Dives Backward had come to the burned tepees of a

Lakota camp circle first. The raiders had killed everyone there, even the children, throwing the bodies into a heap. Dives Backward let out a cry and galloped west toward a Cheyenne circle that had also, from the looks of it, been wiped out as savagely.

The fires in the town itself had nearly burned out by the time Lemuel reached the road that led to the main street. Four survivors had gathered together in front of one house that was little more than blackened timbers. One was a Negro man, one a white man, and two young girls with long blond braids were with them, staring past Lemuel with haunted eyes.

The black man spoke of what had happened, although Lemuel could read some of the events in the ruins of the town and in the ways that the bodies of the dead were strewn over the ground. The raiders had sneaked up in the night. Because they were in the blue uniforms of soldiers of the United States Army, the men acting as sentries might have taken them as friends, or perhaps had not seen them in time to sound an alarm. Some of the raiders had managed to get into the center of town to start the fires, and by then others were attacking the Indian encampments. The raiders had come into town killing everyone in their way, white, black, or red, man or woman, old woman or child. Some of the women had been raped as they lay dying of their wounds.

"Don't know why they didn't kill us all," the Negro said. "Must of been 'cause they saw those folks crossin' over on a ferry." The man gestured toward a group of men loading bodies onto a buckboard. "That's when they finally run off. Musta been two hundred of 'em."

"We should go after them," Lemuel said, knowing that it would be useless, that he did not have enough men to pursue them. The raiders would have scattered by now.

He rode down the main road. Another wagon loaded with bodies lay ahead; the dead would have to be buried quickly, before they began to rot in the heat. The men near the wagon looked up as he approached. They had done their best to lay the bodies out carefully, not to throw them into the buckboard carelessly. A body near the back end of the buckboard, a woman's body in a torn white nightshirt and deerskin boots, had been propped up against the side. Long black hair hid the dead woman's face.

"Katia," he said softly, recognizing the boots, thinking of the times he had run his fingers through her thick black hair. "Katia." He reined in his horse, struggling for breath. He had already known that she was dead, he had felt it when he first caught sight of the burned tepees outside the town. He had always known how precarious the existence of this place was, what a miracle it was that it had existed at all.

He had brought Katia here, to her death.

"What is it, son?" one of the men by the wagon said.

He could not speak. He did not want to look at her body, to read how she had died and what had been done to her through the marks and wounds on her corpse. Katia was not there, in that wagon. Her spirit would not be trapped in that body, to lie with so many others in one grave. Her spirit had been freed, to climb the wind to the Creator, Wakan Tanka.

He tightened his legs around his horse and rode away from that place, thinking of justice and revenge and what he would have to do to get it.

EIGHTEEN

Grigory Rubalev had acquired false papers for Finerty and smuggled him out of Washington in a carriage on a sweltering July evening, taking him to a house in Silver Spring, Maryland. From there, another carriage carried Finerty to Philadelphia. Rubalev had left him in Silver Spring and gone on to another city, perhaps Cincinnati, perhaps someplace farther west, maybe even back to Washington. Finerty's instincts had told him that he did not want to know too much about that gentleman's intentions, or about how he had managed to secure a carriage with a trustworthy driver for them.

Washington might still be the capital of the United States, but it had begun to look like a city under siege, as it had been during the War Between the States. Forts and batteries of heavy and light artillery were again being set up around the city; garrisons of soldiers were living on Capitol Hill, now that sessions of Congress had been suspended for the foreseeable future. There had been fireworks for the traditional Fourth of July celebration, but few celebrants to view them. Acting President McClellan might call himself the Constitution's protector, but Finerty knew of few who would grant him that much legitimacy.

The carriage carrying Finerty had been stopped at the edge of the city on the Seventh Street Road by soldiers. Rubalev left the carriage to speak with them, and within a few moments they had been on their way. Perhaps Rubalev had bribed the soldiers; Finerty knew by then how difficult it was to get out of the city without the proper papers. There had been reports of a few desperate men, a couple of Congressman among them, who had tried to swim the Potomac. The bodies of two such men had been found; the others had simply disappeared.

Why Rubalev had decided to help him, Finerty did not know. Rubalev had refused to take any money from Finerty for the forged papers and had hinted that he was helping others to escape. The man clearly had an interest in flattering and cultivating associates and acquaintances of all kinds, and—although Finerty doubted it—perhaps Rubalev, deep down, was so deeply revulsed by the cabal now calling itself the Council of the United States that he would do anything to help those who might oppose it.

The papers Rubalev had secured for him, identifying him as John Flaherty, a draper from Chicago, were enough to help him secure a train ticket to New York. From there, he would board a train that would take him to Chicago. To try sending a telegraph to his editor Clinton Snowden from Washington would be to risk arrest and incarceration. He would get to Chicago and see what the situation was there, then leave for Omaha and the headquarters of the army's Department of the Platte. He was already certain that Snowden would approve of his change of venue.

He had to go west. War was coming, as General Crook had prophesied. The only question was what kind of war it would be. The army against the Sioux? The United States against any settlers who might want to set up their own autonomous republics, as Texas and California had already done and as Utah was threatening to do? The settlers against one another, ranchers pitted against farmers, or Southern sympathizers against Union supporters? Perhaps some more unlikely coalition would form, united against the usurpers in Washington.

The Chicago *Times* would need a correspondent in the West, and Finerty was curious to see which way General Crook would jump.

Finerty stayed in New York for one day, enough time to purchase some clothes and other necessities, before buying a ticket that would take him to Chicago. He would have to conserve his dwindling funds, but that was not the only reason for deciding to travel to Chicago sitting up on a wooden seat instead of in a Pullman Palace. Being a newspaper correspondent was a very dangerous business these days, and he wanted to remain inconspicuous.

The car in which he found himself was a rebuilt Lincoln car with wooden seats. There were not many passengers, presumably because of the restrictions on travel and the need for papers, genuine or forged. His shabbily-dressed fellow sojourners included a broad-faced man and woman with two young children, five young men who were probably hoping to evade conscription by losing themselves elsewhere, two heavily-painted young women, and three men of indeterminate age who had already begun a game of cards in their seats.

Finerty stowed his bag under an empty seat and sat down by the window. He had bought a clandestinely printed copy of the New York *Recorder*'s latest edition from a newsboy before boarding the train. On the front page was a report from a St. Louis *Post-Dispatch* correspondent, who had been interviewing survivors of a massacre in a Kansas town called Elysium.

He quickly scanned the story. The raiders had worn Union uniforms. They had gone after everyone, murdering white, black, and red people alike, but their greatest animosity was seemingly reserved for the Cheyenne and the other Indians who had been camped on the town's outskirts, whom they had butchered without mercy. A few survivors had heard the blue-coated raiders talking of redskins who did not belong there and who deserved extermination.

Finerty had heard rumors about that incident, and others, before leaving Washington. There could be only one reason for such raids, and that was to demonstrate that the present *modus vivendi* on the Plains would no longer be tolerated. The army was, in this brutal

way, announcing its intention to open up the West again and showing what fate might lie in store for any who had developed sympathies for the redskins.

All of which reminded him more than a little of Ireland, the land
he had fled.

In Ohio, a band of armed men commandeered Finerty's train,
announced that they were members of the Free United States
forces, and rode with the passengers the rest of the way to
Chicago. When he stepped off the train, Finerty found himself in
what might as well have been a foreign country. Groups of men in
makeshift uniforms calling themselves the United States Militia or
the Free U.S. Irregulars were patrolling the streets. Broadsides
were posted on the walls of buildings accusing the Council in
Washington of President Blaine's murder. And most welcome of
all, the Chicago newspapers, in spite of the restrictions on the
press, were being sold openly on the streets.

Out of habit, knowing that what he set down might never see the
light of day, Finerty had passed his time on the train writing out a
long letter to his editor about his experiences in Washington and
his escape from the capital city. Now he was gratified that he had
done so. Finding a way to get to Omaha could wait for a little. He
rode a streetcar to the offices of the *Times* and went directly to
Snowden's desk.

Snowden greeted him as warmly as if he were the Prodigal Son,
sent a boy out for coffee and food, then read his pages quickly. Finerty had omitted any mention of Rubalev's name and any revealing details about the other anonymous men who had helped them
escape from Washington.

"Good work, John," the editor said when he was finished, "and
now I have another assignment for you. Seems the army's command structure is shot all to hell now. The damned Council of the
United States is claiming that Sheridan is in command now and
that all orders will come from him, but a lot of officers out here
don't believe it. They say Sheridan wouldn't have thrown in with
that crowd."

"I don't believe it myself," Finerty said. "Sheridan's in a brig somewhere in the Washington Naval Yards, according to one of my sources. Even if he isn't, they must have him locked up some-where—they're just using his name to hold the army together."

"I want you to get out West and find out what the hell General Crook is up to."

Finerty smiled. "I was about to ask for that particular assign-ment myself."

"And don't cool your heels in Chicago too long," Snowden said. "You won't be the only correspondent heading for Fort Laramie."

"Fort Laramie?" Finerty asked.

"Crook's moved his headquarters there, and Colonel Jeremiah Clarke of Fort Leavenworth is on his way there, too. It might mean war; it might mean Crook intends to break the treaty and present the council with a *fait accompli*." Snowden threw a copy of the Chicago *Tribune* across his desk.

Finerty picked up the paper and saw that this edition of the *Tri-bune* had been published two days ago. He also saw that the byline on the lead was that of R. B. Davenport. Reuben Briggs Davenport wrote for the New York *Herald*, but apparently was now sending dispatches to the *Tribune* as well. Davenport had left St. Paul with Brigadier General Alfred Terry, the Commander of the Department of Dakota, and several battalions of infantry and cavalry to meet with General Crook in Fort Laramie.

"I'll be on my way before tomorrow morning," Finerty said. The knowledge that his competitor Davenport was already hastening toward Laramie would give wings to his feet.

Lemuel still dreamed of Katia. Her spirit came into his soul at night, while he slept, and spoke of what he would have to do.

You cannot stop the war now, she whispered to him, you can only help the Lakota to win it. It will not be enough to have only a new treaty, my people will need a great victory if they are to be safe from the Wasichu.

Even when he was awake, he sometimes heard her whispering to him. He could hear it now as he slapped water on his face. He was sharing Jeremiah Clarke's quarters in Fort Laramie; the colonel had given him a major's uniform and insignia.

Clarke had already left the barracks. Lemuel dressed quickly and went outside. Tents were pitched on the parade ground, and there were others outside the fort's walls; there was not enough room in the barracks for all the men who were here.

Jeremiah was talking to two other officers. He turned toward Lemuel and motioned to him. "Come on," he said without preamble. "General Crook's ready to see you now."

Lemuel followed the other man across the parade ground to the general's headquarters. "Do you have any idea of what he's thinking?" Lemuel asked.

"None."

He had taken a risk by coming here with Jeremiah. Had he left Kansas quickly, he could have been at the camp of Touch-the-Clouds, ready to persuade him not to act rashly. But it would be better to go to the Lakota chiefs as an envoy from General Crook, if he could. There was still a good chance that Three Star Crook would not listen to him, Lemuel knew, and a fair chance that he might consider him a danger and order him placed him under arrest. If that happened, he would try to escape, and if he was shot down in the attempt—well, that would not matter. He would have done all that he could. He would be with Katia once more.

He went into the room. Three Star Crook sat behind a long table with One Star Terry and several other officers. Lemuel wondered if the presence of those officers was a good sign or not.

Crook looked up. Lemuel gazed into the general's pale eyes as Jeremiah took a seat with the other officers.

"We meet again, Rowland," Crook said. "Colonel Clarke has told me that you were living in Elysium, Kansas, when it was attacked."

"I was staying there," Lemuel replied. "I was living in Bismarck, but thought my old friend Colonel Clarke—" He swallowed. "My wife came with me to Elysium. She died in the massacre there." He said those words quickly.

"So Clarke has informed me. The survivors say that men wearing army uniforms carried out those atrocities."

"Perhaps they were United States soldiers, but I wonder about that," Lemuel said. "If they were ordered to break the treaty, they could have found an Indian camp to attack. Or they could have settled for killing the Cheyenne and Lakota there and left everyone else alone. White people might have shed a few tears over the deaths of helpless Indians, but they wouldn't now be forming militias and self-defense forces in the towns bordering the Lakota lands if Indians were the only ones who were slaughtered. If the Council of the United States had wanted to assure people in the West that they wished only to protect them from raids by secessionists, they made a tactical error. Settlers out here now have reason to fear Washington much more than to fear any rebel band, or the Indians, for that matter."

"I am inclined to agree with you," Crook said, "but now I must concern myself with how best to protect the western territories and the states bordering them. The treaty has been broken, by the massacre of friendly Indians camped near Elysium, by the slaughter of the settlers there, and by recent hostilities in the Dakota territory, and the Sioux and Cheyenne might seek revenge for that. They may go after everybody, friendly and hostile whites alike. I must decide which presents the greatest danger to the people out here, the new regime in Washington or the Sioux and their allies."

Lemuel had not known about any fighting in Dakota. Had Touch-the-Clouds, or perhaps another chief, already gone on the warpath? If so, there might be little he could accomplish here.

"Hadn't heard about hostilities in Dakota," Jeremiah Clarke muttered, saving Lemuel from having to ask about that.

Crook glanced at Clarke. "A report came over the wire this morning. About forty troopers were seen riding out from Fort Lincoln by several residents of Bismarck from across the Missouri. At about the same time, a telegraph wire running from that town to an encampment of friendly Sioux was cut. When the troops didn't return to the fort, Colonel Miles declared martial law in Bismarck, stationed soldiers around a workshop and some buildings belonging to an inventor who lives there, had the few Indians living in the town clapped in chains and jailed, and sent out some scouts. Obviously he's expecting something to happen." Crook paused. "A rider managed to get out of Bismarck and across the river and got as far as Deadwood. He killed his horse riding there and damned near killed himself. The message was sent to us from Deadwood."

Clarke seemed about to speak. Lemuel said, "General Crook, let me ride to Dakota."

Crook stared at him for a while in silence. "Why? Do you think you can keep the Sioux from going on the warpath?"

"I can try," Lemuel said. "I know Touch-the-Clouds. If he has already decided on war, he'll be at Fort Abraham Lincoln with his warriors by the time I can get there, and there won't be a thing I can do. But if he hasn't—" He shifted his weight on his feet. "Sir, I am willing to ride to the Lakota and tell their chiefs that you gave no orders to break the treaty, and no orders to attack helpless people. The Lakota and their allies have kept the promises they made at Fort Fetterman four years ago. They will continue to keep them if the new government in Washington doesn't make war against them."

"The government," General Terry said softly. "Usurpers and traitors."

Crook narrowed his eyes. "Rowland, tell your Sioux comrades the following. If they will promise not to break the treaty, I will promise to do what I can to protect their territories. But if they decide to go to war, they will find me an implacable foe. If I hear nothing further from you before the end of July, I will assume that a state of war exists between the states and territories of the United States and the Lakota."

Lemuel nodded. "Yes, sir."

Crook leaned forward. "Go. You have very little time."

"Virgil," Jane Cannary said, "looks like we picked one hell of a time to ride to Bismarck."

Virgil Warrick reined in his horse and stood up in his stirrups. The two of them had stopped at an Arikara camp near Killdeer Mountain two days ago, to hear stories of soldiers attacking an Indian camp. The Arikara chief did not seem to know much more than that, and so Jane and Virgil had continued east to the Missouri River and had followed it south.

From the top of the steep hill where they had halted, Jane glimpsed Bismarck on the other side of the Missouri. On the eastern bank of the river, the rows of plain wooden buildings, the longer and larger structures of the Edison Laboratories and the Lakota Ironworks, and the ramshackle houses on the outskirts of Bismarck looked much as they had when Jane had last visited the town a year ago. South of her, in the distance, along the bluffs overlooking the river valley and Fort Abraham Lincoln, were the tepees and wickiups of well over a thousand Indians.

"Shit," Jane muttered.

Virgil looked through the field glasses that hung from a leather cord around his neck. He had acquired the field glasses from a soldier the last time they had ridden to Bismarck, when Virgil had traded pelts for supplies and Jane had reacquainted herself with whiskey. The liquor had made her vomit afterwards and the tales that she had heard in the saloon had brought her to realize that she no longer had to hide from those who might accuse her of deserting Custer and the Seventh. Custer had decided to live among the Indians, some said; others claimed that he had been adopted by Sitting Bull as a son.

Better for people to believe that, Jane thought, than to know the truth. No one in Bismarck had guessed who she was, and she had left it that way, but it had bothered her that Iron Butt Custer, that shameless self-promoter, had finally become the legend that he had always wanted to be.

Virgil lowered his field glasses. "Almost three thousand," he replied. "That's my guess. Lakota, Cheyenne, some Crow—all of them men."

"A war party," Jane said.

"Surely do look that way, 'cept the warriors ain't got their war paint on yet, so they ain't fighting just now."

War, she thought, and just when she had made up her mind that it was time to leave Virgil's cabin and maybe head back to civilization for good. She had been trying to think of how to tell him that she was not going back to his place. During the winters and the long silences, the days that would pass without having to speak a single word to each other, they had become friends. Maybe it was the silences that had made them friends, the way each of them did what had to be done without having to say anything about it to the other. They had hunted together and patched the chinks between the logs of the cabin together and done a hundred other tasks without ever uttering a word, and gradually she had come to a kind of calming silence within herself.

She had begun to grow restless again that spring. Now, looking at the Indian encampment above the fort, Jane began to think that she had not valued the peace that she had won for herself enough.

Five braves were already riding toward them from the encampment. Jane rested one hand on her pommel. "Shit," she said under her breath, then raised her arms, palms out, careful to keep them away from her holster.

"By Godfrey," Theodore Roosevelt said, showing his teeth, "a veritable multitude of red men has gathered near Fort Lincoln."

Lemuel glanced at the young man. He had ridden to Roosevelt's cabin, to find him raging over the coup in Washington. Two hired hands Roosevelt had sent to Bismarck for supplies had returned to tell him what they had heard from the townsfolk. Lemuel had been certain that the other man would be sympathetic to his mission, but he had not been prepared for Roosevelt's insistence that he become part of that mission.

"We must hasten there at once," Roosevelt added, squinting through his spectacles at the expanse of tepees and shelters.

"They're not yet ready to fight," Lemuel said. "If they were, they would be doing their war dances by now, singing war songs and making medicine and putting on war paint."

Roosevelt turned his head toward him. The man looked faintly ridiculous in his perfectly tailored fringed buckskins and mutton chop whiskers; a mustache had begun to sprout on his upper lip. He seemed unsuited for this land, with his expensive holsters, buckles, and custom-made alligator boots, but he had pushed himself hard during their ride, setting a pace for himself and the men riding with him that had tested Lemuel's endurance.

"I never thought," Roosevelt said then, "that I would find more sympathy within myself for red savages than for men who represent and serve our government." The man had admitted freely to Lemuel that he had come West in the hope of establishing his own ranch, one that would someday be a profitable venture. Sooner or later, the redskins would be forced to bow to inevitable progress, and the railroad so long promised to this region would come, and those who were ready to take advantage of the resources this land offered would become rich. Young Roosevelt would not be the first to break the treaty, he would abide by the restrictions the agreement placed on his activities, but he was convinced that the unrestrained movement of people to the western territories could not be held back indefinitely.

The recent coup in Washington had thrown chaos into the midst of his certainties.

"They have turned us into mere subjects," Roosevelt had muttered back at his cabin, obviously seething. "Those blackguards in Washington have taken a free people, a people who have freely chosen those who govern them, and made subjects of them. They have torn up our Constitution, they have taken our Republic and turned it into an autocracy."

Lemuel looked back at the ten hired hands of Roosevelt's who had ridden there with them. They were a grizzled lot, much given to drinking and the filthiest of curses and mocking remarks about their boss Old Four Eyes in Roosevelt's absence. But in his presence, they responded to him as enlisted men would to an officer.

Roosevelt touched his horse's neck lightly with the crop of his hand-tooled whip. They rode toward the Lakota camp.

White Eagle rode out to meet the Orphan Rowland and to bring him to Touch-the-Clouds. Other men were with him, but Rowland would not have brought them here if they were enemies.

"This is Theodore Roosevelt," the Orphan said as he introduced the man with him. White Eagle stared at the strange-looking man who wore small glass windows on his face. "He has come here as a friend."

Rowland had spoken in English. "I am here as an observer," the four-eyed man said. "Until I know the purpose of these Indians in being here, I cannot call myself a friend."

"We came here," White Eagle said in the same tongue, "because the chief of the Blue Coats here, Bear Coat Miles, sent men to attack us. They rode against my camp." He kept his gaze on Four Eyes Roosevelt. "They would have killed my young daughter, they would have killed my wife and her son, but the thunder spirits came to our aid and fought with us to defeat our enemy. They helped us kill the bastard sons of bitches."

Four Eyes shifted in his saddle. "I see," he said in a voice that was light for a man's. "The man is somewhat more expressive than I expected," he murmured to the Orphan.

"They came to kill us," White Eagle continued, "and so we came here to find out why they cut our talking wire and broke the treaty and attacked my camp. If we do not like the answers—" He made a chopping motion with his hand.

"I have to talk to Touch-the-Clouds," Rowland said.

"He wants to speak to you," White Eagle replied. "I am to take you to him. These men must wait." He gestured at Four Eyes and his comrades.

Four Eyes Roosevelt sat up straight in his saddle. He did not look fearful, White Eagle thought, for a man who had to wear a glass mask in front of his eyes in order to see.

Touch-the Clouds was by himself in his wickiup. White Eagle rode away with his comrades, leaving Lemuel alone with the chief. Lemuel had hoped that other chiefs would be there, men who might listen when he spoke of trying to keep the peace.

Touch-the-Clouds sat in the shadows, facing the shelter's opening, not moving, so still that he hardly seemed to be breathing. He wore only a breechcloth and leggings, but his headdress and a pouch of war medicine and a red war pipe lay on a blanket near him, along with bowls of blue and white and yellow clay for war paint. He wanted to go to war, he was already on the warpath inside himself.

"I have unhappy news," Lemuel said in Lakota as he sat down in front of the other man.

"Say it."

"The woman who was your wife, whom you gave to me, whom I came to love more than my own life, no longer lives."

"I know," Touch-the-Clouds said.

"You were told."

"No, I felt it. I saw it in a dream some days ago. I knew she was gone. I had her last message from the talking wire, spoken to me by a wire warrior, and when I heard it, I knew that those words would be her last words to me." Touch-the-Clouds bowed his head for a moment. "I am sorry, Orphan."

"I loved her," Lemuel said. "Blue Coats killed her, Blue Coats came to where she was and broke the treaty and murdered her. So maybe you will listen to me when I say that you must not make war against the Blue Coats now."

Touch-the-Clouds lifted his head.

"I rode here with a message from Three Star Crook," Lemuel continued. "This is his message. If the Lakota promise not to break the treaty, Crook promises to do what he can to protect your territories. But if you decide to go to war, he will fight you." Lemuel paused. "And if he hears nothing from you before the end of the Moon of Red Cherries, he will assume that the United States and the Lakota are at war."

Touch-the-Clouds held up a hand, a sign to be silent. "White Eagle told me of what has happened in Washington," he said softly. "President Blaine is dead, and the new Great Father is the Blue Coat McClellan. Does it matter to the Lakota which man sits in the White House? Does it matter to us if it is Sherman, Sheridan, or another man who is war chief of the Blue Coats? Sheridan would have come after us if the Great Father and others had not held him back.

Sherman would have rejoiced to see all of us dead. The Wasichu would have broken the treaty sooner or later. Now that they have broken it, we must fight, or else they will keep taking what they want from us until there is nothing left." His hands tightened into fists. "The Wasichu are weaker now. This is the time to strike them, before they can decide how best to move against us."

"What you say is true," Lemuel said, "but if you go to war now, you will have to fight Three Star Crook and all of the forces he now commands. He gave no orders to Miles or to blue-coated raiders to attack helpless people in Kansas. He doesn't want to fight you, but he will if you break the treaty."

"Three Star Crook will fight us when he is ordered to do so," Touch-the-Clouds muttered.

"No. He is angry about what has happened in Washington. He doesn't accept McClellan and Stanton as his rightful chiefs. I don't believe that he would follow them into battle against you. But if he thinks that you are a threat to any of the Wasichu in these territories, he will fight the Lakota."

The chief's eyes shifted slightly. He's uncertain, Lemuel thought, and pressed his advantage. "What did you intend to do here?" he asked quickly.

Touch-the-Clouds smiled slightly. "Surely you can see what I mean to do. Bear Coat Miles has broken the treaty by sending his Blue Coats to kill the people in White Eagle's camp. He has imprisoned eight Lakota men who live in Bismarck in his iron rooms. I will give him a chance to free those men and surrender the fort to us. He will refuse, and then we will attack. I have sent for some of our arrow-rockets, I am only waiting until they are here." He thrust out his chin. "And no one will say that we were the first to break the treaty. I promised to do this, I promised that I would punish those who broke the treaty. That was also part of that agreement."

"Everything you say is true," Lemuel said, "but if you strike at Miles now, all you will have is one victory, and an enemy who might have become an ally. Stay your hand, and you may win much more for yourself."

"So you have a plan of your own," Touch-the-Clouds said. "Tell me what you would do."

"Ask for a meeting with Miles under a flag of truce. I will be your messenger to him. I will tell him that you and your men will leave peacefully if he releases his prisoners and orders the soldiers in Bismarck to return to Fort Lincoln. He will also have to promise that he will abide by the treaty in the future."

"He will refuse."

"He'll listen," Lemuel said, "and if he doesn't, then I will take revenge for his attack on White Eagle's camp. I will count coup on him and kill him myself."

Touch-the-Clouds started. Lemuel had actually managed to surprise him. "Then his men will kill you," the Lakota said.

"Probably. You'll have even more reason then to destroy Fort Lincoln or force a surrender. You see, my friend, to care nothing for one's life can also be a weapon, to be ready to welcome death can be a weapon, as many Lakota warriors have known. I don't much care if I live or not these days, and my death might serve you as well as any advice I can give."

Touch-the-Clouds said, "You are a true friend, Orphan of the East."

Lemuel shook his head. "Your wife—my wife—saw a great victory for you. Her vision was not simply one of your people safe in their lands. She saw victorious Lakota warriors in the street of an eastern city."

"I have seen the same vision."

"You can fight more battles and the men can count coup and your warriors can win many battle honors for themselves, or you can fight a war of conquest and be the greatest of the chiefs. I know which kind of war you have long dreamed of fighting." Lemuel stood up. "I will do what I can to give you the victory my wife foresaw for you." If he failed at that now, Katia's death would have no meaning.

The gate of Fort Abraham Lincoln's wooden wall of pointed logs opened for Lemuel and was closed behind him. He had ridden down the steep hill from the infantry garrison overlooking the fort with White Eagle and five other men after the officer on duty had allowed them to pass, but had guessed that only he would be admitted to Fort Lincoln. He had seen Nelson Miles only twice before, when the colonel had first come there to take command and later in the company of a small delegation from Bismarck, but Miles apparently remembered his name, according to the infantryman who ushered him inside the fort.

Two soldiers took charge of his horse while two others led him across the parade ground to the adjutant's office. Lemuel gave his Winchester to one of the men, then entered. He expected to find the colonel with two or three fellow officers, but Miles was alone. It would have been more difficult to kill him with other men present, although not impossible for an assassin willing to give up his life in the effort. He thought of Frank Grouard, of how he had recoiled from that murder. That had been fainthearted of him. All that he had to do was to remind himself that this was war, and that the war had already claimed Katia's life.

Miles sat behind a plain wooden table. His thick mustache drooped on either side of his mouth. He was a tall, muscular man, but in his blue uniform, without the thick coat trimmed with bear fur that he usually wore in winter, the coat that had given him the name by which the Lakota knew him, he seemed smaller.

Lemuel crossed the room, slowly drew his Colt from his holster, and lay it on the table next to Miles's saber and rifle. Another revolver and a knife were concealed under his coat. The two men posted outside had left the door open, despite the mosquitoes that plagued the valley in summer, perhaps to keep the warm room from getting even hotter, perhaps so that they could watch him. They had a good chance to cut him down before he struck at Miles.

"I see you're in uniform," Miles said. "Hardly appropriate, under the circumstances."

"I served under General Grant," Lemuel replied. "I have earned the right to wear this uniform. Perhaps you've forgotten that. Colonel Jeremiah Clarke provided me with this garment, and General George Crook didn't find it inappropriate when I met with him at Fort Laramie."

Miles's mustache twitched.

"General Crook was concerned enough about what was happening here to allow me to come here, to speak for him," Lemuel continued as he sat down.

"You are here to speak for the Sioux," Miles shot back.

"I am here to preserve the treaty." Lemuel leaned forward. "Those usurpers and traitors in Washington won't keep it. Those words—usurpers and traitors—are not my own. They are the words General Terry used to describe the men who claim to be the government of the United States."

Miles's pale eyes shifted away from Lemuel for a moment. "McClellan and the others are a temporary governing body."

"So they say now."

"According to the Chief Justice of the Supreme Court, they are a duly constituted authority. My wife's uncle was part of that authority until his unfortunate death. He wouldn't have been a part of it unless—"

"General Sherman and I had many differences of opinion," Lemuel interrupted, "but somehow I can't bring myself to believe that he would have been a part of a conspiracy to assassinate President Blaine and then take over the government, especially if Edwin Stanton was involved. His death seems entirely too convenient. I don't believe that Senator John Sherman, your wife's other illustrious uncle, would have approved of such actions, either."

Miles stiffened. "So my wife tells me." He tapped one forefinger against the top of the table. "It doesn't matter. I am a soldier, I must follow the orders of my commanding officer. That means I must follow the orders of General Sheridan, since he has now assumed command of—"

"Sheridan may be dead, too. At best, he's probably under guard. You may not realize that General Crook is already assuming that the chain of command has been broken."

Miles's eyes widened slightly. Now he is afraid, Lemuel thought, but he's hiding it well. "Seems to me," Lemuel went on, "that you should regard Crook as your commanding officer now."

"I was ordered to attack those redskins," Miles muttered. "There they were, with a telegraph line to Bismarck, with a maker of gadgets brought out here to make things for the Sioux—"

"For the Sioux and anybody willing to support his work and leave him free to do it," Lemuel corrected. "Most of the things he's made aren't of much use to the Lakota."

"They would be if they ever went to war. I know what the army's worried about. They're wondering what will happen once the treaty's broken."

"So you decided to break it first."

"I followed my orders."

"You don't even know if Sheridan gave those orders."

Miles leaned back and folded his arms. "Someone in Washington did."

"Of course. The bankers and railroad men have wanted the Lakota lands for a long time. They might have had them by now if there hadn't been more trouble in the South. The only way that they can get them now is to break the treaty and force the Lakota into war."

"The Sioux can't win a war," Miles said.

"No, they probably can't by themselves, not even with their ironworks and the weapons they've bought and made and any new inventions Mr. Edison can devise for them. But they have some friends now, other red allies, other settlers and people who might feel more loyalty to friendly Indians who have kept the treaty than to a government they had no hand in electing. Sheridan and Sherman could have shortened any conflict, I have no doubt about that, but apparently they would rather resist a tyranny than mount a campaign against the Indians."

Miles lifted a brow.

"If Sheridan were still able to do anything," Lemuel continued, "he would be on his way West, and you'd know he was coming."

Miles said, "The Sioux will lose."

"Yes, they probably will lose, even without having to deal with Sheridan, but it would be a long and bloody conflict, and very costly. Do you want to be the man who ignites it?"

"I had my orders." Miles sounded more uncertain.

"Orders given by men who want to use you to line their own pockets. Orders given by usurpers."

"What does Crook want me to do?" Miles asked.

"Whatever Touch-the-Clouds asks of you," Lemuel replied. "He wants the prisoners you're holding freed, martial law lifted in Bismarck, and your promise that you will keep the treaty. You can admit to the Lakota that you mistakenly believed that your orders came from your chief but have since learned otherwise. I would also advise you to make one other gesture."

"And what is that?"

"Restoring the telegraph link to the camp of White Eagle and his men."

Miles's mouth twisted. "Very well. I can't see that I have much of a choice."

"Then perhaps we can prepare to ride to Touch-the-Clouds. He will want to smoke a peace pipe with you and put his mark on a written copy of the agreement." Lemuel let out his breath. How far Miles could be trusted, he did not know, but he would not have to kill the man after all.

"I can do better than that," Miles said. "Brown, Colburn!" The two soldiers standing guard outside came through the open door. "Fetch that gadget maker. We're going to need one of those machines of his. You can tell him he'll be free to go afterwards."

Lemuel shifted in his seat. He should have suspected that Miles would have arrested Edison and locked him up in the guardhouse.

"What does Crook mean to do after I manage to settle matters with these Sioux?" Miles asked.

Lemuel shrugged. "I don't know," he answered truthfully.

"By Godfrey," Theodore Roosevelt said.

"I'll be damned," one of the men with Roosevelt muttered under his breath.

Jane sat next to Lemuel Rowland. She listened as Edison's assistant John Kreusi, standing at the back of his wagon, turned the handle of the machine he called a phonograph.

". . . and the treaty of Fort Fetterman will be kept," the machine sitting in the buckboard said in the voice of Colonel Nelson Miles.

The voice of Touch-the-Clouds began to speak in Lakota, repeating all of the provisions of the new agreement with Miles. The voices sounded a bit scratchier now, possibly because this was the third time the shiny cylinder had been played. There were other cylinders with the same recorded sounds. Thomas Edison had brought two phonographs to the camp of Touch-the-Clouds.

"Lord have mercy," Virgil said.

John Kreusi beamed, looking full of himself, although Edison was the true genius behind this machine. Edison, Lem Rowland had told Jane and the others, was in his laboratory at that very moment, anxious to get back to work after his recent imprisonment. He had not even wanted to come out to the Sioux encampment to make the historic recordings himself.

White Eagle stared intently at the photograph. Other Indians in the encampment, Jane had noticed, had made signs to avert evil after hearing the machine, while others had clapped their hands over their ears and hurried away, but not White Eagle and his comrades.

"Wire Talker Edison has strong medicine," White Eagle said. "If he can make wires sing, and catch voices, maybe he will make a light that can fill a tepee with brightness." The inventor, Jane had heard, was still working on his obsession, a device for illumination that he called an incandescent lamp.

"Oh, you can be sure he will," Kreusi said without a trace of doubt in his voice.

"Kreusi," Roosevelt said, "please do inform Mr. Edison that I would very much like to have a little talk with him about investing in some of his ventures."

The air was still, the summer evening still hot. Several bands of Sioux had already left the encampment near Fort Lincoln; most of the others would leave in the morning, heading west to their traditional lands and their postponed buffalo hunt. Not more than a few hours ago, Jane and Virgil had been sitting in a wickiup as prisoners, contemplating their fate and deeply regretting that they had decided to go to Bismarck. She could go back to civilization after all, Jane thought; there would be no war. Then she glanced at Lem, who had come there to talk to Touch-the-Clouds and to Miles, and saw the sorrow and grimness in his face.

She reached over and touched his arm. "Hey, Lem," she murmured, "I'd like to ask your advice."

He nodded.

"In private."

He got to his feet. Jane motioned to Virgil. She walked away from the group of white men and Indians sitting in front of White Eagle's wickiup. Virgil followed them. She would have no secrets from her Negro friend. Whatever she had to say to Lemuel, Virgil would have to be a part of it.

"Didn't get a chance to say this before," Jane said, "but I hope you'll give my regards to Graceful Swan—I mean, Miz Rowland."

"My wife is dead," he said.

Jane felt a pang of regret. She had meant to call on Graceful Swan the last time she had ridden to Bismarck, but had been so sick from whiskey that she had been ashamed to show her face to the woman. She swallowed hard, afraid suddenly that she might cry.

"I'm sorry," she said.

"Raiders killed her." Lemuel's voice was flat. "We were staying in Elysium, Kansas. We were expecting that there might be trouble, so I was out scouting with another man. While we were gone, raiders wearing army uniforms attacked at night and set fire to buildings and murdered most of the people there."

Jane took a breath, not knowing what to say, and then Lemuel turned toward her and she saw the coldness in his dark eyes. Touch-the-Clouds had that look about his eyes, as had Rubalev the last time she had seen that blond devil. She took a step back from Lemuel Rowland.

"What did you want to ask me?" he said in that same flat voice.

Jane glanced at Virgil, who looked wary of Lemuel. "Ain't told Virgil this, but I was thinking of maybe going back to civilization. I mean staying in Bismarck for a while, then maybe heading out somewheres else." She hooked her thumbs around her holster belt. "Sorry, Virgil."

"I guess I figured you was thinkin' of that, Calamity," the black man said, "so it ain't much of a surprise. Fact is, I'm thinking of settlin' down near a place with more folks myself."

"Trouble is," Jane continued, "I'll need to find work, and I thought maybe you'd know where I could get it. If they need someone to ride shotgun on stagecoaches or maybe on the railroad—"

"The trains aren't running as often," Lemuel said, "so you probably won't find much there. The Union Pacific doesn't run as many trains to California now, and the Lakota will never let tracks be built across their territory."

She did not ask about the southwestern rail lines, such as they were. She had learned from a couple of travelers during her last visit to Bismarck that bands of Mexicans, Texans, Comanches, and Apaches had been claiming more of what they called "tolls," meaning anything that they could steal at gunpoint from the passengers.

"The army might need some scouts," Jane said, "even if there ain't going to be any fighting. Maybe you could put in a word—"

"You asked for my advice," Lemuel said. "Here it is. You two should get whatever you need in town and head back to Montana. You'll be as safe in Blackfeet territory as you would be anywhere else."

"But the fighting's over here," Jane said.

"It's over for now. This peace won't last. Miles may have promised to keep the treaty, but others won't. Men in the East are already looking west again. They believe God meant for this land to belong to them. The treaties are just a delay. All the Lakota can hope for now is that the delay gives them enough time to prepare for the war they'll have to fight."

"If'n there's going to be a war," Virgil said, "maybe we won't be safe in Montana, neither."

"There will be war," Lemuel said. "You can be certain of that. I didn't want to believe it. A part of me kept pretending that war wouldn't come, that the treaty would be kept. Katia knew otherwise; she saw it in her visions. She foresaw her own death and she saw the war that would follow. There will always be wars until there is no one left to fight them. Rubalev told me that, years ago. The Lakota have always believed it."

"Lem—" Jane said.

He turned away from her and Virgil and walked back to where the men were still listening to Edison's phonograph.

NINETEEN

War was coming. Crazy Horse had sensed that even before Plenty Coups of the Crow, Crooked Horn of the Arikara, and Gall, the adoptive brother of Sitting Bull, had ridden to his camp. The three chiefs told him that Touch-the-Clouds was talking of war, had been talking of war ever since the Sun Dance, but Crazy Horse had already dreamed of war and had known what they would tell him.

He had last dreamed of his own death almost a year ago, in the same dream that had come to him from time to time ever since the battle with Custer in the Black Hills. In that dream, he was sitting in the tepee of Touch-the-Clouds when the Blue Coats came for him. They took him to one of their walled forts, and there he saw the warrior Little Big Man wearing the blue coat of a Wasichu soldier. The Wasichu, he realized, were going to put him in an iron cage, a place with barred windows where men were chained like animals. In his dream, Crazy Horse thought, I will run from this place, trance myself into the true world. A Blue Coat came at him then and stabbed at him with a knife on the end of a firestick, and it was when he felt the stabbing of the knife that he would leave his dream and find himself in the world where his death had not happened.

The dream had come to him so many times that he had expected, while drifting into yet another dream of Blue Coats and of warriors, to dream his death once more. Instead, he had dreamed of a camp filled with Blue Coats and Lakota warriors praying over war pipes and painting themselves for battle. His people would be at war soon. It was good that they would fight, since the warriors had been given no chance to display their valor for some years now, and some of the younger men had not yet proven theirs. What Crazy Horse did not understand was why his people were in a camp with the Blue Coats preparing for war and getting ready to fight along-side them. He had awakened after that, and only then had it come to him that he had not dreamed of his death for a long time.

That death, the dream death brought to him by the Blue Coat's knife, would not come to him. Crazy Horse knew that now, yet the dream still existed inside him. It was as if he had dreamed himself into another world and had died there, while the waking world around him was only one of shadows.

Plenty Coups said to him, "Touch-the-Clouds says that we will be at war before next summer."

Crooked Horn said, "Touch-the-Clouds now talks to Morning Star Brother, the Orphan from the East, of war. He seek his counsel. He speaks to him as if the Orphan is a war chief."

Gall said, "Sitting Bull had another vision after the Sun Dance. He saw Blue Coats falling into camp, falling with their heads pointed at the ground, just as he did before the battle against Long Hair Custer in the Black Hills. But there were other Blue Coats with their feet pointed at the ground, standing apart from the battle, and still others falling away from us. Sitting Bull thinks that it means that not all of the Blue Coats will fight against us."

Crazy Horse had known even before the Sun Dance that Sitting Bull would have a vision. After Plenty Coups and Gall and Crooked Horn left his camp, Crazy Horse knew that he had to seek his own vision.

He got up before dawn on the following morning, put on his

hair-fringed shirt, and said to his wife, Black Shawl, "I am riding out today." He had not spoken so many words to her in months, but he had always been a silent man, one who lived largely apart from others. He had never told Black Shawl that he had also dreamed her death, and that of their daughter, that he had seen them wasting away from the evil spirits that sucked the strength from the lungs of people and made them burn with fever. The Wasichu brought such evil spirits, and many had died from them in the past. Crazy Horse had taken his dream as a warning to keep his distance from the white man.

"You will need food," Black Shawl said, handing him some dried meat and a pouch of pemmican. He would not need food, he would be starving himself in order to see his vision more clearly, but he took the food from her because it was simpler than refusing it.

His Oglalas had made camp on the west bank of the Powder River. The women working at hides with their bone tools did not look up as Crazy Horse rode past them. The men grazing the horses and practicing with their bows said nothing to him as he passed.

He rode west, toward Wolf Mountain. He would go to the Greasy Grass, to the river the Wasichu called the Little Bighorn. In years past, he would have ridden to the Black Hills to seek his vision, but Paha Sapa, the Center of the World, which had begun to change after Touch-the-Clouds had his visions, had changed even more since Long Hair Custer had died there with his men. The Blue Coats had come there to look for the yellow metal, and now others came there to take it, to use it for weapons and other tools of the white man that the Lakota wanted, to buy what was needed to make rocket-arrows and firesticks and thunderclap balls to shoot from metal cylinders and to pay the men who knew how to make them. Touch-the-Clouds said that the spirits wanted them to take what they needed from Paha Sapa so that they could defend themselves. Crazy Horse had made his peace with that, yet he ached when he saw the scars miners had left there, and bare places where trees had once grown. His heart grew heavy whenever he climbed to a vantage point from where he could make out the square wooden buildings and dirt roads of Deadwood, so near to Paha Sapa. The Wasichu would have done much worse to the Hills had they exiled the Lakota from that sacred ground, but knowing that was little consolation when he heard the spirits wailing. They wailed now whenever the wind blew through the Black Hills, mourning for what had been lost, and if others could no longer hear them, Crazy Horse still did.

He reached Wolf Mountain by evening and camped there, sleeping under a shelter made with a few tree limbs and a hide. He awoke to the sound of his roan horse pawing at the ground. Another horse was standing several paces from him, a gray horse with no saddle and no bridle. The air rippled around the horse. The sky grew lighter, the horse's gray hide became white, and then the horse began to dance.

He had seen this horse before, as a boy, in the vision that had given him his name. A warrior had been mounted on the horse in that early vision, a warrior with lightning and hailstones painted on his face and body and a red-backed eagle in his hair, the warrior in whom Crazy Horse had seen himself. The spirit-horse was alone now, without a rider.

The spirit-horse trotted west, in the direction of the valley of the Greasy Grass. Crazy Horse mounted his roan and followed the dancing white horse. The thick buffalo grass rippled in the wind, and the trees growing along the banks of the Tongue River swayed, as if they, like the white horse, were dancing.

His visions had shown him the real world, the world of spirits that lay behind the world of shadows in which he dwelled. They had also shown him that there were other shadow worlds beside the one he knew. There was a world in which he had died as a prisoner at the hands of a Blue Coat. There was a world in which Touch-the-Clouds, defeated in battle, had led his people to one of the white man's reservations, there to live out his life in despair. There was a world in which the Lakota fled north to the Grandmother's country, and never again saw the Black Hills. There was even a shadow world in which the white men had never come to the land of the Lakota, where black herds of buffalo too numerous to count roamed over the grassland.

If there was a trail that could lead him from the world in which he lived to another shadow world, Crazy Horse had not yet found it. He could move between this world and the world of spirits, where the white horse was now leading him, but other shadow worlds were closed to him. Still, he could glimpse them in dreams and visions, and what the visions had told him was that every moment, every time a man did one thing instead of another, brought a new shadow world into being. Every step along a trail led a man farther from other trails he might have taken. By glimpsing those he might have followed, he could perhaps see what he might have to do, and where he might be led astray.

War is coming, Crazy Horse thought as he rode after the white spirit-horse. He had learned much from watching how the Blue Coats fought and how they practiced for fighting, how they drilled, how they formed lines, how many supplies they would need if they were to travel deep within Lakota territory to do battle. Now he was thinking of what to tell Touch-the-Clouds about the war that they would soon have to fight.

One way to fight would be to move farther west, to keep as far away from the Wasichu during this coming winter as possible. But if the Blue Coats came after them, they would most likely send one force up from the south and another from the east; they would try to trap the Lakota in their camps, steal their horses and destroy their tents, and leave them without food and shelter during the winter storms. They would not even have to kill them, as Long Hair Custer had when attacking Black Kettle's camp of Cheyennes on the Washita. Crazy Horse had seen such fighting, in many of the shadow worlds, and he did not want to fight that way.

He thought of telling Touch-the-Clouds that they should draw the Blue Coats west, farther from their forts, and then north to the Grandmother's country of Canada. If Three Star Crook became chief of the Blue Coats in the West, he would come after them, and order Miles to break the promises made at Fort Lincoln, but then he would risk provoking the Grandmother's Red Coats and drawing them into battle.

Crook would also have a hard time finding scouts that would help him. That was another thing Crazy Horse had seen in the shadow worlds: more and more of the Lakota and Cheyenne and Crow and Arikara selling themselves to the white man as scouts. If the Blue Coats won a few victories, red men would leave their camps to serve the Wasichu again.

"The Lakota cannot hide in their own lands and expect to win anything in the end," a voice whispered to him. This was a voice he had heard before, that he knew. Crazy Horse looked around, but saw no one who could have spoken the words.

A spirit is trying to tell me what to do, he thought, accepting that; it was why he had come here.

He continued to follow the white horse, stopping only to let his mount graze. He did not eat the food or drink the water his wife had given him. He did not stop to rest, but followed the spirit-horse through the mountain divide and down a steep slope into the valley of the Greasy Grass. By then, he was growing lightheaded, his mouth dry, but he had starved himself for much longer than this in the past while seeking a vision.

The river the Wasichu called the Little Bighorn lay before him. He dismounted, led his roan down a narrow trail to the water to drink, then looked up. The white horse had vanished.

Crazy Horse sighed and touched his wasicun, the personal medicine bundle he wore under his shirt. "I hope I haven't come here for nothing," he said aloud. Although he said little around men, he often grew more talkative in the presence of spirits.

"The Lakota cannot hide in their own lands and expect to win their war."

This was the same voice he had heard before, a woman's voice. He turned around and saw Graceful Swan, the woman that Touch-the-Clouds had given to the Orphan, standing above him on the bank.

"You are dead," he said to her, not that this especially worried him; he had seen and spoken to the dead before. There had been some talk among the men of how Graceful Swan had died at the hands of Blue Coats, of how deeply the Orphan was mourning her. He had pitied the Orphan Rowland for his loss, and thought of how the man from the East had behaved at the Sun Dance.

Rowland had become one of them that summer, taking the name Morning Star Brother. He had even endured having the sticks thrust under his chest muscles by one of the medicine men and dancing for a day with his face turned to the sun. Crazy Horse thought of the shadow world in which he had seen Black Shawl wasting away, of how helpless he had felt, and yet Rowland grieved too deeply for his woman. He had been using the pain of the Sun Dance ordeals not to prove his courage but instead to dampen his grief.

"Yes, of course I am dead," Graceful Swan said. "I wouldn't be here speaking to you otherwise." She wore a dress made out of a buffalo hide with beadwork in the shapes of diamonds and triangles. In one hand, she held a red war pipe, and in the other, a tomahawk, and she bore a shield on her left arm. For a moment, he thought it was his own rawhide shield, with its designs of lightning symbols and a bear and a dragonfly to give him the powers of those spirits. But instead, on the right side of the shield, a Blue Coat with rifle and horse had been painted, and on the left, a warrior in battle dress, and there were other symbols he did not know—a round cylinder, a dome, two lines with more lines drawn between them that made him think of an Iron Horse trail.

"I don't know why you are speaking to me at all, Graceful Swan," Crazy Horse said. "I came here to think about how to counsel Touch-the-Clouds about the war we'll have to fight. The ghost of a woman can't tell me anything about war."

"My last message to Touch-the-Clouds was to tell him that war was coming. He heeded that message even though it came from a woman, and it has turned out to be true. He listens to my husband Morning Star Brother when he speaks of war, and my husband still hears me in his dreams."

"There's something that's bothering me." Crazy Horse sat down on the slope of the bank. "I don't know why the Blue Coats attacked the settlement where you were staying. I don't know why they killed so many people there. Bear Coat Miles going after White Eagle and his talking wire warriors—that I can understand. His chief ordered him to do that, and he had to obey, and if he had killed most of White

Eagle's men and kept the Wasichu medicine man Edison as a captive, it would have been a great blow to us."

"Yes, it would have." Graceful Swan's voice was coming from his left; he turned his head and saw that she was now sitting next to him. "The Lakota would have had to avenge that. They would have had to attack Fort Lincoln and punish Bear Coat Miles for breaking the treaty. Some of the men would have been very angry, and might have killed many people in Bismarck, too, and that would have turned many Wasichu against the Lakota. The war would have started there, and we might have lost it in the end."

"I know." The ghost of Graceful Swan had said only what he was thinking to himself. "That made sense, what Bear Coat Miles did. But it made no sense for the Blue Coats to kill you and all those other people. The Cheyenne and Lakota who were camped there came to that place only because the Wasichu in the town had welcomed them and allowed them to come there to trade. And if the Blue Coats were sent there to break the treaty and kill people, they should have stopped after all of the Cheyenne and Lakota were dead and ridden away."

"Instead," the ghost said, finishing his thought, "they have only enraged both the red man and many white men as well."

Crazy Horse turned her words over in his mind. In some ways, that massacre in Kansas might turn out to be useful to his people. There were Wasichu who would hate the soldiers for what they had done, and that might make them less willing to fight the Lakota. Graceful Swan would not see it that way, of course, nor would the spirits of the people who had died with her, but she had known this war was coming before her death. She might have seen her death coming for her, too, and known that she could not escape it.

"You cannot fight this war alone," Graceful Swan said. "The Lakota and Cheyenne will need all of their allies. I am not speaking only of the Kiowa and Comanche and Cherokee and others who have agreed that red men must not fight among themselves. There may be others besides those red brethren who will fight with the Lakota."

"If we had enough comrades to fight with us," he said, "we

could carry this war away from our grazing grounds. We could carry it east. We could move along the Iron Horse trails and take what we needed along the way. The chiefs of the Blue Coats would not expect us to fight in that way." That was the best way to fight the Long Knives, to keep them from fighting in their customary manner and to fight in ways that they would not foresee.

"That could be done," Graceful Swan said, "but to do it, you must either take what you need from the Wasichu you meet along that trail or have them freely give it to you."

"Surrender, and be spared," Crazy Horse muttered, remembering when Touch-the-Clouds had spoken to him of mercy and terror and their uses in warfare, "or fight, and be destroyed completely. That is the promise we would have to make. We could bring along our rocket-arrows, even if using them is a cowardly way to fight."

"It may be cowardly," Graceful Swan murmured, "but it is effective."

"We wouldn't need wagons with horses to haul them, we could put the rocket-arrows into the Iron Horse wagons. We could shoot those rocket-arrows right up the asses of our enemy."

"You see what you must do, Crazy Horse," the ghost said. "You must win your victory over the Wasichu in the East if the Lakota are to keep their lands."

Touch-the-Clouds, Crazy Horse knew, had been aware of that for some time. Touch-the-Clouds had not brought the Lakota together and made his alliances with other peoples merely to keep what his people already had, or to protect it from the whites. He saw himself as a man like the warrior that Yellow Hair Rubalev told stories about, the warrior who had made his people the rulers of the other side of the world. Maybe that was the only way that the Lakota could keep their lands for all time.

"Yes, you see that," Graceful Swan whispered. He looked toward her and saw that he and his horse were again alone by the river.

Lemuel Rowland had traveled by steamboat to St. Louis and then down the Mississippi to Natchez. A taciturn middle-aged man with a graying beard met him at the dock with horses. Geronimo had deigned to travel as far east as the Red River Valley to meet with Lemuel and Grigory Rubalev. That was the message that had been given to Lemuel in St. Joseph; it had been spoken to him by a rough-looking red-headed young man whom he assumed was one of Rubalev's shadowy acquaintances. Geronimo's concession meant that Lemuel had not had to make a long stagecoach trip to meet with the Apache in Santa Fe, but he had not known that Rubalev was also to be an envoy from the Lakota to the Apache chief.

His guide responded to none of his questions during the four days of their journey, and by the time Geronimo's encampment and his large cattle herd were in sight, Lemuel had stopped asking any more questions. For the Apache to be this far east, near the border between Texas and Louisiana, was unusual, but Geronimo's people were growing more prosperous, had kept their peace with their former Comanche enemies, and often made forays beyond their southwestern homelands. Crossing the Rio Grande, stealing cattle from the Mexicans to herd across the border and then trading or selling the livestock to Texican ranchers had become quite a profitable enterprise for the Apache. From New Orleans up to St. Louis, the Mississippi was again peaceful and clogged with traffic, as Lemuel had seen during his journey, and the people of Louisiana were now more interested in preserving good relations with the Texas Republic than with mounting any resistance to the regime up in Washington.

Geronimo and his men were camped in wickiups outside a small adobe house. The bearded man left Lemuel with Rubalev, then went inside the house.

"He owns this ranch," Rubalev said to Lemuel.

"He didn't tell me that. He didn't say much of anything, not even his name."

Rubalev shrugged. "It is perhaps better if you do not know his name, or anything else about him." The Alaskan was wearing a white Stetson with an eagle feather in the hatband and a well-tailored buckskin jacket that looked as expensive as young Theodore

Roosevelt's. Rubalev jerked his head toward the nearest wickiup. "He may talk to you today, or he may decide that he wants to reach a bargain for his stolen cattle first. I have been waiting here for nearly a week now, and Geronimo has refused to discuss anything with me until you arrived."

Rubalev looked impatient and tired. Lemuel was about to speak when three men came out of the wickiup. One was a sturdily built, handsome man with long black hair; another was a thin old man with a leathery face wearing a sombrero, leather jacket, and breech-cloth with leggings. But it was the third man, small and spare and with close-set piercing black eyes, who drew Lemuel's attention. He wore a plain white tunic covered with dust and a pair of dark trousers; the uneven ends of his black hair reached to his shoulders. He stared at Lemuel in silence, pressing his thin lips together, then made a motion with his hand.

"Geronimo is inviting you to sit down," Rubalev said.

Lemuel sat down on the dusty ground. Rubalev seated himself next to him. Another Apache came out of the wickiup, carrying a jug.

"Chato," the man said, pointing at himself. "I will speak for you," he added in English. "Yellow Hair tells me that you are a red man from the East called Poyeshao, and that you have the ear of the northern chief called Touch-the-Clouds."

Lemuel nodded. "That is so."

"This is Nana." Chato gestured at the old man. "This is Vittorio, who has killed more Mexicans than any of us." He pointed his chin at the third man. "And this is Goyathlay, chief of the Chiricahuas and of the other Apache bands, as Touch-the-Clouds is chief of the Lakota peoples. You know Goyathlay as Geronimo."

Lemuel bowed his head slightly and uttered a greeting, which was translated by Chato. Geronimo said something in his own tongue; Chato passed Lemuel the jug. He hoisted it to his lips, expecting to taste water, and suddenly found his mouth full of whiskey. He managed to swallow the liquor without choking.

Geronimo's lips twitched, as if he were on the verge of laughing. Lemuel offered greetings from Touch-the-Clouds; Chato responded with Geronimo's words of friendship for his brother the Lakota chief. The jug was passed again, and Lemuel forced himself to drink. It might be the middle of winter, but the sun was already growing hot against his back.

"Yellow Hair tells Geronimo that Touch-the-Clouds is in his winter camp," Chato translated for the Apache chief.

"That is true," Lemuel said.

"He says that our northern brothers may soon be at war with the chiefs in Washington."

"That is also true."

"Now you want us to fight with you."

"Touch-the-Clouds has heard rumors that a few of your people went with the Comanche and the Kiowa to join some of the Gray Coats when they began to fight against the Blue Coats again."

"It is said that some of our men went on raids with them," Chato said for Geronimo, "and that they were paid well in loot and cattle, but that is only a rumor. It is said that some of these men also fought with the dark-skinned buffalo people against the Gray Coats when they were not paid what they were promised by the white men, but that is also a rumor. We did not send any of our warriors there, we did not tell them to go, but sometimes men grow restless and do not listen to the counsel of their chiefs. They knew that they were breaking the promises we made to the white chief Gray Wolf Crook, so it is good that no one of those men was caught. If an Apache or a Kiowa had been caught fighting with the Gray Coat guerrillas or with the buffalo people, we would have said that he was not one of us and that the white man would have to punish him for breaking the promises our people made, and the Comanche would have done the same."

"I understand," Lemuel said.

"The Gray Coats to the east of us are tired of fighting," Chato said. "More of the dark-skinned buffalo people are living in their own settlements and keeping away from trouble with the white man. The Texicans have Mexicans to fight against and take land from now. We and the Comanche near here are getting fat with our cattle herds and our horses and our trade with the Texicans. Our young men and our chiefs are content with that. I am content with that."

"Things can change," Lemuel said. "Men can grow restless again."

"Where is the Gray Wolf now?" Chato asked.

"He has gone back to his headquarters in Omaha for the winter. The chiefs in Washington have sent him no orders. He says that he will not fight against the Lakota as long as they keep the treaty."

"But Yellow Hair here tells us that Touch-the-Clouds will be at war soon."

"The white man has broken the treaty. He will break it again, the Lakota are certain of that, and it is again time for their men to prove their courage in warfare. The white man will send his Blue Coat soldiers west, and Touch-the-Clouds does not want to wait until the Blue Coats are near his land. He wants to strike at them long before they get there."

Geronimo studied Lemuel for a long time before speaking again. "It will be useful to our brother Touch-the-Clouds," Chato said for him, "if the Blue Coats have to fight in both the South and against him, and sometimes our warriors grow restless. But if they do grow restless, they will need weapons. They will need other things."

"They will get whatever they need," Rubalev muttered. "I will see to that. I am also in touch with men who will be happy to fight with Apache comrades who will help them in their battle against the Washington chiefs. Your people can increase their wealth greatly by aiding those who once wore the Gray Coat in their actions against the Blue Coats."

Geronimo looked from Rubalev to Lemuel with his sharp black eyes. Lemuel met the Apache's gaze. Geronimo murmured a few words to Chato.

"Will the Gray Wolf fight against the Lakota," Chato asked, "if the Lakota go to war against the Blue Coats to the east?"

Lemuel said, "I do not know."

Geronimo leaned forward and said a word under his breath. "Then guess," Chato said.

"He does not recognize the chiefs in Washington," Lemuel said. "I do not think he will listen to them if they tell him to make war on the Lakota. He will not listen to the Washington chiefs as long as the Lakota remain at peace. If they go to war, and if the Gray Wolf sees them as a threat to the towns and settlements near them, he may have to fight them in order to protect the settlers. And that is all I can tell you."

What was needed now, Lemuel thought, was another outrage like the massacre at Elysium, one that would convince Three Star Crook and One Star Terry and their officers that the men in Washington were now the enemies of even the white settlers in the west. Part of him thought: Let it come, let them strike. Part of him remembered how Katia's body had looked in the back of the buckboard after the slaughter, no more than a lifeless torso and limbs with a shroud of long black hair.

Chato said, "We have fought against the Gray Wolf before. We do not want to fight him again. Some of the men may grow restless as long as the Gray Wolf stays behind his wooden walls and does not ride against our Lakota brothers. Otherwise, they may grow restless only for riding south to steal more cattle and horses from Mexicans."

"I understand," Lemuel said, knowing that this agreement was the best that he could hope for from the Apache.

"Acting President McClellan, the Great Father in Washington—" a man's voice was saying.

"Is he the Great Father?" the voice of another man interrupted. "He calls himself the Great Father, but there are many among you white men who say he is not. There are Blue Coat warriors who follow him and there are Blue Coat warriors who say he is not their chief."

Jane Cannary, nursing a glass of sarsaparilla, listened intently as Titus Oglesby, standing at the bar, cranked the handle of the phonograph while one of Edison's assistants looked on. The saloon's owner had paid a lot to rent the machine and the cylinder that had recorded the voices, even though Edison Laboratories was turning the machines out as fast as possible and had taken the precaution of recording this interview on a few of their cylinders. Businessmen in St. Joseph, St. Paul, and even as far east as Chicago had already paid in gold to buy or rent the devices, but judging by how much Oglesby had taken in this afternoon and how crowded his saloon was with customers paying for both liquor and a chance to listen to the phonograph, his investment was well worth it.

"What I was saying is this." The saloon was quiet as the people in the room strained to hear the other voice on the recording. "Acting President McClellan claims that he is only trying to restore the Union for which he fought, for which so many fought and died." The speaker, Jane knew, was a reporter from the *Rocky Mountain News* named Robert Strahorn. "He says that once the United States are again restored to the unified state they enjoyed in 1869, he will give up his position and allow elections to be held."

"The unified state. I do not know these words."

"That means," Strahorn's voice explained, "many states becoming one nation, one body of people with the same chief."

"The man in Washington who calls himself a Great Father allows the people in Texas and the people in California their own councils. There are white people and dark people in the lands south and east of here who want their own councils. There are people in these lands who want their own councils. I do not see how this can trouble the chief McClellan. Does he say that some can have them and some cannot? Elections means choosing—that much I do know. The people in the place called Bismarck choose a chief, a mayor. The people in your cities choose their chiefs. If my people do not want me as chief, they are free to find another."

Touch-the-Clouds, Jane thought, sounded even better in this interview than he had on the first cylinder Titus had played, an interview with a Chicago newspaperman named John Finerty. The chief also had a point. Couldn't they have their states and territories and republics and still all be Americans? Maybe if they went their own way for a while, they could all get together later. Touch-the-Clouds, with some prompting by Finerty, had said something like that in the first interview, although he had said it in different words.

"Acting President McClellan," Strahorn said, "wants to restore the United States, a republic that reaches from the east all the way to California, that will include all the territory between the eastern and western coasts, and everything from the border with Canada south to the Rio Grande."

"I have heard such words before," the voice of Touch-the-Clouds replied. "To me they have other meaning. To me they mean taking my people's hunting and grazing grounds from us. They mean breaking the treaties the white man made with us."

It amazed Jane that Touch-the-Clouds, a man whom she had feared so much while she was in his camp, could sound so reasonable, even downright understanding, on one of Edison's scratchy cylinders. It was one thing to read such an interview in a newspaper or to hear it read aloud, and quite another to hear the man's actual voice. Now people in Chicago and St. Louis and Kansas City could listen to Touch-the-Clouds speak. From what she had heard, people in those cities, and others, were marvelling at the machines and thinking that maybe the Sioux chief wasn't such a bloodthirsty savage after all.

"I have broken no treaty," Touch-the-Clouds was saying. "The Lakota have broken no treaty. Ask the Cheyenne and the Cherokee and the Arikara and the other red men who are my brothers this question—have you broken a treaty? It is the white man who has broken the treaties."

Rumor had it that Strahorn had also tried to get an interview with Sitting Bull, but the great Hunkpapa chief had refused to come to Bismarck and have his voice captured by the spirits in Edison's machines. Given that Sitting Bull spoke only Lakota, maybe that was just as well, since the need for an interpreter might have made for a tedious conversation. Part of what made Touch-the-Clouds sound so amiable to white folks, Jane was convinced, was his command of the American tongue.

"You know what some will say," Strahorn said. "You can't stop progress. Can't let Indians stand in the way of progress."

"What is progress?" Touch-the-Clouds responded. "You are a man from Colorado. The Wasichu there do not want the red man living in their land, and drove him away, but now they leave us what we have outside their land. There is Utah—the Wasichu who live there had to run there when others of their own people killed their first chief and medicine man and tried to kill them. The Wasichu have taken land from many red men, but that is past. Leave us what we still have, and we will be no trouble."

"Edison must have a mine's worth of gold for his talking machines by now," Jane whispered to Virgil Warrick.

"He wants to be back to work on that incandescent light of his," Virgil whispered back, while keeping his eyes on the phonograph. He had gone to Edison in September, asking for work sweeping up in the laboratories. Now, only eight months later, he was assisting one of the machinists, and getting paid more than she got driving a stagecoach from Bismarck and Fort Lincoln to Deadwood and back. "He's got himself another idea, too, something he calls a kinetoscope, but—"

"What's that gadget going to be?" Jane asked.

"See that photograph?" Virgil gestured toward the bar, where Titus had hung a large poster of a sepia-tinted photograph of Touch-the-Clouds in his ceremonial feathered bonnet and hair-fringed shirt. "What if'n you could see the chief there moving and riding his horse and all, a moving picture? Mr. Edison says that's what a kinetoscope would do, show pictures moving."

"Well, if that don't beat all." Jane stared into her sarsaparilla, wanting a whiskey and trying to ignore that craving. What with a telegraph message that morning about another massacre near Wichita, Kansas, and the voice of Touch-the-Clouds being shipped all over the place, she was beginning to wonder just how noisy the world could get, and now Edison was dreaming of making pictures that moved. Things could get mighty distracting with all those inventions. It was enough to make her think of saddling up and heading back to Virgil's cabin in Montana.

* * *

Finerty found George Crook pacing outside the row of cottages that housed the officers and their wives. None of the wives had come here to Fort Kearney; Crook had ordered them left behind this time. Finerty had followed Crook up the North Platte to Fort Kearney after the news came of the attack on a settlement outside Wichita. Reuben Davenport and Robert Strahorn had probably reached St. Joseph by now; he expected to see the other two newspaper correspondents, and perhaps more reporters, show up here at the fort almost at any moment.

He knew what Crook had to be brooding about now, and it would not just be the massacre near Wichita. Finerty had cultivated a couple of the telegraph operators under Crook's command, and had heard the news only a few minutes after Captain Anson Mills had gone to give Crook the telegraphic dispatch.

Three days ago, saboteurs had set off explosives at a meeting hall in St. Louis, where over a thousand people had gathered to hear a lecture by Lemuel Rowland, blood brother of Touch-the-Clouds, and to listen to the aural recording of Finerty's own interview with the chief. The resulting conflagration had killed three hundred people and destroyed nearly fifty buildings. What probably disturbed Crook the most was that one of the saboteurs had been caught by the St. Louis police, and had admitted to being one of the same men who had ravaged Elysium, Kansas. All of them, he had claimed, were volunteers recruited by the United States Army to carry out operations against those who were considered seditionists and traitors by the Council in Washington.

Those guilty of sedition and treason, Finerty had reflected, apparently included anyone who was willing to listen to Indians talking of peace and independent territories in the West. It had occurred to him then that the members on the Council would consider him, and any other reporter who had interviewed Touch-the-Clouds with some sympathy and forbearance, a traitor. Had there been a chance to interview the army saboteur, he would have been trying to get to St. Louis by now, but a crowd had stormed the jail not long after the man's confession and had lynched him.

Crook wore a long heavy coat against the cold and a fur hat over his closely clipped hair. Finerty rubbed his gloved hands together as an icy spring wind blew toward them from the bare parade ground.

"Sir," Finerty said as he came up to Crook. The general turned toward him, a dark shadow in the night. "I suppose we must be about the same business this evening, contemplating and mulling over the events of the past few days while taking the air."

"This will mean war," Crook said softly. "Both Indians and farmers were killed outside Wichita. Touch-the-Clouds will certainly consider an attack on one of his closest friends, and on people who went to a lecture hall to hear his words, an act of war."

"Yes, he will." Rowland had reportedly said the same thing before departing from St. Louis; the man had been lucky to escape from the hall.

"What I don't understand," Crook went on, "is what the Council in Washington hopes to gain from acts such as this. All they'll succeed in doing is turning even more people against them. Sheridan would have found some other way to provoke the Sioux, and we could have carried any ensuing war into Sioux territory." The Council had recently issued a statement saying that General Sheridan was ailing and had resigned his post, convincing Finerty that Sheridan had probably died while still imprisoned. "Now it's hard to tell where war will break out first."

"You've been saying," Finerty said, "that you don't want war with the Sioux."

"I still don't want war with them. Touch-the-Clouds keeps citing the Constitution while the Council seems intent on scrapping that document, which makes it increasingly difficult to regard the man as a barbarian."

Crook might have been thinking of the chief's comments on the Tenth Amendment. "Your sacred talking paper speaks of your states and their chiefs. The talking paper says that the Great Father cannot take the powers of those chiefs away from them." Finerty suspected that the Iroquois orator Lemuel Rowland was responsible for tutoring his blood brother in constitutional law.

"I'm also puzzled," Crook went on, "as to why I've had no orders from General Pope." Nathaniel Pope had assumed Sheridan's duties as commander of the United States Army. "I still don't know if I am expected to ferret out saboteurs or to prepare for war with the Sioux."

Finerty said, "The Sioux haven't broken the treaty yet."

"No, damn it, they haven't, which makes it even harder to regard them as a potential enemy." Crook cleared his throat. "This conversation is beginning to turn into an interview, Finerty. You may soon have another story for your editor. Lemuel Rowland has sent a message that he is coming here with a party of Sioux under a flag of truce. Even without orders from Pope, I know what the general would probably expect me to do at this point, what Sherman probably would have ordered me to do if he were still alive."

"And what is that?" Finerty asked.

"Tell Rowland to inform the Sioux and the Cheyenne that any Indian who doesn't travel within two months to the reservations allocated to them by the treaty of 1868 will be considered hostile, and will be hunted down by the men under my command."

"That would be rather harsh, General," Finerty said. "Given the disorder in government circles, I doubt that the Department of the Interior could get enough food and supplies to the agencies in that length of time to take care of all those Indians, even if they did decide to give themselves up."

"They wouldn't all give themselves up," Crook said. "The Sioux certainly wouldn't. But the threat of war might drive a wedge through the alliance they have with the Crow and the Arikara. Treachery has its uses in dealing with the Indian, and we could use some Crow and Arikara scouts. But I probably shouldn't be telling you this, given that you've become something of a partisan of Touch-the-Clouds."

Finerty drew himself up. "I am a newspaper correspondent, sir."

"A fact that has never stopped any of you fellows from taking sides."

Four men came out of a nearby barracks and marched toward the gate, bayonets slung over their shoulders. Finerty supposed that they were going on duty as sentries, and then Crook called out to them. "Lieutenant!" The general stepped closer to Finerty. "I'm posting a guard at your barracks until that delegation of Rowland's arrives. It's only for your own protection, Finerty. I wouldn't want you rushing off to get a story to your editor before the outlines of the story are clear. You see, I still don't know what I am going to do."

Finerty let out a sigh.

"Keep this man under guard," Crook said, "and make certain that he doesn't get anywhere near the stable or the telegraph."

The blond man's name was Gregory Rubalev, or so it sounded to Annie Oakley Moses when he introduced himself in the hotel lobby and asked to speak to Buffalo Bill. His slight accent sounded odd to her ears, almost foreign, although unlike her Frank's Irish lilt, and she wondered what state or territory he hailed from.

"Mr. Cody ain't in his room," Annie told him.

"So the man at the desk has told me." Gregory Rubalev swept off his black sombrero and bowed first to her and then to Frank Butler. "I salute the famed Butler and Oakley." The tall blond man glanced from her to Frank, who looked around uncertainly, then got to his feet.

"I saw your demonstration of target shooting today," Mr. Rubalev went on. "You are one of the best sharpshooters I have ever seen." He turned back to Annie. "And you, Miss Oakley, are a match for Mr. Butler."

"She's more than a match," Frank said, sitting down again. "Annie's a much better shot. She won plenty of C-notes from me in contests when she first hooked up with Cody. That's why I finally joined his show and made Annie my wife and my partner—it's cheaper than having her betting against me and beating me."

Annie gazed at Frank gratefully. Technically, she wasn't actually his wife yet, but she loved him for claiming that she was.

"What are you hankering to see Mr. Cody about?" Annie asked.

"A business proposition, Miss Oakley," Mr. Rubalev said. He surely is handsome, Annie thought to herself, and a gentleman, too, and hoped that she was not being disloyal to Frank in her mind. "I represent some performers that he might like to hire for his Wild West Show when he moves on to Cincinnati."

Annie looked at Frank. He was watching Mr. Rubalev. "I don't know as Buffalo Bill needs any more performers," Frank said.

"He most assuredly does not need any more sharpshooters," Mr. Rubalev said with a smile, "since he could hardly do better than Butler and Oakley."

"And I don't know as he's going to Cincinnati right away," Frank said. "He's thinking maybe with things the way they are, it might be better to head out west again."

"The performers I represent," Mr. Rubalev said, "are trick riders and buffalo herders."

"He's got them, too," Annie said.

"Kiowa, Comanche, and Cheyenne riders?" Mr. Rubalev asked.

Annie glanced at Frank. "He is short of them," Frank muttered. "Hell, mister, if you got some genuine redskins for the show, he might damn well be interested." He patted Annie's hand. "Pardon my language." She had heard worse from him, and was grateful for Mr. Rubalev's courtly example; maybe some of his manners would rub off on her man. "But he might have even more trouble taking redskins east now. There's Union soldiers in Cincinnati now, and they say more may be coming, so—"

"Mr. Butler," the blond gentleman said, "all I ask for is some time to speak to Mr. Cody." He unbuttoned his black suit jacket, reached inside his red waistcoat, and pulled out a leather pouch. "A small token of my appreciation for your sharpshooting skills."

Frank accepted the billfold and peered into it. "Those are mighty fine-looking gold coins, mister." He took one out and bit it.

Mr. Rubalev smiled. "Given the present situation in the East, I did not think greenbacks would show my appreciation nearly as well, now that their value is fluctuating so greatly."

"Annie, perhaps you wouldn't mind to have a little supper by yourself this evening." Frank stood up. "Rubalev, you can find Mr. Cody at the Golden Horse saloon, and I'd be pleased to escort you there myself."

* * *

Lemuel had said the words Touch-the-Clouds had asked him to speak, without saying anything about what the Lakota chiefs intended to do. He did not have to tell Crook that the Lakota chiefs had decided to take the warpath. The general would know by now that a war would have to be fought.

Touch-the-Clouds and his brother chiefs were angry. The Lakota considered the recent incidents in Wichita and St. Louis acts of war, even if they did not technically violate the provisions of the Fort Fetterman treaty. Now there were rumors that Washington was finally going to unleash the army upon the Lakota and their allies, to prepare the way for the miners, surveyors, engineers, and settlers who would take their land from them. Lemuel had said all of that, and General Crook had said nothing to deny it.

White Eagle, sitting with Lemuel, was interpreting his words for Crazy Horse and the other men who did not know English. It had taken Touch-the-Clouds, with a plea that had sounded more like a command, to get Crazy Horse to agree to come here to one of the forts of the Long Knives, but the Lakota had needed him here to impress the Wasichu. The newspapermen who had flocked to Bismarck and Fort Lincoln looking for interviews with chiefs and for invitations to visit Indian camps had not had much luck with the Oglala chief. Crazy Horse did not know their language, had no desire to learn it, was not interested in talking to them, and wanted the white man to leave his people alone to live in their customary way. All of that reluctance on his part had only spurred the reporters to write stories about Crazy Horse that had turned him into an admired, legendary, and mysterious figure; Crazy Horse had, the correspondents claimed, sold a lot of papers.

A war, of course, would sell even more newspapers. Lemuel had not been reassured by the presence of the five reporters who had ridden out with Crook and his officers from the fort to parley outside the stockade. Crook's steady, calm gaze had betrayed none of his inner thoughts, but Lemuel was certain that Three Star had decided on his course of action even before Lemuel and the five Lakota men with him were in sight of the walls of Fort Kearney.

General Crook was silent for a long time, then said, "If the Sioux and their allies attack anyone outside of their territories, they will be in violation of the treaty. The army will have to protect all of those who rely on our soldiers for protection."

Lemuel shifted his weight on his buffalo robe. Crook sat on a blanket; the other officers, and the reporters, were still standing with their horses. The reporters wore fur or bearskin coats, as did all of the officers except for Crook. Crazy Horse, who had refused to enter the fort's walls, was mounted on his horse behind Lemuel, wearing only his hair-fringed shirt and leggings, seemingly oblivious to the cold spring air.

"The Council in Washington has given every indication that it intends to fight a war in the West," Lemuel said. "If the Lakota abide by the treaty and wait until they are attacked, they have little chance to keep their lands—perhaps no chance at all."

Crook folded his arms. "We seem to be at an impasse, Rowland."

"Touch-the-Clouds has no intention of fighting you and your men, General Crook, unless you decide to go to war with him. It would sadden my brother Touch-the-Clouds to see you fight for those who would order not just the slaughter of helpless Indians, but also the killing of their own citizens. It would sadden him to see you become the weapon of men who were not chosen by their people to be their chiefs, but who seized that power for themselves."

Crook was silent. The newspaper correspondents scribbled on their notepads. Finerty and Strahorn had been assiduous about getting interviews with Touch-the-Clouds, and extravagant in their praise of his fluency in English and his pointed responses to their questions. Lemuel wondered how sympathetic they would remain to the Lakota chief if their editors, and men with enough money to influence what the newspapers published, decided that it might be more profitable to whip up fear and suspicion of the Sioux.

"I do not wish to go to war against the Sioux," Crook said. "Indian warfare is, of all warfare, the most dangerous, the most trying, and the most thankless, as I found out during my earlier campaigns. In it, you are required to serve without the incentive to promotion or recognition—in truth, without favor or hope of reward."

Crook paused. Lemuel was suddenly certain that the officer had prepared this speech, and he was speaking slowly and deliberately, presumably so that the reporters would have a chance to write his words down accurately. The reporters probably deeply regretted that they lacked the resources to buy one of Edison's recording machines.

"Why would such wars be fought?" Crook continued. "Why have we fought such wars in the past? We fought them in defense of the people of our sparsely settled frontier, who have had but little influence in the East, and whose representatives have had even less voice in our national councils. Their foes were men who were as savages when I fought them, men who thought nothing of taking what they could from agencies and then stealing whatever they wanted from helpless settlers. I saw myself as a soldier defending the weak against the strong."

Lemuel studied the faces of the officers with Crook, but those men were following their commander's example. He could read nothing of what they thought in their grim countenances and pale eyes.

"Yes, that was my charge," Crook said, "to defend the weak against the strong, to defend those who live in the West. I must now decide how best to defend them, how to protect them, and who their true enemies are."

He gazed directly at Lemuel, then at Crazy Horse. "The white men in the East are like birds," Crook continued, keeping his eyes on Crazy Horse. "They hatch out their eggs every year, and they claim that there is not enough room in the East for them, and so they must go elsewhere to build their nests, and they long to come west. For years, they came out west and saw that the Indians had a big body of land that they were not using, and so they said, 'We want the land.' They took what land they wanted, and they will keep taking it, and now I see that there are men in Washington who will not stop even after they have all of the land of the Indians. They will take it from others. They will take it from anyone who dares to stand against them and say that they are not our true leaders."

Crook lowered his voice. "I fought for the Union," he murmured. "I believed that I fought for a just cause, and that it was right to bring the secessionists back into the Union, by force if necessary, even at the fearful cost in blood that we paid." He looked toward Lemuel once more. "You also fought for the Union. It was just to free those who were once slaves, and to pay the price of their freedom in blood. But now, instead of a government that is redeeming the blood that was shed by seeking justice, I see a growing despotism. I see men who have punished the South, but who have done little to seek justice for all who live there. I see people in the West who have no voice in Washington. I am no longer so certain that the Union must be preserved by force. Perhaps it would be better to allow the various communities of this vast and diverse land to go their separate ways, to govern themselves, until they freely choose a Union again. Perhaps the Constitution for which I fought now lives in the hearts of those who do not look to the tyrants in Washington who have claimed to be the Constitution's protectors. And perhaps we cannot expect our people to reunite as a Union until they have leaders who are more worthy to govern them."

Hope leaped inside Lemuel. He will not fight, he thought, he will stand aside and do what he can to protect the Western settlements while the Lakota go to war.

"I have spoken to my officers of my decision," Crook went on, "and told them that in the absence of any other authority in the West, I now consider myself in command of the Department of the Platte and the Department of the Missouri, while General Terry, commander of the Department of Dakota, has acknowledged me as his commanding officer. General Sherman is dead, and I have reason to believe that he never was part of the cabal that used his name. General Sheridan is said to have resigned his command, but I believe that he must have resigned it some time ago, because he would never have agreed to take orders from the man who now calls himself the Acting Commander-in-Chief."

Crook stood up. "The Plains Indians are not a threat to our liberty at present. It is the regime in Washington that threatens the West now. I will not go to war against Touch-the-Clouds and his allies as long as they do not threaten the settlers in the West."

It seemed to Lemuel that everyone present was holding his breath. We won't have to fight Crook, he thought.

"But I will fight once more to preserve what I now consider to be the true spirit of America. I will fight to protect our Western communities. I will fight as the ally of Touch-the-Clouds if he will help in ridding us of the tyranny now trying to rule us."

Lemuel caught his breath. White Eagle was still translating those words as the newspapermen leaped onto their horses. They galloped toward the stockade entrance, Finerty in the lead.

"General," Lemuel said, "if those men get any messages out, we will lose the element of surprise."

"You underestimate me, Rowland." Crook stood up, smiling as he looked down. "They won't be allowed to send their dispatches—at least not until they can do our cause the most good."

TWENTY

"Here is how it will be," White Eagle said to Dancing Girl and Yellow Bird. "We will board the Wasichu paddle-wheel boats with our horses. Some of us will go down the river to Omaha, and the rest of us will go on to St. Joseph, where more warriors from Kansas will join us."

Dancing Girl, sitting outside the talking wire tepee, watched as her father made a long line in the dirt to indicate the Missouri River. "The men with Crazy Horse will ride east from Omaha on the Iron Horse trail, behind Four Eyes Roosevelt and his men. They will go to Chicago, where men who are enemies of the chiefs in Washington now hold the Iron Horse trails, and then continue east from there. The rest of our warriors will go to St. Joseph and ride the Iron Horse east with Touch-the-Clouds and the rocket-arrow warriors." He made more marks in the dirt. "Bear Coat Miles and his soldiers will follow the men going east from Omaha, with Laforte and a company of buffalo soldiers to their rear. I will be in St. Joseph, with Touch-the-Clouds and Morning Star Brother Rowland, and Three Star Crook will be at our rear with his Blue Coats."

Yellow Bird nodded. The son of Young Spring Grass and Long Hair Custer already had the look of a warrior about his eyes. Dancing Girl knew that her adoptive brother was sorry he could not ride to war with the men.

"And One Star Terry," White Eagle continued, "has his men moving east in small companies now, through Missouri. They will go up the Ohio River as far as the Wasichu city of Louisville and move toward the Great Father's city from there on the Iron Horse. The wire warriors will send signals over the talking wires, so that we will all know where our other forces are at any time. We will have to strike hard and fast; we must move and be close to Washington before the chiefs there can know what we are planning and think of ways to stop it. And our victory must be swift."

Her father did not have to explain why. The men would be fighting in unfamiliar territory. They would have to perform this summer's Sun Dance far from their own grounds, without much of the usual ceremony. Although Touch-the-Clouds and the most respected medicine men believed that the spirits would overlook any such changes in custom if they won a great victory, there were those, particularly among the Cheyenne men, who doubted that. The men would not be back in time for the beginning of the buffalo hunt. If they did not finish this war with the Wasichu in Washington quickly, many of the men would grow impatient. Their thoughts would turn more and more to the Plains. They would worry about how their families would fare during the winter. They would no longer want to fight. Many would desert and try to find their way home.

"You will have victory," Yellow Bird said.

"There will be others helping us to fight," White Eagle went on. "The talking wires told us only this morning that more Blue Coats have left Washington to strike at raiders along the Mississippi. Our Comanche and Apache brothers have helped to draw them there."

Dancing Girl drew up her knees and wrapped her arms around them. Except for not joining the rest of their people for the buffalo hunt that summer, and the absence of the men of fighting age, life would not change as much in White Eagle's camp as some feared. Young Spring Grass and some of the other women would still ride to Bismarck to trade; messages from the outside would still come to them over the talking wire. But the people camped to the west on the Plains and by the Black Hills and along the Yellowstone River would see many changes. Chief Joseph's Nez Percé people to the west of the Lakota lands would come east to hunt buffalo for both themselves and the Lakota, while bands of Kiowa to the south would share some of their game with the Cheyenne near them. People could live like that for a while. She did not think that they would put up with it for very long.

"It is good that both of you have learned the speech of the talking wire," White Eagle said, "and are teaching it to some of your friends. We will send you as many messages as we can."

"You will win," Dancing Girl said, wishing that she could feel as certain as she was trying to sound. Her father would not say it, but there was another message he might send, a message telling her that there had been no victory, that the warriors were tired of fighting, even that the Blue Coats had forced them into a retreat. She hoped that such a message would never come. If it did, her people would have to hide in the Lakota lands, and prepare to fight there. And if they lost again, there would be nowhere to run.

"They're good," Lieutenant Hugh Scott said to John Finerty. "Better than I thought."

The lieutenant, Finerty knew, was not just talking about his own men, but also of the Indians who were already moving out in advance of General Crook's forces. He stood next to Scott on the wooden dock, watching as the steamboat carrying men, artillery, and supplies moved down the Missouri toward St. Joseph.

This was probably the most important story he was likely ever to cover, and he still had not been able to telegraph any of it to Snowden, or find a courier willing to risk riding to the nearest town to send it for him, but then the other newspapermen on campaign with Crook and Miles and Terry were equally restricted. One reporter, a fellow named Wasson, who apparently had some expertise in telegraphy, had been caught near a telegraph pole with a small battery and a pocket relay, and had been shot dead. Since then, no newspaperman moved around, ate a meal, relieved himself, or slept without two soldiers at his side.

Lieutenant Scott and a private named Donoghue were usually with Finerty during the day. The thin-faced Scott, at first taciturn, had grown more talkative in recent days.

"Those Injuns will do all right as fighters," Hugh Scott continued. "I didn't know whether to believe that chief, that Touch-the-Clouds, when he said they'd learn to follow his orders. Hell, I know some of them were terrified getting on the train, but they got on without a peep. I just hope they can keep up their courage."

"Oh, I think they will," Finerty murmured. "One might almost think that, by sending them out ahead of your men, General Crook has made certain that they won't lose heart. After all, if they wanted to retreat, they would either have to go through your men or around them."

"You're damn right about that, Finerty."

"And I suspect that Colonel Miles doesn't mind that the Sioux immediately behind Major Roosevelt and his volunteers will probably take more casualties than his Fifth Infantry."

Scott laughed. "Probably not. If we have to fight with the redskins, if we're on the same side this time, fine, but it doesn't mean we have to like them."

Finerty shoved his hands into his trouser pockets. He had been told that he could send a telegraph message from St. Joe, although an army telegrapher would be there to make sure that there was nothing in that message that would give away Crook's plans. He had already made his notes for an innocuous interim story about life at Fort Kearney, but once the invaders—for invaders they were, in a sense—were on the eastern side of the Mississippi and moving rapidly by train, Crook's best efforts would not keep the story from getting out. By the time the Army of the West got to Washington, Finerty would see that his stories got to Chicago by telegraph if possible, and by courier if necessary.

He refused to think of what might happen if Crook's forces were stopped, or worse, driven back.

* * *

The performers in Buffalo Bill's Wild West Show were all in the center of the ring, taking their bows. The people in the stands cheered, stamped their feet, then stood up and waved from the bleachers. Annie Oakley Moses smiled at Frank Butler as he took her hand. They were still mounted on their horses. Annie stood up in her stirrups and bowed from the waist as the crowd cheered the sharpshooting skills of Butler and Oakley.

Well, heck, she allowed to herself, they ain't just cheering for me and Frank, God knows. They were also cheering those Indians Mr. Rubalev had talked Mr. Cody into hiring. She had to admit that they were the best she'd ever seen in "Custer Among the Indians," riding around and standing up on the backs of their mounts and then ducking around the barrels of the horses while they shot at targets. They might not have hit most of the targets they aimed at, but they were dad-blamed great trick riders.

The Indians looked mighty impressive, sitting there on their horses, bare-chested and with feathers in their long black hair and all their war regalia. They might not be Sioux, but they had surely given a good performance as Sioux—or as Mr. Cody's notion of what a Sioux was, anyway. They had even put on war paint, for more authenticity. And Mr. Rubalev, Annie thought, had put on a wonderful performance as Custer, making his stand with his men, then going into battle with his Sioux blood brothers, and he looked just as handsome in his fringed yellow buckskins and Indian head-dress as he had earlier on in his blue uniform costume.

Then she saw the soldiers at the east entrance to the big tent. One line of them marched inside and set up a line, and then a second line of soldiers marched in and lined up behind them. At first, Annie thought they might be some of the performers in the Wild West Show, even though she didn't know their faces, and then she noticed that the people in the audience were getting up all of a sudden and climbing down out of the bleachers.

"What the hell," Frank muttered under his breath.

A man with lieutenant's bars on his shoulders lifted a megaphone to his lips. "Everyone must leave immediately," he announced. "This circus is being closed down."

Annie dug her heels into the flanks of her horse. Her pinto began to step sideways toward Mr. Cody, who was sitting on his white horse near the eastern side of the ring.

A man in a blue uniform with a colonel's gold eagles on his shoulders trotted into the ring on a bay horse. "William Cody?" he said to Buffalo Bill.

Mr. Cody tipped his white hat to the man. "I am that gentleman," he said, "and the proprietor of this show." Annie could not help noticing what a fine figure Mr. Cody cut in his white buckskin jacket and his long golden locks and pointed beard, compared to the mousy little colonel, who sported a weedy moustache and had straggly brown hair.

"I have been ordered to close this show down," the little colonel said.

"Look, I pay my bills, and this is only our first performance in Cincinnati." Mr. Cody's cheeks above his goatee were getting redder. "We've already sold out the next week's performances, and—"

"Cody, keep your hands away from that Colt," the colonel said. Annie made sure that the soldier saw that her hands were still holding her reins. "This show is being closed down, and you and your performers will go with me quietly. You have been charged with sedition, and those Injuns over there are now considered hostiles."

"Sedition?" Mr. Cody was scowling. "What the hell are you talking about?" From the sides of her eyes, Annie noticed that both Mr. Rubalev and Frank had moved closer to Buffalo Bill on their horses.

"The Council of the United States now considers newspaper stories, speeches, or any other public presentation produced, distributed, or performed by Indian-lovers acts of sedition designed to give comfort to the enemy." The colonel puffed out his not very impressive chest. "Because, Cody, the Injuns are now at war with us."

Annie gaped at the little officer. "Since when?" Buffalo Bill asked.

"Since the Council of the United States has ordered General George Crook into action against the Sioux. General George Forsyth is already on his way out there from Virginia with the—"

"Hold on, Colonel," Buffalo Bill said. "The Injuns in this show aren't even Sioux, and what did the Sioux do to provoke a—"

"I don't care what those Injuns call themselves. If they aren't Sioux, they're friends of the Sioux, and they're all redskins anyway. So—"

Someone fired. That's a Remington, Annie thought. The shot had come from close behind her, which meant that Mr. Rubalev might be the one who had fired. Somebody screamed, and then a whole lot of people were suddenly screaming and shouting. A line of soldiers lifted their guns, took aim at the trick riders, and fired.

Most of the people in the audience were still making their way down from the bleachers and over to the exit. They surged toward the openings at the eastern and western ends of the tent. The lines of soldiers broke as they tried to restrain the frightened people. Several shots were fired before the crowds overwhelmed the soldiers.

Annie's horse reared. Frank was next to her. "Better get out of here," he shouted. She rode after him toward the exit on the west, farther from the soldiers. She glanced back. Mr. Cody was right behind her. Amid the fracas, it looked as though some of the Indians were shooting at the soldiers now. She rode past the knots of frightened people and followed Frank outside.

Three Star Crook had sent Gold Eagles Jeremiah Clarke to St. Joseph to seize control of the Iron Horse trails there. By the time White Eagle reached the edge of the city with his wire warriors, Clarke had secured the rail yards. There had been little resistance from the Wasichu in the yards. Some had cheered the Blue Coats. Others had volunteered to follow them to the Great Father's city.

Buffalo Calf Road Woman was the one who told this to White Eagle. "Gold Eagles Clarke now holds the trails of the Iron Horse," she said.

"Then there will be a talking wire room there somewhere," White

Eagle said. "I can send a message back to Bismarck before we leave." Traveling part of the way here on the paddlewheel boat that belched smoke was bad enough, with the men crowded together on the decks and having to keep the horses calm while the deck tilted and moved under them. He did not want to admit how much he dreaded climbing into one of the Iron Horse wagons.

Buffalo Calf Road Woman waved her hand at his face. "No talking wire signals," she said. "Three Star says so. Touch-the-Clouds says so. Morning Star Brother says so."

White Eagle shrugged. He had not been happy that Buffalo Calf Road Woman and Walking Blanket Woman had decided to go to war with the men, but the two had no husbands or brothers to fight for them and no children to look after, so Touch-the-Clouds had allowed them to come. What he liked even less was that Young Spring Grass had wanted to go with them, something White Eagle had refused to allow her to do. "The Wasichu women can shoot firesticks," she had told him. "Unlucky Jane has long and short firesticks and knows how to use them better than most of our men." In many ways, the Wasichu women set a very bad example.

"Then you had better lead us to the Iron Horse corral," White Eagle said.

"I am to lead you there, but you are not to travel in a wagon now." Buffalo Calf Road Woman got back on her horse. "You are to follow the Iron Horse trail to a place not far from here. Morning Star Brother Rowland will take you and some of the men there. Two of our scouts were shot and killed there."

"Then we must avenge them," White Eagle said.

"Touch-the-Clouds and Morning Star Brother mean to do more than that. They will tell all the warriors to destroy that place and kill everyone there. They will have their revenge for our scouts and for the death of Graceful Swan, who was a wife to both of them. You see, Touch-the-Clouds and Morning Star Brother have learned that a few of the men who killed her and so many others in Kansas may have come from that place." Buffalo Calf Road Woman smiled. "And you have to admit that destroying that town will set a good example for any Wasichu who are thinking of fighting against us."

* * *

The Missouri town called Mayville was only a few miles east of St. Joseph and a mile away from the tracks of the Hannibal and St. Joseph Railroad. The town itself was little more than two rows of houses and ramshackle buildings on either side of a dirt road that led to Mayville's center.

There were, Lemuel knew, many good reasons to strike at this place. They did not want saboteurs disrupting the rail lines, as these men might think of doing. They had to punish the deaths of their two scouts. And, he thought darkly, maybe wreaking some vengeance for his loss would ease the knots of pain inside him.

The men struck first at the farmhouse on the edge of town. One of the men crept toward the door and made a sound like that of a wild dog. When a gray-bearded man came to the door, Ghost Dog brought him down with one blow. Soon his wife came out to look for him and Crazy Bull grabbed her from the back and slit her throat before she could scream. By then, three more men had gone in through a window and found two sleeping children. Since they could not take them back to their camps for adoption by their people, the Lakota warriors killed them, too.

The woman and the girl both had long thick hair and scalps worth taking. Lemuel might have ordered the men not to take the scalps, but kept silent. They had to punish those here for what they had done. He knew that he could explain it all to General Crook. He would say that they had to make certain that the tracks were not threatened, that no one else would dare to threaten them.

Touch-the-Clouds had told Lemuel about a young man, not much more than a boy, who had been caught trying to sneak up on an encampment of Lakota warriors. The young man had been brought to him, and had told Touch-the-Clouds stories about the raid on Elysium and other raids and about blue uniforms and money that had been paid to him and to other men to make those raids. He had said that they were told to regard themselves as fighters for the United States and its interests. He had told Touch-the-Clouds where some of his accomplices could be found. He had taken out one of the coins that had been given to him as payment and a silver belt buckle that he had taken from a dead man in Elysium. Then he had told Touch-the-Clouds that the two scouts he was looking for had been shot and their bodies quickly buried so that no one would know what had happened to them. He had said that he was willing to fight with the Lakota and their allies now.

After the man had told him all that he wanted to know, Touch-the-Clouds had taken out his knife and killed the young man himself. A man who would so readily betray his comrades was of no use to him.

Lemuel had no reason to doubt anything that Touch-the-Clouds had told him about that young man and his story. Touch-the-Clouds, like all Lakota, did not lie. They would have had to punish the people here for killing the two scouts, and there was a grim satisfaction in knowing that other hostile acts the men here had committed would also be avenged.

The men took three oil lamps from the farmhouse. They rode toward the town, set a few arrows on fire with the lamps, then shot them at the thatched roofs of two of the buildings. The roofs were soon ablaze. When the first people ran from the buildings into the street, there was already enough light from the flames to shoot them easily with arrows or rifles. A few men came through doorways with rifles of their own, but were quickly brought down.

Lemuel motioned to one of the warriors. The man hurled a burning oil lamp through the wide glass window of one long wooden structure. Except for the sound of wood crackling as it burned, or the brief, intermittent cries of women and children as they ran into the street, the night was strangely quiet. One unarmed man stood in front of a woman, trying to shield her, as two warriors rode toward him, swinging their war clubs. The woman's scream was cut short as a club caught her in the head.

The men here had been foolish, thinking that they would not be found out, doing nothing to protect themselves and this town. They deserved to die for their carelessness and their murderousness. Lemuel watched as the town burned. The flames would make ashes of his grief.

* * *

Reports had been streaming into the offices of the Chicago *Times* by telegraph ever since the departure of the trains carrying the Indians and several companies of the Army of the West. Clinton Snowden had been reading stories from Pittsburgh, St. Louis, Buffalo—stories from just about everywhere except from those newspapermen who were traveling with the Western forces. That was understandable; Crook and the other officers would want the Council in Washington to have as little information as possible about their intentions. Everyone in the big cities knew that the Western forces were on the move by now, moving fast enough that by the time word got out about their presence in one place, they had already moved on to another city.

A couple of days ago, companies of the Army of the West had been sighted in Charleston, West Virginia, and in Dayton, Ohio. There had been some sabotage on sections of track in Iowa and Missouri, which had been followed by retaliatory raids on the nearby towns by parties of wild Indians. Since then, it appeared that any people not overtly sympathetic to the Westerners preferred simply to keep out of their way. Trying to fight for a group of men in Washington who had seized power without the consent of the people was not a cause that was drawing many recruits. Even fewer wanted to provoke savage redskins into raids against defenseless people.

Snowden sighed, and wondered again where the hell John Finerty was.

There was another story out of Cincinnati about the riots there. Apparently all of the trouble there had started when a company of United States soldiers had tried to shut down Buffalo Bill Cody's Wild West Show. From what Snowden could gather, that incident had transformed Cincinnati from an outpost of neutrality into a hotbed of anti-Washington sentiment.

He turned to another story, written by D. Randolph Keim of the New York Herald. Both the Democrats and the Reform Republicans of New York City had issued a statement in support of a resolution passed by the Massachusetts state legislature. The gist of the Massachusetts resolution was that, despite its sympathy for the efforts of the Council of the United States to prevent more states from breaking away from the Union, the legislators of Massachusetts considered the Council an illegitimate and unconstitutional government. Fine, Snowden thought, even if that particular sentiment was being expressed by those New Englanders somewhat late in the day. What interested him more was the appointment of an Emergency Counsel by the New York State government in Albany. The purpose of this Counsel was to "aid and advise the governor during the present crisis," but it was the name of this newly appointed official that had caught his eye.

Ely Parker, former commissioner of Indian Affairs under President Grant, had been named to the post. Ely Parker, Snowden mused, who had so unsuccessfully tried to pursue a peace policy toward the Plains Indians he had regarded as his brothers, and who, Kelm noted in his story, was an Indian himself. It sounded as though the good people of New York had placed their bets on who was likely to win out, and wanted to be on good terms with the victor.

Annie Oakley Moses sat at the edge of a field of tobacco leaves with Frank Butler. Mr. Cody had bribed their way across the Ohio River to Kentucky. All she and Frank had now was their firearms and their horses. It didn't look like Buffalo Bill's Wild West Show was going to make any more appearances.

"I wonder what's taking Bill so long," Frank muttered, looking down the road that ran past the tobacco farm. Mr. Cody had ridden back to Covington to see what he could find out. Annie sighed. All they'd had to eat today, thanks to one of the daughters of the tobacco farmer, were a couple of pieces of pecan pie. Pretty soon she would have to go rustling them up some quail, the way she had hunted to feed her family when she was a girl, after her father died.

"He shouldn't have gone," Annie said. She had tried to talk Mr. Cody out of riding to Covington, not that he would have listened to her. All he needed was to run into somebody who had seen the Wild West Show across the river in Cincinnati, and he might end up being arrested. He might already be cooling his heels in jail, or worse. She thought of how Cincinnati had looked above them while they were making their way down the bluffs with their horses to the ferry. The fires had spread to the waterfront by then. The whole city might have burned if rain had not fallen that night.

"Annie," Frank said, "I want to marry you. I want to make an honest woman of you."

"You asked me that before, and I told you yes before."

"I meant that if Bill comes back and says they aren't looking for us, you'll be my wife right now, I mean as soon as I can find a body in Covington to marry us."

"Why, Frank." She smiled at him.

"Not that I'm any prize catch at the moment."

She saw the cloud of dust down the road before he did, and her sharp eyes recognized the buckskin-clad figure. "Hey, Frank," she said, jabbing him with her elbow, "it's Mr. Cody."

He got to his feet. Buffalo Bill's horse slowed to a trot. Annie could already make out the look of excitement on Mr. Cody's face.

"Mount up!" Buffalo Bill shouted as he neared them. "Most of the rest of the troupe made it to Covington safely. We're mighty short of Injuns, but we can still put on a show. We'll be appearing tomorrow night."

"What?" Frank said.

"In Covington." Mr. Cody looked from Frank to Annie. "Can't do 'Custer Among the Indians' without Rubalev and his redskins, but we can still give Covington its money's worth."

"Hold on, Mr. Cody," Annie said. "What's going on?"

"Tell you what's going on. There's something called the People's Militia patrolling Cincinnati now, and what's left of the U.S. Army's been pulled out. Going by train to Baltimore, so they say, assuming they get there, 'cause it looks like the United States, or what calls itself the United States, is at war with a whole lot of folks."

"Say that again, Bill," Frank said.

"War!" Buffalo Bill waved his hands.

"With Johnny Reb again?" Annie looked around nervously.

"Hell, no, with the West. With General George Crook and Touch-the-Clouds and Sitting Bull and the whole damn Sioux nation and anybody else who decided to come along for the party—maybe even what's left of Custer and his Seventh Cavalry, for all I know. They're going by train across the country, and they even picked up some volunteers along the way. Maybe Rubalev and his Injuns ran off to join them."

Annie tightened the girth of her horse's saddle, then mounted. "Mr. Cody," she said softly, "I don't know as a war is anything to cheer about." It was her Quaker heritage speaking.

"It is if everyone else is cheering. It is if everybody seems to be just letting Crook and the Indians get through without putting up much of a fight." Buffalo Bill grinned. "And if it's over fast enough, the Wild West Show might be making even more money."

The first of Finerty's dispatches had come over the telegraph wires two days ago, telling of General Crook's meeting with Crazy Horse and an Iroquois called Rowland who was a blood brother of Touch-the-Clouds, followed by a brief description of a journey by steamship down the Platte. Old news, Snowden had thought, but still worth printing. Now a newsboy was in front of his desk thrusting a sheaf of folded papers into his hands.

"Man come from Charleston, West Virginia, with this," the boy told Snowden. "Says he got paid to bring 'em here on the train."

Snowden gave the boy a coin, unfolded the papers, and recognized Finerty's handwriting. Good old John, he thought, he found somebody to get this here.

The first dispatch was dated June 20, 1879, two weeks ago, and read: "I am writing this under a half-blanket propped up by a pole near a campfire. Lest the reader think that I am complaining, I am not. Indeed, given that I am now following General Crook and a large company of red Indians east on an expedition that may accurately be called an invasion, I have been able to travel in relative comfort, if one means by that expression being packed into a rail-

road car bereft of any but the plainest benches and filled with soldiers seated shoulder to shoulder. Whenever the train stops, the
neighing of the horses in the adjoining baggage car assaults one's
ears, and we have the choice of opening the windows to admit the
soot and sparks from the locomotive, or closing them to endure a
heat comparable to that of the infernal regions. I have been told
that we are now taking our rest somewhere in southern Illinois,
where we are preparing to dine on some of the hardtack we
brought with us.

"Yet none of these circumstances is a cause for protest. We have
moved rapidly east by train, and thus far have encountered little
resistance. Before the soldiers can become too fatigued, we should
have reached our destination."

Snowden scanned the rest of the page, then turned to the next
dispatch.

"June 23, 1879: Although it is true that the Indians are now allied
with General Crook, one must make allowances for their behavior. It
was our misfortune to have to spend last night in close proximity to
their camp while advance scouts went ahead of us to ensure that the
tracks were clear. During much of the night, the Indians kept up a
tremendous racket, pounding their drums and howling in a way that
would exasperate even the most kindly of men, provided he wanted
to sleep. One of the aboriginals, a comparatively civilized man whose
Sioux name means White Eagle and who speaks a surprisingly fluent
English, explained that his comrades are preparing themselves for
battle by singing war songs, the music of which is fitter for Hades
than for Earth, and uttering various prayers designed to secure the
protection of what they call the wakan beings, or spirits. White Eagle
told me of their various superstitious rituals without a trace of doubt
in his voice, and this from a red Indian who has mastered telegraphy.
It only demonstrates how great the gap is between us and the red
man, and how much savagery exists in even the most civilized of the
breed.

"One exception may be the Iroquois Lemuel Rowland, whose
eloquence and bearing is the equal of many who would be termed
gentlemen. It is he who serves as the intermediary between General Crook and the Sioux chief Touch-the-Clouds, and it appears

that he has the trust of both men. Yet there is an intensity in his gaze, especially when he speaks of those he regards as his enemies, that seems as dark and savage as that of the most primitive of his red brethren."

Snowden turned to another page.

"June 24, 1879: Our hordes continue to thunder eastward along what our red comrades call the Trail of the Iron Horse. What is most strange about our journey is how the people we have encountered along the way have treated us. As we passed through one Indiana town, our train was greeted by a brass band and a crowd of people waving banners that read 'Free Elections, No Dictators' and 'States' Rights and a Union,' among other often contradictory slogans. The few people I was able to query in another Indiana town seemed to think that Crook and his Army of the West are fighting both to restore what they think of as a Constitutional Union and also for the freedom of each state to decide its own affairs. One of them explained this apparent paradox by implying that once each state had exercised its freedom, so to speak, it would then willingly return to the Federal fold.

"Even so, the sight of these people and their good wishes has clearly heartened Crook's troops. At one station that we passed, our train slowed its speed enough so that the townsfolk were able to thrust baskets of pies, roasted chickens, meats, fruits, and other welcome delicacies at us. At a stop in northern Kentucky, we were even treated to a free showing of Buffalo Bill Cody's production of 'Calamity Jane, Squaw Woman,' which featured Miss Annie Oakley in that role and which delighted our Indian brothers in arms as much as it did the rest of us, judging by the caterwauling and ear-splitting whoops they emitted at the conclusion of this performance.

"It is indeed a peculiar sort of invasion where one is treated to cheers and good wishes as opposed to sabotage and resistance. And there is one banner that is especially prevalent among the crowds of well-wishers, one that has excited some comment among the men, a banner that reads, 'May the Spirit of Custer Guide You.'

"If by some chance that fabled soldier turns up among us after his long absence from the scene, to fight at Crook's side, there will be many who will attribute any victory to the valor of George Armstrong Custer."

"Mr. Snowden."

Snowden looked up from Finerty's dispatches. One of the *Times* telegraphers was standing in front of his desk. "What is it?" he asked.

"News just in from Washington City," the man replied. "General Terry's whipped Forsyth and is moving up from Virginia toward Washington, while Colonel Miles is somewhere near Baltimore. And Crook's coming at them from the west." He cleared his throat. "Looks like the Battle of Washington is about to begin."

Crazy Horse thought, I don't know how to fight this war.

He and his warriors, mounted on their horses, grouped together in their warrior societies, were north of the city of the Great Father, but between them and the city lay the white man's fortifications. A row of wooden structures and walls barred the trail leading to the city, guarded by a long line of Blue Coats. To draw the enemy Blue Coats away, to lead them into an ambush, was impossible here. He did not know this terrain. Even if he had, trying to trick the enemy soldiers into pursuing his men would be useless, with Bear Coat Miles and his men behind him and a countryside dotted with Wasichu towns.

Crazy Horse had put on his war paint of lightning bolts and hailstones and wore the feathers of a red-backed hawk in his long hair. He was stripped for battle, clad only in his breechcloth, and still the moist heat and muggy air of this land made his body damp with sweat. A small replica of his shield, with symbols of lightning and a bear painted on it, hung from around his neck, and he prayed that the powers of the bear would protect him. Coming here on the Iron Horse, being so far from the Plains and from the spirits must have driven him mad. He did not understand any of it. He should not have come here. He had not properly listened to what the spirits had told him about how to fight these people.

Rain-in-the-Face rode up to him. "The men are ready to fight," he said to Crazy Horse. "The men want to count coup, they—" and then the spirit of the wind caught Crazy Horse and swept him aloft.

He was in the air, flying toward the city over the battlements that protected it. He soared above an impossibly straight trail that led toward the Great Father's city, and flew on until he was hovering far above a great dome. Along another wide trail, to the west, he saw the white walls of the Great Father's house.

To the south of the city lay the fork of two rivers. The wide river that ran past the western side of the city glittered in the sunlight, a river that seemed made of the yellow metal that the spirits had made for the Lakota in the Black Hills. That metal had helped to bring his people here, to buy them the weapons and medicine they needed to come to this place and demand that the promises made to them be kept. Two trails ran from the city across the wide river, and now he could see that there were boats on the river, floating south on the river of gold. Across the river, on the hills overlooking the city, Crazy Horse saw more warriors on horseback. Some of these men held feathered staffs. As he circled over the city, the warriors on the other side of the golden river lifted their staffs, as if saluting him, and he saw that Touch-the-Clouds was among them, wearing his war bonnet of eagle feathers. Everything looked as the scouts who had forded the wide river had told him it would look. He knew then that they would take the Great Father's city.

Suddenly the wind was pulling him back. Crazy Horse felt himself plummeting toward the ground, an arrow in flight. He found himself astride his horse once more, gazing toward Washington.

He said, "Our men have command of the hills on the other side of the river. There are boats on the river. I do not think the Wasichu here know how to fight, how to defend their great encampment. If we wait—"

But Rain-in-the-Face and the warriors nearest him were shaking their war clubs at him.

Rain-in-the-Face said, "You said that we had to carry the war east."

Feather Earring said, "You led us along the Iron Horse trail."

Standing Bear said, "We did not ride here to sit on our horses like women and wait for the Wasichu to ride out to us and surrender. We rode here to count coup and win battle honors."

"I am a Fox," one of the younger warriors with the Kit Fox society sang. "I am supposed to die. If there is anything hard, if there is anything dangerous, it is mine to do."

Before Crazy Horse could speak, the men were calling out war cries. "Hoka hey! Hoka hey! It is a good day to die!"

"Stop!" Crazy Horse called out, but the men were already riding down the hills toward a long row of Blue Coats and artillery, screaming their war whoops. For a moment, Crazy Horse thought that they might break the line and scatter the Blue Coats, and then he heard the bursts of the white man's spitting guns, the firesticks that could spit out many bullets at once.

The sound was that of a clap of thunder during the most violent of storms. Five thick clouds of black smoke billowed out from the row of Blue Coats. Suddenly the grassy hills below him were a mass of dead and wounded horses and shrieking injured men. One wing of warriors fanned out, as if trying to draw the Blue Coats into following them, and the spitting firesticks tore at the air again.

"Retreat! We have to go back!" a warrior behind him shouted. But there was no place where they could run. Crazy Horse gazed at the field of bloodied men and horses below and listened to the cries of those who still lived. He heard no war cries, no songs of defiant braves cursing their enemy even as they lay dying, only the screams of agonized men.

From the Virginia hills, the Chen brothers, Glorious Spirit and Victorious Spirit, sent their rocket-arrows toward Washington. Some of the rocket-arrows, the ones called Flowering Trees or Blooming Flowers, burst harmlessly above the city in a shower of sparks, in order to frighten those below with their noise and panic the enemy. Others, the Five Eagles Sent to Catch Rabbits or the Mountain Lions Leaping Upon Their Prey, fell toward earth and made craters in the streets and holes in marble walls. Still other rocket-arrows exploded to spread noxious gases through the streets. But it was the Flying Crows with Magic Fire, the rocket-arrows that flew out from the bodies of other rockets, that did the most damage. No one could tell in advance where they would fall after the rockets carrying them burned out. That, for the Chen brothers and their comrades, the Chinese and Scottish engineers who had helped to build them, was the beauty of the Flying Crows; no effective defense could be mounted against them.

The rocket-arrows could also be used against some of the ships that were fleeing down the Potomac. Some of the larger steamships, those flying white banners and the flags of other nations, were allowed to pass. Others became targets of the rocket-arrows and were transformed into blossoms of flame, fiery lilies floating on the river's surface. The rocket-arrows aimed at boats found few of their targets, but the sight of the burning vessels and the sound of the exploding rockets was enough to send other boats toward the Virginia shore waving white flags, ready to surrender.

Glorious Spirit, watching the bombardment with his brother from their pavilion on a hill overlooking the river, thought, These people do not want to fight us. These people have no heart for this battle. They were ready to surrender their city even before we sent our rocket-arrows against them.

But it was good to have a chance to test the arrows in a major battle. The Flying Crows, the arrows that landed where they would after leaving the bodies of their parent-arrows, were especially delightful. For many in the city who believed themselves protected, the sight of a Flying Crow suddenly dropping from the sky would be the last thing they saw, and others would be dead or dying before they could even know that a Crow had found its prey.

"July 14, 1879, to the Chicago *Times*: I am writing this dispatch in Virginia, not far from Arlington, from a hill overlooking the road leading down to the Long Bridge. Below me, General George Crook and a party of officers, trailed by several companies of infantry and cavalry, are crossing the Long Bridge to accept the unconditional surrender of the Council of the United States. At the rear of the last company of cavalry, a party of Sioux, led by Chief Touch-the-Clouds, will follow Crook's men into the city.

"We reached Arlington seven days ago, one day before Colonel Nelson Miles and his troops set out from Baltimore and two days before General Alfred Terry had control of Alexandria to the south. We learned from our scouts that two ships had been sunk on the Anacostia River to the east of Washington, presumably by saboteurs, since these vessels were already sinking by the time Miles and his men reached Baltimore. By blocking the passage of other ships along the Anacostia, the sunken vessels saved the Army of the West from naval bombardment.

"By the time Crook's forces were in control of the Virginia hills, several ships carrying refugees from Washington were fleeing the city. Crook and Terry had decided not to fire upon any vessels that were flying the flags of other nations. Some nations, France among them, will hail our victory over the tyranny, even if they did little to aid us. As for neutral nations such as Germany, better perhaps to preserve their neutrality than to make enemies of them. England, of course, recalled its ambassador immediately after the Council seized power, so Crook did not have to fear provoking the Lion's roar. The British will undoubtedly be content for us now to remain the loose confederation of autonomous republics and states that it appears we are likely to be for the foreseeable future. That is enough to make me hope that the phoenix of the Union will be able to rise from the ashes once again, when representative government is restored and more time has passed.

"It may seem that this battle, one of relatively short duration, was easily fought. It is true that many in the ranks feared that we might have to lay siege to the city, or to attempt to storm it from the Maryland side, an effort that would have cost the Army of the West dearly in blood. It is also safe to say that the sight of Indian campfires ringing the city and the sound of Indian drums and songs in the night might have demoralized even the bravest of men. Certainly the rockets brought here by the Orientals and Scotsmen, whom the Sioux had invited into their territories to build those hideous weapons, did their share of damage. The Smithsonian Institution is heavily damaged, and whether it will be repaired as it was after the fire of 1865 remains to be seen. According to one report, two rockets struck the Willard Hotel, killing many of those who had sought shelter within its walls. The White House, the Capitol, and the General Post Office have all sustained damage, and many houses in Georgetown were consumed in a conflagration apparently caused by exploding rockets. I am told by an officer who served in the Army of the Potomac during the War Between the States that parts of Washington now look much as they did during that conflict. Soldiers are again encamped on the grounds below the Washington Monument, and the Patent Office has once more been transformed into a hospital.

"Yet surely the battle for Washington would have been far more costly had it not been for the ties binding the city's defenders to their brothers in blue besieging Washington. At night, when the Indians troubled to cease their barbaric wailings, I could hear the sounds of ballads being sung by young soldiers, and of bugles being played, and it seemed to me then that all of the soldiers on both sides already longed for the fighting to be over. To fight for the Union, as I once did, is one thing; to give one's life or to take another's in order to maintain the Council in power is quite another.

"Whether or not the bonds of brotherhood helped to bring a quick end to the siege, it is clear that the Indians played their part. The sight of the savages and the sound of their war cries must have terrified Washington's defenders, even if it is now clear in retrospect that the Sioux and their allies were in no danger of entering the city to collect Eastern scalps. The Gatling guns of the city's protectors claimed the lives of, I am told, some seven hundred Indians at last count, and at least two hundred more were felled by cannon fire. I imagine that the sight of pale-faced soldiers must have come as a relief to those defenders of Washington who so quickly dispatched so many of our red allies.

"It is true that the Indians fought bravely, if rashly charging a battalion of artillery that has Gatling guns and cannon with no more weaponry than bows, spears, and rifles can be said to constitute bravery. Certainly the Indians have paid dearly for the right to keep the lands promised to them by treaty, and perhaps will win a few other concessions as well. Even so, one can hear the officers and men of the Army of the West surreptitiously whispering that perhaps it is just as well that there will be fewer Plains Indians to celebrate their victory."

"Harsh words, perhaps, to those of our readers inclined to sympathize with the noble savages of the West. I hasten to add that I am not saying that the Sioux and their allies do not deserve to have their treaty honored. Indeed, it is my earnest hope, after some time spent in close proximity to the Indians, that they return to their own lands as quickly as possible. In the case of the Sioux, it is much easier to maintain kind feelings towards the breed when one does not have to endure their presence for too long a time.

"That said, it is unclear what the intentions of Touch-the-Clouds are at the moment.

"Your correspondent, John F. Finerty."

The first telegraph message about the war's outcome came to the talking wire tepee when Dancing Girl was there to listen to the telegraph. There were few left in her father's camp who understood the signals, and all of them had been taking a turn at the talking wire tent. Yellow Bird was sleeping and Dancing Girl was sewing beads on a deerskin shirt when the telegraph key began tapping out a message.

She listened long enough to hear that the message had been picked up in Bismarck and was being relayed to them, then motioned to Yellow Bird to go and summon everyone in the camp to the talking wire tepee. By the time they were all gathered outside, Dancing Girl had tapped out signals saying that the message had been received.

She came through the tepee's opening, holding the message in her mind. "This is the first message from the wire warrior Gray Horse," she recited in Lakota. "Three Star Crook and the other war chiefs of the Blue Coats have won their battle, and Touch-the-Clouds and his war chiefs have fought bravely to win ours. When the warriors of Washington saw the bands of men who had come there to fight, they became afraid. When they saw that the Lakota and many Wasichu and Wasichu Sapa had ridden against them, the people of Washington knew that there would be no victory for the false Great Father McClellan. Now Washington is ours."

Dancing Girl paused. "Is that all?" Goose Beak asked.

"It is only the first message," Dancing Girl replied.

"And isn't it enough?" Yellow Spring Grass said. "The war is won. Touch-the-Clouds will be a chief among both the Wasichu and our people. And our men will come home."

The talking wire was tapping out another message. Dancing Girl ducked inside and hurried to the telegraph. Others followed her into the tepee.

"This is the second message from Gray Horse," the talking wire was saying now. Yellow Bird crept closer to the telegraph, cocking his head to listen. "We have our victory, but have lost many men. Our warriors showed courage, and the Oglalas of Crazy Horse showed the bravest hearts of all, but courage and even the strongest war medicine cannot protect a man from the spitting fire-sticks of the Wasichu. We have gone to gather our comrades who fell in battle, but it will take all of us to carry them to their last resting place. End of message."

Dancing Girl repeated the message in words. The people in the tepee and outside the open flap were quiet for a while, and then Grass Rope, one of the old men, began to sing a war song.

"The white man rode into our lands," he sang, "and tried to steal them from us. Now we have ridden east to take his lands. The white man called us lice, lice on a dog to be killed before more sprang up. But the white men are now vermin crushed underneath the hooves of our galloping horses."

"There were white men who fought with us," Young Spring Grass reminded old Grass Rope.

"And there are too many of them to be crushed like vermin," Goose Beak added. "I have been to Bismarck, and know how many are there, and the Wasichu to the east of us are greater in number than the ants of an anthill the size of a mountain."

But the old man did not seem to hear them. "They wanted our

land," Grass Rope sang, "they wanted to take it from us and from our uncle the buffalo, and now the buffalo will graze on their lands."

Dancing Girl was remembering that Crazy Horse and his warriors had gone with Bear Coat Miles to war. She thought of how Bear Coat had sent his men against her father's camp. His men would have killed them all. She wondered how many of Bear Coat's men had died in the battle.

They were all in the Cabinet Room, seated around the table, Three Star Crook and One Star Terry and Bear Coat Miles, who would soon wear stars himself. Rubalev, who had turned up in Washington just after the Council's surrender, was there, in a white suit, and Touch-the-Clouds in his war bonnet and leather shirt with fringes of hair. Denis Laforte, who had been Miles's rear guard with his company of buffalo soldiers, was present, along with the famed orator Stephen Douglass, who had survived a strike by a rocket-arrow, although his house on Northeast A Street had not. Young Theodore Roosevelt sat at the far end of the table, decked out in his campaign buckskins, peering around at everyone through his thick glasses. Roosevelt kept talking of preserving the Western lands and of opening them to more development, although it was hard to see how both of those ends could be accomplished. Laforte had become, in the aftermath of battle, such a partisan of his own colored people's rights above all others, even those of the Indians, that he and Rubalev were no longer speaking. There were more men that Lemuel did not know, officers and civilians, men who had managed to convince General Crook that they belonged there to work out terms.

Terms for what? Lemuel wondered. A new republic? Another Union? A loose confederation of autonomous states? Another ruling cabal? Nobody in the room seemed certain of what sort of government they were forming, or exactly what states and territories it would govern.

A vision had come to Lemuel last night. He was walking the

White House grounds, near where the Lakota and Cheyenne had pitched their tepees. The sudden disorientation had come upon him as he came to the gate leading to Pennsylvania Avenue.

Outside the gate, a procession was passing, of chiefs in war bonnets and Blue Coats in dress uniforms. A horse-drawn wagon bore McClellan, Burnside, and Pope, the three members of the Council, also in uniform, along with Edwin Stanton, who looked stooped and wizened in his black justice's robe. Lemuel walked through the gate and followed the procession, past the rows of people who lined Pennsylvania Avenue. No one looked at him as he passed; their eyes were on the men sitting in the wagon.

Below the steps leading up to the Capitol, a gallows with four nooses had been erected. He realized that the four men in the wagon were on their way to their execution, and it seemed that much of Washington had lined Pennsylvania Avenue to watch this procession.

But Stanton was dead; he could not be here. He had been found dead at his home less than a day after Crook's Army of the West had entered Washington. At that thought, Lemuel had found himself back in his own world at the White House gate, gazing out at a quiet, empty street.

Rubalev was speaking again. Lemuel came to himself as he turned toward the Alaskan. "I do not care what you call it," Rubalev said, "the United States or the Provisional Federal Government or something else entirely. I simply want to ensure that all treaties with the Lakota and Cheyenne and Kiowa and any other red peoples will now be kept."

"I have already said that they would be," Crook replied.

"You gave your word as our provisional governor," Rubalev said, "but that does not necessarily bind any government that follows this temporary one."

Lemuel glanced around the table. Deciding on the fate of Generals McClellan, Pope, and Burnside, the men who had made up the Council, had taken the better part of three days. What had seemed so obvious to Crook and his fellow officers as they were rushing toward Washington to do battle, namely that McClellan,

Stanton, and the others were guilty of treason and deserved execution, had become much less obvious in the moments after victory. The generals had acted quickly during a crisis, after President Blaine's assassination, in an attempt to restore order. Their treatment of the South had as its purpose preserving what remained of the Union, and—this was Stephen Douglass's argument—protecting the rights of free Negroes living within the borders of the former Confederacy. Their actions in the West had been misguided attempts to resolve an ongoing financial crisis in the East by opening up more lands to settlement in the West, even if that meant violating treaties. It was also doubtful that some of the worst acts—the massacre at Elysium, Kansas, for example—had been ordered or even known about in advance by the Council's generals. General Sheridan's imprisonment and death, and the somewhat murky circumstances of General Sherman's earlier demise, were probably the handiwork of Stanton, according to one of Crook's aides, who had briefly perused one of the chief justice's diaries before turning all of Stanton's papers over to Crook.

That the worst offenses of the cabal could be attributed to a dead man had left the way open for more mercy toward the living, men who for all their faults had believed that they were acting in their people's best interests. There would have to be some sort of trial, but there was no reason for harsh sentences that would do little to heal America's wounds. Even Jefferson Davis had been treated with forbearance in the wake of the War Between the States, and allowed to go into exile in England; surely McClellan, Burnside, and Pope deserved the same kind of consideration.

Lemuel strongly doubted that Stanton's diaries, whatever they contained, would ever see the light of day. He also wondered if many of the men here would have been speaking of mercy for the Council members had they and their troops, rather than Crazy Horse's Oglalas, taken the brunt of the casualties during the skirmish that was already being called the Battle of Washington.

"I want assurances," Rubalev went on, "that the treaties will be kept by any government that follows your provisional one, General Crook. Allow me to put it this way—we want representation for all

Indians west of the Mississippi in Washington, someone among them who will be their voice here." He glanced at Touch-the-Clouds. "There are more Americans now who have come to sympathize with these people and who would look more favorably on any government that grants them rights, that honors their treaties, that even treats them as fellow Americans."

Miles scowled. "There's not much the Indians can do about it if we refuse to do what you want."

Lemuel, his anger roused, was about to speak when Touch-the-Clouds got to his feet. He had not spoken before, at any of the meetings. The others watched him, waiting to hear what he would say.

"This was my war," he said in his low voice. Two of the officers sitting near General Terry looked toward him apprehensively. "It was I who saw what I would have to do to preserve the lands of my people and those of our red brothers. I said we would have to fight, and Three Star Crook made himself my comrade. We came here on the Iron Horse trail and it is good that we saw friends along that trail. It is good that we did not have to fight a long time. It is good that we sit here now, in the Great Father's White House."

The Lakota chief looked around the table. "But it was red men who did most of the dying here. How many? I hear the Wasichu talking. I hear them say, not so many are dead in Washington, not so many were killed even by the rocket-arrows. We are most of the dead, and I think that all of you are at peace inside yourselves because we are most of the dead."

General Terry cleared his throat. "I would like to say—"

Touch-the-Clouds shot Terry a fierce look that silenced the general immediately. "If the treaties are not kept, the Wasichu will fight us again. They will have to fight Lakota, Cheyenne, Kiowa, Comanche, Apache, and others who have become brothers. They will have to spend very much of the yellow metal to fight this war. They will have other Wasichu saying to them, Do not fight this war. They will see many of their people die. They will see their world become dust."

Touch-the-Clouds paused. No one filled the silence with words, or even any sounds. "I am now chief of the Plains people, chief of all those who live on the lands of Uncle Buffalo. I do not say my words only for Lakota, but for all of those people. The Great Father in Washington will powwow with me as he does with other nations. If he does not, and breaks the treaties, we will come east again, and strike at Washington again, and you will not fight men with horses and firesticks. You will fight men with even bigger rocket-arrows and spitting firesticks and the medicine of Talking Wire Man Edison. Break the treaty, and we will know you are men who will not keep your promises until you are all dead."

Crook plucked at his beard. "You see what the chief wants," Rubalev said. "There should be an ambassador in Washington to represent the red people of the Plains. The treaties must be kept, and no people allowed to settle in Indian territories without the consent of the Indians who live there. That is not so much to ask, and doing it will make you more popular among some of those you will govern."

"I don't think," Crook said, "that any government that succeeds this provisional one will be in any position to fight another war, at least not right away."

"Then you will have nothing to lose by granting Touch-the-Clouds what he wants," Rubalev said.

Touch-the-Clouds went to his tepee after the meeting, followed by Rubalev. Lemuel trailed the two men. The Lakota chief refused to sleep behind the walls of the Great Father's house, and was living in one of the tepees in front of the White House. Rubalev had offered Lemuel a room at his house, but he had refused the offer. He preferred to stay among the soldiers and Indians bivouacked on the White House grounds. In Rubalev's house, he would only be reminded that Katia had once lived there.

Lemuel expected Rubalev to say his farewells and leave for his Washington house, which was untouched by the rocket-arrows, but instead he followed them both into the tent of Touch-the-Clouds. Two men guarding the tepee, White Shield and Elk Thunder, came in after Rubalev.

The air was still and moist, oppressive even with the tent flap tied up and open. Rubalev took out a match and lit the lamp hanging from the center pole; it seemed that he wanted to stay for a bit.

The five men sat down, with Touch-the-Clouds facing the entrance. "When do we leave this Wasichu swamp," Elk Thunder asked in Lakota, "this hive built on a marsh?"

"The men are saying that they do not want to have the Sun Dance so close to this place," White Shield added. "The Iron Horse can carry us back to our own lands before this moon is past. We should go home."

"You will want to secure your interests before you go home," Rubalev said in English.

Lemuel was sitting across from Rubalev. He had to know that White Shield and Elk Thunder knew no English.

"You will need an ambassador," Rubalev continued. "You will need someone here who can look out for your people and who knows the territory of Washington. You need someone who will give you what you want."

"I have what I want now," Touch-the-Clouds said in Lakota.

"You know what I mean," Rubalev said in English. "You can be the American khan, the one who will be like your brother to the east, who ruled a great empire. This is the start of your empire. It is a good start, you can keep the Plains for your people. As time goes on, you can take —"

"Do you say," Touch-the-Clouds interrupted, in English this time, "that I must break the treaty the Wasichu made with me?"

Rubalev rested his hands on his knees. "Your vision told you that you would rule in the East as well as the West. You know your people, they will have to keep fighting, they are warriors. You can settle for what you have, or you can reach for more. You know what will happen if you do not, the white men will live peacefully with you for a while, and then they will want to steal what you have again."

"That will not happen," Touch-the-Clouds said, and then in Lakota, "Grab Yellow Hair's arms."

Rubalev threw himself back, but did not move fast enough. Elk

Thunder and White Shield had him by the arms. Touch-the-Clouds pulled out his knife and slashed the Alaskan's throat. Lemuel had barely grasped what was happening when Touch-the-Clouds said, "Don't worry, Orphan. I am not about to kill you."

The blood pumping out of Rubalev's neck looked black in the dim light of the lamp. He fell forward as the two men holding his arms let him go. "That's good hair," Elk Thunder muttered, putting his hand on Rubalev's head. "Do you want it?"

"No," Touch-the-Clouds said, "and you will not take it either. The men in the Great Father's house treat me as one of themselves now. I will not have them calling me and my men—" He paused. "Savages," he finished in English.

"Where do we take him?" White Shield asked.

Touch-the-Clouds answered in Lakota, "Roll him up in a blanket. Morning Star Brother Rowland will find a place for him, maybe at the bottom of the Potomac."

"Why?" Lemuel managed to say.

"He called himself my brother, he spoke to me of my visions, he told me of the great chief on the other side of the world. His deeds helped to bring me to the house of the Great Father. But now I see he was another Wasichu who thought he could make me his weapon, use me as his war club to take what he wanted."

"And what did he want?"

Touch-the-Clouds lifted his war bonnet from his head. "His northern land. Revenge on the ones who took it from him. More of the yellow metal I gave to him to buy us weapons. To be a man set at the head and front of other men, a man of much power. I do not know all of what he wanted, and he can no longer tell me." The Lakota grasped Lemuel's shoulder. "There is another reason for him to die. He brought death to Graceful Swan, he sent death to her and to those with her. Who do you think bought those men who went raiding in blue coats? The man who was brought to me before we went east on the Iron Horse told me who paid him and the others to raid and kill. Now Yellow Hair has been punished for that, for being a spider with his spies and his bought men and his schemes. He wanted a war, he made it come about, he had his war, and now that war is over."

Lemuel supposed that he should rejoice that Rubalev was dead, that the man who had used Katia for his own ends, traded her, cast her aside and then caused her death, was dead. There was nothing left inside him to feel satisfaction at this revenge.

"My vision was a true one," Touch-the-Clouds said as White Shield and Elk Thunder put a blanket over Rubalev's body. "I saw it clearly. Yellow Hair did not. I will be the great chief, this khan, this man he saw in his vision, but I will follow my own trail to that end."

Lemuel rode across the Long Bridge toward the hills of Arlington. The sentries posted at the Virginia end of the bridge saluted him as he passed. He remembered that he was still wearing his officer's coat, the one he had worn to the meetings in the White House. His horse carried him up the hill as he followed the road toward the place where so many had been buried.

Rubalev would not lie here. Lemuel had taken the body to Rubalev's house in a hired carriage, paid the driver well with some coins from the dead man's purse, and carried the blanket holding Rubalev's body inside. There was no one in the house; the servants had fled during the siege, and Denis Laforte would not come there now. He had taken the body down to the cellar and concealed it behind a shelf of wine bottles and barrels. Eventually the body would be found, but Lemuel had taken the buffalo hide blanket with him; there would be nothing to connect the death of Rubalev with the Lakota camped around the White House.

He came to a path that wound among the trees. In the shade under the trees, the late afternoon air was cooler. Above him, he heard women's voices singing in Lakota: "We came east along the Iron Trail to the home of the Great Father. We sent our arrows against those who had taken the Great Father's home from him. Now Uncle Buffalo is calling to us again, calling us home."

Lemuel emerged from under the trees. On an open field of grass, hundreds of graves had been erected on poles. The body of each fallen warrior had been wrapped in a robe or a blanket and laid to rest on one of the wooden platforms atop the poles. Every man had been brought here in a wagon or on a pony drag in a long procession through the streets of Washington and across the Long Bridge. Crazy Horse had demanded that. They could not bring the bodies of the dead back to the Plains, but at least here they would be closer to their western lands; so Crazy Horse had reasoned. Many in Washington had turned out to watch the strange procession, to peer at the Indians in their beaded and fringed shirts and feathered headdresses who rode with their dead comrades.

All of them, Lemuel knew, had been prepared to die in battle. They would have been satisfied to know that victory had followed their deaths. But the way that they had died held little honor or glory.

"We kill from afar with our rocket-arrows. Our enemy kills from afar with iron balls and spitting firesticks. How can a man prove his courage with such weapons? Can a man count coup on an enemy killed from a distance? Does a man send others to ride in front of him, as our Blue Coat comrades did, and watch them die? The battle is over, the victory is ours, but there is no honor in it for a man."

That was the kill song Crazy Horse had sung as he led the procession of the dead through Washington. However bewildering the world of the white man was to the Oglala chief, Lemuel thought, he had seen this battle, and the kind of battle it was, very clearly.

Buffalo Calf Road Woman and Walking Blanket Woman were mounted on their pinto ponies, gazing out at the field of raised platforms holding the dead. "Uncle Buffalo is calling to us again," Walking Blanket Woman sang, "calling us home."

A small herd of Indian ponies grazed under the graves. Lemuel rode past groups of warriors sitting under trees toward the northern side of the grassy field. Two men were there on a gently sloping hill, sitting on horseback, unmoving. One of them wore a long feathered war bonnet and held a pipe in his hand. The other man was barechested and wore hawk's feathers in his long hair.

Lemuel rode toward Sitting Bull and Crazy Horse and reined in his mount. "I have come to tell you," he said in Lakota, "that if it is your wish, I will go to the Great Father's house tomorrow and ask for an Iron Horse and wagons to carry your men back to their hunting grounds."

Crazy Horse shook his head, but did not speak. Sitting Bull lifted his pipe. "How could it not be our wish to go home?" he asked.

"Both of you have the right to be at the meetings in the Great Father's house," Lemuel said. "Touch-the-Clouds would welcome you there."

Sitting Bull shrugged his shoulders. "I do not want to sit behind walls and listen to men babble in speech I do not understand. Anyway, I would be useless at such meetings. Touch-the-Clouds has made himself a chief over many chiefs. He has made himself the head and front of our people and other peoples as well. He does not need to have me sitting with him in a room full of Wasichu so that he can pretend in front of them that he still listens to other chiefs."

"Touch-the-Clouds has won," Lemuel said. "The Wasichu will not break the treaty. They will not steal your lands from you. They know how much it would cost them to do so, and they do not want to pay the price. They will form a new council and the treaty will be kept as long as the buffalo graze. They will keep it because Touch-the-Clouds has made himself a great chief."

"Yes, he has won what he wanted," Sitting Bull said, "and now I want to go home." The Hunkpapa chief was silent for a while. "What will you do, brother to Touch-the-Clouds? Where will you go?"

"Touch-the-Clouds wants me at his side during the meetings. After that, I suppose some post will be found for me." Lemuel was suddenly overcome with longing for the wooded hills and green land of Tonawanda, for the places he had known as a child.

"Touch-the-Clouds thinks that we will go on riding our horses and hunting Uncle Buffalo," Crazy Horse said. Lemuel started, surprised to hear the voice of the Oglala chief. "He thinks that we will go on as before, but coming here has changed us, the battles we fought have changed us. The air of this place smells of farts and rotting plants and Wasichu sickness, and I will take it into my lungs and carry it home with me, and others will breathe of it, and it will change us all."

Lemuel was about to ask the Oglala what he meant, but Crazy Horse and Sitting Bull were already riding down the hill toward the dead.

TWENTY-ONE

The crowds had begun to filter into the park next to Independence Hall at dawn. By midmorning, hundreds of Philadelphians were standing shoulder to shoulder as the dignitaries made their way past the crowds to the grandstand that had been set up for them.

Lemuel Rowland, from his seat on the speakers' platform, estimated that more people were here today than for President Crook's appearance earlier that summer, during the 1884 Independence Day celebration. George Crook was more a master of the concise statement as opposed to the stemwinder, nor was he much of a politician; but like his predecessor General Grant, he did not have to be. His campaign for president had brought together the northern states east of the Mississippi along with Nebraska and Kansas, and his election had dampened separatist sympathies in those regions. Crook had not wanted to run again, but he was a president who had saved the South from the excesses of the Council's generals, and thus a candidate who was likely to win most of the former Confederacy's electoral votes.

There was a Union now, if a fragile one. The largely Negro popu-
lation of northern Mississippi had attracted more black residents,
some of whom wanted autonomy. The Republics of Texas and
California, as well as Utah and the southwestern territories of New
Mexico and Arizona, considered themselves independent, although
that might change if their hostilities with Mexico grew more heated
and they needed more men to defend their borders.

As for the Plains—Lemuel glanced at the other scheduled speakers on the platform. The romance of the Plains, which his fellow
speakers had done their share to cultivate and promote, had drawn
this mass of listeners to Independence Hall. There, sitting at his left,
was Calamity Jane Cannary, with her new associate Susan B.
Anthony, prepared to speak on the subject of woman's suffrage.
Lemuel had noticed a few boys hawking copies of Jane's ghostwritten autobiography, *Scouting and Stagecoaches: My Life and Adventures
on the Plains*, at the edges of the crowd. There was Theodore
Roosevelt, running for Congress from New York and likely to win his
seat largely because of his own book, *Hunting Trips of a Ranchman*,
and his lectures on that subject. Next to Roosevelt sat Ely S. Parker,
Secretary of the Interior, with one of his duties being the maintenance
of diplomatic ties with the West. And there was Lemuel himself,
although he was probably the least important member of this assemblage, being merely Consul and Trade Representative of the Dakota,
Montana, and Wyoming Territories. Both President Crook and
Touch-the-Clouds had preferred to keep his title vague. President
Crook's advisors could maintain the appearance that the territories
were potentially a future part of the United States, while Touch-the-
Clouds remained free to regard Lemuel as the envoy of an independent nation.

Surveying the audience, Lemuel easily saw which of the speakers had most attracted the crowd. The men with small children sitting on their shoulders, the women shielding themselves from the
sun with parasols, the Philadelphia dignitaries in the grandstand—
all of them were looking toward the Lakota chief who sat between
Roosevelt and Ely Parker.

The American khan, the ruler of these lands—that was the destiny Grigory Rubalev had seen for Touch-the-Clouds. The Lakota looked the part of such a ruler today, in his elaborately beaded buckskin shirt and fringed leggings and a headdress of eagle feathers that fell to his waist; a leather shield with painted symbols of past battles—two painted hills, the wall of a fort, an arch that was probably meant to represent the Capitol Dome—rested next to his chair.

Would Touch-the-Clouds ever be an American khan? Lemuel wondered again, as he more often did these days, whether Rubalev's dream for Touch-the-Clouds had, in some sense, already been fulfilled. For a man who had sought and gained guarantees that his people would be free to live in their own way in their own territory, Touch-the-Clouds spent a good deal of time in the East. He had published his own ghostwritten autobiography two years ago, *Touch-the-Clouds Speaks: The Wisdom of a Lakota Warrior*, copies of which still sold almost as soon as they came off the presses, thanks partly to the praise lavished on the volume by Mr. Mark Twain and also by Mrs. Elizabeth Custer, who would soon contribute to her husband's legend with the publication of her own memoir. Touch-the-Clouds had also authorized the publication of several dime novels in which he was featured as the hero. He had become a popular lecturer and had appeared in Buffalo Bill's Wild West Show for a season, and those who had not seen him had probably heard a phonograph recording of his voice. He had, as much as General Crook, become the victor at the Battle of Washington and had been invited to parade down New York's Fifth Avenue in full regalia with some of his warriors. Among the children who dreamed of the West and imagined themselves as George Armstrong Custer, Buffalo Bill Cody, or Calamity Jane Cannary were many more who imagined themselves as Touch-the-Clouds, a man who owed nothing to anyone and who was truly a free individual. If he did not rule them as chief, he had gained a foothold in the territory of their hearts and minds.

The crowd applauded as Calamity Jane was introduced by a Philadelphia suffragist. Jane approached the lectern; she wore a Stetson and one of her denim jackets, but had bowed to convention by donning a riding skirt instead of her usual trousers. Her speech was both colorful and brief, the gist of it being: I've scouted for Custer, headed up a mule train, ridden shotgun on a stagecoach, and know how to use a gun, and you can say the same for a lot of ladies out where I come from, so we ought to be able to vote. There were a few catcalls from the crowd, but no boos, and Lemuel suspected that Jane's remarks might convince even more people of her cause's rightness than would Susan B. Anthony's eloquence and reason.

There was more applause at the end of her speech than there had been at its beginning. Jane looked relieved as she sat down again. The crowd had quieted down enough to listen to Miss Anthony. As she spoke, Lemuel gradually grew conscious of whispering on his right. Roosevelt was saying something to Touch-the-Clouds. Ely Parker leaned over to murmur in an undertone to the two other men.

They would have much to talk about, Lemuel thought, as they always did. Buffalo and cattle ranches, railroads, gold mines, rocket-arrow building and development, Edison's laboratories— Bismarck was still the only town on the continent with electric lights—all of those enterprises would draw more people to the West. That the Lakota people and their allies had anything to say about such matters was the doing of Touch-the-Clouds, who was now almost as wealthy and influential as any Wall Street magnate.

And it was my doing as well, Lemuel reminded himself, again wondering what he had wrought and what the Lakota had actually won for themselves.

The boards under his feet shifted, and he found himself alone on the platform. The crowd of people gradually faded from view, and then the distant buildings, until all that was left was an empty meadowland of trees and grass and horses grazing in the distance. Perhaps that would come, that dream some Indians still held of a land without Wasichu, a land inhabited entirely by those who might have come from the other side of the world to this continent. Perhaps it even existed somewhere. Sometimes it eased the pain inside him to think that such a place did exist and that Katia might be still alive there.

The sound of applause banished the vision. Lemuel came to himself. Susan B. Anthony was returning to her seat. Lemuel felt Jane's hand on his arm. He turned and saw the look of sorrow on her face.

"I know what you're thinking, Lem," she said softly without turning her head. "You're thinking about what brought us here. You're thinking about what it cost."

Fighting for the Union, for the Lakota to keep their lands—he felt as though he had spent much of his life battling in the service of illusions. Sometimes, at the moment of waking or just before drifting off to sleep, he even remembered the world differently. President Grant was still alive; the South and the North had become separate nations; the West had never been settled; he had stayed in Tonawanda and lived out his life there. His mind would insist on the delusions; even later, he would sense the details of an earlier illusion forcing themselves back into his mind. Some shift of the shadow play before his scrutiny would take away one scheme and replace it with another.

Not one of the illusions had given him a Katia who was still living. Had he found her, he would have clung to that shadow world with everything in him, whatever horrors that world might contain.

The mayor of Philadelphia was introducing him now. Lemuel stood up and walked to the lectern. He offered a few brief remarks about his life just after the Civil War, the combination of disillusionment and curiosity that had taken him to the Plains; he had made the statements so often that he could now say them without hearing himself.

"Today I stood before your Liberty Bell," he continued, "or perhaps I should say our Liberty Bell, with that crack in it that reminds us of how fragile our nation is. The conflict between the North and the South helped to fracture that bell, but did not break it. The discord between the East and the West fractured that bell, but did not destroy it. The red men of the Plains lifted their war clubs against that bell, yet now their chiefs come here in peace."

Lemuel paused. "This country, with its institutions, belongs to the people who inhabit it. Whenever they shall grow weary of the existing government, they can exercise their constitutional right of amending it, or their revolutionary right to dismember or over-throw it." He glanced toward the bleachers, then at the people standing below the platform. "Those words were spoken by President Abraham Lincoln, and as it happens we have spent the better part of the past twenty and four years exercising that revolutionary right. Now—"

His throat locked. He had suddenly lost the rest of his speech. Lemuel knew that he should feel embarrassment at least, shame, even panic as he looked into the expectant faces waiting to hear his next words.

Then the words he needed came into him. "What has changed in these past few years is this," he went on. "Among the people who inhabit this country are the red men of the West. It can be said that, if they are deprived of the constitutional rights that some might argue should be theirs, they will necessarily be forced to exercise their revolutionary rights. That could mean refusing to acknowledge any authority Washington might have over their territories. That could mean barring settlers from their lands. That could even mean, if the crimes against them once again become as great as they have been in the past, that the nation of red men might finally acquire the means to ride against their enemies and set themselves up as the rulers of us all."

His words, he realized even as he was speaking them, were nothing less than a threat. He gazed into the faces looking up at him, expecting to see shock, even anger, but already their eyes were shifting from him to the man seated behind him on his right. Lemuel turned toward him and saw Touch-the-Clouds nod at him in agreement. He would rule these people, one way or another.

He knew whom the crowd had come to see. Lemuel uttered a few words of introduction and then stepped back as the sound of hands clapping and people cheering. Touch-the-Clouds walked toward the lectern, holding his hands palms out and high above his head, and the cheering became a roar, rising toward the bright blue sky.

This was the worst of the shadow worlds, the one that kept coming to him, the one that he could not escape. The vision of this world had come to Crazy Horse in his dreams at first, disturbing his sleep, and now he saw it even when he was awake. It was a world of people moving in rows like ants toward a fort of stone that belched black soot from tall towers. It was a place where the Iron Horse trails crisscrossed the grazing grounds of Uncle Buffalo. It was a place where the endless plain of grass could not be found, only fences and fields of grain.

Crazy Horse had followed the Yellowstone River southwest, away from his camp. Alone, riding near the edge of the sandstone bluffs that banked the river, he had thought that he might hear the spirits once more. For two years now, he had kept far away from Bismarck, that place that was eating up the land with its houses and fields and long buildings, that place where the medicine man Edison and his comrades made their talking machines and burned glass torches that turned night into day and summoned spirits that could speak through wires with human voices. Near the sacred Black Hills, Deadwood had begun to sprawl like Bismarck, drawing men willing to dig out the yellow metal for the Lakota and other men who had come to help make rocket-arrows or to labor in the ironworks. Now White Eagle and his wire warriors were putting up their poles and stringing their talking wires from Bismarck west to the Yellowstone River.

The Lakota had won their victory. Touch-the-Clouds had told him that many times. They were free to live on the Plains and follow the buffalo, to live as they always had. But Touch-the-Clouds did not live that way anymore. Touch-the-Clouds went east and spoke with the Great Father and other Wasichu chiefs and told his stories and returned with more Wasichu medicine men and more settlers.

"I do what I do," Touch-the-Clouds had said to him, "so that you can live as you do." Remembering those words brought pain, because Crazy Horse knew the truth of them. He had seen for himself how numerous the Wasichu were after following the Iron Horse trail to the East, how they lived crowded together, and he had known then that there would be many Wasichu who would dream of the empty lands in the West. If the Lakota did not trade with them, if they refused to travel even a short distance down the white man's road, the Wasichu would come in swarms and take what they wanted. Crazy Horse knew that, too.

All along the horizon to the north and the south of him, he saw metal towers and bright shiny panes that reflected the sun. He watched as a great bird of metal rose and climbed to the sky, leaving a trail of pale smoke. In the distance, metal carts with wheels but no horses to pull them moved across long black trails. Crazy Horse had grown used to seeing such strange sights, to having them come upon him unbidden.

What would happen to the young men who had not yet tested themselves in raids and in battle? Who would they fight? In the shadow world, he had seen young men in the blue coats of the Wasichu, and had wondered if they were fighting their own battles or those of the white man. He thought of how Bear Coat Miles had sent so many Indian warriors before him, how quickly they had been cut down, and how few of Bear Coat's men had died.

He reined in his horse, willing the shadow world to disappear, and at last the glittering towers and the metal carts crawling along black trails faded from view. A man was riding toward him from the west, the legs of his horse concealed by clouds of dust.

Another Lakota, Crazy Horse thought when he could make out the beaded patterns of the man's shirt, a Minneconjou. The man rode up to him, greeted him, told him that his name was Kicking Bear, and was silent for a while after Crazy Horse spoke his own name.

"You fought in the Great Father's city," the young man said at last. Crazy Horse nodded; the other man would have been no more than a boy when that battle was fought. "I wish I could have fought there."

"No, you don't," Crazy Horse replied.

"I was told that you shun the Wasichu."

"I do," Crazy Horse said, "and so does Sitting Bull."

"I live as far away from the Wasichu as I can get," Kicking Bear said, "and now I am on my way to the camp of Sitting Bull. I have much to tell him. I have been to the place where the Fish Eaters live, and I have seen the man that the Wasichu call the Christ in the camp of the Fish Eaters, and I have also seen the dancing ghosts."

"If you are going to see Sitting Bull," Crazy Horse said, "then I'll ride with you."

They began to follow the river east. Sitting Bull, he knew, was camped at the fork of the Yellowstone and Tongue Rivers. He did not speak, sensing that Kicking Bear was one who liked to talk and that he would tell Crazy Horse more about the vision of the Christ that he had seen among the Paiutes when he felt like it.

"There were others there," Kicking Bear said at last, "Blackfeet and Crow and a few Cheyenne. There weren't that many of us, but more will go to that place when they know what I saw among the Fish Eaters. We waited for three days, and then the Christ appeared to us, and he was a red man, not a white man as the Black Robes and the other Wasichu medicine men claim that he is. He showed us the wounds the Wasichu made in his hands when they nailed him up, and he taught us how to dance a dance that will bring back the dead, that will restore our fathers to us, that will make the earth as it was, without any Wasichu in it."

Crazy Horse said nothing.

"If we dance this ghost dance," Kicking Bear said, "the spring will come and the earth will heave and bury all the white men. Every red man who dances the ghost dance will be taken up into the air by a great wind and held there while the Wasichu are swept from the earth forever."

Crazy Horse grunted. "You can climb such a wind just as easily," he muttered, "as you can banish the Wasichu from this world."

"The ghost dance will free us of the white man," Kicking Bear said. "We will dance and another spring will come, and when the grass is green the white men will be gone. Then the buffalo will return everywhere, not only in the lands given to us by the treaty. All of the wild horses will come back. All of our ancestors will be resurrected to live among us again if we dance the ghost dance the Christ of the Fish Eaters taught to us."

Crazy Horse thought about that. Maybe the ghost dance was a way to get into a shadow world he had not seen for some time, the world where the Wasichu had never come to this land. Maybe the ghost dance would finally rid him of the visions of that other shadow world of metal towers and black soot and scarred land empty of buffalo.

"I will teach you how to do the ghost dance," Kicking Bear said, "and then I will go to tell Touch-the-Clouds of the Paiute Christ. For keeping the white man from stealing our lands, for riding east and punishing those who broke the treaty, he made himself the greatest of our chiefs. He will make himself an even greater one when he dances and makes the white men disappear."

From the sides of his eyes, Crazy Horse saw a field of snow covered with the bodies of dead Lakota. He blinked, and the vision disappeared. Another shadow world, he thought, one that could not be his own, that could not be real.

"You will teach us the ghost dance," Crazy Horse said, "but I wonder if Touch-the-Clouds will be willing to learn it." He would do whatever he could to bring this ghost dance medicine to his old friend, but if Touch-the-Clouds had gone too far along the white man's trail to learn it for himself, it did not matter. Crazy Horse would dance the ghost dance. He would dance to the limits of his strength, dance even if Touch-the-Clouds clung to his Wasichu ways and medicine and refused to dance. He would dance and would not stop dancing until he had climbed the wind and danced himself into the world the Paiute Christ had promised.

Afterword

"The United States," historian David Herbert Donald writes in *Liberty and Union*, "was a historical impossibility. From Aristotle to Montesquieu, political theorists agreed that democracy was an unstable form of government, tending to distintegrate into anarchy, which in turn led to despotism."

Pondering this statement makes one think that our actual history is one of the least likely of possibilities, that it may be a less likely alternative history that has branched off from a more plausible continuum.

To wrestle with alternative history is to contend with two ideas. One is the notion that a change in the fate of a particular individual, especially an important person, or a small change that alters the outcome of a certain event, can produce great subsequent changes. The other is the idea that there are fundamental events that cannot be altered, regardless of an individual's actions. One of the pleasures in reading an alternate history is in considering how different one's own history might have been. Another is in viewing how much that other world might still resemble our own, even with those differences.

A number of individuals contend with fundamental events in the pages of this novel. Because *Climb the Wind* is fiction, I have taken many liberties with the people and the events of this story. Of the characters, Lemuel Rowland, Katia Rubalev, Grigory Rubalev, Denis Laforte, Virgil Warrick, Jeremiah Clarke, Soaring Eagle, White Buffalo Woman, White Cow Sees, White Eagle, Caleb Tornor, Glorious Spirit, Victorious Spirit, and Dancing Girl are my own invention. A number of others are historical figures. In our world, the "shadow world" that constitutes our historical reality, here is what happened to some of these people:

Ely Samuel Parker was a Seneca who studied civil engineering at Rensselaer Polytechnic Institute, collaborated with the pioneering American anthropologist Lewis H. Morgan on his groundbreaking study *The League of the Iroquois* (published in 1851), served with Ulysses S. Grant during the Civil War, wrote out the terms for surrender at Appomattox, and became the first Native American Commissioner of Indian Affairs during President Grant's first term. As commissioner, he worked to rid his bureau of fraud and corruption, making many enemies as a result. He resigned that post in 1871, after being charged with misconduct in office and then subsequently exonerated of all charges by Congress, moved to New York City and became a prosperous businessman. He died in 1895.

Touch-the-Clouds was a comrade of Crazy Horse and a Lakota chief and warrior for whom I have imagined a much more significant historical role. As a young man, he apparently saved Crazy Horse from being killed by the jealous husband of Black Buffalo Woman, who had left her husband for Crazy Horse. In 1877, the Touch-the-Clouds of our history surrendered at the Spotted Tail agency in Nebraska and lived out his life as a reservation Indian.

Crazy Horse fought against the United States Army for most of his adult life, and was the chief Lakota tactician at the Battle of the Little Bighorn. After losses and setbacks for the Lakota in several subsequent battles, he went to the Red Cloud agency in Nebraska in 1877 with his wife, Black Shawl, who was dying from tuberculosis. His request for permission to take her to the Spotted Tail agency for medical treatment was refused. In desperation, he left Red Cloud and went to Spotted Tail, where he was arrested by Indian police employed by the U.S. Army and taken to Fort Robinson. At the sight of the jail cell awaiting him there, Crazy Horse panicked, was bayoneted by an infantry officer, and died on September 5, 1877, at the age of thirty-five. He is the only lifelong enemy of the United States to be honored on a U.S. postage stamp.

General William Tecumseh Sherman and General Philip H. Sheridan implemented an early version of the military strategy of "total war," in which entire civilian populations are made to suffer the effects of armed onslaught, during the Civil War, notably during Sheridan's Shenandoah Valley campaign of 1864 and Sherman's destructive "March through Georgia" in 1865. Later, in combination with standard army procedures, the tactics of total war and surprise were used against Indians and approved by Sherman, as commanding general of the army, and by Sheridan, as commander of the Military Division of the Missouri, in 1876–77. Especially effective were surprise raids on Indian villages and encampments, during which the army would capture Indian horses and goods, forcing their victims to surrender or take refuge in other camps; often women and children were killed in these attacks, since the men had no time to mount a defense. Sheridan, who ordered Custer to attack Black Kettle's Cheyenne camp along the Washita, was responsible for the statement, "The only good Indians I ever saw were dead," later to enter American folklore as: "The only good Indian is a dead Indian." An equestrian statue of Sheridan stands in front of the New York State Capitol Building in Albany, New York, the city where Sheridan was born.[1]

---

[1] It is worth noting here that between 1862 and 1867, wars with the Cheyenne, Sioux, and Navaho cost the United States government an estimated one hundred million dollars for several hundred Indian casualties, including women and children. According to the records of the Military Division of the Missouri, the total cost of the war against the Sioux and Cheyenne from 1876 to 1877 was $2,312,531.24. In 1990 dollars, this amount would equal approximately $27,663,242, or about $185,000 for each Indian killed.

Calamity Jane Cannary married James Butler "Wild Bill" Hickok in 1870, gave birth to their daughter Jean Hickok in 1873, then gave Jean up for adoption. She reportedly accompanied Custer and his Seventh Cavalry on the Black Hills expedition of 1874, and divorced Hickok in 1876, shortly before his death in a gunfight. In 1893, she joined Buffalo Bill's Wild West Show, touring the eastern United States and England. During the last few years of her life, she often went on drunken benders, and was thrown out of at least one town, Billings, Montana, for shooting up a saloon. She died of pneumonia in 1903 near Deadwood, South Dakota, and was buried next to the grave of Wild Bill Hickok.

William McKay and Horatio Nelson Ross did in fact accompany Custer on the 1874 expedition in the Black Hills.

George Armstrong Custer, Thomas Custer, Isaiah Dorman, Charley Reynolds, Donald McIntosh, and Bloody Knife all died at the Battle of the Little Bighorn in 1876. Luther Hare, John Burkman, and Frederick Benteen survived that battle. Elizabeth Bacon Custer published three volumes of memoirs and devoted her long life and widowhood to preserving her husband's memory until her death in 1933 in New York City.

Buffalo Calf Road Woman fought against the forces of General George Crook at the Battle of the Rosebud River, the battle that preceded Custer's defeat at the Little Bighorn by eight days. At the battle by the Rosebud, Buffalo Calf Road Woman saved her brother's life by riding into the midst of the fight to rescue him when his own horse was shot out from under him. That battle was known among the Cheyenne afterward as the Battle Where the Girl Saved Her Brother.

Walking Blanket Woman fought against Custer's Seventh Cavalry at the Little Bighorn to avenge the death of her brother. It is said that she wore the full war dress of a man and carried her dead brother's shield.

Monahseetah (or the Young Grass That Shoots in the Spring, which I have rendered as Young Spring Grass) was a Cheyenne woman who survived Custer's massacre of Black Kettle's people camped along the Washita in 1868. She was reportedly at the Battle of the Little Bighorn with her aunt, who found Custer's body and broke the dead man's eardrums with her awl so that he, who had ignored the warnings of the Indians, "could hear better in the next world." The legend persists among some Native Americans that Monahseetah had a son by Custer, named Yellow Bird, while she was living with and scouting for Custer in the late 1860s. If so, he would have been Custer's only child and direct descendant.

Sitting Bull was nominated as paramount chief of all the Lakota Nation in 1866. Before the Battle of the Little Bighorn, this chief and medicine man had a vision of white soldiers falling into camp, the vision that warned him of the Seventh Cavalry's approach and foretold his people's victory. That victory was the prelude to a series of defeats for the Lakota, and in 1877, Sitting Bull led his Hunkpapa Lakota to Canada, where they remained for four years before surrendering to the United States Army in 1881. He was imprisoned at Fort Randall for two years and then released into the custody of the Standing Rock agency in South Dakota. In 1885, he became a major attraction in Buffalo Bill's Wild West Show. In 1890, General Nelson A. Miles ordered the arrest of Sitting Bull, whom the army now considered a "fomenter of disturbances" for encouraging the Ghost Dance religion among the Lakota. When Indian police, backed by a squadron of cavalry, went to Sitting Bull's cabin to arrest him, they were surrounded by a crowd of Ghost Dancers. Although Sitting Bull was prepared to leave peacefully, two of the Indian police shot him and killed him.

Samuel Langhorne Clemens, as Mark Twain, became one of America's most popular, most enduring, and most authentic writers.

Frank Grouard was General George Crook's chief of scouts during the Plains Indian campaigns of 1876–1877. The son of a Polynesian woman and a French missionary, he came to the United States, lived among the Lakota for several years, and was adopted by Sitting Bull.

William F. Cody was a Pony Express rider, hunter for the Kansas Pacific Railroad (where he killed so many buffalo to feed the railroad workers that he was immortalized as Buffalo Bill), was featured in a number of dime novels by writer Ed Judson (who wrote as Ned Buntline), and began a career in show business in 1872, appearing in

"Scouts of the Plains." After that, except for a brief return to the Plains in 1876 to scalp Chief Yellow Hand in revenge for Custer's death, he became an impresario, produced his Wild West spectacles, toured the United States and Europe, became a millionaire, went bankrupt, and spent his last years touring with a circus. Buffalo Bill died in 1917 and is buried in Colorado, where a bronze equestrian statue of himself marks his grave.

John F. Finerty, born in Ireland and the son of an Irish editor, fled his homeland in 1864, but remained a lifelong advocate of Irish independence. He served in the Ninety-fourth New York Regiment during the Civil War, moving to Chicago after the war. He worked as a reporter and then as city editor of the Chicago *Republican* from 1868 to 1872. Until 1875, he worked for the Chicago *Tribune*. In 1876, the city editor of the Chicago *Times*, Clinton Snowden, assigned Finerty to cover the 1876 Sioux campaign for his paper. Finerty traveled with the troops of General George Crook during the war against the Lakota and later covered the Apache campaign in the Southwest. From 1879 to 1881, he was the Washington correspondent of the Chicago *Times*; from 1883 to 1885, he represented a Chicago district in Congress. When he died in 1908, several hundred army veterans and members of a number of Irish societies were part of his mile-long funeral procession. He was the author of *War-Path and Bivouac*, published in 1890.

Thomas Alva Edison had 1093 patents to his name. Among his many inventions were the vote recorder, the automatic telegraph, waxed paper, the mimeograph, the phonograph, the electric light, and the kinetoscope, a precursor of the motion picture projector.

Theodore Roosevelt, then vice president, became president of the United States in 1901, after the assassination of President McKinley. His love of the outdoors, which flowered during the time he spent in the Dakota Badlands in the 1880s, led him to espouse the cause of conservation and to set up a system of national parks.

Schuyler Colfax was elected vice president of the United States in 1868, in Ulysses S. Grant's first term. After being implicated in the Crédit Mobilier stock scandal, he was dropped from the Republican ticket, retired from politics, and had a successful career as a lecturer.

James G. Blaine was Speaker of the U.S. House of Representatives from 1869 to 1875 and was elected to the U.S. Senate from Maine in 1876. He ran for president as the Republican candidate in 1884, but lost to Grover Cleveland. He served as Secretary of State in 1881 during the administration of James Garfield, resigning that post after Garfield was assassinated and Chester A. Arthur, an ally of Senator Roscoe Conkling (a political enemy of Blaine's) became president. In 1889, Blaine was again appointed Secretary of State by President Benjamin Harrison, and died in 1893.

Edwin M. Stanton was appointed Secretary of War in 1862, resigned after the assassination of President Abraham Lincoln, but was persuaded by Lincoln's successor, President Andrew Johnson, to remain at his post. Stanton's support of Radical Republicans in Congress, and of a harsh and punitive policy of Reconstruction in the defeated South, brought him into conflict with President Johnson. After Johnson demanded his resignation in 1867, Stanton refused to resign; Johnson then suspended him, appointing Ulysses S. Grant as Secretary of War *ad interim*. When the Senate declined to approve Stanton's removal, citing the recently passed Tenure of Office Act (which prevented the president from removing a Cabinet officer and which was designed to limit Johnson's powers), Stanton resumed his post as secretary but resigned after the attempt to impeach Johnson failed. In late 1869, friends persuaded President Grant to appoint Stanton to the Supreme Court, but Stanton died a few days after receiving the appointment. An unsubstantiated rumor at the time claimed that Stanton was a suicide. Another rumor, never proven, was that he was involved in the assassination of President Lincoln.

George B. McClellan was a West Point graduate who was appointed major-general in the U.S. Army in 1861, but after reverses in battle against the Confederate forces, he was relieved of command in 1862. He became active in the Democratic party and ran for president in 1864, but lost to Abraham Lincoln, the incumbent. He was elected governor of New Jersey in 1878 and held that office until 1881.

George Crook, called by General Sherman "the greatest Indian fighter in the history of the United States," was a field commander in campaigns against the Paiute, Apache, Sioux, and Cheyenne. He became known for using mules instead of cumbersome wagons for hauling supplies and resigned the mule pack to allow the animals to carry more weight. A master of guerrilla tactics against the Indian, he also had sympathy for his foe, and became one of the few white men trusted by the Sioux. In 1886, during his last campaign against the Apache, Crook persuaded Geronimo and his Chiricahuas to surrender by promising them that they would be released after imprisonment in the East for two years, and then allowed to return to their own lands. The War Department in Washington refused to honor this promise, Geronimo fled into Mexico, and Crook was severely reprimanded for negligence, for offering unauthorized terms to the Apache, and for his tolerant attitude toward Indians. Crook immediately resigned and was replaced by an old rival, Nelson A. Miles. Crook died in 1890. Geronimo surrendered later in 1886 for the last time, spent the rest of his life as a prisoner of war in Florida, Alabama, and Fort Sill, Oklahoma, and died of pneumonia in 1909.

Nelson A. Miles fought in the Civil War and rose to the rank of major-general of volunteers. In 1866, he left the volunteers and became colonel of the Fortieth Infantry. His wife, Mary Hoyt Sherman, whom he married in 1868, was the niece of William T. Sherman and Senator John Sherman, a family connection Miles readily exploited. He began fighting Indians as a colonel of the Fifth Infantry, and his persistence in pursuing the enemy was in large part responsible for the final defeat of the Sioux. He disagreed, often publicly, with George Crook over the treatment of Indian prisoners; he also oversaw operations on the Sioux reservations before and after the massacre at Wounded Knee. In 1895, he became commander general of the U.S. Army, but his increasing altercations with President William McKinley made him lose favor, and he was a political liability by the time Theodore Roosevelt became president. He retired in 1903 and died in Washington, D.C., in 1925.

Alfred H. Terry, trained as a lawyer with a degree from Yale, fought in the Civil War and was commander of the Department of the Dakota from 1866 until his retirement in 1888. As a field commander, he fought during the Great Sioux War of 1876–1877. In 1877, he was sent to Sitting Bull, then in exile in Canada, with orders to promise the great Lakota chief a pardon if he and his people surrendered their horses and firearms and returned to the United States. Sitting Bull, having reason to distrust these promises, refused the offer and remained in Canada until 1881.

Frederick Douglass was an escaped slave who became a gifted and celebrated orator, abolitionist lecturer, and supporter of women's rights. His intellect was so impressive that opponents of abolition often refused to believe that he was a former slave. He helped to raise a regiment of black soldiers, the Massachusetts Fifty-fourth, to fight for the Union during the Civil War, served as U.S. marshal for the District of Columbia from 1877–1881, was recorder of deeds for the district from 1881–1886, and was minister to Haiti from 1889–1891. He was also the author of a classic autobiography, revised several times, *Life and Times of Frederick Douglass.* He died in 1895.

James Wormley and his family, prominent members of Washington's African-American community in the years after the Civil War, owned and managed the Wormley Hotel, which was established in 1871. The hotel was considered by many to be the best and most elegant of all Washington hotels in the 1880s, and many celebrated people and crowned heads of nations were among its guests.

Annie Oakley married Frank Butler, an Irish immigrant and trick shooter, in 1880; he soon retired from their act of "Butler and Oakley" to become his wife's manager. The couple toured North America and Europe with Buffalo Bill's Wild West Show. Annie Oakley was adopted into the Lakota nation by Sitting Bull in 1885, presented to Queen Victoria of England in 1887, and shot a cigar out of the mouth of Crown Prince Wilhelm of Germany without injury to the prince. After giving demonstrations of rifle shooting for U.S. soldiers in 1918, she retired from public life in 1922 and died in 1926. Butler, whose management of his wife's career helped to make her a legend, also died in 1926.

Kicking Bear was the Minneconjou Lakota who brought the

news of Wovoka, the Paiute Messiah, to Sitting Bull. Wovoka's Ghost Dance religion quickly spread among the despairing Sioux and led to the massacre at Wounded Knee in 1890. There, while troops of the Seventh Cavalry were attempting to herd a group of unarmed Ghost Dancers back to the Standing Rock agency, a shot was fired, and the soldiers then opened fire upon the helpless Indians. It is estimated that some three hundred Lakota men, women, and children died at Wounded Knee. Twenty-five Blue Coats also died, most of them killed by army bullets or shrapnel.

Several people deserve acknowledgment for their aid and moral support during the writing of this novel. First and foremost are my editor John Douglas, whose support and patience approached the superhuman, and George Zebrowski, for his strong encouragement. Others who helped me more than they perhaps realize include Jack Dann, my literary agent Richard Curtis, Richard Miller, Rebecca Springer, Nancy Hanger, Shirley S. Darmer, Kenneth I. Darmer, Connie Sargent Jensen, and the staffs of the Albany Public Library and the New York State Library and Archives. I am grateful to all of them.

—Pamela Sargent

About the
Author

Pamela Sargent sold her first published story during her senior year in college at the State University of New York at Binghamton, where she earned a B.A. and an M.A. in philosophy and also studied ancient history and Greek. She is the author of several highly praised novels, among them *Cloned Lives* (1976), *The Sudden Star* (1979), *The Golden Space* (1982), *The Alien Upstairs* (1983), and *Alien Child* (1988). Her novel *Venus of Dreams* (1986) was selected by The Easton Press for its "Masterpieces of Science Fiction" series; Gregory Benford described it as "a sensitive portrait of people caught up in a vast project. It tells us much about how people react to technology's relentless hand, and does so deftly. A new high point in humanistic science fiction." *Venus of Shadows* (1988), the sequel, was called "a masterly piece of world-building" by James Morrow and "alive with humanity, moving, and memorable" by *Locus*. *The Shore of Women* (1986), one of Sargent's best-known books, was praised as "a compelling and emotionally involving novel" by *Publishers Weekly*; Gerald Jonas of the *New York Times* said about this novel: "I applaud Ms. Sargent's ambition and admire the way she has unflinchingly pursued the logic of her vision." *The Washington Post Book World* has called her "one of the genre's best writers."

Sargent is also the author of *Earthseed* (1983), chosen as a Best Book for Young Adults by the American Library Association, and two collections of short fiction, *Starshadows* (1977) and *The Best of Pamela Sargent* (1987). Her novels *Watchstar* (1980), *Eye of the Comet* (1984), and *Homesmind* (1984) comprise a trilogy. She has won the Nebula Award, the *Locus* Award, and has been a finalist for the Hugo Award. Her work has been translated into French, German, Dutch, Spanish, Portuguese, Italian, Swedish, Japanese, Chinese, Russian, and Serbo-Croatian.

Ruler of the Sky (1993), Sargent's epic historical novel about Genghis Khan, tells the Mongol conqueror's story largely from the points-of-view of women. Gary Jennings, bestselling author of the historical novels *Aztec* and *The Journeyer*, said about *Ruler of the Sky*: "This formidably researched and exquisitely written novel is surely destined to be known hereafter as *the* definitive history of the life and times and conquests of Genghis, mightiest of Khans." Elizabeth Marshall Thomas, author of *Reindeer Moon* and *The Hidden Life of Dogs*, commented: "Scholarly without ever seeming pedantic, the book is fascinating from cover to cover and does admirable justice to a man who might very well be called history's single most important character."

Sargent is also an editor and anthologist. In the 1970s, she edited the *Women of Wonder* series, the first collections of science fiction by women; her other anthologies include *Bio-Futures* and, with British writer Ian Watson as co-editor, *Afterlives*. Two new anthologies, *Women of Wonder, The Classic Years: Science Fiction by Women from the 1940s to the 1970s* and *Women of Wonder, The Contemporary Years: Science Fiction by Women from the 1970s to the 1990s*, were published in 1995; *Publishers Weekly* called these two books "essential reading for any serious sf fan." With artist Ron Miller, she collaborated on *Firebrands: The Heroines of Science Fiction and Fantasy* (1998).

At HarperPrism, *Climb the Wind: A Novel of Another America* will be followed by *Child of Venus*, the third novel in her Venus trilogy. Pamela Sargent lives in upstate New York.

Pamela Sargent's World Wide Web site is located at:
http://www.sff.net/people/PSargent/default.htm